Humphrey Bold
A Story of the Times of Benbow

by

Herbert Strang

Double 9
BOOKS

Humphrey Bold
A Story of the Times of Benbow
by Herbert Strang

Copyright © 2024

All Rights reserved.

ISBN: 978-93-62767-09-7

Published by

DOUBLE 9 BOOKS

2/13-B, Ansari Road
Daryaganj, New Delhi – 110002
info@double9books.com
www.double9books.com
Tel. 011-40042856

ABOUT THE AUTHOR

George Herbert Ely (1866–1958) and Charles James L'Estrange (1867–1947), two English writers who worked together on several children's adventure books, wrote under the pen name Herbert Strang. In the late 19th and early 20th centuries, the pair contributed to the boys' fiction genre with a variety of books written under the collective pen name Herbert Strang. Charles James L'Estrange was born in Hampstead, London, on November 6, 1867, and George Herbert Ely was born in India on October 24, 1866. They were both students at London's Dulwich College. Young readers were drawn to Herbert Strang's adventure stories because they frequently dealt with themes of bravery, patriotism, and discovery. By using a pseudonym, the writers were able to continue building a steady reputation for themselves in the boys' literature market while producing a large body of work. They have several popular series, such as "The Adventure Series," "The Airship Boys Series," and "The Marooner's Island Series." The books added to the canon of young reader adventure fiction because of their captivating characters and thrilling stories.

CONTENTS

Chapter 1
The Wyle Cop

'Tis said that as a man declines towards old age his mind dwells ever more and more on the events of his childhood. Whether that be true of all men or not, certain it is that my memory of things that happened fifty years ago is very clear and bright, and the little incidents of my boyhood are more to me, because they touch me more nearly, than such great matters as the late rebellion against His Majesty King George, whom God preserve.

Especially does my thought run back to a day, fifty-six years ago this very summer, when by mere chance, as it would appear to men's eyes, my fortunes became linked with those of Joe Punchard, who is now at this moment, I warrant, smoking his pipe in the lodge at my park gates. I was eleven years old, a thin slip of a boy, small for my age, and giving no promise, to be sure, of my present stature and girth. The neighbors shook their heads sometimes as they looked at me, and wondered why Mr. John Ellery, if he must adopt a boy--a strange thing, they thought, for a bachelor to do--did not choose one of a sturdier make than poor little Humphrey Bold. They even joked about my name, averring that names assuredly must go by contraries, for I was Bold by name, and timid by nature. The joke seemed to me, even then, a very poor one, for a boy must have the name he is born with, and I have known very delicate and white-handed folk of the name of Smith.

Mr. Ellery, a bachelor, as I have said, adopted me when my own father and mother died, which happened when I was still an infant and, mercifully, too young to understand my loss. My father, as I called him, was a substantial yeoman whose farm and holding lay some three miles on the English side of Shrewsbury. He was well on in years when he adopted me, and dwells in my memory as a strong, silent man who, when his day's work was done, would sit in the inglenook with a book upon his knees. This taste for reading marked him out from the neighboring farmers, with whom, indeed, he had little in common in any way, so that he was rather respected than liked by them. But he was wonderfully kind to me, and if my love for him was qualified with awe, it was from reverence, and not from fear.

My frail appearance, on which the neighbors jested, caused my father to look on me sometimes with an anxious eye, and he would question the housekeeper and the maids about my appetite, and whether I slept well o' nights. On these matters he need not have had any concern, since I ate four hearty meals a day, with perhaps an apple or a hunk of bread in between; while as for sleeping, Mistress Pennyquick was wont to declare, five out of the seven mornings in the week, when she woke me, that she knew I would sleep my brains away. This prediction scarcely troubled me, and since the motherly creature never disturbed me until I had slept a good nine hours by the clock, I do not think she was really distressed on this score.

Until I reached my eleventh birthday I did not go to school, being taught to read and write and cipher by my father himself. But one day he set me before him on his horse and rode into Shrewsbury, where, after a solemn interview with Mr. Lloyd, the master, I was put into the accidence class at King Edward's famous school. As we rode back, I remember that my father, who was generally so silent, talked to me more than ever before, about school, and work, and the great men who had been in past time pupils in the same school, notably Sir Phillip Sidney. And from that day I used to trudge every morning, barring holidays, into the town, and say my *hic, haec, hoc* as well, I verily believe, as the rest of my schoolfellows.

But with the opening of my school days I began to know what misery was. My lessons gave me little trouble, and the masters were kind enough; but among the boys there were two who, before long, kept me in a constant state of terror. They were older than I by some four or five years, and in school I never saw them; but outside they used to waylay me, tormenting me in many ingenious ways. Looking back now I see that much of my terror was needless. They seldom ill-treated me in act; but knowing, I suppose, that the imagination is often very apprehensive in weakly bodies like mine, they took a delight in threatening me, conjuring up all manner of imaginary horrors, and so working on me that my sleep was disturbed by hideous nightmares. I told nobody of what I suffered, and when Mistress Pennyquick noticed that I was pale and heavy-eyed sometimes in the morning, she did but suppose it was due to a closer application to books than I had known formerly, and forthwith increased my daily allowance of milk.

My father, if he had known of these doings, would doubtless have taken strong measures to put a stop to them, for the older, though not the worse, of the two bullies was a nephew of his own. His sister was married to Sir Richard Cludde, of a notable family whose seat lay north of Shrewsbury, towards Wem, and it was his only son, named Richard after his father, who made one of this precious couple of harriers. There was little coming and going between the houses of the two families, for Mr. Ellery had not approved his sister's match, Sir Richard's character being not of the best, and heartily disliked the fine-lady airs which she put on when she became wife of a baronet; while she on her side resented her brother's cold looks, and nourished a special grievance against him when he adopted me and announced that he would name me his heir. I make no doubt that she gave tongue to her feeling in the hearing of her son Dick, for among the many taunts which he and his boon fellow Cyrus Vetch cast at me was that I was what they pleased to call a "charity child."

I have mentioned Cyrus Vetch. If I feared Dick Cludde, I both feared and hated his companion. Cyrus was the son of a well-to-do merchant of the town--a man little in stature, but stout, and wondrous big in self esteem. He was the owner of much property, already one of the twelve aldermen, and ambitious, folk said, to arrive at the highest dignity a citizen of Shrewsbury could attain and wear the chain of mayor about his bulldog neck. He doted on his son, who certainly did not take after his father so far as looks went, for he was a tall, lanky fellow with a sallow face, the alderman's countenance being as red as raw beef.

Hating Cyrus as I did, and not without cause, as will be seen hereafter, I may be a trifle unjust in my recollection of him; but I seem to see again a weasel face, with a pair of little restless cunning eyes, and lips that were shaped to a perpetual sneer. As to the sharpness of his tongue I know my memory does not play me false: Dick Cludde's taunts bruised, but Cyrus Vetch's stung.

I had been less than a year at the school when an event happened which had a great bearing on my future life. It was in the autumn of the year 1690. I left afternoon school, and walked up Castle Street, intending to turn down by St. Mary's Church as I was wont to do, and make my way by Dogpole and Wyle Cop to English Bridge and so home. But just as I came to the corner I spied Cludde and Vetch waiting for me, as they sometimes did, at the back end of the church. To avoid them, I went on till I came to the corner of Dogpole and Pride Hill, hoping thereby to escape. But Cyrus Vetch's keen eyes had seen me, and when I came to the turning by Colam's, the vintner's, there were my two tormentors, posted right in my path.

"Aha, young Bold!" says Cyrus, clutching me roughly by the arm, "so you thought to give us the slip, did you?"

I could not deny it, and said nothing.

"Hark 'ee, young Bold," Cyrus went on, "you're to bring us tomorrow morning a good dozen of old Ellery's apples, d'you hear?"

"A good dozen, young Bold," says Cludde, with the precision of an echo.

"Let me go, please, Vetch," I said, endeavoring to wrench my arm away.

"Not so fast, bun face," says he, giving my arm a twist. "You'd best promise, or it will be the worse for you. Now say after me, 'I, Humphrey Bold, adopted brat of John Ellery'--Speak up now!" "Please let me go, Vetch," said I, wriggling in his grasp.

"You won't, eh? You're an obstinate pig, eh? You defy us, eh?" and with every question the bully twisted my arm till I almost screamed with the pain.

"Don't be a ninny," says Cludde. "What's a few apples! Why, old Ellery's trees are loaded with 'em."

Vetch's grip somewhat relaxed while Cludde was speaking, and, seizing the opportunity, I wrenched my arm away with a sudden movement and took to my heels. Being thin and light of foot, I was a fleet runner, and though they immediately set off in pursuit, I gained on them for a few yards, and had some hope of distancing them altogether. But just as I came to where Dogpole runs into Wyle Cop, a stitch in the side, which often seized me at inconvenient times, forced me to slacken speed. Seeing this, they quickened their pace, and in a few moments they would have had me at their mercy.

But in that predicament I heard Joe Punchard whistling, through the open door of the shop where he did 'prentice work for old Matthew Mark, the cooper. I knew Joe well; he had often brought barrels to our farm, and once or twice on my way home from school I had gone into the shop and watched him at his work.

Now, as a fox when the hounds are in full cry behind him will run for shelter into any likely place that offers, so I, hard pressed as I was, rushed panting into the shop, too breathless at first to explain my need.

"Hallo! What's this!" cried Joe, who was just rolling down his sleeves before closing work for the day. "What be the matter, Master Bold? You be all of a sweat and puffing like to burst."

"They're after me! Keep 'em off, Joe!" I gasped.

"After you, be they! Some of your schoolmates worriting of you, eh? Don't be afeared, lad. I be just going home, and I'll see you safe to Bridge.

"Ah! there they be," he added, as my pursuers appeared in the doorway.

"Good afternoon to you, and what might you be pleased to want?"

"Out of the road, Joe Punchard!" cries Cludde, walking into the shop. "I'll teach that little beast to run away."

And he came forward to where I stood, sheltering myself behind Joe's thick-set body.

"Bide a minute," says Joe, lurching so as to shield me. "What ha' Master Bold bin doin' to you?"

"What's that to you?" says Cyrus Vetch, edging round him on the other side. "He's a young sneak, that's what he is, and wants a good basting, and he'll get it, too."

"Not so fast now," says Joe, sticking out his elbows to broaden himself. "I know you, Master Vetch, and 'tis my belief you and Master Cludde are just nought but a brace of bullies, and you ought to be ashamed of yourselves, Master Cludde in particular, seeing as the little lad be your own cousin."

"You shut your mouth, Joe Punchard!" shouts Cludde in a passion. "He my cousin, indeed!--the mean little charity brat!"

"And a blubbering baby, too!" says Vetch, "cries before he is hurt."

"'Tis not much good crying after," says Joe with a chuckle, before I could protest that I was not crying; I always did hate a blubbering boy.

"Now you two boys be off," Joe went on. "I'm going home, and I'll see to it you don't bait Master Bold no more this side of the Bridge. And what's more, I tell you this: that if I cotch you two great chaps worriting the boy again, I'll take and leather you, both of you, and that's flat."

"Try it, bandy-legs," said Vetch with a sneer. "We'll do as we please, and if you dare to lay a hand on either of us, I'll--I'll--"

"What'll you do, then?" says Joe, who all this while had been spreading himself in front of me. "What'll you do then? D'you think I care a farden what you'll do? You'd better behave pretty, Master Vetch, or 'twill be worse for you, my young cockchafer."

At this the two boys backed a little, and Joe, thinking them daunted by his threatening mien, turned to take down the key of the shop from its nail on the wall. But he had no sooner left my side than Vetch sprang forward, and catching me by the arm, gave it a cunning twist that, in spite of myself, made me shriek with pain. Joe was round in an instant, and made for my tormentor, who with Cludde ran towards the door. But in their endeavor to escape they impeded each other: Vetch tripped, and before he could recover his footing Joe had him in an iron grip, and began to shake him as I had many times seen our terrier shake a rat he had caught in the barn.

"Let me go!" yells Cyrus. "Help, Dick! Kick his shins!"

But Cludde, though a big fellow enough, was never over ready to put his head in chancery. He stood in the street, shaking his fist, and writhing his face into terrible grimaces at me.

"Let me go!" cries Vetch again.

"You young viper!" says Joe, shaking him still. "You'll misuse the little lad before my face, will you? And squeal like a pig to be let go, will you?

"Aha! You shall go," he says with a sudden laugh. "Dash me if 'twere not made o' purpose."

Joe Punchard, I have forgotten to mention, was short of stature, standing no more than five feet three. But he was very thick-set and heavily made, with massive arms and legs, the latter somewhat bowed, making him appear even shorter than he was. It was these legs of his, together with his big round head and shock of reddish hair, that inspired some genius of the school with a couplet which was often chanted by the boys when they caught sight of Joe in the street. It ran:

O, pi, rho, bandy-legged Joe,

Turnip and carrots wherever you go.

But bandy-legged as he was, Joe had the great strength which I have often observed to accompany that defect of nature. So it was with exceeding ease he lifted Cyrus Vetch, for all his struggles, with one hand, and dropped him into a barrel that stood, newly finished, against the wall--a barrel of such noble height that Vetch quite disappeared within it. Then, trundling it upon its edge, as draymen do with casks of beer, he brought it to the street, laid it sidelong, and set it rolling.

Now the Wyle Cop at Shrewsbury, as you may know, is a street that winds steeply down to the English Bridge over the Severn. Had it been straight, the bias of the barrel would doubtless have soon carried it to the side, and Joe Punchard might have risen in course of time to the status of a master cooper in his native town. But when I went to the door to see what was happening, there was the barrel in full career, following the curve of the street, and gathering speed with every yard. Joe stood with arms akimbo, smiling broadly. Cludde was racing after the barrel, shouting for someone to stop it.

If I had not already been in such mortal terror of the consequences of Joe's mad freak, I should have laughed to see the wayfarers as they skipped out of the course of the runagate, not one of them aware as yet that it held human contents, nor guessing that the end might be more than broken staves.

By this time Joe himself had come to a sense of his recklessness. He gripped me by the hand, and dragged me down the hill at so fierce a pace that in half a minute all the breath was out of my body. I wondered what he purposed doing, for the barrel was now out of sight past the bend, and could scarce have been overtaken by the wearer of the seven league boots. But as we turned into the straight again, just by Andrew Cruddle, the saddler's, we again espied the terrible barrel, rolling with many bumps towards the head of the bridge.

And then I verily believe that my heart for some seconds ceased to beat, and I am sure that Joe shared my dismay, for he tightened the grip of his great strong hand upon my puny one until I could have sworn it was crushed to a pulp. At the bridge head were two gentlemen, who had to all appearance been engaged in chatting, for one still sat on the parapet, while the other stood within a foot or two of him. They were not talking now, but gazing at the barrel rolling down towards them, and the one who was seated wore the trace of a smile upon his face.

But the other--Heaven knows what terror seized me when my eyes lighted upon him: it was none other than Joshua Vetch, the father of the boy who, as I feared, was being churned to a jelly; and he stood full in the path of the barrel.

Mr. Vetch, as I have said, was a small but corpulent man, and stood very upright, with a slight backward inclination, to balance, I suppose, the exceeding greatness of his rotundity. His countenance habitually expressed disapproval, and his shaggy brows were drawn down now in an angry frown. I perceived that he said something to his companion, and then I saw no more for a while, a mist seeming to gather before my eyes.

When I regained possession of my faculties, dreading what might have happened, I found myself on the skirts of a group of five or six, and heard the loud voice of Mr. Vetch bellowing forth words which, for modesty's sake, I forbid my pen to write. He was not dead, then, I thought, nor even hurt, or assuredly he would not have had the strength to curse with such vigor. But what of Cyrus?

"I'll have the law on the villain! Run for a potticary! D'you hear, you gaping jackass? Run for Mr. Pinhorn and bid him come here!"

And then followed a string of oaths like to those I had heard before. The group parted hastily, and out came Dick Cludde, with a face as white as milk, and sped up the town as fast as his long legs would carry him. No doubt he was the "gaping jackass" whom Mr. Vetch had so addressed in his fury.

Pushing my way through the townsmen who had gathered, and whose numbers were swelled every moment by the afflux of aproned grocers, and potboys, and 'prentices, and others from the streets, I saw Cyrus laid on his back by the parapet, white and still, his father pacing heavily up and down, and his friend Captain Galsworthy fending off the prying onlookers with his cane.

"I'll thrash the villain to a pulp! I'll send him to the plantations, I will! I'll break every bone in his body!"

So Mr. Vetch roared and, much as I disliked him, I could not but feel a certain compassion, too, for all the world knew how he doted on his son. I looked around for Joe Punchard, to see whether he was in hearing of these threats, but he was not among the crowd.

By and by came Mr. Pinhorn, the surgeon, and some while after him four lads bearing a stretcher, upon which the unconscious form of my enemy was conveyed slowly up the town to Mr. Vetch's house on Pride Hill. I followed on the edge of the crowd until I saw the doors close upon the bearers, and then I betook myself home, in sore distress at the fate in store for my friend Joe Punchard, and in some terror lest I should share it, the mad freak of which he was guilty having been performed on my behalf.

Chapter 2
Joe Breaks His Indentures

It was so much later than my usual hour for returning from school that I was not surprised to see Mistress Pennyquick at the gate of our farm, shading her eyes against the westering sun as she looked for me up the road. I endeavored to compose my countenance so as to betray no sign of the excitement through which I had passed; but the attempt failed lamentably, and when the good creature began to question me, I burst into tears. This was so rare an occurrence with me that she was mightily concerned and adjured me to tell all, promising that if I had done wrong she would shield me from my father's anger. And when in answer to this I told her what Joe Punchard had done to Cyrus Vetch, and the terrible things I had heard the alderman threaten against him, she laughed and said I was too tender hearted for a boy, and Joe Punchard would be none the worse for a basting, and a deal more to the same tune, which almost broke through my determination to say nothing of what had caused the mischief; for, after all, Dick Cludde and Cyrus Vetch were my schoolfellows, and, in my day; for one boy to tell on another was the unpardonable sin.

My father came in soon after, and when he heard so much of the story as I had told Mistress Pennyquick he drew his fingers through his beard and said in his quiet way: "To be sure, barrels were not made for that kind of vetch!"

And then we sat down to supper. We had hardly begun when there came a smart rap on the door, and, with the freedom of our country manners, in walked a visitor. My heart gave a jump when I saw it was none other than Captain Galsworthy, the gentleman with whom Mr. Vetch had been in converse at the bridge.

We knew the captain well; he was, in a way, one of the notable persons of our town. We boys looked on him with a vast admiration and reverence, not so much for his title--for there are captains and captains, and I have known some who have done little in the matter of feats of arms--as because he bore on his lean and rugged countenance marks which no one could mistake. A deep scar seamed his right temple, and on one of his cheeks were several little black pits which we believed to be the marks of bullets. He spoke but rarely of his own doings, and until he came to Shrewsbury a few years before this he had been a stranger to the town: but it was commonly reported that he had been in the service of the Czar of Muscovy, and since that potentate was ever unwilling that any officer who had once served him should leave him (save by death or hanging), it was supposed that the captain had made his escape. He lived alone in a little cottage on the Wem road, and, not being too plentifully endowed with this world's goods, he eked out his competency by giving lessons in fencing, both with singlesticks and swords.

Well, in comes the captain, cocking a twinkling eye at me, lays on the table the cane without which he never went abroad, and, placing a chair for himself at the table, says:

"'Tis to be hoped we are not in for a ten years' Trojan war, Master Humphrey."

Though I understood nothing of his meaning, I knew he made reference to the recent escapade, and I felt mightily uncomfortable. My father looked from one to the other, but did not break his silence.

"They haven't put you to the Iliads yet, I suppose," says the captain, helping himself to a mug of our home-brewed cider, "but you know, neighbor Ellery, 'twas an apple that set the Greeks and Trojans by the ears, and 'tis apples, or rather the want of 'em, that is like to put discord between some of our families hereabout."

"You speak in riddles, Captain," says my father at last; "and why are you eying Humphrey in that quizzical way?"

"Why, bless my soul, don't you know? I thought it had been half over the county by this."

"I know that that 'prentice lad Punchard hath half-killed young Vetch, and richly deserves what he will no doubt get tomorrow."

"And is that all? Have you told only half your story, Humphrey?"

This direct question made me still more uncomfortable, especially as my father's eyes were sternly bent upon me. He hated lies, and half truths still more, and I could see that he was dimly suspecting me of a complicity in Joe Punchard's action to which I had not confessed. But Captain Galsworthy was a shrewd old man, and he saw at once how the matter stood.

"No peaching, eh, lad?" he said kindly. "I've an inquisitive turn of mind, and after that performance with the barrel--and it was a monstrous comical sight, Ellery, to see the little alderman skip out of the way when the barrel made straight for his shins, but not so funny when he pulls at the shock head sticking out and finds it belongs to his own son--after that performance, I say, I caught young Dick Cludde by the ear, and made him tell me the story. And it begins with apples--like this excellent cider of yours, Ellery."

He quaffed a deep draught and leaned back in his chair, giving me another friendly wink. The captain was ever somewhat long winded over his stories, and I could see that my father was growing impatient; but he sat back in his chair with his hands upon the arms and said never a word.

"Young Cludde and Cyrus Vetch, it seems, have a sweet tooth for your apples, Ellery," said the captain, "and Cludde told me with a fine indignation that Humphrey flatly refused to fill his pockets for their behoof. They were proceeding to enforce their requisition, I gather, when the boy broke from them, and, finding himself hard pressed by and by, took refuge behind Joe Punchard's bandy legs. And Joe must needs take up the cudgels on behalf of the oppressed, and chose an original way of punishing the oppressor. And thus the rolling of the barrel is explained."

At this Mistress Pennyquick broke out into vehement denunciation of the two boys, but my father silenced her. Quietly he began to question me: he would take no denial, and drew out of me bit by bit the whole story of the bullying I had suffered from those two of my schoolfellows.

And then he was more angry than I had seen him ever before. He smote the arm of the chair with his great fist, and vowed he would not have me ill used; and though he said but little, and never once raised his voice, I knew by the set of his lips and the gleam of his eye that it would go hard with anyone who baited me again. Then the captain made a proposition for which I have been thankful all my life long.

"The moral of it is, Ellery, that Humphrey must be a pupil of mine.

"Give me your arm, boy.

"Ah!" says he, feeling the muscle, which was soft enough, no doubt, seeing that I was only eleven and had never done anything about the farm. "We must alter that. Let him come to me twice a week, Ellery, and he shall learn the arts of self defense, first with nature's own weapons, for boxing I take to be the true foundation of all bodily exercise, and afterwards, when he is a little grown, the more delicate science of swordsmanship, which demands bodily strength and wits, and to which the other is but a prelude. And I warrant you, if he have the right stuff in him, that by the time the schoolmaster has done with him he shall be able to hold his own against any man, and will need no succors from Joe Punchard or anyone else."

Hereupon Mistress Pennyquick set up a cry about the wickedness of teaching little boys to fight, and the state she would be in if I was some day brought home mangled and disfigured, and a great deal more to the same effect. The captain tapped the table until she had finished, and then, with a fine courtly bow, he said:

"Spoken like a woman, ma'am. Humphrey will suffer hard knocks, to be sure; yes, please God, he shall have many a black eye, and many a bloody nose, and we shall make a man of him, ma'am: a gentleman he is already."

"Yes, to be sure," says the simple creature, "and his mother was a born lady, and--"

"Tuts, ma'am," the captain here interrupted. "I was not alluding to his pedigree. The boy has suffered torment for months without breathing a word of it to betray his schoolfellows; from that I deduce that he has the spirit of a gentleman, and I want no further proof."

"'Tis time the boy was abed," says my father. "Run away, lad."

I got up at once to go, guessing that my father wished to have some private talk with Captain Galsworthy. My ears were tingling, I confess, with his praise of me, and my heart throbbed with delight and pride at the thought of being the captain's pupil. I could not sleep for thinking of it. I imagined all manner of scenes in which I should some day figure, and saw myself already holding off five enemies at once with my flashing sword. These visions haunted my dreams when at last I slept, and it was after a bout of especial fierceness that I found myself lying awake, in a great heat and breathlessness.

And then I was aware of an actual sound--a sound which no doubt had entered into my dreams as the clash of arms. It was a soft and regular tapping, a ghostly sound to hear at dead of night, and like to scare a boy of quick imagination. I lay for some moments in a state bordering on panic, unable to think, much less to act.

Tap, tap, tap--so it went on, like the ticking of the great clock on the stairs, only louder and more substantial. It ceased, and I held my breath, wondering whether I should hear it again. Then it recommenced, and I was about to spring from my bed and run to tell Mistress Pennyquick when a sudden thought held me: What would Captain Galsworthy think if he knew I had fled from a sound? Would he regard me as the right stuff of which to make a man?

The captain's good opinion was worth so much to me now that I crushed down my fears and sat up in bed (yet keeping a tight clutch upon the blanket), and tried to use my reason.

The tapping, I reflected, must be caused by some person or thing. A ghost is a spirit, and insubstantial, and I had never heard that the ghost which some of the townsfolk (chiefly servant maids) had seen in St. Alkmund's Churchyard had done more at any time than glide silently among the tombs. And even as I decided that the sound must have a natural cause, I had startling confirmation of my conclusion in a new sound--nothing else than a sneeze, sudden, and short, and stifled. The tapping ceased, and while I was still trying to collect my wits I heard a groan, and immediately afterwards a voice calling my name, and then a new tapping, only quicker.

It was now clear to me that some one was at my window, though, seeing that my room was some twenty feet above the ground, I was at a loss to imagine how the tapper had mounted there.

My fears now being merged in surprise, I got out of bed, stole to the window, and pulled the blind an inch aside.

"Master Bold! Master Bold!" came the voice again, and, venturing a little more, I put my head between the blind and the window, and saw a dark form against the clear summer sky.

"Master Bold, 'tis me, Joe Punchard," said the voice in a whisper. "Canst let me in, lad, without making a noise?"

Without more ado I lifted the sash gradually, for it was heavy and creaked, and I feared to rouse the household. When it was high enough for Joe's bulky form to pass through he clambered over the sill, and stood in my room.

"How did you get up, Joe?" I asked in a whisper.

"Got a ladder from the rick yard, lad. I bin tapping for nigh half an hour, I reckon. You be one of the seven sleepers, for sure."

"But what do you want, Joe? You can't stay here, you know."

"Nor don't want to. I be come to tell you, lad, I be going away."

"Going away, Joe?"

"Yes. No one knows it but you, and I wouldn't ha' telled you only the old mother will be in a rare taking when she finds me gone, and I want you to tell her as I've come to no harm."

"But why, Joe?"

"Vetch--that's why. 'Tis no place for me now, lad. He bin cursing and swearing he'll send me to the plantations for that business with the barrel, and he'll keep his word. And so I be going to run for it."

"But where, Joe? And what about your 'dentures?"

"That's where it is: my 'dentures must go too. If I be catched, there's a flogging and prison for that. But I don't mean to be catched. Before the sun's up I'll be on my way to Bristowe."

"That's ever so far."

"So 'tis, but not further than a pair of legs can walk."

"And will you get a place with a cooper there?"

"No, no; no more coopering for me; I be done with barrels for good and all. I be going to sea."

"To sea! What ever made you think of such a thing?"

"One thing and another. And I won't be the first, not even from such an upland place as Shrewsbury. Why, haven't we heard Mistress Hind tell time and again how her brother John Benbow ran away to sea nigh upon thirty years ago?"

"True, and so did Sam Blevins, and hasn't been heard of since, Joe."

"Well, if Vetch ships me to the plantations you may be sure no more will be heard of Joe Punchard, so 'tis as broad as 'tis long."

"'Tis all my fault, Joe. If I hadn't run into the shop this wouldn't have happened, and you'd have worked out your 'dentures, and maybe risen to be a partner with Mr. Mark. I wish I had let them catch me, Joe, I do."

"Now don't you take on, Master Humphrey. As for partners, I be sick of making barrels for other folks' beer, that's the truth, and by what I've heard there's riches to be picked up in the Indies, and many a sea captain is a deal better off than Matthew Mark. And I'm set on trying it, lad, the more so as, by long and short, I dursn't stay in Shrewsbury no longer. So you'll be so good as go and see the old mother tomorrow, and tell her I be gone to sea, and I'll send her home silks, and satins, and diamonds, too, maybe, and I'll come home some day rich as creases, as I heard parson say once."

"I hope you will, Joe. Will you write to me and tell me how you are getting on?"

"Bless your life, I can do no more than make my mark. But maybe I'll light on some scholar who'll write down out of my mouth, and I'll make him limn a barrel on the paper, and then you'll know for sure 'tis me."

This conversation had proceeded in whispers, but Joe's whisper was sonorous, and I was in some fear lest Mistress Pennyquick, whose room was hard by, should hear the rumble and take alarm. Yet I could not refrain from keeping him while I told of the matter so near my heart--the offer of Captain Galsworthy to take me as a pupil. Joe listened very sympathetically.

"'Tis an ill wind blows no one good," he said. "That there barrel makes a sailor of me; maybe 'tis to make a sojer of you."

"And what of Cyrus Vetch?" I could not help saying.

"Ah! Cyrus Vetch!" muttered Joe, looking troubled. "I be afeared 'twill make him a downright enemy to you, lad. But you'll grow, and captain will learn you how to ply your fists, and when it comes to a fight, mind of my fighting name, and punch hard."

Then, having promised to see his mother and do what I could to console her, I wrung his hand and wished him well, and he climbed out again by the window, and in the starlight I watched him carry the ladder across the yard; and then with a final wave of the hand he vanished into the night.

Chapter 3
I Meet The Mohocks

At breakfast I said nothing of Joe's midnight visit, reckoning that it would not be long before the news of his flight got abroad. It was indeed the subject of a great buzz of talk among my schoolfellows, who flocked about me as I walked down Castle Street, demanding to hear the full story from my own lips. I could tell them nothing that they did not know, save only my leave-taking with Joe Punchard, which, of course, I had resolved to keep very close. I learned from them that Cyrus was abed, and like to stay there, said Mr. Pinhorn, for a week or more. His father was in a desperate rage, and had sent horsemen along all the roads in pursuit of the runaway, and I had some fear that my good friend would be caught and brought back to receive his punishment.

However, nothing had been heard of him by the time school was over, so that I had great hopes that he had got himself clean away. I went to see his mother as I had promised, and said what I could to comfort her; but the good woman was mightily upset, and declared in a passion of weeping that she was sure she would never see her Joe again.

That evening at supper my father was even more quiet than his wont. Mistress Pennyquick told me afterwards that he had been to see his sister Lady Cludde and her husband at Cludde Court, and given them a piece of his mind. What passed between them I know not, but I do know that my father never set foot in Cludde Court again, nor did his sister come any more to the farm, even when her brother lay a-dying. His visit had this good effect, however, that I suffered no more bullying at the hands of Dick Cludde or Cyrus Vetch. Dick eyed me with a malignant scowl whenever he met me, and as for Cyrus, who did not come back to school for a good ten days, he looked over my head as though I did not exist, which gave me no discomfort, you may be sure. At the end of that year they were both taken from school, Cludde going to Cambridge, and Vetch to assist his father, who was a grain merchant in a substantial way, as all Shrewsbury supposed.

It would be a tedious matter were I to tell all the little happenings of the next few years. Whether it was due to my constant exercise under Captain

Galsworthy's tuition, I know not, but certainly, from that very summer, I grew at an amazing rate, shooting up until I was as tall as boys three or four years older, yet hardening at the same time. Twice a week regularly I betook myself to the captain's little cottage on the Wem road, and spent an hour with him in mastering the principles and practice of what he called the noble arts of self defense. He was pleased to say that I was quick of eye and nimble of body, and, being on my side very eager to learn, I was speedily in his good books, and he seemed to take a special pleasure in teaching me.

At first I found our bouts at fisticuffs a severe tax. The captain, though well on in years, was still hale and active, and, being tall and spare, he had a great advantage of me. With the long reach of his arms he could pummel me without giving me the least chance of reprisal, and many's the day I crawled home after our encounters bruised and sore, provoking indignant remonstrances from Mistress Pennyquick. But I refused to let her coddle me, and as my appetite never failed, and I throve amazingly, the good woman at last ceased to lament, and, as I discovered, was wont behind my back to vaunt my growing manliness.

By the time I was fifteen I was as tall as the captain himself, and then my share of bruises ceased to be so disproportionate. In skill, whether with the fists or the foils, he was always vastly my superior; indeed, to this day I have never met his equal. But I had youth on my side, and sometimes the old man at the end of a particularly arduous bout would sigh, and wish he were younger by a score of years.

No one could have been more generous in encouragement and praise. It would have amused an onlooker, I am sure, to see him, when I had had the good fortune to tap claret, mopping the injured feature and all the time maintaining a flow of complimentary remarks.

"Capital, my lad!"--after fifty years I can hear him still--"on my life, a neat one, Humphrey; I shall make something of you yet, my boy."

And then we fall to it again, and, being somewhat overconfident, perhaps, after my success, I fail a little in my guard, and the captain sees his opportunity and lands me such a series of staggerers that I see a thousand stars, and there am I dabbing my nose while he cries again: "Capital, my lad! A Roland for an Oliver! And now we'll wash away the sanguinary traces of our combat and allay our noble rage with a mug of cider."

And thus, giving and receiving hard knocks, we continued to be the best of friends.

These years brought changes in their train. One day Joshua Vetch, Cyrus' father, died suddenly of an apoplectic fit, brought on, folk said, by disappointment at Mr. Adderton the draper being elected mayor over his head. And then it was found that, so far from being wealthy as was supposed, he had been for years living beyond his means, being ably assisted in his expenditure by Cyrus. His affairs were in great disorder; Cyrus himself was totally unprovided for, and but for his uncle, John Vetch, a reputable attorney of our town, who took pity on him, and gave him articles, God knows what would have become of him.

At this change of fortune I could not but remember how, years before, he had sneered at me as a "charity brat." I fancy he remembered it too, for when I met him face to face one day, as I returned from school, coming out of his uncle's office, he flushed deeply and then gave me such a look of hatred that I felt uneasy for days after.

Cyrus had never borne a good name in Shrewsbury, and after his father's death he seemed to grow reckless. Dick Cludde was still at college, though I never heard that he did any good there, and in the vacations he and Cyrus consorted much together, and became in fact the ringleaders of a wild set whose doings were a scandal in Shrewsbury for many a day. Cludde, it seemed, had made a jaunt to London with other young bloods at the end of the term in the December of this year 1694, to see the great pageant of Queen Mary's funeral.

The adventure did him no good, for when he returned to Shrewsbury he formed, with Vetch and others of his kidney, a gang in imitation of the Mohocks, as they were called-- the band of dissolute young ruffians who then infested London, wrenching off knockers, molesting women in the streets, pinking sober citizens, and tumbling the old watchmen into the gutters. Our streets at night became the scene of riotous exploits of this kind, and our watch, being old and feeble men, were quite unable to cope with the rioters, so that decent folk began to be afraid to stir abroad after dark. Though they disguised themselves for these forays, it was shrewdly suspected who they were; but they escaped actual detection, and indeed, they were held in such terror by the townsfolk that no one durst move against them openly, for fear of what might come of it.

Things grew to such a height that one Saturday the mayor, with half a dozen aldermen, walked out to the little cottage on the Wem Road, and besought Captain Galsworthy's aid. The captain and I chanced to be in the thick of an encounter with the foils, and neither of us heard the rap on the door which announced the visitors. A gust of air when the door was opened apprised us that we had onlookers at our sport; but the captain's eyes never left mine until with a dexterous turn of the wrist, which I had long envied and sought in vain to copy, he sent my foil flying to the end of the room.

"Capital, capital!" cried he, removing his mask and wiping his heated brow.

"Good morning, Mr. Mayor," he added; "we have kept you waiting, I fear; but we were just approaching the critical moment: the issue was doubtful, and there is little satisfaction in a drawn battle.

"Your looks are portentous, gentlemen: is this a visit of state, may I ask?"

Whereupon the mayor, an honest little draper, made a speech which I am sure he had diligently conned over beforehand. He passed from a recital of the woes under which Shrewsbury suffered to a most flattering eulogium of the captain's prowess, to which my good friend listened with an air of approval that amused me mightily. And then the mayor came to the point, and in the name of the corporation and all decent citizens of Shrewsbury besought the captain to suppress the disturbers of their peace.

"Hum! ha!" said the captain, rubbing his nose reflectively. "I am an old man, Mr. Mayor: methinks this is work for younger blood than mine."

"No, no!" cried the company in chorus.

"We seed tha knock the steel from the hand of Master Bold there as 'twere a knitting needle," says the mayor, whose speech was as broad as his figure.

"Well, well," says the captain, "I'll think of it, my friends. You do me great honor, and I thank you for your visit."

The captain and I talked over the matter between ourselves, and the upshot of our consultation was that we got together a little band of his former pupils, and for several nights in succession we perambulated the streets of Shrewsbury from the English to the Welsh Bridge and from the Castle to the Quarry, with naked swords and a martial air. But we had our exercise for nothing. The town was as quiet as a graveyard, and the only disturber of the peace that engaged our attention was poor Tom Jessopp, the drayman, who, one night, having drunk more old October than was good for him, encountered us as he was staggering home down Shoplatch, and invited us, first to wet our whistles, and, on our declining, to fight him for a pint. We escorted him home and put him to bed, not without some difficulties and inconveniences, and that was the first and last of our adventures, the captain declaring that to deal with topers was no work for a man of honor.

The very night after our company was thus dissolved the mayor was knocked down at the foot of Swan Hill by the Town Wall, gagged and trussed, and laid upon his own doorstep, where he was found by the maidservant in the morning, having wrought himself to the verge of apoplexy by his struggles to rid himself of his bonds. He besought the captain with tears of outraged dignity to resume his guardianship of the town; but the old warrior merely rubbed his nose and spoke of rheumatism.

The outrages occurred only at intervals, and ceased altogether during the college terms, when Dick Cludde was absent, so that we were not far wrong in our inference that he was the fount and origin of the deeds of lawlessness. The townsfolk, you may be sure, did not love him; nor did the high and mighty airs Sir Richard and my lady chose to assume in their dealings with the citizens win them many friends; so that when it became known, about the time when Dick left Cambridge finally, without a degree, that his father had suffered serious reverses of fortune in his adventures in oversea trade, there were few who felt anything but satisfaction.

At this time I was midway in my seventeenth year--a big strapping fellow standing five feet ten, having quite outgrown the delicacy of my childhood. I was high up in the school, on good terms with the masters, though my Latin and Greek was never considerable: on better terms with the boys, for, I must own, my inclinations were rather towards baseball and quoits than towards the nice discrimination of longs and shorts. I had developed in particular an amazing strength of arm, which stood me in good stead in wrestling bouts, and led to my being counted two in our tugs of war. It was this same strength, I fancy, that made my schoolfellows chary of provoking me to wrath, for which I was somewhat sorry, having always loved a fight.

During these years no tidings came to us of Joe Punchard. His poor mother, who earned a living by washing for some of our Shrewsbury folk, feared the worst from his long silence. But Mistress Nelly Hind, who kept a coffee shop in Raven Street, called Mistress Punchard a croaker and bade her be of good cheer, for she had neither seen nor directly heard from her brother John Benbow for twenty years; yet he was alive and well, and captain of a king's ship, if rumor were not a false, lying jade.

"Not that your Joe will ever rise to such a height," she added.

"Sure he's a better boy than ever your John was," said Mistress Punchard, up in arms for her offspring.

"John's legs are as straight as the bed post," retorted his sister, and then the two women began a war of words, in the midst of which, having drunk my dish of coffee, I slipped away.

I rarely speculated on my future, and my father never spoke of it. We took it for granted that I should succeed him in his little property, and during the school holidays I sometimes accompanied him to market, and learned to handle samples of grain and to discuss the points of his fat cattle.

It was when I was approaching the end of my seventeenth year that I began to think of the future more nearly. My father had suffered long--though Mistress Pennyquick and I had known nothing of it, he being so reticent--from a disease which nowadays physicians call angina pectoris, a disease that grips a man by the chest, as 'twere his breastbones are ground together, with breathlessness and exquisite pain. As he grew older, the attacks recurred more frequently and with greater violence, and after one of them, the first I had seen with my own eyes, he sent for Mr. Vetch, the attorney, and was closeted with him a great while in his room. Mistress Pennyquick's face was very grave when she spoke to me about it afterwards.

"'Tis a bad sign when a man sends for his lawyer, Humphrey," she said. "I can't abide 'un, for they always make me think of my latter end. Your father have made his will, I'll be bound, and I wish he spoke more free of things. But there, 'tis always the way; empty barrels make the most noise, as the saying is, and I will groan with the toothache while the poor master will suffer his agonies without a word."

One night as we were sitting reading, my father had an attack which terrified us. All at once, without a moment's warning, he dropped his book, and stood up, bending forward, his face blue, his eyes almost starting from his head. We hastened to him, but he motioned us away, and then Mistress Pennyquick bade me ride for Mr. Pinhorn. I snatched my cap, and, knowing that with my long legs I could reach the town by the fields more quickly than on horseback by the road, I did not stay to saddle Jerry, but set off at full speed across five-acre, vaulted the gate into the spinney, and so on till I gained the bridge, by which time I was blowing like a furnace.

It was dark, being October, and though I knew every yard of our ground, I marvel now to think how I escaped breaking my leg in a ditch or coming to some other mishap. I raced on to Raven Street, where Mr. Pinhorn lived, and by good luck found him just alighting at the door from his nag. I told him my errand in gasps; the good surgeon understood without much telling, and he leaped again into the saddle (his foot never having left the stirrup) and galloped away.

My knees shook so violently with the exertions I had made that I would fain have rested awhile before returning. But the thought that my father might die in my absence struck me with a chill, and I set off at a swinging stride after the surgeon.

I had gone but a few yards, however, when ahead of me, by the light of a flickering oil lamp, hanging from a bracket before one of the houses,

I saw a group of some five or six, youths by their build, gathered about a doorway. Immediately afterwards I heard from the same spot a harsh sound as of rending wood, followed by guffaws of laughter. The party then moved quickly on for a few paces, and again came to a halt at a doorway, whence in a few seconds the same sound reached my ears.

Passing the door at which I had first seen them, I noticed that where the knocker should have been there was nothing but a few bent nails and a splintered panel. After former experiences my suspicion scarce needed this confirmation: without doubt these were our Shrewsbury Mohocks, out for a night's frolic. I had never before seen them at their diversions, my patrolling of the streets with Captain Galsworthy having been a mere parade, as I have related, and now I was in no mood to encounter them, having the trouble of my father's illness on my mind. But I perceived that they were engaged in wreaking their knavery upon the sign board of Nelly Hind, and my blood waxed hot at the thought of the poor woman's distress, and my fingers itched to strike a blow on her behalf.

Strong as I was, I knew 'twould be mere folly to attempt single-handed to engage half a dozen, and I was thinking of running quickly to some of the members of the Captain's disbanded force and enlisting their help when the situation was changed by the arrival of old Ben Ivimey, the feeblest of the ancient watchmen to whom the peace of Shrewsbury was confided. He was past sixty and stone deaf, and his bent old figure, with a lantern in one hand and a staff in the other, came round the corner all unsuspecting what was in store for him.

The Mohocks, intent upon their mischief, did not observe the coming of the watchman. He was a little man, but must have been of some mettle in his day, for, perceiving what is afoot, he toddles up in his odd headlong gait, and laying his hand on the arm of one of the roisterers, formally arrests him in the name of the mayor.

The fellow swings round at the touch, and bursts into a roar of laughter. He was masked, as were all his companions; but I knew him by his make to be Cyrus Vetch. Well, he laughs, and shakes off the watchman's feeble grasp, and springing back, draws his sword; and in another instant there was old Ben, the center of the group, skipping this way and that to avoid their sword points, protesting, threatening, appealing, escaping one merely to run upon another.

I will say this for them, that they intended to do him no harm; their lunges were sportive and not in earnest; but diverting as the sport was to them, it was the very contrary to the old man, whose cries proclaimed that he thought his last hour was come.

All this happened in the space of a few moments. I was unwilling to leave old Ben to the mercy of his tormentors while I ran for assistance, as I was intending; yet it was clear I could do nothing alone.

"John Kynaston," thinks I, "lives only a couple of hundred yards away: he and I together might account for the ruffians."

I was just turning to make my way to Kynaston's house, when a cry of pain from the old man drove out all considerations of prudence. In dodging one of that ring of steel points it would appear that he had stumbled full upon another, and the weapon, by accident or otherwise, had pierced his arm. My blood was up; I clean forgot my design of running for help. I had no weapon with me, but, hastily scanning the dim-lit street for a something to wield, my foot kicked an object in the gutter. In a trice I had seized it in both hands, barely conscious of its weight. Then I ran with it the few yards that separated me from the scuffle, and, lifting my weapon above my head, hurled it at the nearest of the group. There was a sound of fury from the fellow at whom I had aimed, and from the two beyond him--a sound muffled and all but inarticulate, for the missile which had fallen like a bolt among them was a large wooden bin filled with household refuse, and placed in the gutter for the coming of the early morning scavenger.

Chapter 4
Captain John Benbow

Our Mohocks suffered some discomfort, I fear, as the contents of the bin hurtled upon them. Household refuse hath, to be sure, no sweetness of savor; and the shower of bones, eggshells, cabbage stalks, potato parings, rinds of bacon, and what not, with a plentiful admixture of white wood ash, served to stay their activity in deeds, though I must own it did but enhance the fury of their tongues. But the diversion gave me a breathing space in which I drew old Ben within the shadow of a doorway and took his staff from his fainting hands--not without resistance on his part, for the mettlesome old fellow refused to yield up his insignia until I brought my face within an inch of his dim eyes, and he recognized me for a friend.

"Spring your rattle, man!" I cried, and then to the din of curses and roars for vengeance there was added the sharp crackle of his alarm signal.

By this time the leaders of the rioters had rubbed the dust from their eyes and came towards me, the foremost of them, Cyrus Vetch, shouting to his comrades to spit me like a toad. He had recognized me, and sprang towards the doorway where I stood with staff aslant, the trembling watchman still whirling his rattle behind. Mad with rage he cut at me with his sword, which bit deep into the staff, by that very fact becoming for a brief moment useless.

Before Vetch could recover his weapon, I had withdrawn mine, and lunging fair upon him, I dealt him a thrust that sent him spinning halfway across the street. But I was now beset by his comrades, who made at me from both sides of the porch, but for whose shelter I should in all likelihood have been overborne.

They had some sense of fair play, however. They returned their swords to the scabbards, and were for trusting to their fists alone. I contrived to give one of them a smart tap on the crown before they came to close quarters; but ere I could recover myself they were upon me, the staff was wrenched from my grasp, and I was as hard put to it as a stag bayed by hounds. I made what play I could with my fists, and got home at least one blow for two; but the odds were too heavy against me, and when at length a fellow as big as myself slipped round to my back and gripped me hard by the neck, all my struggles did not avail to prevent my being shoved and pulled and hustled out into the middle of the street.

Vetch had picked himself up, and now came running towards me in a frenzy. In his rage he had plucked off his mask, revealing his distorted features to all the good folk who, I doubt not, by this time had their heads out at their windows, viewing the scene from a secure altitude.

"Out of the way, Mytton!" he screamed, his voice shrill with passion. "Out of the way, I say; I will crop his ears, the cur!"

Burt Mytton, the fellow who had me by the neck, and some others of the band, were not for pushing things to such extremities. They closed about to protect me, and even Dick Cludde caught Vetch's arm and expostulated with him. Another meanwhile had snatched old Ivimey's rattle from him, and ever and anon amid the din I caught the sound of his quavering voice calling, "Help for the watch! O my sakes! O my bones!"

Then a cry arose:

"To the river! Give 'em a ducking!" and in another moment there we were, myself and Ivimey, being lugged at a quick scuffle down the street towards the Severn. There was no hope of escape, and I had resigned myself to the imminent bath, when at a turn in the narrow roadway we found the path blocked by two pedestrians.

With Mytton's hand forcing my head downwards I did not at first see them, but I heard a loud voice call, "Hold, rascals!" breaking in upon the watchman's feeble cry, "O my sakes! Help for the watch!"

"Out of the way!" cried Vetch; but the next moment I heard a clatter of steel upon the cobbles; and guessed that the stranger had struck my enemy's sword from his hand. Then my neck was released, and looking up I saw my captor himself captive in the grip of a tall man in riding cloak and high boots, while Vetch was struggling with a short, thick-set fellow who had his arms about the other's body.

Bullies are ever cowards at heart, and the rest of the band, finding the tables thus turned upon them, had taken to their heels and disappeared into the night.

"Let me go, hound!" yelled Vetch, and at the answer I started with a thrill of pleasure.

"Let ye go! Not for all the aldermen in the country. 'Twas your tricks drove me out of Shrewsbury, and seemingly ye're at 'em still. You ha'nt learnt your lesson, Master Vetch; more fool you."

It was Joe Punchard's voice. If I had doubted it I should have been assured by a word that fell from his companion.

"Haul him to the watch house, Joe. I'll bring this fellow!"

"And the bag, Captain?" says Joe.

"Give it to this long fellow," says the other, with a hard look at me.

And I found a large bag thrust into my arms, which Joe had been carrying and had dropped on the road at the encounter.

By this time a crowd had assembled, the good folk who had been craning their necks at the windows having swarmed out, now that the danger was past. And as we thronged up the street a score of voices poured into the ears of the man Joe had called "captain" the full tale of the Mohocks' doings.

I walked among them, shouldering the bag. I perceived that Joe had not recognized me, which was not to be wondered at, seeing that when he last saw me I was a pale slip of a boy, whereas now I was a tall brawny youth with cheeks the color of a ripe russet. And Joe himself was not quite the 'prentice lad I had known. His legs indeed were no less bowed than of yore; nor was his hair less red; but the round face appeared rounder than ever by reason of a thick fringe of whiskers. His body had filled out, and he moved with a rolling gait that caused him to usurp more than one man's share of the narrow street.

When we had laid the two ruffians safely in ward, the captain said to Joe:

"Now we'll go visit Nelly, and 'gad, my limbs yearn for bed, Joe. This fellow can still carry the bag; 'tis worth a groat."

I grinned, and stepping alongside of Joe, whose head did not reach much above my elbow, I looked down on him, and said:

"Don't you know me, Joe?"

His start of surprise set me a-smiling. His round face, somewhat more weatherbeaten than when I saw it last, expressed amazement, incredulity, and half a dozen more emotions in turn.

"Bless my soul!" he cried. "Sure 'tis little Humphrey Bold, growed mountain high. Give me the bag, sir; God forbid you should bear a load for Joe Punchard."

"No, no," I replied. "I'll earn my groat, now I've begun. And right glad I am to see you, Joe; I had thought never to look on your face again."

"And would not, but for my dear captain," says he.

"Captain, 'tis Master Bold, the boy I told ye of. 'Twas him I saved from the hands of Cyrus Vetch the last day I was at home, and sure 'tis a wonderful thing that the very night of homecoming we save him again. Vetch needs another turn in the barrel, methinks. I wonder if my old master has one that will hold his long carcass.

"But look 'ee, Master Humphrey, this be Captain Benbow, Mistress Nelly's brother, and my dear master. Oh, I've a deal to tell 'ee of, and a deal to hear, I warrant me. Is my old mother yet alive, sir?"

"Yes, and hale and hearty, Joe, though she has well-nigh given up hope of the silks and satins you promised her."

"Bless her heart, she shall have 'em now. We have rid from Bristowe, sir, the captain and me, and we stayed but to put up our horses at the Bull and Gate, where I left my bag filled with good store of things for the old woman. Won't she open her eyes! Won't she thank Heaven for bandy-legged Joe!"

We had now reached the door of Mistress Hind's house, and as I set down the bag a great oath burst from Captain Benbow's lips.

"Split me!" says he, eying the splintered panel and the gap where the knocker had been. "Had I those villains on deck they should have a supper of rope's end, I warrant you."

His voice was rough, and his tongue had a keen Shropshire tang, which indeed it never lost, giving thereby evidence to confute those who afterwards claimed for him kinship with a noble family. In truth Benbow was the son of an honest tanner of our town, and took no shame of his origin: his greatness was above such pettiness of spirit. He had run away to sea at an early age, and for some years lived a hard life before the mast. But his native merits in time triumphed over adverse fortune, and before he was thirty he became master and in a good measure owner of a frigate which he called The Benbow.

It is said, I know not with what truth, that his fortunes date from an adventure that befell him in the year 1686. In the Benbow frigate he was attacked by a sallee rover, who boarded him, but was beaten off with the loss of thirteen men. Benbow (I tell the tale as I heard it) cut off their heads and threw them into pickle. When he landed at Cadiz, he brought them on shore in a sack, and on being challenged by the custom house officers as importing contraband goods, he threw them on the table with, "Gentlemen, if you like 'em, they are at your service."

This saying so tickled the humor of the king of Spain that he recommended Benbow to our King James, and thus led to his promotion in our Royal Navy. The captain was now somewhat above forty years old, straight but slight in build, not ill looking, save that his nose was a trifle over big--a defect not uncommon, I have remarked, among great commanders.

Well, as I said, we had arrived at Mistress Hind's door, and the captain was in a great rage at the havoc wrought by Vetch and his crew. He rapped on the door with the hilt of his sword, and out pops Mistress Nelly's head from the window above ('twas in a night-cap), and she screams:

"Out upon you, you vagabones! You've done mischief enough for one night, drat you, and if ye be not gone inside of half a minute I'll empty the slops on ye, that I will."

Benbow laughed.

"The family spirit!" he says under his breath to Joe. "Speak to her; don't tell her I'm here."

"Oh, Mistress Hind," says Joe in a mournful voice, "here's a welcome to a poor worn-out old mariner as you used to befriend."

"Who in the world are ye?" she asks.

"Who but Joe Punchard, ma'am, that went away for rolling a barrel, and has been a-rolling ever since."

"Ay, now I know your voice. Back like a bad penny, are ye? Come and see me tomorrow; I'm abed now."

"But I've brought a friend with me--another poor old mariner"--with a wink at Benbow--"who wants a night's lodging."

"Can he pay?" asks Mistress Hind.

"To be sure: his pockets are full of pieces of eight and other sound coin."

"Then I'll come down to you; but ye must bide a minute or two till I throw a few things on, for I'd die rather than show myself to a mariner in my night rail."

Benbow laughed again.

"'Tis twenty years or more since I saw Nell," he said, "but I'd know her tongue in any company."

And now the remembrance of my father's illness, which the subsequent excitements had driven from my mind, returned with a sudden force that made me take a hasty leave of the two travelers, though both asked me to wait and drink a dish of coffee with them. So I did not see the meeting of brother and sister, but learned from Joe next day the manner of it.

Mistress Hind did not recognize the captain, never having seen him from a boy, until, sitting at table with a dish of coffee before him, and she standing over him, bidding him haste that she might return to bed--sitting thus, I say, he took up the dish and began to blow into it to cool it, as children do.

"Why," says Mistress Hind, "tha blows it round and round to make little waves, just like my brother John."

"Nelly!" says the captain, setting the dish down.

"And there they were," said Joe in telling me the story, "in each other's arms, and when she'd done drying her eyes she says,

"'John, and I needn't ha' minded about the night rail!'"

It was nigh eleven o'clock when I got home--a very late hour in our parts, and Mistress Pennyquick was in a great to-do, imagining all kinds of evil that might have befallen me. Mr. Pinhorn had remained with my father a long time, she said; he was now asleep and was not to be disturbed. I was myself fairly tired out, and fell asleep the instant my head touched the pillow.

Chapter 5
I Lose My Best Friend

There was a crowded courthouse next day when Ralph Mytton and Cyrus Vetch were brought before the Mayor and charged with breach of the peace and malicious damage to the property of lieges. It was the first time that the Mohocks had been caught in the act, and their being well connected added a spice to the event.

The two prisoners bore themselves very differently. Mytton, a nephew of the member of Parliament, assumed an air of bravado, smiled and winked at his friends in court, evidently trusting to his high connections to get him off lightly. Vetch, on the other hand, was sullen and morose, never lifting his eyes from the floor except when I was giving my evidence, and then he threw me a glance in which I read, as clearly as in a book, the threat of venomous hate. Both he and Mytton were very heavily fined, and the Mayor was good enough to compliment me on the part I had played.

As we were leaving the court, a tipstaff came up to Joe Punchard, and formally arrested him as a runaway 'prentice; at the instance, I doubt not, of Vetch himself. But the matter ended in a triumph for Joe, for Captain Benbow accompanied him before the Mayor and declared that as a mariner in the King's navy he was immune from civil action. Whether the plea was good in law I know not. The Mayor did not know either, and the clerk, to judge by his countenance, was in an equal state of puzzlement. But Benbow was clearly not a man to be trifled with, and Joe had certainly had a part in bringing the Mohocks to book, and for one reason or another he was given the benefit of the doubt. When he left the court he was mightily cheered by a mob of 'prentices among the crowd, and would have accepted the invitations to drink pressed upon him but for the peremptory orders of his captain, who was no wine bibber himself, being therein unlike many of the navy men of his time.

The fines levied on Mytton and Vetch were the least part of their punishment. The incident of the dust bin brought on them open ridicule; they became the laughingstock of Shrewsbury. The school wag, who afterwards became famous for his elegant Greek verses at Cambridge, pilloried them in a lampoon which the whole town got by heart, and for days afterwards they could not show their faces without being greeted by some lines from it by every small boy who thought himself beyond their reach. It began, I remember:

> Come list me sing a famous battle,
> A dustbin and a watchman's rattle;
> The hero he was nominate Cyrus,
> The scene was Shrewsbury, not Epirus.

The rhymester introduced all the characters; for instance:

> Another who the dust has bitten
> Was a brawny putt by name Ralph Mytton;
> And Richard Cludde, a Cambridge lubber,
> He ran away home to his mam to blubber;

and so the doggerel went on, chronicling the details (more or less imaginary) of the fight, the entrance of Mr. Benbow and Punchard on the scene:

> And Nelly Hind's bashed portal closes
> On bandy legs and Roman noses;

and ending thus:

> *Carmen concludo sine mora:*
> *"Intus si recte ne labora,"*

which being the school motto (dragged in by the hair of the head, so to speak), pleased Mr. Lloyd, the master, mightily.

The rage of the persons chiefly concerned knew no bounds, and this good came of it, that the Mohocks troubled Shrewsbury streets no more.

Captain Benbow, and with him Joe Punchard, stayed but a few days in the town. They had come on a flying visit in an interval of the war against the French on the high seas, and very proud we were that the captain, one of ourselves, was winning himself a name for prowess and gallantry in his country's service.

Before he departed, however, I got from Joe a relation of what had befallen him since the night he stole away. He arrived in Bristowe footsore and ragged, and there came nigh to starving before he found employment. One shipmaster swore his hair was too red: it would serve for a beacon to French privateers; another, that he was too bandy: his legs would never grip the rigging if he essayed to go aloft. But at length he obtained a berth on a tobacco ship trading to Virginia, and suffered great torture both from the sea and from the harsh and brutal ship's officers. He made other voyages, to the Guinea coast, the Indies, and elsewhere, and one fine day, being paid off at Southampton, he chanced to hear that Captain Benbow was in port, and making himself known to that officer as a fellow townsman, he was taken by him to be his servant, and had never left him since.

"And have you pickled any pirates' heads?" I asked, remembering the story, and bethinking me of the silver-mounted cup possessed by Mr. Ridley, the captain's brother-in-law, which was said to have once covered the head of a sallee rover.

"Pickled fiddlesticks!" says Joe. "Dunnat believe every mariner's tale you hear, Master Humphrey."

And then he proceeded to tell me a fearful and wonderful tale of a sea serpent, and was mightily offended when I said it was all my eye.

Joe went away with his captain after a few days, and I own I envied him, and for the first time felt a secret discontent in the prospect of a life among pigs and poultry, a feeling which was heightened when Dick Cludde soon afterwards departed with a commission from His Majesty. Dick was a lubber and, I believed then, though I had afterwards proof to the contrary, a coward; and matching myself against him I knew I would do the king's navy more credit than he. But I kept my thought to myself--and next day made a sad bungle, I remember, of my construe of Thucydides' account of the sea fight at Salamis.

So months passed away. I saw with grave concern that my father was ailing more and more. The attacks of his terrible disease came more frequently, and Mr. Pinhorn owned that he could do him no good. He bore his pain with wonderful fortitude, never suffering a complaint to pass his lips. Many a time in after years I recalled his noble courage, which helped me to bear the lesser sufferings which fell to my lot. He seemed to know that his end was approaching, and one day called me to his private room and talked to me with a kindness that brought a lump into my throat.

Much of what he said is too sacred to be set down here; I can truthfully say that his assurance of having made ample provision for me seemed of little moment beside his earnest loving counsel, which made the deeper impression because he had so rarely spoken in that strain.

The end came suddenly, and with a shock that stunned me, for all I was so well prepared for it. A few brief moments of dreadful agony, and the good man who had been more than a father to me was no more. Never once during his long illness had his sister Lady Cludde visited him; neither she nor her husband accompanied his remains to the grave: and when we had left him in the churchyard of St. Mary and returned to the house, I was roused for a little from my stupor by the sight of Sir Richard among those assembled to hear Mr. Vetch read the will.

A great wave of anger surged within me when I saw him sitting in my father's chair, his fat hands folded upon his paunch, and his bleared eyes rolling a quizzing glance round upon the little company. So enraged was I that I took little heed of Mr. Vetch at the table, and heard nothing of what he said as he drew from his pocket a long paper sealed and tied with tape. No doubt I watched him untie the knots and break the seal, and spread the document on the table before him; no doubt I heard his cry of amazement, and saw Sir Richard and the few friends of my father who were present rise from their seats and crowd about him; but I remained listless in my place until a shriek from Mistress Pennyquick woke me to a sense that something was amiss. Then I heard Sir Richard say, in his loud blustrous tones:

"Then my lady inherits?"

"Not so fast, not so fast, Sir Richard," said Mr. Vetch in a tone of great perturbation. "She is, it is true, the heir-at-law, but our departed friend left his house, messuage, farm and all its appurtenances to his adopted son Humphrey Bold, with an annuity of fifty pounds per annum to his faithful housekeeper Rebecca Pennyquick: I took down his instructions with his own hand, and engrossed the will myself.

"There is some mistake, gentlemen, something inexplicable. I must ask you, in all fairness, to postpone your judgment of the matter until I have made search in my office. Never in my forty years' experience has so untoward a thing happened, and I must beg of you to give me time to solve the mystery."

"I will wait on you tomorrow, Mr. Attorney," says Sir Richard. "Meanwhile I claim this property for my Lady Cludde."

And with that he takes his hat and stick and marches from the room.

The neighbors followed him, giving me commiserating glances, one or two of them shaking me by the hand and speaking words of condolence. Mr. Vetch remained for a time staring at the paper before him; then he folded it and came to me.

"Some devilish prank," he said hurriedly. "Never fear, my lad; all will come right. I will see you tomorrow, my boy."

And then he too went, leaving me alone with Mistress Pennyquick, who had done nothing for some while but sob and rock herself to and fro on her chair.

"That wicked man!" she moaned. "But he will be punished--he will be punished, Humphrey. What does the good Book say about them that despoil widows and orphans? Oh, my poor master!"

"What is it, Becky?" I asked, with but little curiosity for her answer.

"'Tis the doing of that wicked man and his wife! I know it is," the poor creature sobbed. "And they wouldn't come near the poor soul when he was in his agony. And now they want to rob us--to rob you, my poor boy, and me who served him faithful these twenty year. God will punish him!"

"But what have they done, then?" I asked again.

"Done! Lord knows what they haven't done. I knew summat would happen when I saw Mr. Vetch come to your poor father a while ago--you mind, I told you so. Lawyers are all no good, that's my belief. Don't tell me Mr. Vetch didn't know what he was a-carrying. He's in league with the wretches, I know he is, for all his mazed look. Don't tell me he didn't know the paper was as white as the underside of a fleece. Fleece is the very word for it: he's fleeced us, sure enough, and I'll come on the parish, and you'll be a beggar, and they unnatural wretches will wallow in their pride, and--oh! I can't abear it, I can't abear it!"

And the poor creature burst into a passion of weeping, so that it was some time before I could learn the cause of her distress. It was amazing enough. When Mr. Vetch unfolded the document which he believed to be my father's will, the paper inside was as clean as when it came from the scrivener's. There was not a single mark upon it.

Chapter 6
I Take Articles

We were at breakfast next morning, Mistress Pennyquick and I, when Captain Galsworthy, after a herald tap on the door, walked into the room.

"What's this cock-and-bull story that's running over the town?" he cried without circumstance.

Before I could reply, Mistress Pennyquick began to pour out her tale of woe, roundly accusing Sir Richard Cludde and Lawyer Vetch of conspiring to defraud me of my rights.

"I haven't slept a wink the whole night through, sir," says the poor soul, "and I've wetted six--no, 'tis seven handkerchers till they're like clouts from the washtub, and I can hardly see out o' my eyes, and--"

"Stuff and nonsense and a fiddlestick end!" cries the captain angrily, "dry your eyes, woman. Of all God's creatures a sniveling woman is the worst. Vetch has been wool gathering:

"*Quandoque dormitat Homerus*--eh, Humphrey?--

"Which means, ma'am, that you sometimes catch a weasel asleep. Depend on't, he engrossed the wrong docket, and by this time has discovered the true will in one of his moldy boxes. Gad, it'll ruin him, though--if his nephew has not done it already. A family lawyer can't afford to be caught napping.

"Put on your cap, Humphrey: we'll go and look into things and hint that we must change our attorney."

So he and I set off together. But, early as it was, Sir Richard Cludde had been before us. When we entered Mr. Vetch's office, there was the burly knight with his hand on the door, flinging a parting word at the lawyer, who sat behind his desk with his wig awry, the picture of harassment and woe. Sir Richard gave a curt nod to the captain, but vouchsafed me not a glance.

"You understand, Mr. Attorney?" he said. "The present occupants will vacate the premises within a week, and you will bring me the keys."

Then he strode away, banging the door after him. The captain whistled.

"Sits the wind--the whirlwind, I might say-in that quarter? Where's the will, Vetch?"

"I would give my right hand to know," said the lawyer. "There is Mr. Ellery's box"--he indicated a case of black tin with the name John Ellery printed in white letters on its side; "'twas there I laid it, with the title deeds and other documents. I searched it through yesterday. I spent half the night in ransacking every other box in the room, all to no purpose."

"You did not lay it aside when you had drawn it and afterwards engross a blank paper like folded, think you?"

"Sir, 'tis impossible. I drew the will at a sitting: it was not a long one; folded, engrossed, and tied it with my own hands. Nothing short of witchcraft could undo my handiwork."

"Or your nephew," snapped the captain. "He is the boon fellow of young Cludde; 'tis the Cluddes who gain by the disappearance, and mightily glad they will be of the property if all is true that's said of Sir Richard's affairs. Where's your nephew, Vetch?"

"At home and abed, Captain, suffering from a catarrh. I did ask him if he knew aught of the matter, and he laughed and denied it, reminding me that I had never trusted him with the keys. He is wild, I own, sir; heady and self willed, a sore trial to me sometimes; but he is of my name, and that name is honorable in Shrewsbury."

"'Tut, man, nobody but a fool would suspect you of evil dealing, and if your nephew had a hand in this it might be nought but a boyish prank, though a deuced indecent one. But now to the practical question: in the absence of the will, how does Humphrey stand?"

I shall never forget the poor lawyer's look of misery when this question was put to him, sharp as a pistol shot. He bent his quill in his hand till it cracked; he fidgeted on his stool; he began a sentence three times and left it unfinished.

"In a word," says the captain, who was ever for directness, "he is a pauper?"

The lawyer bowed his head, but said never a word. Captain Galsworthy began to drum on the table with his fingers, as his manner was when perturbed. I sat silent, still too much under the shadow of my great loss to comprehend the full bearing of his words.

"Did you put it to Cludde?" he asked suddenly.

"I did, sir, with all the force of which I was capable. I begged him to acquiesce in the known wishes of our friend, to accept the draft of the will--here it is--taken 'down by myself from his lips. Sir Richard looked at it, pished and pshawed, said he had never held John Ellery's wits in much account, and declared that my instructions were a clear proof of his feeble mindedness. When I protested that I had never known a man with a clearer head or of sounder sense he bellowed at me: what, did I think it sound sense to will away to a stranger property that had been in the family for generations?

"'No stranger,' I said, 'indeed, by marriage a kinsman of your own, Sir Richard.'

"'No kinsman of mine!' he said, 'nor of my lady's neither. When I married Susan Ellery I did not wed her brother, nor any beggar's brat'--those were his words, sir--'any beggar's brat he was fool enough to keep off the parish. If you had the will I'd dispute it against all the attorneys in England.'

"He is a hard man, Captain. He demands possession in a week."

"And your draft has no value in law?"

"Not a whit, I am sorry to say."

"Then devil take the law," the captain snapped out.

"Hang me, I'll go myself and see Cludde and tell him what I think of him."

"Not for me, Captain," said I, feeling my face burn. "I'll take nothing from Sir Richard Cludde, beggar's brat as I am."

"You won't be a fool, Humphrey," said the captain. "Half a loaf is better than no bread, and if I don't wring an allowance out of the rogue, I'm a Dutchman."

The captain would have his way, in spite of my protestation. But he returned from his visit to Cludde Court in a towering passion. The knight refused point blank to acknowledge any claim upon him, and swore that if Mistress Pennyquick and I were not out of the house by the day he named, he would come with bailiffs and constables and fling us out neck and crop.

Captain Galsworthy was more concerned than I was at the failure of his well-meant intervention. In my ignorance of the world, and how hardly it uses those who have nothing, I did not foresee, as my wise old friend did, the arduous course I was to follow, nor the many buffets in store for me, but thought, like many lads before and since, that with the equipment of health and strength I could ride a tilt against circumstance. Youth is green and unknowing, as Mr. Dryden hath it, and sure 'tis a mercy.

Before the day was out, we had a piece of news that confirmed the captain's suggestion as to the disappearance of the will. Cyrus Vetch had vanished, together with the contents of his uncle's cash box. When Mr. Vetch went home to his dinner, he found the cash box broken open, and Cyrus gone. I could not doubt now that 'twas my old enemy had wreaked on me the vengeance that had smouldered in his breast ever since Joe Punchard sent him down Wyle Cop in the barrel, and was fanned into a flame by my action on the night of the adventure in Raven Street. Mistress Pennyquick was firm in her belief that the Cluddes were party to the crime, but that I could not credit then, and never will.

Mr. Vetch himself came to see me the next day. The poor old man was quite broken down. He humbly begged my forgiveness for the trouble he had brought upon me, for so he chose to regard it; and he confessed to me, what I am sure he never revealed to a living soul beside, that Cyrus had been for years a thorn in his flesh. He was a spendthrift and a gambler, and had bled his uncle many a time to discharge what he called his debts of honor. This drain upon the lawyer, together with losses he had sustained in the failure of Chamberlain's Land Bank scheme--that monstrous attempt of the Tories to set up a rival to the Bank of England--had brought him to the verge of ruin, and with tears in his eyes he expressed to me his fear that the matter of my father's will would bring him into such ill repute that the Shrewsbury folk would no longer trust him and would give their business into other hands.

This set me a-thinking, and during the week I was allowed to remain in the old farmhouse I turned over in my mind a plan which, I own, mightily pleased me. It was clear that I must do something for myself. I had never had any great liking for farming work, and now that the position of a yeoman on my own land was denied me I was not inclined to accept service on the land of another. Mr. Lloyd, the master of the school, when I went to take leave of him, was kind enough to say that he would use his interest to obtain for me a servitorship at Oxford or a sizarship at Cambridge, which would put me in the way of making a livelihood as a tutor or perhaps as a parson. But I was not in the mind to be any more subsistent on charity, even of this modified sort, nor had I indeed any hope of achieving excellence in the classical tongues, so I thanked him, but declined his offer.

The idea that had entered my noddle was that I might join Mr. Vetch, and do something in the practice of law to make amends for the ill fortune which, unwittingly and indirectly, I had been the means of bringing upon him. When I had made up my mind, I mooted the project to Captain Galsworthy, who laughed at it as quixotic, but confessed that he saw no better course open to me.

"I had liever you took up a more active trade--one in which you could put to use the sciences you have learned of me," said the old warrior. "But that would take you from Shrewsbury, to be sure, and I should miss our little bouts, Humphrey boy. And when you come to think of it, a man needn't be the worse lawyer for a passable dexterity with the small sword."

Mr. Vetch was quite overcome when I set my proposal before him. He embraced it eagerly, drew out my articles at once, and swore that I would be his salvation. And as I must needs have somewhere to live, he insisted on my taking up my abode with him; he had a roomy house, he said, and I need not occupy Cyrus' chamber unless I pleased.

"But what about poor old Becky?" I said. "She is really harder hit by this unlucky affair than I, and 't would break her heart to go to the poor house."

"Let her come, too," said Mr. Vetch. "My housekeeper is leaving me; the fates are conspiring in our favor, you see. Let her come and mother us both, and I will give her twenty pounds a year."

I had as yet broken nothing of my designs to Mistress Pennyquick, foreseeing trouble in that quarter. It was pitiful to see her, who had been such a bustling housewife, sitting the greater part of the day with her hands in her lap, or dabbing the tears from her eyes, and to hear her melancholy plaints, which grew the more frequent as the time drew nearer for leaving the old house. After concluding my arrangement with Mr. Vetch I went back to the farmhouse, flung my cap into a chair, and, sitting across the corner of the table, said:

"Only two days more, Becky."

"And what will become of us I don't know," says the old woman. "'Tis the poor house for me, and water gruel, and I've had my rasher regular for forty year. And as for you, my poor lamb, never did I think I'd live to see you put on an apron, and say 'What d'ye lack, Madam?' to stuck-up folks as'll look on ye as so much dirt."

"What's this talk of aprons?" says I, laughing.

"How can ye laugh?" she says, the tears rolling down her cheeks. "Beggars can't be choosers, and ye'll have to ask Mr. Huggins to have pity on ye and take ye into his shop, and ye'll tie up sugar and coffee for Susan Cludde belike, and--oh, deary me!"

"Nonsense, Becky," says I. "I shan't have that pleasure. I'm going to join Mr. Vetch."

"What!" she shrieks.

"'Tis true. Mr. Vetch has given me my articles, and instead of tying up coffee and sugar I shall tie deeds and conveyances and become a most respectable lawyer."

"Oh! 'twill kill me!" she moans. "Of all the dreadful news I ever heard! And wi' Lawyer Vetch, too; the man as devours widows' houses and makes away with good men's wills! I wish I were in my grave, I do!"

"Wouldn't you rather be with me, Becky?" I said, smiling at her.

"'Tis cruel to talk so," she cried, sobbing. "How can I be with 'ee? What you get from Lawyer Vetch won't keep two--if you get anything at all. They say his nephew has ruined him--the wretch! Indeed, if you ask me, I say you'll get more from Mr. Huggins than from the lawyer. You'll have enough to do to keep yourself, without being saddled with a poor, forlorn old widow woman."

"But won't you come? I am going to live with Mr. Vetch."

"Live with the devil!" she screamed, lifting her hands with a gesture of utter despair. "It is downright wicked of you, Humphrey--and your poor father not a week in the grave. Sure the end of the world be coming, when the leopard and the kid shall lie down together, and the lion shall eat straw like the ox."

"And donkeys won't bray, I suppose," says I. "There, I don't mean you, Becky, though you are an old goose. Mr. Vetch wants a housekeeper, and you are to come with me and mother us both, he says, and he'll give you twenty pounds a year."

The good creature's look sent me into a fit of laughter. She stared solemnly at me for a while through her tears, saying never a word. Then the drooping corners of her mouth lifted; she folded her hands across her plump person and said:

"Your father only gave me eighteen, Humphrey: are you sure 'twas twenty the lawyer said?"

"Quite sure. The devil isn't as black as he's painted, eh Becky?"

"Ah! you never know a man till yon've lived with him. Pennyquick was--but there, he's gone, poor soul, as we all must, and tis ill work saying anything against one as can't answer ye back: not that Pennyquick was ever much of a hand at that, poor soul!"

I heard no more vilification of Mr. Vetch. Becky recovered her old activity with surprising ease, and went about the house collecting such personal belongings of her own and mine as the lawyer told us we might remove without question. He himself came to the house on our last day, and made an inventory of the articles we removed, and having seen these safely bestowed in a pannier on the back of Ben Ivimey's son, who came to carry them away, we shut the doors of the old place, Mr. Vetch pocketed the keys, and we set off for the town.

Mistress Pennyquick shed a plenitude of tears, and I had a monstrous lump in my throat that threatened to choke me if I tried to speak. With a discretion that raised him mightily in Becky's esteem, Mr. Vetch fell behind, leaving us two together; and so with full hearts we took the road, going into our new life hand in hand.

Chapter 7
A Crown Piece

This turn in our affairs was a nine days' wonder in Shrewsbury. And whether it was that some chord of sympathy was touched in our townsfolk, or that Mr. Vetch worsted his only rival, Mr. Moggridge, in a case of breach of covenant that was tried at the next assizes, I know not; but certain it is that my friend's business took a leap upward from that very time. Clients flocked to him; he soon had to employ an additional clerk; and Mistress Pennyquick, who was twice as tyrannical as before on the strength of her extra two pounds a year, declared privately to me one day that she wished for nothing now but that she might live to see me a partner with Mr. Vetch, in a house of my own, with a sensible wife and five pretty children.

But I have come to believe that as an Ethiopian can not change his skin, nor a leopard his spots, so a man can not alter the bent of mind he was born with, nor follow any course with success but the one to which his nature calls. I entered Mr. Vetch's office with the best will in the world to please him, and to master the principles of legal practice and procedure; but I found it hard to reconcile myself to the atmosphere of a stuffy room filled with musty tomes, and to the unvarying round of desk work--copying from morning to night agreements, deeds and other documents bristling with a jargon unintelligible to me.

I soon tired of freehold and copyhold tenure, of manorial rights and customs, and the hundred and one legal fictions connected with actions at law and bills in chancery that constitute the routine of an attorney's profession. I yearned to breathe an ampler air; and when one day I saw Dick Cludde, returned home on leave, strutting past with Mytton and other boon companions, in all the bravery of cocked hat, laced coat and buckled shoes, I flung down my pen and donned my cap, and set off, with bitter rage and envy in my heart, to pour out my soul to my constant friend, Captain Galsworthy.

"Halt!" cried the captain, when I was in the midst of a tirade. "We'll have a bout."

And forthwith we donned the gloves, and for a full quarter of an hour we sparred, he with the cool mastery that never deserted him, I with a blind rage and fury which had its natural end. In the third round I aimed a blow at my adversary's neck with my right hand, but failing in my reach, he returned it full swing with his left, and dealt me such a staggerer on my cheekbone that down I went like a ninepin and measured my length on the floor.

"Capital!" says the captain, sitting down (the old fellow was puffing not a little). "Capital! That was a settler, eh, my boy? Now you can get up and talk sense."

I got up, rubbing my cheek, and grinning a rueful smile, as the captain told me. We remained long in talk; never had my old friend been wiser or more kindly. He listened to me with patience as I told him--quietly, for he had fairly knocked my rage out of me--how desperately sick I was of my occupation, and how I longed to stretch my limbs and do something.

"I knew it, my boy," he said. "I had seen it coming. I understand it. Haven't I been through it myself? I was bred for commerce: you might as well have harnessed a pig. One day--I was younger than you-I took French leave and a crown piece and trudged to London. I enlisted in old Noll's army, shipped to Flanders and served under Lockhart--he was a man, sir!--at the siege of Cambrai, deserted when the campaign was at an end, and roamed over half Europe; took service with the Emperor; fought with the Swedes against the Poles, and the Poles against the Swedes; fell in with Patrick Gordon, and was beguiled by him to Muscovy; and should have been with the Czar Peter at this day if he hadn't called me a fool when he was sober; we paid no heed to what he called us when he was drunk.

"Ah! I see your eyes glistening, you young dog. You were never born to be tied up with red tape."

This brief account of his life, and he never told me more, had indeed set my heart leaping. What would I not give, I thought, to see what he had seen, and do what he had done!

"But now to be practical," said the captain. "You want to go: very well, go. But you won't sneak off like Cyrus Vetch; you can't go with a commission like young Cludde. How much money have you got?"

"A few guineas I have saved."

"Well, keep them; you may be in a tight place some day, and find 'em handy. You have a hankering for the sea, you say. Then tramp to Bristowe, as your champion Joe Punchard did, and hitch on to John Benbow if you can find him. He'll work you hard, if all that's said about him is true; but he'll either make you or break you. That's my advice."

Advice that jumps with one's own inclinations hath ever a comfortable appearance of soundness. I told the captain that he had hit on the very scheme I had proposed to myself, adding, however, that I had thought to go a-horseback.

"A-horseback!" he cried. "What want you with a horse? You don't own a horse, and to hire one you would expend all your guineas and have nothing to feed either him or yourself. No, go on your shanks; there's a world of knowledge to be gained by footing it on the open road."

And so we settled that Captain Galsworthy should himself come to our house on Pride Hill and break the news to my good friends there. They were both downcast when they heard it, Mr. Vetch more than Mistress Pennyquick, which somewhat surprised me. He plied me with innumerable reasons for remaining with him, spoke of the long miles I should have to trudge before I reached the port, described the perils of the road, even foresaw that I should be arrested as a vagrant and clapped into jail! He conjured up dismal pictures of the seafaring life, and waxed quite eloquent in drawing a contrast between the bare windswept deck and the cosy fireside, the dangers from storm and pirates and the serenity of our quiet town. And then the captain broke in upon his speech with a great laugh.

"Gad, Mr. Attorney, you have o'ershot your bolt," he cried. "Mark you the sparkle in the boy's eyes and the catch in his breath? The bogies you raise are beacons to him. D'you think to frighten him as you would a girl? Spare your breath, man, to cool your porridge; what fellow of spirit would be deterred from a life of action by your vision of slippers and a basin of gruel?"

And indeed the lawyer's eloquence fell on deaf ears; or rather, as the captain said, all his reasons did but whet my eagerness until I fairly tingled with the imagined delight of matching myself against the hostility of the elements and man. And so he at last desisted, and gave a grudging compliance to my purpose; and Mistress Pennyquick concluded the discussion with a shot at Captain Galsworthy.

"This is all along o' you, Captain," she cried. "This is what comes of teaching little boys to fight. I knew years ago 't'ud have a bad end, and I told his poor father so, and I'm sure I hope you are satisfied."

"Abundantly, ma'am," says the captain, bobbing her a bow. "My pupil does me credit, and will do me more."

My preparations were soon made; indeed, I had nothing to prepare save a few garments, which poor Becky blessed with a copious baptism of tears. Then, one fine spring morning, when the buds on tree and hedge were bursting and the air was full of song, I set off on my long journey. Captain Galsworthy accompanied me for a few miles on the road--across English Bridge, past our old farmhouse (now held by a tenant of Sir Richard Cludde's), through the beautiful vale of Severn, till at Cressage my way led me southward from the river. Then he held me fast by the hand and looked me in the face.

"God bless you, Humphrey," he said. "Live clean, and--and--hit straight from the shoulder, my boy."

And then he turned away--not before I had seen a film of moisture gather in his eyes.

Now I was fairly started on my travels--in a customary suit of plain gray homespun, with worsted hose, knit for me by Mistress Pennyquick, a pair of stout shoes, a round hat, and a stout staff in my hand. I carried a few extra garments in a knapsack strapped to my back, and my few guineas were safely stowed in a wallet beneath my belt.

For a mile or two after leaving the captain I was in as black a fit of the dumps as ever beset a man. I was but halfway through my eighteenth year, and had as yet never gone more than ten miles from my native town, nor slept a night away from home. 'Tis true, no close ties of blood now bound me to Shrewsbury, but it held dear memories and kind friends, and I felt a natural heart sickness at thus cutting myself adrift from all and ranging forth alone into the great unknown world. But healthy youth can not long lie under such an oppression; my low spirits lasted just so long as it took me to gain the crest of the hill towards Harley, and when I had turned and taken a parting look behind--at the fields in their fresh green, and the spires of Shrewsbury beyond, and the Severn winding like a bright ribbon through the vale--when I had fed my eyes on this charming scene, and breathed a prayer that in good time I should behold it again, I set my face once more to the south, and stepped briskly down the slope that hid my home from sight and stood as the dividing line between my past and my future. And as I trudged on between the bright hedgerows, and heard the song of birds all about me, and felt the warm sunbeams on my face, I began to exult in my youth and strength, and the words of a song from one of my father's play books came to my mind, and I hummed them aloud:

A merry heart goes all the day,

A sad tires in a mile a.

About half a mile out of Harley, the road makes a long ascent to the market town of Much Wenlock. I was pretty warm by the time I arrived there, and mighty hungry, so I repaired to the inn where my father was wont to eat on market days, and where I had several times been with him, and ordered a dinner of bread and cheese and ale. The innkeeper, Mr. Appleby, was not a little surprised to see me, and was fairly staggered when I told him I was off to Bristowe to seek my fortune. To the stay-at-home folk of the countryside Bristowe was as distant as Brazil, and he would have heard that I was starting for the ends of the earth with but little more amazement.

"Betsy," he called through the half-open door into the little parlor behind, "here be young Master Bold a setting off to Bristowe."

"Bless us!" cried his wife, bustling out, and bringing with her an odor of roast meat that somewhat slacked my appetite for bread and cheese. "Deary me! You doesn't say so now! Well, to be sure! 'Tis a fearsome long way, by all accounts; but there, you be growed a great big chap, Master Bold, and I'm sure I wish 'ee good luck. Come away in, sir, dinner's just off the jack, and me and my man 'ud be main proud if you'd eat a morsel with us afore ye goes."

I was nothing loath, and found the roast of mutton a deal more to my liking than the frugal fare I had ordered. I was still but halfway through my second helping when there came through the door a great clatter of hoofs from the street, and then a loud voice crying "Appleby! here, sirrah, stir your stumps!" with an oath or two by way of seasoning.

My host got up in a hurry and ran to the outer door, and I laid down my knife and fork, and I think my cheeks must have gone a trifle pale, for Mistress Appleby asked me anxiously what was amiss. I hastened to reassure her, but begged her to close the door into the inn place which her husband had left open. She wonderingly complied, but was enlightened a moment afterwards, when she saw Dick Cludde swagger in, followed by the two naval captains whom his lady mother had been entertaining.

"I understand your feeling, sir," said the good wife. "'Tis a sin and a shame ye lost the farm, which was yours by right; but doan't 'ee let 'em spoil your dinner; I can't abear mutton half, cold."

A more important matter, however, than the cooling of my mutton was troubling me. I had heard Cludde call for wine and dice, from which it was clear that he did not intend to leave yet awhile. There was no way out except by going through the inn taproom, and I was not inclined to face Dick Cludde there, for he would of a certainty make some sneering or belittling remark, and my temper being not of the meekest I feared things might come to a brawl. Not that I cared a fig's end for Cludde, or feared any ill result from a personal encounter; but I knew the inn was a property of Sir Richard's, who would speedily find a new tenant if Dick got a broken head there.

There was nothing for it but to stay where I was, and bear with what patience I might the interruption to my scarcely begun journey. So I sat in my chair, and even through the closed door could hear the loud voices of the naval men and the rattle of the dice on the board. They called often for more wine, and grew more and more boisterous as their potations lengthened, giving me a hope that they would by and by be so fuddled as to make it possible for me to escape unrecognized. But this hope was soon dashed.

"Let's have another bottle!" cried one of the three; his speech was very thick. "Let's have another."

"No, no," said another. "You've had enough, Kirkby; and Cludde there is half asleep already."

"Ads bobs, Walton," returned the man addressed as Kirkby, "are you growing like Benbow? No wine, no gentlemen! What's things comm' to, I say, when a fellow like Benbow, no gentleman"--(he pronounced it "gemman")--"flies his flag on a king's ship!"

And then, being perfectly tipsy, he launched out into violent abuse of Joe Punchard's captain, who was, it is true, a rough and ready seaman, and, I must own, somewhat uncouth in his manners. From his words I learned that Kirkby had been a lieutenant on Benbow's ship, and was deeply incensed that any one who was not a "gemman" should have had the right to give him orders. For a full half hour he inveighed against that brave man, the head and front of whose offense appeared to be that he rated bravery more highly than blood, and seamanship than breeding, and often took sides with the tars against their officers.

"Why, what d'ye think of this now?" cried Kirkby. "'Twas on Portsmouth Hard, and a dirty old apple woman shoved her basket under my nose and begged me to buy, and wouldn't be denied, and followed me whining up the road, and out of all patience I turns round and tips up her basket, and all the apples roll into the mud. A tar who was smoking against the wall says something under his breath and begins to gather up the apples. 'Leave that, sirrah!' says I. He begs my pardon and goes on as before.

"I up with my cane and was laying on for his insolence when Benbow roars out ('twas under the window of his inn) 'What be you a-doin' of?' That's how he speaks. 'What be you a-doin' of?' says he.

"'I'm a-teachin' of him manners,' says I.

"'I'll teach you manners,' he roars, and orders me back to my ship, and humiliates a gemman before a lout with hair as red as fire and legs that made a circle."

"Why, sure 'twas Joe Punchard," cries Cludde, "a fellow that near killed a friend o' mine," and he breaks into the old School distich--

O, pi, rho, bandy-legged Joe,

Turnip and carrots wherever you go."

and the others screamed with maudlin laughter.

"I know who was the gemman," whispers Mistress Appleby, who had heard it all.

Shortly afterwards, being in high good humor after vindicating their quality as gentlemen, the three called for their reckoning and went round to the stables to see to their horses. I seized the opportunity to make my escape, taking leave very heartily of my kind host and hostess. I was not sorry to get upon the road again, having purposed to cover at least twenty-five or thirty miles before night. It was downhill now, and I was swinging along at a good pace when I heard horses behind me and saw, with annoyance, that I might not escape unnoticed, after all. Cludde and his companions were cantering down the hill, at the risk of mishap, for naval officers are notoriously bad horsemen, and one of them-- Kirkby, I doubt not--was swaying in his saddle. I stepped down to the side of a brook which skirted the road, hoping they would pass me by; but my lanky body was not one to escape remark, and Kirkby himself as he came up threw a jest at my height. Cludde gave me a glance, and a malicious smile sat upon his face.

"Poor beggar!" he said in an undertone, but loud enough for me to hear, and he flung me a coin, which struck my arm and rolled to the brink of the brook. In a trice I was up the bank, hot with a mad rage to come to grips with the fellow. But he had anticipated the movement, and setting spurs to his horse was beyond my reach. I disdained to pursue him; indeed it would have been vain; I could but stomach the affront. But I was not yet seasoned to petty slights, and in my bitterness of spirit I sat down on the grassy bank and for a while gave the rein to my feelings, brooding moodily on my wrongs. Then I chanced to spy the coin which he had flung to me as a man might fling a bone to a dog. I picked it up: it was a crown piece. For a moment I was tempted to pitch it into the brook; but on a sudden impulse I bestowed it in a little inner pocket apart from the rest of my money.

"There it is, Dick Cludde," I muttered between my teeth, "and there it shall remain until the day when I return it you, with interest."

After that I felt more composed, and walked on with a lightened heart.

Chapter 8
I Fall Among Thieves

For some time past the sky had been clouding over, and the wind blowing up with a threat of rain. Before long it began to fall in a steady drizzle, and I saw that if I would not be drenched to the skin I must renounce my purpose of completing thirty miles, and seek a shelter for the night. Coming to a small hamlet of two or three cottages, I inquired of a laboring man whom I saw entering one, how far I must go to find an inn. He told me that there was one a mile or so on, just before coming to Morville, and thanking him, I hastened on my way.

But before I had gone a mile I espied a ruined barn in a field by the roadside, and being already tired and little inclined to encounter strangers, I turned into it to see if it would afford me sufficient protection against the weather. The interior was cosier than the outward aspect promised, and finding a quantity of clean hay at one end, I stripped off my coat, set down my knapsack for a pillow, and, rolling myself in the hay, was soon fast asleep.

I was roused while it was still dark by the sound of voices. Being wide awake in an instant, I had sufficient presence of mind to avoid betraying my whereabouts by a rustling among the hay, and lay and listened, wondering who the intruders might be, and fearing lest they should approach my end of the barn to seek a couch for the remainder of the night. But they made no movement in my direction, and before many minutes had passed I understood by their voices that they were three, and gathered from their talk that they were poachers who had been plying their stealthy trade in the coverts of a neighboring park, and had turned into the barn, which they evidently knew well, for a brief rest before making for their homes at Bridgenorth.

I hoped that they would leave before daylight, without discovering me; but just as the sparrows on the roof were twittering a greeting to the dawn, as ill luck would have it, one of the men spied my coat, spread on staddles against the wall to dry. He uttered a sharp exclamation, and called to his comrades. I heard them come in my direction, and guessed by their silence that they were looking warily around for the owner of the coat. But they did not see me, being completely covered by the hay; and, remarking that it looked a "rare good coat," one of them put his hand into all the pockets in turn, and from the inner one fetched out Cludde's crown piece.

"A silver crown, Jo," he says.

"Bite it," said another.

"Good as gold," returned the first. "This be rare luck."

Now, if I had been a few years older and more expert in dealing with men, I should doubtless have parleyed with the fellows; but in the heat of youth and inexperience, indignant at the freedom with which they were handling my belongings, I sprang out of the hay, made for the man who held the coat, and peremptorily called on him to drop it.

His answer was a sudden well-planted blow which sent me incontinently backward into the hay from which I had risen. I was up in an instant, and then began a struggle, short and decisive. The three men were all shorter than I, but thick-set and powerfully made, and struggle as I might I soon had to own myself beaten, and was borne to the floor, one holding my head, another my feet, and the third discommoding me very much by sitting on my middle.

"What be you a-doing here?" says the man called Job.

"I might ask you the same question," I replied, again choosing the wrong method of dealing with them.

"You might, but you wouldn't get no answer," was the grim retort. "You've heard what we've a-said?" the fellow went on.

I replied that I had heard it all. The men joined in a chorus of oaths, and then began to discuss among themselves what they should do with me, with a freedom and a disregard of any view I might hold on the matter which in other circumstances I might have found amusing.

"If we lets him go," said the man called Job, "he peaches, sure enough, and then 'tis the collar for us all," by which I understood he meant the hangman's noose. "If we don't let him go we must ayther take him with us or tie him up, and then belike his friends will find him, and 'twill be the same end for us."

"Rest easy on both points," I said, having recovered somewhat of my composure. "I won't peach, and I have no friends within twenty miles."

"'S truth?" said the man.

"It is quite true," I replied.

Whereat they burst into a guffaw, and I knew that I had made another mistake.

"He bain't over ripe," said the man on my middle.

"True, he was born young," said Job. "Well, now, I'm a gemman, I am, and fair exchange is no robbery, and as I've took a fancy for this 'ere coat, being a trifle newer nor mine, I'll chop with you; me being a trifle older nor you makes all square, I reckon. Bill, what about the breeches?"

"To be sure, Job, mine be worn thin; I'll have measter's breeches."

"And what's for me?" growled the man at my feet.

"There's only the shirt and the boots left," said Job, "for bein' gemmen we can't let him go bare. You take the boots, Topper."

And having thus apportioned my habiliments, they proceeded to divest me of boots and breeches, threatening to knock me on the head if I made any resistance. In stripping me they came upon the wallet in which my precious guineas were stowed. Job opened it in a twinkling, and I had the mortification of seeing all the money I possessed divided among these three ruffians.

When the exchange of clothing had been effected, I found myself attired in a dirty, greasy coat much too small for me, my arms protruding far beyond the sleeves, a pair of grimy patched leather smalls, that left an inch or two of bare flesh above my stockings, and boots that, rent and battered though they were, cramped my feet terribly.

"How we have overgrowed!" quoth Job with a leer.

The others laughed; then suddenly the man called Topper looked at Job with a frown and said:

"Fair's fair; that there silver crown--I want a bit of that, Job."

This set them squabbling, though they kept a wary eye on me all the time. In the end they decided to settle the ownership of the coin by the arbitrament of chance. Job first spun it; Bill called "heads" and lost. At the second spin Topper called "tails," and was about to pocket the crown when I made a suggestion.

"Gentlemen," I said, in a conciliatory tone which I ought to have adopted before, "I value that crown piece more highly than all the guineas you have appropriated. 'Tis clear you are sportsmen"--I glanced at the hares that lay on the floor, the booty of their night's depredations. "I make you an offer which as sportsmen you will not refuse. Let Mr. Topper and me fight it out, man to man, and the coin go to the winner."

"Spoke like a man; what dost say, Topper?" said Job.

"Done!" says Topper, forthwith flinging off his coat, and rolling up his shirt sleeves.

It was clear that I was incurring a risk, for the muscles of his arms stood up like great globes; but if I could not match him in strength, I hoped at least to have some little advantage of him in science, thanks to the lessons of my good friend Captain Galsworthy. I pulled off my coat, or rather Job's, starting a seam as I did so, and then, the other two men standing between us and the door, Topper and I began our bout.

I could see that he, as well as his companions, expected to win an easy victory. But when at the end of the first round, we stopped at Job's call for a breather, neither of us had got home more than a few body blows, and Topper was patently chagrined, more especially as the others could not forbear twitting him. He began the second round with an impetuosity that kept me wholly on the defensive, and pressed me so hard that I gave back and failed to counter a blow that sent me spinning on to the hay behind. This afforded the others much satisfaction, and at the call of time, they encouraged Topper with a cry to give me a settler and have done with it.

But this was his undoing. He came at me with the same ferocity as before, and, confident of a speedy victory, gave me an opening of which I was quick to take advantage. In a trice I was within his guard; I dealt him a right-hander with all my force; he staggered, and before he could recover, a left-hander got him on the point of the chin, and over he went with a thud on to the floor.

His companions bent over him in consternation. At that moment I could have made my escape, I doubt not, had I chosen to dash for the door, and indeed, I was on the point of doing so when I was stayed by some feeling that it would be hardly becoming to take flight then. Besides, the coin for which I had fought was still in the fallen man's pocket.

He got up by and by, somewhat dazed and rubbing his head. He glowered at me for a moment, then flung the crown towards me with a curse.

"Who said he was green?" he muttered, allowing Job to help him on with his coat.

"He's a viper," said Job consolingly. "We won't tell no one, Topper."

It was light by this time, and Bill remarked that they had best be getting back to Bridgenorth, or they would find folk astir. They looked at me with some hesitation; then Job said:

"We're a-going to make you fast, my bawcock, and don't make no mistake. Ads bobs, if ye come to Bridgenorth Fair we'll find some 'un to down you, strike me if we don't."

They bound my legs and arms with withes that are used for tying trusses of hay, and left me.

I felt some natural satisfaction in the issue of this fight; but it made poor amends for the loss of my clothes and my guineas. Luckily my knapsack, hidden in the hay, had escaped the poachers' observation; and the recovery of Dick Cludde's crown piece gave me a good deal of pleasure.

The moment the poachers were gone, I began to try to free myself from my bonds, but it was only after much painful wriggling and straining that I at length released my hands. My clasp knife had departed with my breeches; Bill's pockets were empty; but after some search, crawling about the barn, I discovered a broken slate wherewith to cut the fastenings of my feet. And then, when I stood upright, and with leisure for thought became fully aware of the sorry figure I cut, in foul garments a world too small for me, I was nigh overwhelmed with a feeling of despair, and was almost ready to wait until nightfall, and slink back by byways to Shrewsbury. But after a while I got the better of this heartsickness, and, rating myself for a poltroon, I strapped on my knapsack and issued forth from the barn, doggedly resolved to pursue my journey.

It was many an hour since I had eaten, and, once more in the open air, my stomach cried out for breakfast. When a man has never had to want for food, it is with a disagreeable shock he realizes that he must be hungry. True, I had the crown piece, and before the sun had mounted I was sore tempted to spend it; but the vow I had inwardly made to keep it for its owner, together with a shame-faced reluctance to appear in my present condition before a fellow man, helped me for a time to bear my hunger. Yet I knew that I could not go long without food, and it would soon become imperative that I should pocket my pride and either change the crown or seek some means of earning enough to buy myself a meal.

For a time I trudged through the fields, avoiding the public eye. Coming at length to a road, which I took to be the highroad, I set off along it, stiffening my resolution to ask for a job at the first village I reached. But just as a row of cottages came in sight, and I was considering in what terms to make my request, a parson and a lady on horseback turned into the road from a by-lane, and when they had passed I heard a ripple of laughter from the lady, no doubt in response to some jest from her companion on my ridiculous appearance.

This set my blood a-boiling; I flung away in a rage, leapt a stile into a field, and felt that I would rather starve than ask assistance of a living soul. I sat down beneath a hedge, utterly woebegone, and chewed the bitter cud of my misfortunes until for sheer weariness I fell asleep.

When I awoke, the sun, which had shone brilliantly all day, was already sloping to the west. My rage was gone now, and I cursed myself for a fool. A pretty spirit I had shown indeed! What was I good for if I could not bear a little ridicule?

"Let 'em laugh, and go hang!" I cried, and up I sprang, resolved to accost the first person I met, whoever it might be, and at any rate earn a crust.

I walked along the field, took a long draught from a clear brook that crossed it, and coming into the road, spied a large house lying some way back amid trees. True to my resolve, I made towards it, entered an iron gate that stood open, and was marching up the broad gravel walk leading to the house when I was checked by a voice.

"Hi, you fellow, what do you want here?"

I turned, and saw a well-dressed boy of about my own age coming out of a shrubbery into the walk. I stopped, feeling a certain awkwardness, and stood before him, looking sheepish enough, no doubt. He eyed me for a moment; then burst out a-laughing.

"You have no business here; get you gone, fellow," he said, when he had recovered.

I gulped down the wrath that rose in me, and said quietly:

"I was but on my way to ask if I might do something to earn a meal and a night's lodging."

He looked at me curiously, perceiving that in mode of speech I was somewhat different from the low tramp I looked. But youth is often impatient and hard; my appearance consorted so little with my tongue that he had much excuse for regarding me as a ne'er-do-well, the less deserving of pity because he probably owed his plight to vicious courses.

"There's the poorhouse for tramps, and the lock-up for rascals," he added. "Be off with you!"

"Pardon me, sir," said I, as quietly as before, "I have eaten nothing for thirty hours or longer, and if you would but give me speech with the master of the house, I doubt not he would allow me milk and bread, for which I would willingly do a turn of work in the morning."

"D'you hear me, sirrah!" cries the boy. "You're a poacher if the truth were known. We want no lazy louts here, and if you're not outside the gates instantly I vow I'll set the dogs on to you."

And with that he came up to me and gave me a shove with his shoulder. He had courage, for he was smaller than I. 'Twas the spirit that prompts a gentleman, however puny, to despise the churl, however big.

His words I had borne patiently enough, but I could endure no more. Wrenching myself away, I dealt him a buffet that stretched him flat on the ground.

This scene had passed within a few paces of the gate, and I had been so preoccupied that I had not heard the clatter of an approaching horse, and in consequence was taken utterly aback when a loud voice behind me cried, "What's this? What's this?" and immediately afterwards the lash of a whip fell smartly on my back, causing me to spring round in a heat of indignation. A gentleman had just ridden in at the gate, and, taking in the situation at a glance, had begun the chastisement which he had much reason to suppose I deserved.

What with my hunger, the boy's insults, and the sting of the lash, I was now roused to as high a pitch of fury as I had ever in my life reached. I had taken a step towards the horse, to drag the rider from his saddle, and he had raised the whip once more to strike, when a voice from the direction of the house caused us both to pause.

"Don't, uncle; oh, please don't!"

Involuntarily I turned, and saw a young girl flying down the path, her long unloosed black hair streaming behind her. She came to us with flushed cheeks, and breathless with running.

"It was all Roger's fault," she cried. "I saw it, heard it all. The poor man is starving and wanted to work for food, and Roger was rude to him."

Her uncle looked at her, and at me, and at the boy, who had risen from the ground, wearing a sullen and crestfallen look.

"Is that the right of it, Roger?" asked the gentleman.

"He said so, sir," he replied, "but he looks such a villainous tramp, and you know what lies they tell--why, look here!" He stooped and picked something from the ground. "He said he was hungry, and look at this!"

He held up my crown piece, which in the violence of my movements, I suppose, had sprung out of my tattered garment. I felt my cheeks flush hotly, and was stricken dumb in the face of this mute evidence giving me the lie. The girl gazed at me for a moment; then, her lip curling with disdain, she turned her back and walked up the path towards the house.

"Well, rascal?" said the gentleman sternly.

"It is mine, truly," I said. "But--"

"Go fetch the men," he said to the boy.

"As sure as I'm alive I'll commit you for a rogue and vagabond, for mendicancy and assault."

He drew his horse across the gate so that I could not escape, while the boy hastened to the house.

"You are a magistrate, sir," I ventured to say, "and sure 'tis not your custom to condemn your prisoners unheard."

"Adzooks, you teach me my duty?" he cried in a rage. "You insolent scoundrel!"

I held my peace, and in a few moments the boy returned, with two stablemen.

"Take this fellow to the coach house," said their master.

"I'll go where you please," I cried hotly, "but if those men lay a finger on me I'll crack their skulls for them."

My height and my fierce aspect so well promised that I could perform my threat that the men held off and eyed their master dubiously.

"Lead on, Roger!" he cried with an oath, too much incensed for further speech.

The boy led the way. I followed, the two stablemen stepping behind me, but at a reasonable distance, and the horseman brought up the rear. Thus in procession we went round the house to the back; I entered the coach house, and the gentleman having dismounted, came in after me, and commanded me to give an account of myself.

Chapter 9
Good Samaritans

During the short passage to the coach house I had been trying to consider my course: but my state of famishment and the agitation into which I had been thrown had bereft me of all power of consecutive thought; so that when the gentleman called upon me, in no gentle tones, to give an account of myself, I stood like a stock fish before him. Then I was amazed to feel my legs giving way under me; I stretched forth my arms in an instinctive attempt to steady myself, and, clutching at empty air, fell heavily forward on to the stone floor.

When I came to myself, I saw a kind, motherly face bending over me, and was aware of a hot taste in my mouth.

"Are you better now?" said the lady, in tones the like of which I had seldom heard.

I smiled, and she held a spoon to my lips, and I swallowed its contents--a mixture of rum and milk, I think--as obediently as a baby.

"Poor boy! he must have been starving," said the lady.

"And what right had a fellow to be starving with a crown piece in his pocket?" said the gentleman behind.

"He will explain by and by," replied the lady. "He must not be vexed tonight, James. I have made up a bed in the loft, and Martha is preparing some food.

"Can you walk, my poor boy?" she asked me.

"I am quite well, ma'am," I said, staggering to my feet. "I don't know what came over me."

She told me that I had fainted, which surprised me mightily, though when I came to reflect it was not much to be wondered at, seeing that never in my life before had I been for more than four hours without food.

"The gentleman asked me to explain--" I began, remembering what had preceded my fall.

"Never mind about that now," said the lady. "You will go to bed, and when you have had some food you will sleep, and you can tell my husband all about it in the morning."

And then she directed the two stablemen who were standing at the door to help me up the ladder into the loft of the coach house. A bed, spread with linen as good as ever I lay on, was arranged at one end; and, dropping on to this, I was asleep immediately. They told me next morning that the mistress had herself brought up the posset which her servant had prepared; but, finding me in such deep slumber, had carried it away again, saying that sleep was as good as food to me then.

The sunlight, streaming in at the little window above my bed, wakened me early. I was at first perplexed at my unfamiliar surroundings, but, recollecting at length the happenings of the previous day, I got up and descended the stairs. At the door of the coach house one of the men I had already seen was swilling the wheel of a big coach with pails of water, whistling the while. He grinned when he saw me, and said:

"Mistress said you was to go straight to kitchen when you waked, and fill your stomick."

"I am mighty hungry, to be sure, but I should like to wash first," I replied.

"Why, you do look 'mazing grimy," he said with another grin. "Do ye feel better this marnin'? You went into a faint like as I never did see--a real female faint it was. I reckon as how you be overgrowed, young man."

"Where shall I find the pump?" I asked, restive under this reference to my unhappy attire.

"Ho, Giles!" he called, "take the young man to the poomp."

At this cry, Giles, in whom I recognized the second man whose skull I had threatened to crack, appeared from round the corner of the coach house. His face also wore a grin.

"Ay, true now, you do want the poomp," he said. "Come, and I'll show 'ee. It do make a young feller weak-like when he overgrows his strength. There was my sister Jane's Billy, to be sure, shot up like a weed, he did, was for ever falling into fits, and a bit soft in his noddle, too, poor soul.

"Here's the poomp; be 'ee strong enough to draw for yourself, think 'ee, or shall I do it for 'ee?"

I was strongly tempted to catch the fellow by the middle and give him a back throw which would enlighten him as to my physical aptitude; but I forbore, and allowed him to pump for me, which he did with great willingness, discoursing the while on the infirmities of all his kin. Refreshed by my ablutions, I was nothing loath to follow him to the kitchen, where a red-faced little dumpling of a cook set before me such a breakfast as would have made Mistress Pennyquick stare.

"Eat away," she said, setting her arms akimbo and eying me up and down as I ravenously began my meal. "Lawks! I don't wonder ye fainted if 'tis true, as they say, that ye hadn't had bite or sup for a week. You've a big body to keep a-goin', to be sure; overgrowed your strength seemingly. The likes of me don't faint."

And at this Susan the housemaid, who had just come in, giggled, and put her hand over her mouth, and I felt as if my ears had rims of fire. Would they never have done with their personal allusions? Mentally I cursed Job and Bill and Topper very heartily, and as heartily wished that my inches were a little less.

Luckily I was not born without a certain sense of humor. It had deserted me under stress of what I had gone through during the last two days, but when my cavities had been well filled with Martha's excellent viands, I was suddenly able to see myself as I must appear to others, and I astonished the servants by laying down my knife and fork, leaning back in my chair, and emitting a long ripple of laughter.

"Goodness alive!" exclaimed Martha. "Giles said a' was a natural, and I believe a' spoke true."

"No, no," I spluttered. "My noddle's sound enough. I think; 'tis only that--that I'm overgrown!"

And with that I laughed again, and my merriment was infectious, for the round little cook laughed until she dropped exhausted into a chair, and the housemaid uttered shrill little titters from behind her hands, bending forward at each explosion, opening her hands to take a peep at me, and then "going off," as they say, again.

In the midst of this hilarity there sounded suddenly a jangling and creaking of wires in the neighborhood of the ceiling, followed by a clang.

"Measter's bell!" cried Susan, and, smoothing her apron, and settling her countenance to a wonderful demureness and sobriety, the little rascal tripped away. She was back in a minute.

"Measter wants to see tha," she said.

I got up and followed her from the room and up the stairs, comfortable in body and mind, for sure, I thought, such cheerfulness was of good augury: the master of such happy servants could not be a very terrible man.

Susan showed me into a large and well-furnished room, where, though it was summer time, a big fire was crackling merrily in the grate. On one side of it sat the master in a deep chair, smoking a pipe of tobacco; on the other the kind mistress was knitting. She smiled at me as I approached, and I knew that she was not thinking of my strange garb. The master hummed and hawed, as if in embarrassment how to address me; then, in a jovial tone intended to set me at my ease he said:

"Had a good breakfast?"

I assured him that I had never made such a meal in my life.

"That's right. Now, we want you to tell us your story in your own way; but mind, no beating about the bush."

I had already resolved to tell just so much as was necessary, without naming names, so I began:

"I was on my way to Bristowe, sir, and two nights ago, being overtaken by the rain, I sought shelter in a decayed barn near the roadside, and slept among some hay. Before morning three men came in whom I soon discovered from their speech to be poachers. They found me, robbed me of my money--not a vast sum--and forced me to exchange garments with them."

Here the flicker of a smile crossed the gentleman's face.

"They left me tied hand and foot, and when I released myself I was in such a taking at the scarecrow figure I must cut that I shunned the sight of men, and kept to the fields. But I had not eaten since noon of the day of my misadventure, and, being desperately hungry, I entered your gate to beg a meal, purposing to pay for it by some service for you."

"Hum! What then of this crown piece which you confessed was yours? Why need ye starve with that in your pocket?"

"To that, sir, I have no answer, save that I would not spend it till the last extremity."

"Hum! How old are you?"

"Somewhat past seventeen, sir."

"Just the age of our Roger," said the lady.

"And what's your name?"

At this I hesitated. I could not be more than thirty miles from Shrewsbury, and if I told my name perchance it might travel back, and I was in no mind to have my mischances retailed in the town. The gentleman saw my hesitation.

"Well, well," he said, "no matter for that. You have run away, eh?"

"No, sir. I have no relatives, and I came with full consent of my friends."

"And what think you to do at Bristowe? Have you friends there?"

"No, sir. I purposed to find employment on a ship."

"The old story!" quoth the gentleman with a grunt. Then, with a shrewd look at me, he said: "*Contra mercator, novem jactantibus austris.*"

"*Militia est potior,*" I said, capping his tag from Flaccus' first satire, without reflecting whereto he was luring me.

"I knew it!" he cried, waving his pipe triumphantly at his wife. "And you haven't run away from school?"

"Indeed I have not, sir. I left school some months ago."

The lady smiled at his crestfallen look. It was plain that, in talking over myself and my situation, he had declared with the positiveness which I found was part of his character, that I had fallen into some trouble at school and fled the consequences.

There was a brief silence; then he said:

"You spoke of work. What can you do?"

"Little enough, sir," I replied. "But I lived for some years on a farm, and could do something in that kind."

Husband and wife glanced at each other, and the gentleman said:

"Well, well, go downstairs now; presently I will send for you again."

I went down, and found my way, by the back of the house, the door standing open, into the garden. I had not taken more than half a dozen paces down the middle path when a big dog of the retriever kind came barking towards me. Stooping down, I patted his head and tickled his ears, a thing which all animals love, and then went on, the dog trotting by my side in most friendly wise.

And at a turn of the walk I came without warning upon the girl who had interposed to save me from a thrashing and had then gone scornfully away, thinking me a liar. The consciousness of my ridiculous appearance rushed upon me in a flood, and, having but small experience of womankind save as represented by Mistress Pennyquick and our maids, I must stand stock still, red to the roots of my hair.

The girl had been walking towards me, swinging by its riband a garden hat, for the air was hot. The dog ran to her, with a bark that might have been of reassurance. She stopped, and, with a pretty shyness far short of embarrassment, said:

"Are you better now, poor man?"

I mumbled something, I know not what, and she smiled and passed on.

Then I felt I would have given anything to live that moment again.

"Dolt! Fool! Jackass!" I called myself. "What a baby she must think me! 'Poor man!' she said. Good heavens! Does she think I am forty?"

And thus fuming at my tongue-tied awkwardness, I went along the path.

I walked up and down for some time, and was still pacing along with my back to the house, when I heard a light footstep behind me, and for a foolish moment fancied it was the girl whose aspect and kind words had lately put me in such a commotion. But on turning about, I felt relief and disappointment mingled (the disappointment was, I think, the greater) to see that it was only Susan.

"Measter wants tha," she said.

I stepped along in silence beside her, she taking three steps for my one, and giggling to sicken a man.

"Tha'lt never get a sweetheart," she said by and by.

"Oh! and why not?" I asked.

"'Cos tha'rt such a great big feller," she said.

"What in the name of all that's wonderful has that to do with it?"

The minx looked archly up into my face.

"Tha'rt too high for a maid to kiss," says she.

To this I made no answer, being no whit inclined to bandy words with this pert young housemaid. And so we came to the house.

"We have been considering your case," said the master, when I again stood before him. "Are you still set on going to Bristowe?"

"Truly, sir, I have seen nought to change my mind."

"You know you are miles out of your road?"

"'Tis through coming over the fields," I said.

"Well, if you are bent upon it, I will furnish you with money enough to take you there, and trust to you to repay me in good time."

"'Tis good of you, sir," I said, guessing, and not wrongly, I think, at whose persuasion he made that offer.

Then I was silent. The name "charity brat," bestowed on me years before by Cyrus Vetch, still rankled in my soul, and though, now that I look back upon it, there was nothing that need have wounded my pride in accepting the proffered loan, I was loath to be beholden to any man. Maybe my feeling on this point was complicated with another of which I was as yet hardly conscious; but certain it is that, after standing silent for a brief space, I said suddenly:

"I thank you heartily, sir, but I had liever earn the money."

"Pish, lad!" cried the gentleman. "'Tis easy to see you are not of laboring rank, and as for the money, I shall not break if I never see it again."

That was the worst argument he could have devised. My pride was up in arms now, in good sooth, and I said firmly:

"With your leave, sir, I will earn what money I need."

"Didst ever see such an obstinate youth?" said he testily, turning to his wife. "Well, as you will. I warrant you will soon sing another tune. Go and see my steward, one of the men will take you to him, and tell him what you know of husbandry; 'tis no more, I warrant, than you have learned out of Vergil's *Georgics*.

"Stay," he added, as I turned to go, "we must have a name for you. You can not be a mere cipher in my estate books."

"Call me Joe, sir," I said, he thinking me of my friend Punchard.

"Joseph in the house of bondage," says he with a laugh, "Well, Joe it shall be."

I was some paces towards the door when remembrance came to me.

"May I have my crown piece, sir?" I said, turning back.

"God bless the boy! Here, take it; 'tis the same that jumped from your pocket. And now I bethink me, those poachers' tatters sit very ill on your long carcass.

"We must find something better suited to his frame, mistress."

"We will have, a clothier from Bridgenorth," said the lady.

"I trust you will be very happy with us the short while you stay, Joe," she added with her gentle smile, and I went from the room with my heart very warm towards her.

Chapter 10
The Shuttered Coach

Thus I entered on a period which I look back upon, after fifty years, as one of the happiest in my life. The steward, Mr. Johnson, an active, silent man, employed me alternately in practical work upon the estate--felling trees, repairing fences, and so. forth--and in keeping his books, for which latter duty my service with Mr. Vetch had in some sort fitted me. For a week I saw nothing of my master, and caught but fugitive glimpses of the members of his family. I suspected, and rightly, as it turned out, that he was deliberately keeping out of my way, but receiving careful reports of me from Mr. Johnson.

His name, I learned, was James Allardyce, and his rank was something above that of a yeoman. He was choleric in temper and hasty in judgment, but the soul of kindness and generosity, and the servants loved him. The boy I had felled was his only son, just home from the school at Rugby; and his niece, Mistress Lucy, as everyone called her, had but lately become a member of his household. She was an orphan. Her father had been a planter with large estates in Jamaica, and on his death she had been brought to England at his wish by an old nurse, and delivered into the care of her mother's brother. She had another uncle, it was said--a squire, her father's brother, who lived somewhat north of Shrewsbury. 'Twas Susan who told me this; she was a chatterbox, and would have talked all day to me had I not discouraged her, and then she said I gave myself airs.

But it was from Roger Allardyce I learned things so surprising that I wonder I did not betray myself. About a week after I came to the Hall (so the house was called) I was returning early one morning from bathing in a stream that crossed the estate, when I met the boy face to face. He was striding along, whistling, with his towel over his shoulder, and gave me a look aslant as he passed, then halted and called after me: "I say, Joe!"

I turned at once, and knew that he bore me no malice for the blow I had dealt him at our first meeting.

"I say," he repeated, "how did you manage to keep your crown piece when those poacher fellows bagged your money?"

I could not forbear smiling at this blunt manner of holding out the olive branch. I told him of my fight with the man called Topper.

"Wish I had seen it," he said, laughing heartily. "And I wish it had happened a day or two before, for if you had been settled here then you could have plied your fists to some better purpose."

I asked him to explain.

"Why, a lubber of a fellow rode over from Shrewsbury; he's a cousin of mine, more's the pity, and a king's officer, by George! There were two other officers with him, and they had been drinking, and they insisted on coming in, and stayed ever so long playing the fool. Father was in Bridgenorth, and Giles with him, and the other men were not at hand, and we had to put up with their tomfoolery, which soon drove mother and Lucy from the room: but if you had been there we could have contrived to fling them out between us."

"I would have done my best," I said.

"How is the water?" he asked.

"Fresh, with a wholesome sting," I replied, and then, giving me a friendly nod, he went on to his bath.

Here was strange news, I thought, as I returned to the house. I could have no doubt that the obnoxious visitors were Dick Cludde and his friends: for it was hardly possible that three other king's officers should have ridden out of Shrewsbury in this direction on the same day. If Cludde had come once he might come again, and should he catch sight of me my story would not only be known to my employer, but would be spread all over Shrewsbury--a thing I could not contemplate with satisfaction. It crossed my mind that 'twould be safer to leave Mr. Allardyce and seek employment with some other yeoman; but from this course two reasons deterred me: first, the liking I had taken for him and his family; second, an obstinate reluctance to allow Dick Cludde in any way to alter my plans. It would not be difficult, I reflected, for one in my humble position to avoid him should he come to the house, and if I needs must meet him, I should even welcome the occasion for bundling him out neck and crop if he proved a troublesome visitor.

My resolution was strengthened a few days afterwards. Since the morning when Roger Allardyce had first addressed me, a friendship had sprung up between us, with a rapidity only possible to boys. We bathed together of mornings; he would come and chat to me when I was at my work; and the hours of work being over, he would lug me into a little outhouse he kept as his own, and show me his treasures--guns, and fishing tackle, a breastplate worn by his grandfather in the Civil War, an oak-apple from the tree in which King Charles had hidden after the battle of Worcester. He treated me as his equal, and once, when I alluded to my dependent position, his curiosity, which with excellent well-bred delicacy he kept in check, got the better of him, and he begged me to tell him all about myself, swearing never to reveal it to a soul. But I cleaved to my determination; all I would tell him was what he knew already, that I was a penniless orphan bent on making my way in the world.

Well, one evening, when I returned from my work in the fields, I found him waiting for me with excitement plainly writ on his open face. He dragged me to his outhouse, and having shut the door, said:

"I say, Joe, there's a storm brewing, and we may need your fists. You remember I told you about my cousin riding over from Shrewsbury? Well, his father came today--Sir Richard Cludde, a big red-faced bully of a man. He's Lucy's uncle, you know; her father was his brother, and they quarreled, and hadn't seen each other for twenty years. But now he declares that he is Lucy's legal guardian; his brother died suddenly and left no will, and he came today to claim her as his ward. Father wouldn't hear of it; but told him Lucy had been brought here by the express command of her father, and he refused to give her up. The squire was in a terrible rage: 'tis said he has fallen on evil times, and is set on getting a hold on Lucy's property in Jamaica, and making a match between her and his son Dick--the lubber I told you of. There was an angry scene 'twixt him and father, you could have heard him roaring all over the house, and he went away in a towering passion, swearing that we'd not heard the last of it, and he'd go to law, and he'd beat us even though it cost him his last penny, and more to the same effect. Father makes light of it, but I know he is uneasy: he has been several times of late to see his lawyer in Bridgenorth, and 'tis by no means clear how the law will decide. There will be trouble, for Sir Richard is an obstinate man, and I'm glad you are here, for we are not going to let Lucy leave us, and if he comes one day to take her by force we'll make a fight for it, Joe. And I'll tell you what: you must teach me how to use my fists. Shall we begin now, Joe?"

I smiled at his eagerness, and though I was tired after my day's work I would not disappoint him, but stripped off my coat, and then and there began his instruction in what my old friend the captain called the noble art of self defense. He proved an apt pupil, and I a conscientious teacher, pleasing myself with the thought that by making him expert in boxing I was maybe gathering interest on Dick Cludde's crown piece. And being then of the age when romantic ideas get some hold upon a boy's mind, I flattered myself also that by staying on at the Hall I became in some sort a defender of fair Lucy Cludde, who was far too good, I vowed, for that pudding-headed lubber Dick.

After this Roger and I became faster friends than ever. We had constant sparring matches and some practice also with singlestick and foils; and Mr. Johnson would let me off sometimes of an afternoon to go a-fishing with the boy. Before I had been a month at the Hall there were few likely streams for miles around that I did not know. All this time I had seen very little of the other members of the family. Mr. Allardyce was putting me to probation, inquiring of my diligence from Mr. Johnson, and hearing somewhat of me from his son. As for Mistress Lucy, I deliberately avoided her. I had cut anything but an heroic figure at our two meetings, and though I was ready to engage in mortal fray as her champion, the recollection of my abashment before her caused me to hold aloof. She and Roger would sometimes go riding together, and I thought with a bitter envy that, but for the misfortune that had befallen me, I might have made one of the party, though in truth I remembered, a moment afterwards, that but for this same misfortune I should very likely never have seen her.

Thus matters went on for upwards of a month. My wages, which I had scrupulously saved, amounted to something above twenty-five shillings--enough to pay my way to Bristowe. There was no reason why I should remain longer at the Hall, and indeed I was beginning to grow restive under my servitude, light as it was, and to think more and more eagerly of my interrupted purpose. One day, therefore, I sought an interview with Mr. Allardyce, and told him that having now enough money for my needs I wished to leave his service and set forth on my way. He laughed and said:

"I wondered how long 'twould go on. You are still bent upon your travels, then?"

I assured him that such was the case, thanked him for his kindness, and asked to be allowed to go on the following Monday: it was then Friday.

"Well, Joe," says he, "I won't stay you. Mr. Johnson has given me good reports of you, and as for Roger, he is never tired of singing your praises. According to him, you are a past master in exercises of arms, and I confess I had hopes you would give up your scheme and return to your friends and take the position you were clearly bred for: then Roger and you might have been companions still. But 'twas not to be; very well; on Monday we shall bid you our adieux, and we shall look to see you someday when you have made a name for yourself--which to be sure will not be Joe."

I was up early next morning, and was going off for my customary swim when, on crossing a stile, I saw a figure draw back into a coppice bounding the field. Thinking it was Roger who had been before me, I called to him, but receiving no answer, and wondering who could be abroad at that early hour--for the men of the estate were engaged in their duties elsewhere--I sprang down and strode off to the coppice, moved by some little curiosity. But though I walked to and fro among the trees for some time, I saw no one, and concluding that it was probably some poacher returning home from his night's work I went on to the bathing place, resolved to give a hint to Mr. Johnson.

Roger joined me presently, with a glum face.

"Oh, I say, Joe," he said, "this is deuced bad news. Father says you are leaving us on Monday."

"Yes, I have been here long enough," I said.

"Of course, I didn't expect you to work here forever, but I did think you would change your mind and remain friends with me."

"We shall always be friends, you and I, I hope," I said, "but it will be on a different footing. I could not work here forever, as you say: and if I mean to do anything in the world 'tis time I set about it. Maybe five years hence I shall return, and you will not be ashamed to own me for a friend."

"Ashamed! When was I ever ashamed? Why, we think a world of you, father and mother and Lucy, too. When father told us last night, they were sorry, yet glad, too, I own. Mother said she was sure you would get on, and I know you will, but all the same I wish you were not going. I say, tell me your real name, and if you have a bother with your people I'll go and see them, I swear I will, and persuade 'em to forgive you."

How surprised he would have been, I thought, if I had told him that the people whom I had not wronged, but who had done me wrong, were relatives of his own! But I would not tell him, and when we had finished our swim and were returning to the house, he declared that he also would leave home; there was no fun in being a yeoman, he said: and if a fellow like Dick Cludde could be an officer in the king's navy, so could he--or in the army, and he would persuade his father to let him go, by George he would! And he asked me to write to him, so that he might know where to find me when his great plan came to execution.

On Monday morning at half-past seven, after a good breakfast, I was at the gate, girt and equipped for my journey. The poachers' garments had, of course, long been discarded, and I was clad in the suit of serviceable homespun obtained for me from Bridgenorth in the first days of my service, and now but little the worse for wear. All the family was at the gate to bid me farewell, even Mistress Lucy, in her riding habit, for she was wont to go for an hour's canter on fine mornings, before breakfast at half-past eight. The adieux were said; all wished me well; Mr. Allardyce, as a parting shot, said that I should always find a job on his estate if I fell in with more poachers, or if my fortunes at Bristowe did not turn out to my liking; and then, my heart warm with their kindness, I set off up the road.

Six or seven miles lay between me and the highroad to Bristowe through Worcester and Gloucester, but I knew of a short cut four miles from the Hall, which would bring me into the road at the turnpike at Deuxhill, some way farther south, and save a good three miles of the road. I had learned of this short cut in the course of my fishing expeditions with Roger; it was the nearest way to the Borle Brook, where our angling had ever the best success- -a narrow track striking off to the right, very rutty and rough, bordered by hedges, and uphill but not steep.

I had tramped three miles or more, at a good pace, when I heard galloping horses behind me, and the rumble of wheels. Turning about, I saw a coach drawn by three horses, with a postilion on the leader, approaching at a great rate, jolting and swaying in a manner that bespoke desperate haste.

I stood aside to let it pass, holding my nose against the whirling dust cloud it raised, and giving it but a glance as it rattled by. The shutters were up; I could not see whether it held anybody; and when it had passed I again took the middle of the road, wondering idly what necessity there might be for so great speed. Only a minute or two afterwards I heard a light patter close at my heels, and looking back without stopping, I was surprised to see the big black retriever which belonged to Mistress Lucy, and with which, since my first meeting with him in the garden, I had been on friendly terms. The dog uttered a low bark when he recognized me, fawned upon me, and then set off running ahead. I noticed now that the beast left a thin trail of blood on the ground. He had not run far when he stopped, turned round, and barked as if to invite me on, not waiting, however, to see whether I responded.

For a moment I was too much taken up with wondering by what mishap the dog had been wounded to connect his appearance, and his evident wish to urge me on, with the coach that had lately passed. But then the connection struck upon me in a flash, and I began to run with all my might. The dog had doubtless accompanied his mistress on her morning ride; he could only have been wounded in defending her; she must have been waylaid, and, thought linking itself with thought, I guessed that Sir Richard Cludde had taken this means of asserting his claim to her guardianship, and the man I had seen in the coppice a few days before was an emissary of his. Without a doubt she was now a prisoner in the coach, being carried against her will to Shrewsbury.

The road here ran steeply downhill, and the coach was out of sight round a bend. Without pausing to consider the chances of overtaking it, I leapt rather than ran forward, soon outstripping the dog, which had done his best, poor beast, but was now well-nigh exhausted. I flung away my staff, that encumbered me, and tore headlong down the hill, till, coming to the bend, where the road sloped upwards, I caught sight once more of the coach, no more than half a mile ahead of me. This surprised me, for neither the ascent nor my speed could account for its nearness, and I wondered, as I pounded after it, whether I had after all been mistaken.

But the matter was explained when I came to the inn that stood at the point where my short cut branched off. I saw wheel tracks to the right, crossed by similar tracks back again to the road, and I guessed that the postilion had intended to drive his horses down the byroad, but having found it too rough or too narrow had been compelled to return, even at the cost of loss of time in backing.

My heart leapt with exultation; the kidnappers were not making for Shrewsbury after all; they purposed driving southward, with what design I could not guess, nor did I stop to consider, for in a twinkling I saw a possibility of intercepting them. Dashing into the inn, much to the amazement of the innkeeper, who had sometimes served Roger and me with a pot of ale as we returned from fishing, I told him my suspicions in quick, breathless gasps, and bade him send to Mr. Allardyce for assistance, and to follow me, if he could, along the byroad to Deuxhill. The man was not too quick-witted, and I could have beaten him for his slowness to comprehend the urgency of the affair. But some glimmering of it dawning upon him, he promised to borrow a horse from Farmer Grubb close by, he having none of his own, and to send a messenger back to the Hall. Without further parley I left him, and set off along the byroad, scarce giving a glance to the poor dog limping painfully towards the inn.

Chapter 11
I Hold A Turnpike

Could I reach the turnpike in time? I wondered. I had lost perhaps three minutes at the inn. The coach must already have reached the crossroads, and was now, without doubt, speeding southward on a course parallel with my own, but downhill, whereas the byroad, though shorter, was for the most part uphill, and so rough that I risked spraining my ankle on a stone or in a rut.

And even supposing I gained the turnpike before the coach, would the keeper be persuaded to close his gates against a three-horsed vehicle on the highway? I knew the man, and luckily had done him a slight service which perchance he would be willing to repay. Once, when Roger and I had gone to the Borle Brook to fish, we came upon a little girl some five years old sitting by the brink, weeping bitterly. One foot was bare, her little shoe was floating down the stream, she had lost herself, and was so frightened that it was long before we could make out from her sobbing answers to our questions that she was daughter to the turnpike man. Then Roger rescued her shoe, and I set her aloft on my shoulder, to her great contentment, and she was laughing merrily when we reached the turnpike, and gave her into the hands of her distracted mother. Remembering this, I raced on at my best speed, resolved, if only I arrived in time, to turn this little incident to account.

It did but add to my anxiety that the highroad was nowhere visible to me as I ran, so that I could not measure my progress with that of the coach, but was forced to go on at the same break-neck pace, not daring to moderate it in any degree. And I could almost have cried with vexation when that plaguey stitch in the side seized me, and I had to stand a while to recover my breath. Then I raced on again, desperately anxious to make up for the lost time. My work upon the Hall estate, and my exercise with Roger, had kept my body in good condition: yet to run for four miles or more at a stretch with the mind in a ferment would tax any man, and by the time I came in sight of the turnpike I was fairly overdone, dripping with sweat--'twas a sunny day in July--and trembling in every limb.

And then I heard, or fancied I heard, the rattle of the coach on my left, and I picked up my heels and scampered along the last half-mile at a pace which, in other circumstances, I should have deemed impossible, the loose stones flying from beneath my feet.

I emerged upon the highroad, threw a glance over my left shoulder, and gave a great gasp of relief when I spied the coach plunging down the road, but nearly a mile distant. I had had no clear notion of what I was going to do beyond attempting to keep the gate closed, and now I realized with a sinking heart that, even if I should succeed therein, the coach could scarcely be delayed long enough for help to arrive. But certainly that was the first step, and I dashed straight into the keeper's cottage, the door of which stood open, and found Mistress Peabody, his wife, paring potatoes at the table, her little girl by her side.

"Where is Peabody?" I blurted out.

"Sakes alive!" cried the woman, "but you did give me a start. Whatever be amiss?"

What more I said I know not, but at my demand that she should refuse to open the gate for the coming coach the poor bewildered soul dropped her potatoes and declared she could never do it; 'twould cause terrible trouble with Peabody, and maybe bring about his dismissal by the justices, and where he was she did not know, and she had told him many a time he would get into a coil if he left his duty and went so often to the King William a-fuddling himself with--

"For God's sake, woman," I broke in, exasperated, "take the child into the garden and leave it to me."

I fairly pushed her out at the back door, the little girl clinging to her skirts, terrified at my appearance and the fierceness of my words. I shut the door upon them, whipped the key of the gate from its nail on the wall, flung it into the pan of water among the potatoes, and then, a desperate expedient coming into my mind, sauntered leisurely out of the front door, picking up as I passed a stick of wood from among a heap with which the child had been playing on the floor.

I climbed the gate, and sat upon the topmost bar, with my feet on the third. Then, having pulled the broad brim of my hat down over my eyes, I took out my clasp knife (it had been given me a few days before by Roger as a memento) and began to whittle the stick, whistling a doleful tune.

The coach was by this time within a hundred yards of me.

"Gate! gate!" shouted the postilion, but I paid no heed. There was now a man on the box; I suppose he had been picked up at the crossroads. He joined his cry to the postilion's, and together they roared "Gate!" with many imprecations of the kind that men who deal with horses have at command.

But I still went on whittling my stick, not without some feeling of insecurity, for the coach was approaching at a furious speed, and it seemed impossible that the postilion could draw up in time to prevent the horses from dashing themselves against the barrier. He accomplished that feat, however, and the leading horse came to a standstill within little more than a foot of me; I could feel its hot breath on my hand. Like the other two, it was covered with foam, and their sides were heaving like a bellows.

"Gate!" roared the postilion, looking in at the open door, and receiving no reply he turned his head towards me and demanded with an oath to know where the turnpike keeper was.

"He bin gone out," I said, in the broadest Shropshire accent I could muster.

"The mischief he is! Who be in charge of the gate then?"

Sputtering with wrath the postilion cursed me and demanded to know what I meant by sitting a-top when travelers wished to pass through. I assumed the vacant grin that rustics wear, and said:

"The toll be tuppence, measter."

"Here it is," says the man, flinging the coins on the ground, "and be hanged to you."

I descended from my perch (the man abusing me for my slowness), picked up the money, and went into the cottage as if to get the key.

"Be quick about it," roared the postilion after me.

"Coming, measter," I replied, sitting on the table, out of his sight. In a little he cried to me again:

"What be doin' of? Stir your stumps, I say."

"Coming, measter," says I, knocking my knife against the potato pan to signify bustle. The man's language grew more and more violent as the minutes passed and still I did not reappear, until, having consumed as much time as I thought becoming, I went to the doorway, and said, in the manner of stating a simple fact of no importance,

"Key binna hangin' on nail, measter. The nail be proper plaace for it: can ya tell me where to look?"

My drawling tone seemed to incense the man to the verge of apoplexy. Hurling abuse at me, he ended with a threat to horsewhip me within an inch of my life if I did not instantly find the key and open the gate. At this I shrank back, putting up my hands to guard my head with great affectation of terror, and withdrew once more into the cottage. As I did so, I heard the shutters on the far side of the coach let down, and a voice demanding the reason of the delay.

"The pudding-headed scut cannot find the key, sir."

"Tell him," said the voice in a louder tone (and I tingled as I recognized it)--"tell him that if he keeps us waiting another minute we will break the gate down."

I laughed inwardly at this foolish threat. The gate was a stout barrier, that would do more damage than it could receive from any attempt of theirs.

"Bring out the key, rascal," roared the postilion again.

"An' you please, measter," says I, appearing in the doorway, "I be afeared the key bin lost."

Then the man on the box scrambled down, and ran into the cottage. With him I hunted in every nook and corner of the room, and there being no sign of the key we went out, and to the other side of the coach, and there I heard the coach door open, and the voice cried:

"Hold the leader, Jabez; and you, Tom, go to the wheelers' heads. I'll blow in the cursed lock with my pistol."

Slipping back so that I might not be seen, I peeped through the window and saw Cyrus Vetch, pistol in hand, moving towards the gate. Here I was in a wretched quandary. I glanced anxiously up the road: there was never a sign of Mr. Allardyce or any other pursuer. To blow in the lock would be the work of a second: then nothing I could do would prevent the coach from passing through and getting clean away.

I was ready to despair when a possible means of checkmate flashed into my mind. Vetch was within a yard of the gate; his two men were at the horses' heads, to hold them when the report of the pistol came; their eyes were fixed on their master. As lightly as I could (my boots being heavy, as the long service required of them demanded) I darted through the doorway, my right hand clasping my knife, hid behind my back. Running to the side of the horse nearest me I set to a-hacking with all my strength at the leathern trace. Thank Heaven my knife was new and unblunted! But I had not succeeded in cutting the leather through when the pistol cracked and the lock burst. The startled horses immediately began to rear and plunge, so violently that the single man at the wheelers' heads could not hold them. Vetch ran to assist him; none of them had noticed that the violence of the horses' straining had completed my unfinished work: the trace snapped in two.

Pulling itself free the horse swung round, and plunged more violently than before, keeping the man Tom employed and serving also to screen me from view. Now was my opportunity. I wrenched open the shuttered door, and saw a man leaning with his body out of the other door, watching the movements of Vetch. And between us, shrinking back on the seat, was Mistress Lucy. She turned her head as I pulled the door open, and holding on to it to preserve my balance, for the coach was being swerved this way and that by the frantic horses, I whispered:

"'Tis I, Mistress Lucy: jump out!"

And quick as thought--'tis a blessing when a woman's wits are keen-- she made one spring for the roadway, by a hair's breadth eluding the grasp of Dick Cludde, who had turned about at my whisper. I caught the girl as she touched the ground, and, pulling her away from the wheel, just in time to save her foot from being crushed by it, I seized her hand, and dragged her--willing captive!--towards the doorway. I pushed her into the cottage, with a roughness for which I afterwards asked her pardon, and hastened in after her.

Before I could close and bolt the door I heard a crash and a cry of pain, and caught a glimpse of Cludde, who, in leaping from the coach, had fallen awry and lay sprawling in the dust. Then I shut him from sight and ran to the other door, by which Mistress Peabody had gone into the garden. This I slammed and barred, dashing afterwards to the window to do the like with it. Luckily it was already fastened, and I was hastily drawing the shutters over it, when Vetch, his face livid with passion, came up to it, drove his pistol through the glass, and threatened to shoot me if I did not instantly unbolt the door.

I have always had reason to thank Heaven that my brain is quickest and my resolution most cool at the moments of greatest stress. Vetch had fired his pistol through the lock of the turnpike gate; being busy with the horse he had certainly not had time to recharge it, nor to get another; so I thought that I might safely defy him. Whispering to Mistress Lucy to find some hiding place in the cottage out of view from the window, I stood with my hand on the shutter, and said:

"What will you do if I yield?"

The answer was the heavy pistol, hurled straight at my head. It struck my temple and fell with a crash to the floor. I gave back a little, half stunned by the blow, and Vetch seized that moment to smash another pane of the window, preparing to leap on the sill and into the room, But I had sufficient strength to anticipate him. Throwing my whole weight on the shutter I drove it into its place, taking a certain pleasure in the knowledge that I had at least bruised the fellow's knuckles. Then I dropped the bar into its socket, and in the half darkness called to Mistress Lucy that all was well.

Immediately there began a heavy battering on the door, but not so heavy but that through it I heard Cludde order his men to splice the broken trace. 'Twas lucky it was so, for had all four of them come with one mind to force my frail defences, the brief siege would, I fear, have had but a sorry end. The door was a stout one, and finding it resisted their blows, Vetch and Cludde soon desisted, and I supposed that they had withdrawn altogether. But after a short interval, a violent crash on the back door, which was of much slighter timber, warned me that I must still be prepared to fight against heavy odds.

I looked round for Mistress Lucy: she was standing beside an oaken clothes press, the largest article of furniture in the room.

"Help will come, I hope," I said to her; "if not, I can keep them at bay, and I will."

A moment after I had spoken, I heard a shout from the road. The blows upon the door ceased; I caught the sound of scurrying feet, and running to the window, I unbarred the shutter and opened it so that I might glance out. The coach was moving: the postilion was in the saddle, the other man was on the box. It passed through the gate: the horses were lashed to a gallop, and the equipage disappeared down the road in a cloud of dust. Flinging the shutter wide, I craned my neck out of the broken panes and looked in the other direction. Not half a mile away three horsemen were pressing a gallop towards us.

"You are safe," I said, turning to the girl.

She came eagerly to my side, and in another minute the horsemen--the innkeeper and two men whom I did not know--leapt from their saddles when I hailed them, and came to ask if all was well.

Chapter 12
I Come To Bristowe--And Leave Unwillingly

The presence of the innkeeper and his friends--a neighboring farmer and one of his sons: another son had ridden to acquaint Mr. Allardyce at the Hall of the kidnapping--relieved me of a certain embarrassment I felt, now that the stress and excitement were over. As yet Mistress Lucy had spoken scarce a word; but she had looked at me with great kindness, and I knew that she was but waiting for an opportunity to thank me for the service I had rendered her. With the shy awkwardness of my age I wished to avoid this, and so I willingly related to the innkeeper all that had occurred, and had barely ended when Peabody came back in haste from Glazeley, where I fear he had been fuddling himself as his wife had suggested. To him the story had to be told over again, I meanwhile itching to get away before Mr. Allardyce could arrive.

When I announced my determination to proceed at once on my journey there was a great outcry from the men: would I not wait and see the Squire and be suitably rewarded? Mistress Lucy herself, who had remained in the cottage while we conversed outside, came to the door at this point of our discussion, and with bright color in her cheeks beckoned me and asked whether I would not stay until her uncle's arrival. But my mind was made up.

"You are in safe hands," I said, "and I have far to go."

"I shall not forget what you have done for me--Joe," she said, and for the second time gave me her little hand. I could say nothing, but when I was once more upon the road I thought of her kind look and manner, and glowed with a deep contentment.

I had not walked above a mile when I heard a galloping horse behind me, and Roger's clear voice calling me by name. I halted, and he sprang from the saddle and caught me by the hand.

"By George! 'twas mighty fine of you, Joe," he cried, with kindling eyes. "I'll break Dick Cludde's head for him, I will, if ever I see him again. Who was the other villain? Lucy says there were two."

"'Twas--" I began, but suddenly bit my lip; if I named Cyrus Vetch my own secret, which I had so carefully guarded, would soon be known, and I was resolved (maybe without reason) that they should not know me as Humphrey Bold until I had done somewhat to win credit for the name. "'Twas a long weasel-faced fellow," I said, after so slight a pause that it escaped Roger's perception.

"And weasels are vermin," cried Roger, "and he has killed Lucy's dog! But come, Joe, what nonsense is this! Father insists that you shall come back; he declares this trudging to Bristowe is sheer fooling, and had already got half a dozen fine schemes in his head for you. Mount behind me, man: the mare will carry you though you are a monster; come back and we'll be sworn brothers."

I confess the boy's generosity touched me, and the offer was tempting; but I steeled my soul against it, and, strange as it may seem, 'twas the remembrance of Mistress Lucy that put an end to all wavering. Once I had had no higher aim than to win Captain Galsworthy's praise; now I felt--but dimly--that I would endure the toils of Hercules to win a lady's favor. 'Twas the budding of young love within me--and I never knew that a lad was any the worse for it.

So I thanked Roger as warmly as I might, but held to my purpose against all his reasons. The boy was impulsive and quick tempered, and finding me obdurate after ten minutes' battery of argument, he flung away in a huff, got up into the saddle, and bidding me go hang for an obstinate mule he galloped back to the turnpike.

And so I set my face once more for the south. Missing my staff, which I had thrown away in my haste, I cut myself a large hazel switch from a copse by the roadside, promising myself a stouter weapon when I should arrive at a town.

My heart was light: had I not begun to pay Dick Cludde interest on his crown piece? I was inexpressibly glad that I had been able to defeat his outrageous scheme, and thinking of this, I wondered why he had driven southward instead of to his father's house beyond Shrewsbury. My conjecture was that, knowing what a hue and cry Mr. Allardyce would raise if he believed his niece had been conveyed thither, the Cluddes had arranged to remove her to a distance until the legal matter then pending should have been decided in their favor. I remembered hearing Dick once speak of some relatives at Worcester, and in all likelihood that had been his destination.

To have encountered me within so few miles of Shrewsbury must have mightily surprised him. He had known of my intention in setting out; 'twas common talk in Shrewsbury; and, having passed me at Harley near two months before this, must have supposed (if he thought of me at all) that I had long since reached my destination. What he would infer now I did not trouble to consider, and as he was to have rejoined his ship about this time, I did not expect any news of my adventure would be carried back to Shrewsbury. It crossed my mind that he might possibly seek to waylay me on the road and take vengeance for his discomfiture, but reflecting that he would scarcely suppose my journey, interrupted for so long, would be resumed at once, I was in nowise disquieted; only I resolved again to buy a stout cudgel, to have a weapon in case of need.

By noon I arrived at Bewdley, where, being mighty hungry, I made a good dinner of beef and cabbage at an inn. When I started again, I had the good luck to get a lift in a farmer's gig, which carried me for several miles, so that I reached Worcester without difficulty that night. After a sound sleep at the Ram's Head I sallied out, bought a fine staff of knobby oak at a shop in the High Street, and after viewing the outside of the cathedral (the doors were not yet open), a building that surpassed in beauty anything that I had before seen, I set off for Gloucester.

No mischance, nor indeed any incident of note, befell me during the remainder of my journey. I passed the next night in a wagon, swaddled in a load of fresh mown hay, the driver with rustic friendliness inviting me to keep him company on his dark journey. On the third night after my departure from the Hall I trudged, weary and footsore, into Bristowe, and sought a bed at the White Hart in Old Market Street, this tavern having been recommended to me by the friendly hay-cart man.

Next day, when I went out to view the city of which I had heard so much, I was struck with wonderment, not merely at its size, wherein it dwarfed Shrewsbury and all the towns through which I had passed, but at its noise and bustle. Shrewsbury was a sleepy old town, where life went on very placidly from day to day, and the sight of these busy, though narrow, streets with their many fine buildings and their swarms of people, the dogs drawing little carts of merchandise, the river with its bridges, the floating basin with many tall ships, the quays thronged with sailors and lightermen, filled me not only with wonder, but with a sense of loneliness and insignificance.

Among all these folk, intent upon their various occupations, what place was there for me, I wondered? I got in the way of a line of men on the quay side carrying large bales which I presumed had been unloaded from a ship there moored. One of them hustled me violently aside, another made a coarse jest upon me, and, raw and inexperienced as I was, bewildered by the strangeness of it all, I felt a sinking at the heart, and questioned for the first time whether I had been wise in forsaking the scenes I knew and venturing unbefriended into this outpost of the great world.

I was standing apart, gazing at the shipping, when an old, weather-beaten sailor, smoking a black pipe, came up and accosted me.

"Lost your bearings, matey?" he said in a very hoarse voice, which yet had a tone of friendliness.

No doubt I looked foolish, for I knew no more than the dead what he meant.

"Lor' bless you," he went on, "I knows all about it. 'Tis fifty year since I made a course for that 'ere port from Selwood way, and I stood like a stuck pig--like as you be standing now. Be you out o' Zummerzet, like me?"

I told him I came from Shrewsbury.

"Never heard tell of it," he said, "but seemingly they grow high in those parts. And what made ye steer for Bristowe, if I might ask?"

Mr. Vetch had warned me against confiding in strangers; but there was something so honest in the old seaman's look that I, who have rarely been wrong in my instinctive judgment of men, determined to trust him, and told him so much of my story as I thought necessary.

The result was that he took me under his wing, so to speak. He spent the whole morning with me, explaining to me the differences in build and rig between the vessels lying there, telling me a great deal about the duties of a seaman and the ways of life at sea. He counseled me very earnestly to give up my design and seek an employment on shore.

"Sea life bean't for the likes of you," he said. "I don't know nothing about lawyers, saving them as they call sea lawyers, and they're rogues; but you'd better be a land lawyer than go to sea. 'Tis all very well for them as begin as officers, but for the men the life bean't fit for a dog. Aboard ship you'd meet some very rough company--very rough indeed. I don't pretend to be better nor most, but there be some terrible bad ones at sea. Of course it depends mostly on the skipper, but even where the skipper's a good 'un--and there be good and bad--he can't have his eyes everywhere, and I've knowed youngsters so bad used on board that they'd sooner ha' bin dead. Not but what you mightn't stand a chance, being a big fellow of your inches."

What the old fellow said did not in the least shake my resolution. The only effect of it was to turn my inclination rather in favor of the merchant service than the king's navy, to which I had inclined hitherto. In a king's ship

I might certainly share in some fighting, which has ever great attractions to a healthy boy; but then I should have little chance of seeing the world unless specially favored by circumstances, for the ship might be kept cruising about, looking for the French who never came. Whereas in a merchant ship I might see India, and even China, and my new friend told me fine stories of the fortunes to be made in those distant parts by the lucky ones, besides which I felt a longing to see strange and far-off lands and peoples for the mere pleasure of it. To take service with an East Indiaman most hit my fancy, and when the sailor told me that London and Southampton were the ports for the East India trade, I began to think of working my passage to one or the other of them.

John Woodrow, as he was named, advised me not to be in a hurry, and when I explained that my little stock of money would be exhausted in a few days by the charges at the inn where I had put up, he recommended me to a widow living towards Clifton, who would give me board and lodging for a more modest sum. My anxieties on this score being removed, I resolved to follow Woodrow's advice, and not be in too great haste to take my first plunge. He promised to let me know of any decent skipper who might be sailing to Southampton or London if, when I had had a few days to think things over, my mind remained the same.

Next day a great king's ship of three decks came into the river, and I passed the whole morning in gazing at her, watching what went on upon her deck, and the boatloads of mariners that came ashore from her, envying the officers, and wavering in my design to join a merchant vessel. The vessel was named, as I found, the Sans Pareil, and though I had little French (the dead tongues being most thought of at Shrewsbury), I knew the words meant "the matchless," and certainly she outdid all the other ships around her.

The only vessel, indeed, that any way approached her was a large brig which, as my friend Woodrow had told me the day before, was a privateer that was being fitted out by certain gentlemen and merchants of Bristowe for work against the French. The Bristowe merchants had suffered great losses from the depredations made on their ships by French corsairs. Many a vessel loaded with a rich freight of sugar, or tobacco, or other produce of the colonies, had fallen a prey to the enemy, who swooped out of St. Malo or Brest, as Woodrow said, and snapped up our barques almost within sight of their harbor. 'Twas not to be wondered at that those who had suffered in this way should make reprisals.

The Sans Pareil had such a fascination for me (never having seen a king's ship before) that I was only awakened to the passage of time by the crying out of my stomach. I had promised Mistress Perry, the widow with whom I had taken up my abode, that I would return punctually at noon for my dinner, and now the church clocks (no less than my hunger) told me it was long past that hour. She would be mightily vexed, and the joint would be burned black, and I neither wished to offend her nor to eat cinders. So I now hurried away as fast as my legs would carry me, and soon came to the footpath leading to Clifton.

As I turned the corner by Jacob's Well, I stepped hastily aside to avoid a man who was coming fast in the opposite direction. He also moved at the same moment, and, as I have often known to happen at such sudden encounters, the very movements made to prevent the collision brought it about. We both moved to the same side, and jostled each other, and I, being the more weighty of the two, gave him a tough shoulder and well nigh upset him.

"Clumsy h--" he was beginning, but he got no further, and 'twas well he did not, for if he had uttered the word "hound" that had all but come to his lips he would scarce have gone on his way without my mark upon him. But he did not say it, being indeed startled out of his self possession. No doubt he had as little expected to see me as I to see him: it was Cyrus Vetch.

We both turned after jostling each other. The impulse seized me to take him by the neck and drub him for his rascally dealing with Mistress Lucy--and to settle at the same time some little private scores of my own. But he was in truth so pitiful a creature, and looked so scared, that I let him alone; besides I felt that I might one day have a greater account to pay off, to which settlement Dick Cludde must be a party.

He on his side, to judge by his pale cheeks, expected a rude handling, and when he found that I made no movement towards him, a look of relief crossed his countenance, followed by an expression which at the moment I was unable to fathom. Then, as by mutual consent, and without having exchanged a word, we turned our backs on each other and went our several ways.

As I expected, the joint of beef was done to shreds, and Widow Perry rated me soundly for being so late, asking me whether I expected her dog to keep turning the jack till doomsday. ('Twas a strange custom of the Bristowe housewives to employ dogs for turning their roasting jacks). With all humility I expressed contrition, and vowed amendment, and I kept my word. While I ate my dinner my thoughts were busy with my late encounter with Vetch, and I wondered what he was about in Bristowe, and whether Dick Cludde was still with him. I did not doubt they were in a desperate rage with me, and if they should be here together I was pretty sure they would take some means of avenging themselves; but confident of my strength and my skill of fence the prospect gave me rather a pleasant expectancy than any alarm.

So three days passed--days which I spent for the most part with Woodrow the old mariner, plying him with questions innumerable about shipping and life at sea, and learning many things by my own observation. I saw no more of Vetch, nor did anything give me cause of uneasiness. On the second day Mistress Perry, indeed, threatened a slight discomfort by wishing me to share my room with a new lodger she had just taken; but she gave in when I flatly refused to bed with a stranger, and grumblingly accommodated the man--a rough-looking sea dog--in a little closet off the stairs.

On the third afternoon, when I returned to the quay after my dinner, Woodrow told me he had found a skipper who would sail for Southampton at the end of the week, and was willing to take me as ship's boy. He assured me that I could hope for nothing better to begin with, and the voyage would be long enough for me to try my sea legs, and, as he believed, to cure me of my fancy for a sea life. I was to visit the skipper at the Angel tavern that evening, and if he liked my figurehead, as Woodrow put it, the matter could be settled there and then.

Accordingly, about seven o'clock, I met Woodrow at the corner of the Bridge, by the Leather Hall, and accompanied him to the Angel in Redcliffe Street, where he presented me to his friend, Captain Reddaway. After the usual jocose allusions to my height, to which I was now fairly inured, the skipper asked me a great many questions about navigation, feigned a vast surprise at my ignorance, and supplied the answers himself, to impress me, I suppose, with his own stores of knowledge.

Then the two mariners settled down over their pipes and beer to a conversation in which I was not expected to take a part; indeed, it consisted chiefly of reminiscences of voyages they had made together, and, though entertaining enough at first, by and by became insufferably tedious. For politeness' sake they included me in the conversation from time to time by waving their pipes at me, and I did not like to risk hurting the feelings of my new employer by showing how wearied I was, or by leaving them; so that it was not till near ten o'clock that I managed to escape, and then only because they had both fallen asleep.

The night was warm, and my lungs being filled with the reek of their strong tobacco I determined to walk down by the river before returning to my lodging, in the hope of getting a breath of fresh air blowing in from the sea. The river side was deserted and silent; the lights of the vessels at anchor increased the darkness around; and I was walking slowly along, wondering which of the lamps hung on Captain Reddaway's vessel, when suddenly I found myself surrounded by a group of men who seemed to have sprung from nowhere. Before I knew what was happening, much less make any movement of defence, I was being dragged by rough hands to the edge of the quay. I shouted lustily for help, only to receive a crack on the head from one of the men, while another clapped his hand across my mouth. I wriggled desperately, tripped up one fellow, and used my feet to some purpose on the shins of another; but there were so many of them that I was soon overpowered, and was quite helpless in their hands when they lugged me down the steps into a boat that lay moored below.

Throwing me into the bottom they pulled off; in a few minutes they came under the quarter of a large vessel in midstream; I was hauled up the side, and, more or less dazed with my rough handling, heard without understanding a loud voice giving orders. In two minutes I was lying bound hand and foot in the fore part of the vessel, and there I remained, exposed to the open sky, until morning dawned.

Chapter 13
Duguay-Trouin

'Twas little sleep I got that night, my body smarting with the ill usage I had suffered, and my mind in a ferment of rage and dismay. This was the third and the worst mischance that had befallen me since I left Shrewsbury, and no one would blame me overmuch, perhaps, had I given way to utter despair. Old Woodrow had told me stories about such tricks of kidnapping, but, just as when we hear a parson denouncing sin we are apt to apply it to our neighbor and not ourselves, so I had never dreamed that I myself might be the victim of such an outrage. And remembering what Woodrow had said, I broke out into a sweat of apprehension, for I knew that I could not have been impressed as a mariner to serve aboard a privateer, as was often done; only tried mariners were seized with that intent, and certainly no one would wish to teach a raw landsman his duties on a vessel engaged in such a perilous and desperate business.

I could only conclude, then, that the design in kidnapping me was to ship me to the American or West Indian plantations, whither every year hundreds of poor wretches were sent to a dismal slavery. Woodrow had pointed out to me one day in the street a high magistrate of the city, who had made great wealth in the sugar trade, and did not disdain to add to it by selling flesh and blood.

My imagination racked with this fear, I lay sleepless, save for brief intervals of restless dozing. Soon after dawn I heard movements about the ship, and by and by some of the sailors came and looked at me, making all manner of jests in language fouler than I had ever heard. The features of one of them seemed familiar to me, though at first I could not recall place or time when I had seen him before. But after a while, as I watched him, I recognized him in spite of some change in his garb: it was the lodger whom Mistress Perry had wished to place in my room.

My kidnapping was then, I thought, a carefully arranged plan, and I remembered that before leaving the house I had told Mistress Perry in the man's hearing where I was going, and that I might return somewhat late. He had doubtless lodged there to spy on me, and I was sore tempted to speak to the fellow and ask him how much he had got for the dirty job.

But an hour or two afterwards I had fuller enlightenment as to my plight. The master of the vessel came aboard; he had spent the night ashore; and his foot no sooner touched the deck than he stepped to where I lay, and ordered one of the men to loose my bonds and stand me on my feet. And as I rose, staggering, I saw behind him the grinning faces of Cyrus Vetch and Dick Cludde. The meaning of it all flashed upon me; this was their revenge; and the knowledge heated me to such a fury that I leapt forward and, before I could be stopped, dealt Vetch a buffet that sent him spinning against the foremast. Cludde, ever chicken-hearted, turned pale, expecting a like handling, but he was spared, for the master cried to his men to seize me, and I was in a minute again pinioned and laid where I had been before.

"Hot as pepper," says the master, with a grin to Vetch.

"Yes," I cried, with an impetuous rage I could not check, "and 'twill be hot for you some day. You've no right to bring me here against my will, and I demand to be set free."

"Too-rol-loo-rol!" hummed the master, smirking again. "What a bantam cock have ye brought me here, Mr. Cludde?"

"He was a desperate fellow at school, Captain," said Cludde. "Why, when he was only eleven he pretty nearly murdered my friend Vetch here."

"Split my snatch block, you don't say so! We shall have to watch the weather with him aboard."

"D'you hear?" I cried, incensed beyond bearing. "Let me free, or I promise you you shall suffer for it, and those curs too."

"Didst ever see such a brimstone galley! I'll soon bring you to your bearings," and with that he gave me a cuff on the head which made me dizzy.

He left me then with the others, and soon afterwards I saw Cludde go over the side, taking farewell of the captain, and, to my surprise, of Vetch also. Still more astonished was I when, the order being given to throw off, the vessel dropped down with the tide, having Vetch still aboard. We made the mouth of the river, and stood out to sea; it was clear that my old enemy and I were to be shipmates, though I could not guess the purpose of his crossing the ocean.

During the ship's slow beating out I had had leisure to look about me, and I now knew that I was aboard the Dolphin, the privateer whose fitting out I had watched from the quayside. Despite my sorry situation I felt a stirring of interest and excitement; a privateer would scarce put to sea for nothing, and the thought that ere many days were passed I might be in the midst of a sea fight helped to drive my grievances from my mind. Withal I was puzzled: if slavery was not to be my lot, what had my enemies gained?

But I was soon, in sooth, in no state either to feed my imagination or to nurse my wrongs. The unaccustomed motion of the vessel produced on me the effect which but few escape; and we were no sooner fairly out in the Channel than I turned sick, and suffered the more severely, as I was told afterwards, because I had had no food for upwards of fifteen hours. For a whole day I lay in helpless misery: but then Captain Cawson (so he was named) himself came to me, hauled me to my feet, and with an oath bade me go and scrub the floor of the cook's galley. At the time I thought him a monster of brutality, driving me to my death; but I soon learned that nothing prolongs sea sickness, or indeed any sickness, so much as brooding on it, and the activity thus forced upon me had some part, I doubt not, in hastening my recovery.

From that time I was the ship's drudge. At everybody's beck and call, I was employed from morning till night in all kinds of menial offices. It was a hard life, and the treatment meted out to me was rough; but having got the better of my first rage and indignation, I resolved to make the best of my situation and to show no sullenness; besides I honestly wished to learn all that I could of a sailor's duty, and felt some little amusement in thinking that, if my enemies had sought this way of crushing me, they had very much mistaken their man. My activity and strength of limb stood me in good stead and won me a certain rough respect from officers and men, together with the real goodwill of a few of the better disposed among them.

After a day or two one old salt, named John Dilly, took me in a manner under his wing, and I made shift with his guidance to bear my part in shortening and letting out sail. Fortunately the weather was mild, and the early days of my apprenticeship were not so terrible as they might have been had the vessel encountered the storms that are commonly experienced in those seas, and especially in the Bay of Biscay, in which we beat about for nigh a week in the hope of sighting a Frenchman.

From John Dilly I learned that Vetch's position on board was that of purser, he having been introduced to the captain by Dick Cludde. Vetch attempted no active measures of hostility against me; indeed, he kept religiously out of my way, fearing maybe that I might seize an opportunity to settle accounts with him. Sometimes I saw him grin with malicious pleasure when he caught sight of me tarring ropes or engaged in some other arduous or unsavory task; but I never gratified him by giving sign of resentment or humiliation.

I had to take my watch with the rest of the crew. One morning, some ten days after leaving Bristowe, the captain came on deck at two bells and ordered me to the mizzen cross-trees to keep a sharp lookout, at the same time sending Dilly to the fore cross-trees. It was his practice, I had learned, to give a money bounty to the first man who sighted an enemy if the discovery resulted in a capture, and I was eager to win the prize, not more for its own sake than as a means of standing well with the captain.

The sun rose over the hills of France as I sat at my post. For a time I was entranced with the beauty of the sight, watching the changing hues of the sky, as pink turned to gold, and gold merged into the heavenly blue. But the morning air was chilly, and what with the cold and my cramped position I was longing for release when my eye was suddenly caught by what resembled the wing of a bird on the horizon about west-southwest. Was it the sail of a ship, I wondered, roused to excitement, or merely a cloud? Had old Dilly observed it?

I durst not cry out lest I were mistaken; but, straining my eyes, in the course of a few minutes I made out the speck to be beyond doubt the royals of a distant ship.

"Sail ho!" I cried with all my might.

"Where away?" shouts the captain, and when I answered "About west-sou'-west," he went to the companion way, reached for his perspective glass, and, mounting the rigging, climbed as high as the royal yard.

He took a long look through the glass, and then, shutting it up with a snap, he cries:

"You're right, my lad, smite my taffrail if you're not. She's a Frenchman, sure enough, and the bounty's yours if it comes to a battering and grappling. I'm a man of my word, I am."

The stranger was yet a good way off, and the captain, instead of altering the brig's course and standing in pursuit, shouted to the men to brace the yards round, and, the wind being due north, headed straight for Bordeaux, whither the vessel was to all appearance making. At the same time he hoisted French colors at the mizzen, and then ordered one of the anchors to be dropped over the stern and about fifty fathom of cable to be paid out, the meaning of which I did not understand till Dilly explained that 'twas to check the way on the brig and allow the stranger to overhaul us. Then he cried to us to lie flat on the deck and keep out of sight, and he sent one of the best hands to the wheel, wearing a red cap, which was, Dilly told me, to make him look like a Frencher.

There was only a light six-knot breeze, and Dilly said that the anchor dragging astern took quite two knots off our speed, so that in the course of an hour the stranger came clearly into view. She was a big barque, deep in the water, and the men chuckled as they peeped at her, for 'twas clear she was full of cargo. Every sail was set, alow and aloft, and she came on steadily at a good rate, not altering her course a point, from which 'twas plain she had as yet no suspicions of us.

I noticed that a buoy had been fixed to the end of the cable inboard.

"What's that for?" I asked Dilly, who lay at my side.

"'Tis ready to be flung over," he replied, "so as to mark the position of our cable when it is sent by the board. We'll come back for it anon."

When the vessel was about a mile distant, our captain gave the order to fling the cable overboard, then shouted:

"Hard up, wear ship."

We sprang to the braces, the ship spun round, and there we were on the starboard tack heading straight for the stranger. 'Twas clear then that she thought something was amiss, for she tried to put about and run for it; but being greatly hampered by her stern sails and the press of canvas she was carrying, by the time she had come round we had gained a good quarter mile upon her. The wind had freshened, and in some ten minutes our captain gave the order to haul the tarpaulin off Long Tom, the biggest of eight guns we carried, and give the Frenchman a pill. The gun was already loaded, and Bill Garland, the best shot aboard, of whose skill I had heard not a little from his messmates, laid it carefully and took aim, and then for a minute I could see nothing for the cloud of smoke. I sprang up in my excitement; 'twas the first shot I had ever seen fired, and the roar of it made me tingle and throb. But old Dilly pulled me down.

"Not so fast, long shanks," he said. "Our turn's a-coming."

"Did he hit her?" I asked, dropping down beside him.

"Clean through the mizzen topsail," he replied, "but done no more harm than blowing your nose."

The gun was reloaded, and Bill was about to fire again when the captain sang out to him to wait a little, for we were sailing two feet to the Frenchman's one, and drawing rapidly within point-blank range.

"He's loaded with chain shot this time," said Dilly, "and that's a terrible creature for clearing a deck or cutting up rigging. If Bill have got his eye we'll see summat according."

The gun spoke, and when the smoke had cleared we saw that the shot had cut through the Frenchman's mizzen and main weather rigging, bringing down the top masts with all their hamper of sails. Even to my inexperienced eye it was clear that the barque was crippled and lay at our mercy. She still kept her flag flying, however, and as we drew nearer we could see a throng of soldiers upon her decks, she being without doubt a transport returning from the French possessions in the West Indies. She fired a shot or two at us, but they fell short, her ordnance plainly being no match for ours, so we had nothing to do but heave to and rake her at our pleasure. After a couple of broadsides that made havoc on her decks, she suddenly struck her flag, and of our crew I was perhaps the only one who did not cheer, for it seemed to me that none but a craven would have yielded so easily, and I was longing for the excitement of boarding. We ran up to windward of her, and Captain Cawson, keeping the port broadside trained on her in case of treachery, sent an armed boat's crew in charge of the first mate to take possession of her.

I was not among those who were told off for this duty, but the fever of adventure had got such a hold upon me that I was hungry to take a share in what was toward. So I contrived to slip into the boat at the last moment, at some peril of a ducking, and mounted the Frenchman's deck with the rest. Then I wished that I had not been so impetuous, for the sight that met my eye was more terrible than anything I had ever imagined, and explained the surrender. Scores of wounded and dying men were strewn over the decks; their groans and piteous looks turned my heart sick. But such sights were no new thing to the rest of the crew. They set to work with amazing coolness to clear the decks, and get the vessel into trim, our captain having ordered the mate to rig jury masts, under which he hoped to sail the prize to England.

This seemed to me, I own, an enterprise of much danger, for we were near the French coast, and might easily fall in with a French frigate, or even a squadron of the enemy's vessels. But the prize was exceedingly valuable, and Captain Cawson was no more unwilling than any other English seaman to run a certain risk. Accordingly the soldiers and passengers on board the Frenchman were sent below and battened under hatches, and the crew was made to assist our men in cutting away the rigging and splicing and setting up the weather shrouds. The lighter sails were stripped off the foremast, the mate thinking to bring her into port under mizzen and main sail, together with all the fore and aft canvas that could be safely set.

'Twas the work of several hours to get things shipshape, the Dolphin meanwhile lying by to give us countenance and protection. When all was trim and taut we set a course for our own shores, following the Dolphin about three cables' lengths astern.

'Twas drawing towards sunset when she signalled to us that a sail was in sight. This news caused much commotion among us, still more when our own lookout cried that the vessel bearing towards us under press of sail out of the west was beyond doubt a frigate, and in all likelihood a Frenchman. I knew our case would be parlous if indeed it was so, for neither the privateer nor the merchant barque we had captured was armed in any wise to match a line-of-battle ship. Moreover 'twas unlikely that in our partly crippled condition we could out-sail the vessel: and when the mate, taking a look at the stranger through his perspective glass, declared that she was certainly French, our only hope was that darkness might shroud us before she came within striking distance--a slender chance at the best, for, though 'twas drawing towards dusk, the sky was wonderfully clear.

We held on our course, there being nothing else for us to do. The frigate loomed ever larger, and my heartbeats quickened as I wondered what the event would be. I did not dream that we should strike our flag as the Frenchman had done, and thought that we, having two vessels against one, would at least make a fight of it. But I was struck with mingled indignation and dismay when I saw the Dolphin crowd on all sail and bear away northwards, leaving us to our fate. I thought it a scurvy action on the part of Captain Cawson, and Dilly could not persuade me that he could have done us no good by remaining.

But the mate was not a whit discomposed. He swore a little, as did the men, yet without any heat: indeed they joked among themselves about the prison fare they would soon be starving on; and when a shot from the frigate fell across our bows, the mate merely spat out the quid he was chewing, and ordered the flag to be hauled down. Ten minutes after, the frigate was on our weather quarter, and dropping a boat, sent a crew aboard.

I was bitterly chagrined at this reversal of our fortunes, and when the Frenchmen who had been our prisoners were released, I went very sullenly with the rest into the boat that conveyed us to the frigate. We were clapped under hatches, and confined in the hold, a noisome close place, lit by a single oil lamp that stunk horribly.

"Smite me if it bean't Doggy Trang!" said the mate when the squat towsy-headed seaman who had conducted us below had left us. "I seed him at Plymouth a year or two ago."

I thought he was referring to the seaman, but it turned out that he meant the captain of the vessel, a young Frenchman named Duguay-Trouin, who was known to our men as a daring and courageous corsair. Two years before this, they told me, when commanding the royal frigate La Diligente of thirty-six guns, he had run among a squadron of six English vessels in a fog, and after a stout resistance was forced to yield, not before a ball from the Monk had laid him low. He was carried prisoner to Plymouth, whence he had cleverly escaped one night by scaling a wall and putting off in a little boat.

My companions soon accommodated themselves to their surroundings and fell asleep; but I was in too great a ferment to take matters so equably. I had no love for the buccaneers who had kidnapped me at Bristowe, to be sure: but my English pride was hurt at our capture by the French, and I quailed at the prospect of a long imprisonment in France. Surely, thought I, I must have been born under an unlucky star, for misfortune has dogged me ever since I left my native town.

The old seaman brought us some food by and by. He knew a little English, and in answer to a question from the mate explained that his captain was now hotly chasing the vessel which had run away, and if he caught it, the dogs of English would be sorry they ever showed their noses off the French coast. The captain being Duguay-Trouin, we knew that if it came to an action his ship would be well handled, and we had noticed that she carried far heavier metal than our own vessel. But the Dolphin had got a good start of her, and we did not suppose it possible that she could be overtaken.

I had never spent a more uncomfortable night than those hours in the hold. I could not sleep; the light went out; and in the darkness rats scurried hither and thither, and I had to keep my legs and arms in motion to ward them off. There was no glimmer of light from the outside, and it was only when the seaman again appeared with food that we knew morning had dawned. He told us with a grin that our vessel was fast being overhauled, and assured us that she had certainly made her last privateering voyage under the English flag. The mate cursed him vigorously, rather from habit than from ill temper, and the seaman shut us in, leaving us once more in total darkness.

My fellow prisoners talked among themselves, using language that made me shudder. I rested my head on my hands, stopping my ears and giving myself up to a dismal reverie. From this I was suddenly startled by a dull report overhead, and a slight trembling of the vessel.

"Ads my life!" cried the mate: "they've caught her."

"Maybe 'tis another vessel," said one of the men.

"Shut your mouth!" was the reply, "and list for an answer."

In a few moments there came a muffled report through the timbers.

"There's to be a fight, sure enough," said the mate, "though what the captain can be a-thinkin' of beats me altogether."

"I would do the same," I said, "and so would any Englishman worth his salt."

"Then you'd be as big a fool as he is," was the blunt retort.

It was a tantalizing position to be in. Here we were, boxed up in the darkness, condemned to listen to a duel of firing at long range, without any means of knowing what its effects were, hoping that our countrymen would win, yet aware that if the vessels came to close quarters a shot might plunge among us and send us all into eternity. We could tell that the vessel was racing through the water at a great rate, but, to judge by the reports that reached our ears, the distance between the combatants was not diminishing. The alternation of shots continued for some time; then suddenly the ship swung round with a violence that threw us all in a heap, and caused me to bump my head hard against the wall.

"Helm's hard up," said the mate, "she's going to try a broadside."

And in a few seconds there was a thunderous roar above, and a shock that made the vessel stagger. There was no reply save a single shock, from which I judged that the Dolphin was holding her course; and it was clear that the broadside had done little or no damage, for the ship again swung round, and the duel of single shots began again. But we could tell that the vessels were now nearer to each other, and after a time we heard a series of dull reports, followed by a thud or two and the sound of rending and tearing woodwork above and around. 'Twas a broadside from the Dolphin. But before we had time to rejoice at the success of our comrades, or to hope that their shots had brought down enough of the French ship's spars to disable her, the vessel shook again under a terrific discharge of her ordnance, and we, knowing how vastly superior was her armament to that of our own ship, were in no little anxiety as to the effect of this second broadside at shorter range. Another and another broadside followed from each combatant: and then came to our ears from the deck above a great yell of triumph. My heart sank within me; the mate let out a volley of oaths; 'twas impossible to mistake the meaning of that shrill cry.

The cannonading ceased. For a time that seemed endless there was silence, save for a shout now and then, and a thud that might be caused by the work of replacing or repairing an injured spar. Suddenly the hatch above was lifted, raised, and when our eyes became accustomed to the light we saw men swarming down the ladder into the hold. A French seaman among them relit the lamp, and we recognized the faces of some of our comrades on the Dolphin. Among the first I saw old Dilly, and behind him came Cyrus Vetch, his countenance black with rage. As soon as he was among us he launched out into bitter complaints at being herded with common seamen--he who by right and courtesy ought to have been classed with the officers and allowed the hospitality of a cabin.

"'Tis infamous," he cried; "'tis a scandal to treat a gentleman with such indignity. Duguay-Trouin was not so served when he was brought prisoner to Plymouth."

"Stow your jab!" cried the mate angrily. "Ain't we good enough for you? What's a land lubber like you doing here at all? We ain't aboard the Dolphin now, I'll let ye know, and here we're all equal, and smite my eye, if you complains of your company, and gives honest seamen any more of your paw-wawing, 'ware timbers is what I say to you, my gemman, or I'll rake you fore and aft."

From which it may be concluded that Vetch was by no means a favorite with the crew of the Dolphin.

Chapter 14
Harmony And Some Discord

From Dilly I learned that the Dolphin had suffered severely in the engagement. A third of the crew had been killed or wounded: Captain Cawson himself was dead. The survivors had been divided, some being left in the Dolphin, the remainder being brought to the Francois; among these were the more severely wounded, who were tended with much humanity in the sick bay.

Now that the chase and the fight were over, we were allowed on deck a few at a time, a boon for which I was very grateful. I was surprised at the youth of our captor, the renowned Duguay-Trouin. He looked little older than myself, and was in fact, as I afterwards discovered, but twenty-three years of age.

His youthful appearance somewhat heartened me. Here was a man (so ran my thought) but little my senior, yet he had already won a great name for daring and courage; he had been captured and imprisoned, but had escaped, and was now again active in his vocation. Other men as well as I had their mischances and surmounted them: why should not I? Thus it happened that, when, a few days later, we arrived at the French port of St. Malo, and were handed over to the authorities of the prison there, I was not so depressed in spirits as I had expected to be.

This was fortunate, for the lot to which we were condemned was miserable in the extreme. We had wretched quarters, foul and unhealthy; some five hundred prisoners, most of them captured in merchant vessels, were herded in a space not large enough for the comfortable habitation of half that number. In my heart I fully sympathized with Vetch's objection to being classed among the seamen, for they were in the main a sorry lot, filthy in their habits and base minded. Some, like old Dilly, were of a higher type, and these consorted together as much as possible.

The conditions at St. Malo were so bad that I was not sorry when, after some few weeks there, a great number of us were marched out under an armed guard to a castle about fifteen miles to the southeast. A very woebegone battalion we must have looked as we tramped to our new quarters--many of us suffering from prison fever, all more or less in rags, and half starved. The change was due to no compassion on the part of the authorities, but to an alarm in the town. A sloop had come in, it appeared, with news that an attack was intended against the port by no other than Benbow, and it was feared that the prisoners might seize this opportunity for a mutiny. I did not learn this until after we had reached our new prison; it came out through one of our jailers, a talkative fellow who liked to air his little English, otherwise I should not have felt so much pleased at the change of quarters; though even if Benbow had assaulted the town and we prisoners had risen, it was improbable that we could have found a means of escaping to him.

The new prison was, as I have said, a castle, or to speak more precisely, the ruins of one. It had once been a place of considerable dimensions and of great strength; but it was now far gone towards demolition. The outer walls still stood, completely encircled by a moat, the only entrance being by way of the drawbridge which, to judge by its moss-grown edges, had not been raised for many a day. Marching over it, and through an archway, we found ourselves in the courtyard, a large area roughly square in shape, and open to the sky.

At the farther end, built against the wall in the intervals between three round towers, a kind of wooden barracks had been erected for our accommodation, the only habitable portion of the castle being the keep, flanking the entrance, and this was devoted to our guardians. Our barracks was in two stories, the lower being intended for use by day, the upper, which was reached by a ladder, containing our sleeping apartments. The rooms on the ground were lit by windows opening into the courtyard; the sleeping rooms only by narrow gratings in the wooden wall. I did not learn all this at once, of course; but I have set it down here for convenience sake.

On arriving at the castle we were marshaled in the courtyard, and taken into the keep one by one. There, with the aid of the loquacious sergeant as interpreter, we gave our names, ages, and descriptions to the commandant, a sour-visaged fellow, who entered the particulars in a book. Then we were severally assigned our sleeping quarters, and I found myself one of a squad of ten, none of whom was known to me with the exception of Vetch and Dilly. Vetch once more protested against being ranked with common seamen, and demanded to be released on parole; but the commandant ordered him gruffly to be silent, and he went away very sullen and wrathful.

Our sleeping apartment, I found, was a small room at the right-hand corner of the barracks--so small that I foresaw our nights would not be comfortable. There were five truckle beds ranged against the wall; 'twas clear that each of us would have a bedfellow. The bedding consisted of a hard straw mattress and a single woollen coverlet which, judging by its tenuity, had already seen service with generations of sleepers. Luckily it was early autumn; we should not need to dread the winter cold for some time to come; and I was young and lighthearted enough to flatter myself with the fancy that we should either be released as the sequel to some terrible defeat of the French, or that we should find some way of escape.

Being myself long and broad, I made matters even by choosing as my bedfellow a little fellow named Joseph Runnles, lean as a rake, and of a quiet and melancholy countenance, thinking that such an one would not discommode me in either body or mind. My choice was justified; he neither kicked nor snored, and was so reserved and silent that I believe I did not exchange with him a dozen words a week.

Our new quarters proved a deal less dreary than those we had left at St. Malo. The weather was fine; there was ample elbow room in the courtyard, and though we were closely watched by the guard constantly set at the gate, we had our liberty during the day. At night, when we repaired to our dormitories, the doors opening on the courtyard were locked, and we could dully hear the tramping of the sentry along the battlements above our heads.

In a few days we had settled down in our new life. Some of the men passed all the daylight hours in throwing dice or playing games of chance, not without frequent quarrels, which our guardians ignored so long as they remained short of fighting. Others, more industriously inclined, occupied themselves in fashioning toys from wood supplied them, which were afterwards sold in neighboring villages, the proceeds (after a very liberal commission had been subtracted) being devoted to the purchase of additions to their meagre fare.

As for me, the idea of escape was already beating in my mind, and as a first step I resolved to pick up a knowledge of the French tongue, of which I was almost wholly ignorant. Accordingly I lost no opportunity of conversing with soldiers of the guard, with whom I ingratiated myself by showing them some of the tricks of fence taught me by Captain Galsworthy. The only work which all the prisoners had to perform in turn was the drawing of water from a well in the keep. The water of the moat, as I had seen when we crossed it on entering, was covered with a green scum, the rivulet which fed it not being of sufficient volume to keep it in circulation.

A few days after our arrival I was laid low by a mild attack of jail fever, of which I had doubtless brought the seeds from St. Malo. I kept my bed for a couple of days, being tended with much kindliness by a little old surgeon attached to the garrison. I should not have mentioned this trifling sickness but that it prevented me from witnessing the arrival of a fresh batch of prisoners; so that when I descended on the third day into the courtyard I was mightily surprised to see, at that very instant carrying a bucket of water across from the keep, no other than my old friend Joe Punchard.

"Joe!" I cried, beyond measure delighted at seeing a familiar face.

Down went the bucket with a clatter upon the stones, and Joe looked around as though scarce trusting his ears. Then seeing me he waddled across, seized my hand, and shook it with a hearty goodwill that was somewhat over vigorous for my enfeebled condition.

"Ods firkins, sir!" he cried, "my head spins like a whirligig. How dost come here among these heathen Frenchies, and all the way from Shrewsbury, too?"

Before I was halfway through my story, one of the soldiers ran up and ordered Joe to fill his bucket again and wash out the lower rooms.

"Ay, I'm a swab again, sure enough," says poor Joe, going off ruefully to his task.

He was soon back, and when he had heard me through my account of what had befallen me since I saw him last, he broke out into vehement denunciation of Cyrus Vetch and all the race of Cluddes. Vetch himself happening to pass at that moment, wearing the hangdog look habitual to him since fate had made him a prisoner, Joe bursts out:

"Ay, you may well look ashamed of yourself, you villain! Where's that will, rogue? What have you done wi' 't?"

Vetch turned a shade paler, I thought. I had never said a word to him about the loss of my father's will, and had no intention of doing so, biding my time, and I was a little vexed that Joe in his impetuous espousal of my cause had let the fellow know of our suspicions. He halted a moment, then with a "What are you prating about, turnip head?" he turned on his heel and walked away.

Joe, in a great rage, was for springing after him, but I caught him by the arm and begged him to let the matter rest.

"Snatch my bowlines!" he cried, in a tone reminding me of Captain Cawson; "he'd better 'ware of running across my course. If I come athwart his hawser I'll turn him keel upwards, I will."

I diverted the current of his anger by asking him how he had become a prisoner of the French.

"Why, in a deuced unlucky way," says he. "Captain Benbow--he's now rear admiral, but will always be captain to me--he had a mind to draw alongside that there place they call St. Malo, and cut out a frigate of Doggy Trang he believed to be there, and he sent me and some more by night to take the bearings of the harbor. We was in a skiff, and a gale came on and beat us about all night and split our sails and drove us ashore in the very teeth of a crew o' Frenchies. There was a tight little scrimmage, I promise you, but they were two to one, and grappled us close, and clapped a stopper on our cable, hang 'em. They chained us together, the dogs, and marched us into St. Malo with scarce a rag to our backs, and yesterday they sent me and some more here."

"And right glad I am they did, Joe. But surely Captain Benbow did not send you in charge of the party?"

"Well, no, if you put it so, he didn't. We was in command of Lieutenant Curtis."

"And is he here, too?"

"No. He happened to have a pocketful o' money, and so they let him sling his hammock in the town, where he could spend it. When it is gone, belike they will send him to join us."

"And let us hope that we'll be gone as soon as his money, Joe. I am mighty glad you are here; for if we put our heads together we can surely find some way of getting free."

"Bless your eyes, don't I wish we may. Maybe there's a fate in it, sir. Fate jined you and me when it made me set Vetch a-rolling in the barrel, and 'tis fate has jined us all three here. Ay, please God, sir, one day we'll slip our cables, clap on all canvas, and steer for the north, though how, whereby, and by what means we can do it beats Joe Punchard."

The companionship of Joe, at a time when I was weak from my sickness, mightily cheered me, and we spent much of each day together. Our longing to be free did but increase as the days passed. The monotony of prison life fretted us, Joe perhaps less than me, for his life had been harder than mine, and as the days grew shorter, and the nipping cold of winter by degrees overtook us, we began to know what real wretchedness is. By day we could warm ourselves with exercise and active sports in the courtyard, but at night we shivered under our thin coverlets, and I found myself by and by wishing that my bedfellow Runnles had a little more flesh on his bones, for a lean man is no comfort in bed on a bitter night. Joe was not in my dormitory, or I should certainly have bedded with him.

Above everything else, I think, the wretched food made us unhappy. If a man be but well fed he can endure much hardship and trouble, and I had never wanted in this respect. The prison food was bad, ill cooked, and meagre; and though Joe, for one, might have procured better if he had chosen to employ himself in his old trade of coopering, he refused to do so after making one barrel, the price of which, after the soldiers' commission had been deducted, was something less than a fourth of what it would have been in England.

"'Noint my block!" he cried, when the pitiful sum was placed in his hand. "Dost think a Shrewsbury man 'll be done out of his dues by a codger of a Frenchman what he don't vally no more than pork slush or a stinking dogfish? Split my binnacle if I be!"

And he flung the money at the amazed Frenchman, and kept his word to work at his old trade no more.

I think this sturdiness of his raised him somewhat in the estimation of our jailers, and in spite of the opprobrious epithets he applied to them (which to be sure they did not understand) he was soon as popular with them as Vetch was the reverse. Joe was blessed with a great fund of good humor, which withstood all privation and restraint. He growled and groaned at being compelled to take his turn in scouring the floors and other menial tasks, but after emitting a stream of hot language, which ever appears to flow very freely from the lips of sailor men, he went his way with great cheerfulness. He joked with his fellow prisoners, and being of a loquacious turn, had many things to tell them of the doings of his hero, Captain Benbow.

Vetch, on the contrary, was what the Scriptures call a "continual dropping." He kept himself apart, sulking the livelong day, scarce ever speaking, and when he did speak using a tone which the Grand Turk might employ towards a beggar. It was true enough that the prisoners were inferior to him in quality, but, their lot and circumstances being the same, it was decidedly a mistake to make the others feel their inferiority, and, as I think, a mark of ill breeding to boot. His few words were sneers, and he had a contemptuous way of looking at a man that made one itch to thrash him. At length he was thrashed, and very smartly, by a man in our dormitory, and after that he was utterly ignored, by general consent. It happened in this wise.

One bleak day of mud and rain, when we were driven by the weather out of the courtyard into the lower rooms of the barracks, and were sitting in doleful dumps, at a loss how to pass the time, Joe Punchard cried out of a sudden:

"Come, souls, what's a spell of foul weather to men that have sailed the salt seas! Haul forward your stools, mates, and we'll have a concert and make all snug. I warrant some of you can troll a ditty, though ye be too modest to own it; and not being plagued wi' modesty myself, I'll heave anchor first."

I knew, nothing of Joe's musical powers, and it was with no little surprise I discovered that he had an excellent voice of the pitch they call barytone. He began:

Of all the lives, I ever say,

A pirate's be for I;

Hap what hap may he's allus gay

And drinks an' bungs his eye.

For his work he's never loath;

An' a-pleasurin' he will go;

Tho' sartin sure to be popt off,

Yo ho, with the rum below.

At the conclusion of the stanza his audience broke into loud applause. And then, with a sheepish air that set me a-smiling, Joseph Runnles, my bedfellow, the little silent man of whom I have spoken, drew out of his pocket the parts of a flute, and putting them together, set it to his lips and accompanied Joe through the next stanza, picking up the tune with a facility that spoke well for his musical ear.

In Bristowe I left Poll ashore,

Well stored wi' togs and gold;

An' off I goes to sea for more,

A-piratin' so bold.

An' wounded in the arm I got,

An' then a pretty blow;

Comes home I finds Poll flowed away.

Yo ho, with the rum below.

"Adad, brother," cries Joe, clapping the little man on the shoulder, "why have you stowed away your noble talents so long under hatches? I've sailed the seas for many a year; east, west, north and south, as the saying is; Blacks, Indians, Moors, Morattos, and Sepoys; but smite my timbers, never such a man of music have I drawn alongside of before."

Runnles blushed like a girl, and said never a word, but blew the moisture out of his flute, ready for the next stanza.

An' when my precious leg was lopt.
Just for a bit of fun,
I picks it up, on t'other hopt,
An' rammed it in a gun.
"What's that for?" cries out Salem Dick.
"What for, my jumpin' beau?
Why, to give the lubbers one more kick!"
Yo ho with the rum below.

By this time the other men had got the hang of the song, and when Joe started the next stanza they joined in, trolling the tune (they knew not the words as yet) in voices high and low, rough and coarse for the most part, and with more heartiness than melody. This happy thought of Joe's cured our dumps and put us all in a good temper, and for the rest of that morning we sat singing songs, and listening to the tootling of Runnles' flute, when the little man could be prevailed on to treat us to a solo.

"You be mighty bashful for a sailor man," said Joe at the end of the concert, "partickler as your name be Joe like mine, but we won't let 'ee hide your talents any more, split my braces if we will."

It was on the night of that day that Vetch got his thrashing. We had gone early to our dormitory because of the rain, and being unable to sleep for the cold, one of the men suggested that Runnles should give us a tune.

"'Tis comfortin' to the spirits," said the man, a big fellow known to us as the bosun: his name was Peter Wiggett.

Runnles, evidently gratified at this mark of appreciation, put his flute together and began to pipe the tune of Mr. Ackroyd's famous song of the fight in '92 when Admiral Russell beat the French. This, to be sure, was rather inspiriting than soothing, and thus perhaps there was a shadow of excuse for Vetch when he called out from under his coverlet (he lay in the next bed):

"Cease that squealing, hang you, and let a man get to sleep."

"Belay there!" shouted the bosun.

"Pipe away, Runnles, and we'll love you, my hearty."

Runnles struck up again, but he had not gone far (it was to the line, "To meet the gallant Russell in combat on the deep") when the fluting suddenly ceased, and we heard a cry that was certainly a squeal. Vetch had got out of bed in the dark and, snatching the flute from Runnles' hand, caught him by the throat. I sprang up from Runnles' side, but the bosun from the bed beyond was before me.

"Avast, you lubber!" he cries, flinging himself on Vetch; "I thought we should grapple one day: now I'll bring you up by the head, you swine."

And with that he took Vetch with the left hand, and belabored him with the right until the poor wretch fairly howled for mercy. Then he threw him on to his bed (with some damage, I fear, to Dilly, who shared it), and bade Runnles play up: but the little man was so much upset at the turn affairs had taken that he declared his lips were too dry to blow a note, and indeed it was several days before he could be prevailed on to flute again.

Chapter 15
The Bass Viol

Where one leads, others are sure to follow. It was wonderful how many of the prisoners discovered a talent for music after Punchard and Runnles had thus led the way. Our jailers encouraged this pastime; it was not merely harmless in itself, but it had a quietening effect on the temper of the men, and the squabbles and brawls among them notably diminished. One of the Frenchmen unearthed an old fiddle, and though one of its strings was wanting, a man named Ben Tolliday contrived to scrape very passable melody out of it. Old John Dilly announced that he had played the cornet in his youth, and before very long an instrument was found for him, and after a few days' practice (during which we had to suffer a variety of discordant and ear-splitting noises) he recovered something of his former skill. An old drum with a very loose membrane was found in the lumber room of the keep, and this the bosun appropriated, though being quite destitute of a sense of rhythm he made but an indifferent performer. Some of the men fashioned original instruments for themselves, one of these, a mouth organ, being a real triumph of ingenuity.

I, alas, had no singing voice, and was totally ignorant of music; but Joe kindly informed me that any fool could play the bones, and made two pairs of castanets for me out of beef bones supplied by the soldiers (we had no joints ourselves, but only a bullock's cheek now and then) so that I too was able to bear my part in the concerts which now became of daily occurrence.

The soldiers of the guard often came and listened to our performances, and even the sour-faced commandant once condescended to form part of our audience, and smiled broadly when Dilly, who was a Devon man, sang with much expressive pantomime the pleasant ditty of Widdicombe Fair, though the Frenchman did not understand a word of it.

This condescension on the part of the commandant emboldened me to proffer a request which I had been meditating for some days. I had by no means given up the hope of escaping from the castle, but the more I thought of it, the less likely it appeared that I could succeed without assistance. Of course, Joe Punchard should accompany me, and when I talked the matter over with him, neither of us had the heart to scheme for our own freedom without regard to those of our fellow prisoners with whom we had become more closely connected through our musical interests.

"There is old John Dilly," I said one day, when we were discussing the subject, "he was good to me aboard the Dolphin; I shouldn't like to leave him behind."

"True," says Punchard, "and Runnles is a quiet, good soul; besides his name is Joe."

"And the bosun, he's as strong as an ox, and might be a useful man."

"And Tolliday, he's for ever sighing about Molly, his sweetheart; 'twould make two folks happy (maybe) if he got away among us."

Thus we ran over the list of our friends very seriously, though it tickled my sense of humor when I remembered that we had not as yet the ghost of a notion how this escape we talked of was to be contrived. But having thus selected our partners in the attempt we were resolved to make some day, we decided that it would be a step in the right direction if we all shared the same dormitory. We might then talk over the matter without the danger of it being blabbed among the whole body of prisoners.

Accordingly I took advantage of the commandant's gracious appearance among our audience to ask him (having now picked up enough French to make myself understood) to allow all the members of the band to sleep together, explaining that we should attain to greater efficiency if, after the lower doors were locked for the night, we could practice for an hour or so together before the sun went down. His grim face relaxed into a smile at the serious manner in which we took our diversion, and he readily granted the permission we desired. By this change we got rid of Vetch, who was glad enough to leave us, I doubt not.

The first step having thus been gained, I began to devote myself earnestly to the problem of escape. I did not make light of the difficulties. The only entrance to the castle precincts was, as I have said, the gateway at the end of the drawbridge, and this was so stoutly guarded that escape in daylight was impossible. At night we were locked in the dormitory nearly thirty feet above ground, with a thick stone wall between us and freedom, and supposing we could make a hole in the wall, which seemed unlikely, there was still the moat to be reckoned with. It was not only too far below for any one to dive into it with safety, but it was, as I had learned from the soldiers, choked with mud to within a very little of the surface, so that I could not but doubt whether it were possible even to swim across. But I did not despair of crossing it if we could only get down: that was the difficulty, and for long tedious weeks it seemed to me insuperable.

Before we had hit upon a plan, we were thrown into a great excitement by the disappearance of Vetch. I had missed him for a day or two from the courtyard, but thought little of it, supposing that he was confined to his dormitory by a touch of fever, as happened not infrequently among the prisoners. But on Punchard's remarking one day that he believed Vetch was malingering, it came out that he had not been seen by his roommates for nearly a week.

Was it possible that while we had been merely thinking of escape, Vetch had found a means of escaping? It seemed impossible, and when I was having my daily conversation with the soldiers of the guard, I asked point blank what had become of him. They laughed and chuckled, and amused themselves for some time by giving all manner of fantastic explanations, which improved my knowledge of French, but were mightily vexatious. At last I made out, from hints and half statements, that the commandant had been discreetly inquiring among some of the prisoners for a man who was well acquainted with the river Avon. Since these inquiries ceased and Vetch disappeared about the same time, I was free to conclude that in Vetch the commandant had found his man. Had he purchased his freedom at the price of treason to his country? Were the French meditating an attack on Bristowe? These were questions I could not answer; but you may be sure the knowledge that Vetch was gone acted as a whip to my determination, and I was more than ever resolved to find some way of leaving these walls behind.

We had concluded, Punchard and I, that our only course must be to pierce the castle wall and let ourselves down to the moat by means of a rope. The latter portion of this scheme being manifestly the more likely, we decided to secure our rope first. This was easier said than done. Our coverlets were of such thin and rotten material, we should need to tear up several of them before, even carefully knotted, they would serve our purpose, and we could not risk the detection that would surely follow if any of them were missed by our guards. When I went next to take my turn at drawing water from the well I carefully examined the rope by which the bucket was let down, thinking it might be possible to cut this one night at an hour when its loss would not be discovered till next day and the birds had flown. But a close inspection showed that it was very rotten; evidently it had seen long service; and while it was still strong enough to stand the strain of a bucketful of water, I could not flatter myself it would safely bear my weight, to say nothing of the bosun, who was a deal heavier.

But since a rope we must have, I pleased myself with the fancy that if I should succeed in procuring that it might be taken as a good augury for success in the more difficult feat, the piercing of the wall. Could we make a rope, I wondered? We had a fair quantity of bast, in the mats that formed the only covering of the floor of our barracks, but not near enough to form a rope sufficiently stout to bear the weight of even the lightest of us; besides the tearing up of the mats could not fail to be discovered.

Racking my brains for some means of overcoming the difficulty, I suddenly bethought myself of trying a ruse. I said nothing of my intention to Punchard (to the others I had as yet not breathed a word of our purpose) but the next time I went to the well I took a knife with me, and, choosing a portion of the rope where it was much frayed, I carefully sawed through one or two of the strands with the blunt edge. The result was that when I was drawing the full bucket up, the rope snapped, the bucket fell to the bottom with a clatter, and I (to make the accident more convincing) toppled over on my back. Up came one of the guard, and rated me soundly for my clumsiness, employing a succession of abusive terms which I stored in my memory for use in case of need.

I picked myself up slowly, rubbing my back, and, putting on the most innocent air in the world, I pointed to the frayed rope and asked whether my corrector could expect such a thing as that to last for ever. The man grumbled a good deal, but the condition of the rope admitted no answer to my question, and I had the satisfaction next day of seeing a brand new rope attached to a brand new bucket. I even had the pleasure of using it for the first time, for the old rope having broken when I was on duty, I was condemned to the punishment of drawing water for a week afterwards, an extension of my task which I bore with wonderful cheerfulness.

When I told Punchard of what I had done he laughed with great delight, but immediately became very sober.

"'Tis all no use, sir," says he gloomily. "For why? I can't swim."

This was a difficulty I had not foreseen. How is it, I wonder, that so many men who go down to the sea in ships do not master that most useful art--the very first, one would think, that should engage their attention? 'Twas true, the depth of water above the mud in the moat was so little that even the best swimmer would be at a bad pass; but I hoped that with the coming of the spring rains this would be remedied. Yet if Punchard and any of the others were unable to swim, the moat would be impassable were it dredged to the bottom; and since we must descend the rope singly, and the water came right up to the wall, I could not see for the life of me how this disability could be got over.

Finding our purpose thus stopped in this direction (though but for a time, for my resolution was in nowise weakened), I began to devote myself earnestly to what I had felt all along was the crux--the breaking through the wall. So deeply was I preoccupied with this baffling problem that I fear I clattered my bones but half heartedly in our musical concerts. Yet it was during one of these concerts that some good genie flashed upon my invention a plan which promised (if it could be carried out) to solve the very difficulty I had almost given up as insoluble. I say it was a good genie that suggested the idea to me, for, looking back upon it, I can account for it in no other way.

I was watching Tolliday sawing away at his fiddle, and marveling (being ignorant of music) at the loud tones which he produced from so small an instrument. 'Twas clear that the hollow belly of the fiddle had some part in the effect, and then I remembered the big bass viols I had seen used in the church at home, and reflected that the larger the instrument the deeper and more powerful the tones.

And here came in the genie to supply the link which led to the formation of my plan. In my mind's eye I saw a big hollow vessel shaped like a bass viol floating on the water of the moat, and Joe Punchard clinging to it, and I wished with all my heart that one of our jailers would discover such an instrument, and hand it to us for the use of our band. 'Twas but a step from wishing to devising. We had no bass viol; could we not make one? No one would oppose us; the band was highly popular with the garrison, and I was sure that they would willingly provide us with material for the construction of yet another instrument.

Accordingly, next morning I suggested that we should ask the commandant to give us some planks of wood with which to make an instrument of a new model. The men were amused at the notion, never suspecting that I had any other design than to enrich the harmony of our ensemble. 'Twould be good fun, they agreed, though they had great doubt (as I had myself) whether our unskilled workmanship would produce anything but a useless monstrosity so far as music was concerned. They were willing to try, however, the attempt would help us to kill time; and the commandant proving perfectly agreeable to humor us, we gut the planks, borrowed some tools from the soldiers, and set to work.

The next following days saw half a dozen of us busily employed in the courtyard in knocking together a long shallow box, in the upper side of which we pierced S-shaped holes like those of the fiddle, with a notched bridge at about one-third of its length for holding four strings, and wooden screws at the other end for stretching them taut. Joe Punchard, good fellow, was the most ardent of the artificers, plying the tools with a dexterity born of his work for master cooper Matthew Mark years before. We got from the soldiers, who showed a great interest in our task, cords of different thickness, and several lengths of iron wire which we twisted together somewhat after the manner of the thickest string of the fiddle. We then stretched this and three cords over the bridge on the top of the box, screwed them to a high tension, and plucked them to see if they emitted notes that could be called musical.

The result surpassed my expectations. Tolliday, our fiddler, declared that the notes were true music, though to be sure not very resonant, and he undertook to tune the strings in fifths, so that it might be able to take a proper part in our next symphony. Having no bow with which to scrape the strings, he said that they could only be strummed with the finger and thumb, and when he offered to teach one of us thus to handle it, there were many candidates for the place, which in the end fell to a man named Winslow. The men were all mightily pleased with the success of our work, and I was secretly delighted, not with the instrument as a producer of music, but at knowing that we had a box which might serve those of us who could not swim as a raft.

We had now at command (if we could secretly purloin it) a rope to let us down, and a raft to ferry us over the moat, but we had still to find a means of getting beyond the wall, and to this I bent all my energy of mind. In this, too, I took Joe Punchard into consultation, and we discussed all kinds of plans. With the sentry on guard throughout the night in the courtyard there was no hope of escape by the gate and drawbridge. There was no opening in the wall. The only possible means of exit was to cut a hole in it, and this would be a matter of great toil, the wall being, as some one had told us, ten feet thick. It consisted, so far as we could tell from the inside, of solid blocks of stone cemented together, and when, at an odd moment when no one was looking, I tried to scrape away some of the cement between two of the stones, I found that it was almost as hard as the stone itself.

To cut through ten feet of such solid material was a task that might have caused any one to despair. Still, it was the only course open to us, and I have never known any task too hard for patience and determination. Joe and I decided that we must gradually scrape away the cement around one of the blocks until we could remove this altogether, and then work at the next one, and the next, until we had pierced right through to the open air.

Apart from the toilsomeness of the task, there were risks to be feared and provided against. First; one or another of the soldiers inspected our dormitory every day. This inspection, 'tis true, had become somewhat perfunctory, the man being content, as a rule, to mount the ladder until his head was a foot or two above the level of the floor, throw a hasty glance around, and descend again. The second risk was more serious. Since we could hear at night the tramp of the sentry going his round of the battlements, it was probable that, however quietly we might work, the sentry would hear the sound of scraping as he passed above. If the wall had been wainscotted, he might suppose such sounds to be caused by the gnawing of mice; but there was no likelihood of mice making their habitat in a thick stone wall. Further, even if we should so contrive that our task of scraping was interrupted when the sentry passed, there was still the danger that the sound might attract the attention of the men in the adjoining dormitory. If they should get any suspicion of what was toward, it would soon be common talk among the whole body of prisoners, and some whisper of it would certainly reach the ears of the guard.

In order to lessen this risk, Joe and I decided to begin our work at a stone measuring three feet by two, in the right-hand corner of the dormitory, farthest removed from the partition dividing us from the next, and a foot or two above the floor, so that a bed could be pushed against the wall and hide all signs of our operations in case a sudden visit of inspection was made.

These preliminaries having been settled by Joe and myself, the time was come for taking our roommates into our confidence. I did not disguise from myself that we were staking a great deal on their loyalty, and even more on their silence, for the slightest whisper of the plot outside our own little company would be fatal. There were ten of us bandsmen altogether. At first I thought of speaking to the men individually, and thus testing their courage and enterprise. But on reflection I decided that what was most requisite to our success was a corporate spirit, which could be best engendered by opening the matter to them as a body. Accordingly, one evening, when we were assembled in the dormitory for a practice, I took the fateful plunge.

I am not an orator, and I shall not set down here the words in which I addressed them. Suffice it to say that they listened very attentively, not at first perceiving the full drift of my meaning, so careful was I to feel my way with them. They held me in some special consideration, which I no doubt owed partly to Joe Punchard, who had told them something of my story, and when at length I declared plainly our intention to escape, asked them if they would join hands with us, and impressed on them the necessity of maintaining silence about it, they one and all promised that never a word should pass their lips.

As to the scheme itself, when I unfolded its details, they were somewhat dubious, and, strangely enough, the most enthusiastic in its favor was little Runnles, the melancholy flute player, and the most doubtful was the bosun, whose physical courage was equal to anything, but who was daunted by what appealed more particularly to the moral qualities of patience and endurance. He dwelt lugubriously on the difficulties I have already mentioned, and shook his head when I combated his objections; but he agreed to throw in his lot with the rest of us, and said that if we once got clear of the walls, and there was any fighting to do, he would break any Frenchman's head as soon as look at him.

Nothing remained now but to begin operations, and I soon found that the demands upon our patience would be even more exacting than I had supposed. We divided our company of ten into five watches, each to take a spell of two hours' work. One night, as soon as all was quiet, Joe and I set to work, he with a chisel which he had used in making our new instrument, I with my clasp knife. Very gently, so as to avoid noise, we began to scrape away at the mortar between the block of stone we had selected for removal and the one below it.

Runnles hit upon a capital way of warning us of the approach of the sentry within earshot. He tied a string to Joe's leg, and gave it a tug when he heard the tramp of footsteps above. Then we desisted for a minute or two, resuming our work when the footsteps had died away.

At the end of our two hours' spell we were disappointed at the little we had been able to do. Two small heaps of dust lay at the foot of the wall, but the impression on the hard mortar or cement had been but slight, and I was appalled to think of the weeks that must elapse before we had cut completely round the stone. But I professed myself well satisfied with the start we had made, and we handed over our tools to Dilly and Tolliday, the next couple, with encouraging words.

Chapter 16
Across The Moat

It would be tedious to chronicle the stages of our progress, the hopes and fears, the anxieties and suspense, which in turn laid hold of me. Night by night for a week, in pitch darkness and bitter cold, we scraped away the cement, carrying away in the morning in our pockets the dust that fell, and disposing of it in the sweepings of the courtyard.

Once we had a great scare. In the dead time of night we heard footsteps, and voices in the room below our dormitory, and gave all up for lost. We stole into our beds, and lay in that painful state of shortened breath and quickened pulse which the expectation of ill induces. But by and by the voices ceased; we heard the closing of the door below; whatever their errand had been (and we never knew it) the men of the guard had returned to their quarters, and after a few minutes' pause we were again out of bed and at our work.

At the end of a week it happened as I had feared. The men's patience gave out. The bosun was the first to yield. After his two hours' spell of labor he rose from the cramped position it entailed and swore he would do no more. The men whose turn it was to follow refused to get out of bed, and Joe and I, who, having worked our spell were fast asleep, knew nothing of the mutiny until the morning. Then, though I was nigh despairing, I affected cheerfulness, said that we had all been working too hard, and declared for a couple of nights' holiday.

I did not blame or expostulate, and the wisdom of my course was vindicated on the third night, when, without a word being said, the bosun and Runnles took up their tools and set to work again. I learned afterwards that Runnles had employed himself during the two days in quietly encouraging the others, and I think it was the persistence of the little man that shamed them into perseverance.

Night by night for three weeks we toiled on, and then were bountifully rewarded. We had scraped away the cement between the stone we had selected and those around it, and by prying it with our chisel and one or two other tools we had now procured, we gradually forced it inwards and at length lifted it out and laid it on the floor. It was the middle of the night, but all the men were awake, and in the excitement of the occasion the bosun uttered a shout of triumph, cursing himself immediately afterwards for his folly. The sentry above stopped, and by and by a soldier came into the room below and up the ladder and demanded what was the matter. Luckily I had the presence of mind (and by this time sufficiency of French) to make answer pat.

"'Tis the big man in a nightmare," I said with a laugh, "dreaming he heads a boarding party."

"Mad dream!" says the Frenchman with a chuckle, and went down again without entering the room.

We longed for daylight to reveal the full extent of our success, yet dared not wait for it, for the stone was heavy, and it would take some time to replace it, and since we were always visited soon after daybreak we feared to be intruded on before we had put it back and removed the traces of our work. So we set it again in its place and for the rest of the night slept the sound sleep of contentment.

But this success spurred me on to devise some means of easing the work yet to be done. The stone was two feet broad; if the wall was ten feet thick there were four more like it still to be removed, and at the same rate it would be three months before we could tunnel through to the air. And thinking of this my heart fell, for there was not room in the cavity left by the stone for two men to work abreast, so that it might indeed be four months before we saw the end of our toil. I determined, therefore, by some means or other to procure a light, by whose aid I could explore the hole and see if the next stone was cemented with the same care.

It chanced that that day we had for dinner a very fat piece of beef. I took advantage of this to pocket some lumps of fat, intending to make a candle with it and a wick composed of some twisted threads from my shirt. The difficulty was to kindle the candle when made, for none of us had a tinder box, though we had steel in our chisel and could easily break a piece of stone from the slab we had loosened.

Tolliday was equal to this, however. He pretended that one of the screws of his fiddle had swelled, so that it would not turn freely in the hole, and he got us to ask one of the soldiers to lend him his tinder box, so that he might make a fire of shavings and heat a skewer red hot, with which to burn away the hole. All unsuspicious, the man lent him the box, which, when it was returned to him had somewhat less tinder in it than before.

That night, and during the remaining weeks of our work, we had a candle. We screened the light very carefully, you may be sure, so that it should not shine through the grating in the wall on the courtyard, and attract the soldiers' notice.

The stone having been removed, I crawled into the opening, holding the candle, and could scarcely check a cry of joy as I perceived that our task would henceforth be much lighter than I had supposed. At the end of the hole, instead of another stone cemented like the first, as I expected, there was a mass of rubble. I could not doubt that the whole of the interior of the wall consisted of this material, and that we should encounter no more blocks of stone until we came to the outer layer of the wall.

It was easy to understand now why castles deemed impregnable were sometimes battered down. A thickness of ten feet of stone might withstand any bombardment, but once the outer stones were pierced, the lighter material would offer but little resistance to cannon shot.

That was an afterthought, however; my reflection at the moment was that liberty was nearer to us by several weeks. Being acquainted with my discovery, my comrades made no ado when I suggested that we should now remove another of the stones of the inner wall, so that we might more easily get at the rubble. Filled with a new spirit of cheerfulness, they worked with such ardor that in ten nights we were able to lay a second stone alongside of the first.

But we were now confronted with a new difficulty. It had been easy enough to dispose of the cement dust: it was quite another thing to get rid of the vast quantity of small stones and pieces of brick which now had to be removed. Further, if we cleared all the rubble from the middle of the wall between us and the outside, there would be no support for the slabs of the battlement above, and however firmly they were cemented, it was not improbable that they would sink in and betray us.

The latter predicament we could but ignore for the present. For the disposal of the rubble, after some thought I hit upon a plan that proved entirely successful.

When all was quiet one night, Joe and I descended the ladder which led from our dormitory to the room below, and lifted, after some trouble, one of the planks of the floor. As I had hoped, it was not laid immediately on the ground; a space of two feet deep had been left. Into this hole night by night we cast the rubble we scooped out from the wall, carefully replacing the plank when we had done. We moved always with bare feet, carrying the stuff in our pillow cases. When I consider how many slight accidents might have marred our work and utterly undone us, I can not but think that we were in some sort watched over by Providence. Our life aboard ship had made us sure footed; but that we were able to work for weeks without betraying ourselves by a sound or the neglect of some precaution I ascribe to something higher than ourselves.

To come to an end of this part of my story, after several weeks' work at the rubble we once more encountered stone. Before attacking this, we waited for a night or two. We no longer had any fear of the slabs of the battlement falling; the cement was clearly strong enough to bear the weight of the passing sentry; but I had some apprehension that as he tramped along the man might discover the hollowness below him by the ringing of his feet on the stones. But two nights sufficed to banish this fear also, and then we started eagerly on the last portion of our task.

The flight of time passes almost unnoticed when the moments are well filled. Winter had given place to spring, and spring was now merging into summer. We had no almanac, and kept no account of the days; it was by the lengthening daylight and shortening darkness and the new warmth in the air that we knew summer was at hand. The long nights of winter would perhaps have been more favorable to our escape, but, on the other hand, we should suffer more from exposure, and moreover, I fancy no man is ever so brave in cold weather as in warm. We prisoners, at any rate, worked now with more zest than ever, heartened by the knowledge that if we did win to freedom, we should find ourselves in a pleasant, sunny world.

One night when Runnles and the bosun were at work, the chisel of the former met with no further obstacle. Enlarging the hole he had made, he set his eye to it, and whispered to the bosun to blow out the candle. Then he crawled back into the room and told me in his quiet way that he had seen the stars. Before morning the cement round a stone somewhat larger than the one we first removed had been scraped away, or pushed out into the moat, and we knew that when we had hauled the stone back through the tunnel into the room we should have made a hole large enough for the biggest of us to pass through.

My fears for the success of our enterprise were never greater than at this moment when the way seemed open. The men were in so wild a state of excitement that I was consumed with anxiety lest their demeanor should arouse suspicion among our guardians. Before I went down to the courtyard I spoke to them very earnestly, begging them to keep a watch on themselves, and not betray by word, look or sign that anything had happened to break the monotony of our life.

They obeyed my injunctions almost too well, for a more silent, morose, hangdog set of fellows could never have been seen; they provoked jests from the prisoners of the other dormitories, who declared that sure their music had made them all melancholy.

"It must be tonight, Joe," I said, when, our morning tasks being done, he and I went apart from the rest for a little private talk. "If we delay it, I cannot answer for their behavior."

"That is all very true, sir," said Joe; "but I can not see how we are to manage it. There's a hole in the wall, to be sure, and a new rope on the windlass of the well: but how we be going to get the rope where 'tis needed is more than I can guess."

"Don't you think that by tonight our drum will want washing?" I said.

He looked at me, clearly puzzled at what seemed a sudden change of subject.

"'Tis very dirty, to be sure; but washing it won't make it sound no better, I reckon."

"I rather think it will," I replied, and then I told him what I had in mind.

"'Tis a main risky trick, sir," he said dubiously. "If they should happen to want another bucketful of water we're lost men."

"We must risk something, Joe," I answered, "and fortune has so well befriended us hitherto that I can't think she will balk us now."

But I own that my anxieties increased as the day wore on, and my melancholy countenance was doubtless a good match with the faces of my comrades. When one of the other prisoners twitted me on my lugubrious mien, I had an inspiration.

"We are saving our cheerfulness for the concert tonight," I said. "'Twill be the best we have ever given, and we shall never give a better."

And for the rest of the day there was a great buzz of talk among the men about the announcement I had made, and a great deal of laughter at our mournful preparation for a cheerful entertainment.

Late in the afternoon, when water drawing had ended for the day, I went to one of the soldiers and asked if I might be allowed to wash our big drum.

"Why, 'twill spoil it," he cried. "You'll get no sound out of a wet skin."

"I shall only wash one side," I replied, "and it will give a thicker sound than the dry one, and so add to the variety of the piece we are going to play."

"Well, wash it then," he said, and went off grinning to tell his comrades of this latest whimsy.

I fetched the drum from the corner of the room where it lay, and carried it to the well within the keep. The members of the band were in the secret, and I had asked them to hold the attention of the other prisoners while I set about my task. The well was situated in a somewhat gloomy corner, and, there being none of the garrison at hand, I was able to accomplish my purpose unobserved and without interference. Having drawn up a bucketful of water, I unhooked the bucket, unwound the rope until there were but a few feet still left upon the windlass, then cut it, made a gash in the side of the drum, and coiled the lower and longer portion of the rope in the interior of the instrument. Then I tied the bucket to what remained of the rope, and lowered it into the well, where it hung only a few feet from the surface, but quite out of sight in the darkness. This done, I carried the drum across the yard, turning its broken side away from the soldiers, who stood smoking against the wall, and who laughed when they saw the water dripping from the instrument upon the flagstones.

The prisoners were all grouped in a ring about Joe Punchard, who was amusing them with a strange dance of his own invention. He bent his knees till he was almost sitting on the ground, and in that position danced a sort of hornpipe--a feat that must have imposed a terrible strain upon his inwards, but which he seemed to perform with consummate ease. The men were so intent upon his antics that I passed them by unnoticed, and gained the lower room of the shed, where I whipped the rope out of the drum and ran with it up into the dormitory, hiding it under one of the beds. I was down again in a minute, and then, tearing the membrane jaggedly to disguise the fact that it had been cut, I went out into the yard, and when Joe had finished announced with an air of vexation that I had unluckily made a hole in the drum. At this my fellow bandsmen abused me with a fine show of anger, the bosun in particular storming at me with a violence at which I had much ado not to smile.

The other men laughed, and made fun of our mishap, which boded ill for the success of our concert. But when we had eaten our evening meal, we got our instruments and played until the sun went down, with a gusto which certainly we had never shown before. For the nonce I gave up the castanets to the bosun, and beat the drum myself, thumping it on its sound side joyously. The soldiers gathered round and gave us very hearty applause; and when Runnles, to conclude the program, played them on his flute the air of *Au clair de lune,* which he had picked up from one of them, they cheered him to the echo.

I hoped that there was nothing ominous in the choice of this old song to end our concert. Moonlight would be fatal to our enterprise; and I was quite ignorant whether the moon rose early or late. But we had gone so far that our attempt must be made this very night, for with the morning the cutting of the rope would without doubt be discovered; the alarm would be given, and the ensuing search would bring to light not merely the severed rope, but our operations upon the wall.

We went up into our dormitory, taking with us our instruments as usual, among them the bass viol of our invention. This was to serve as our raft. We waited for several hours with feelings painfully tense. None of us was inclined to talk; my nine comrades were, I doubt not, wondering as anxiously as I myself what the issue of our attempt would be.

When all was quiet, the strongest of them removed the stone at the inner end of the tunnel, and set it down with many precautions on the floor. Then Runnles, being a little man, crawled to the other end and looped the rope about the loosened stone there. This we hauled inwards an inch at a time, stopping after every pull to listen. It seemed endless work to drag it into the room, but at last it was done, and we set the stone alongside the other.

Our way was now clear. I had insisted on being the first to descend, though Joe Punchard and two other men volunteered for that office, pleading that they were mariners of longer standing than I, and therefore fitter for the climbing work. But this I would by no means agree to--the suggestion and the plan being mine, it was meet that I should be the first to face what perils it might involve. Accordingly, I first crawled through the tunnel to see whether the aspect of the sky favored an immediate descent, and, being reassured on that point, I went back into the room to make the final preparations.

We stripped a plank from one of the truckle beds and placed it across the opening, one end of the rope being knotted about its middle; the knots were firm, you may be sure, as none but sailors can make them. Then, taking the other end of the rope, I went to the outward end and lowered it very gently towards the moat, knowing that it would not be seen in the darkness by the sentry on the battlements above even if he chanced to look over, and to that he would have no temptation.

There was a good deal of doubt among us as to whether the rope was long enough for our purpose. The bosun, who had crawled after me, whispered he was sure it was too short. And when I had let it down to its full length and drawn it up again, as yard after yard it came dry through my fingers I began to fear that the bosun was right. But at last the rope left a slimy wetness upon my hands, and I rejoiced to find that two or three yards of it had fallen into the water.

Our next step was to draw the rope wholly into the dormitory and fasten its wet end to the bass viol. On the top of this, it will be remembered, there were two S-shaped openings which we had cut to make it serviceable as a sound board. These Joe had now covered over with the broken skin of the drum, to make the box water tight. We pushed it through the tunnel, and I let it down into the moat, very slowly, so that it might not strike the wall and draw the sentry's attention. When the rope was paid out to its full length I wrapped a coil of bast about my shoulders, and, having suspended from my neck a short plank from the head of the bed, I bade the men in a whisper to remember the further plan we had arranged, and made my way down the rope--a feat that offered no difficulty to a seaman even so little practiced as I.

Coming safely to our musical raft, I was not long in discovering it to be a very cranky thing, so that I had to keep my hold of the rope in order to maintain my balance. But in a short time I was able to defeat the raft's attempts to turn turtle, and then, kneeling on it, still gripping the rope, I looked anxiously for signs that the attention of the sentry on the battlements had been awakened. But I heard his footsteps approach and recede at the same measured pace; 'twas clear he suspected nothing; and without more delay I began to work the raft towards the far side of the moat, using the short plank I had brought with me as a paddle. So that no sound of splashing might rise to betray us, at every stroke I dug the paddle into the mud, which, as I had suspected, came to within a little of the surface; indeed, the depth of water was barely sufficient to float the raft, with my weight on it.

A most unsavory odor resulted from the stirring of the mud; but a greater inconvenience was the tendency of the raft to lurch. Holding on to the rope with one hand, I instinctively pulled upon it to maintain my equilibrium when I felt myself toppling, with the result that the raft moved backward, and I had to begin my punting again. Fortunately, the width of the moat was little more than thrice the length of my crazy craft, in spite of whose instability I succeeded in reaching the opposite side.

Here, however, I found that my difficulties were by no means over. The water was low in the moat, and the bank, perfectly free from vegetation, rose almost vertically to a height of six or eight feet. On a moonlit night I must have been seen if the sentry had glanced in my direction; dark as it was, I feared it was not so dark but that my moving shape might be descried. I waited: not hearing the sentry's footsteps, I began to fear the worst; but finding after a time that no alarm had been given, and that all was still about me, I first fastened the coil of bast I had brought on my shoulders to the end of the rope where it was knotted about the raft, and then began to clamber up the bank, somewhat incommoded by having to keep a hold of the bast with one hand.

Careful as I was, I yet dislodged one or two clods of earth as I climbed, which fell with a dull splash into the water. I went cold with apprehension, and clung to the face of the bank, not daring to make a movement. There were no fowl upon the moat; the splash I had made was louder than any frog could have made; surely the unaccustomed sound must this time have caught the sentry's ear! But all was silent; maybe he was asleep; and in another few moments I gained the top of the bank, breathless, rather, I suspect, from excitement than exertion.

It seemed a very long time since I had left my comrades above: doubtless it had seemed even longer to them. So, after the briefest of pauses to recover my breath, I gave three sharp tugs upon the bast line, which were immediately answered by three similar tugs: this was the signal I had arranged with Joe. The tension on the line was relaxed; Joe, hauling at the rope, was drawing the raft gently back across the moat to its former position at the foot of the wall. There was a short interval; then I knew from the jerking of the bast line that a man was descending the rope, and when he was almost level with me I saw his form very dimly. When I learned from the cessation of the jerks that he was safe on the raft, I hauled in my line, ferried the man across, and, leaning over, gave him a helping hand up the bank. It was little Runnles.

"I've got my flute, sir," he whispered with strange inconsequence as he came to my side.

"Lie on the ground and don't stir," I whispered back.

Again I gave three tugs, and the same sequence of events ensued. One by one the men came down the rope, crossed the moat on the raft, and joined me on the bank. We had no difficulty with any of them but the bosun, whose massy frame so much depressed the raft that it took the united exertions of six of us to haul it through the upper layer of mud.

Joe Punchard came last of all. When with his arrival our little party of ten was complete, we crawled on hands and knees one by one to the shelter of a thicket that stood some fifty yards away, and then consulted in whispers how we were to shape our course.

Chapter 17
Exchanges

I have been many a time surprised to observe the strange volatility of sailormen. They will pass in an instant from jollity to woe, and, when just snatched from the jaws of death, will give the rein to jests and sportiveness as if life were nothing but a perpetual holiday. Some of my comrades were perfectly hilarious, and began to talk and laugh as freely as they might in the forecastle, far from a hostile shore. I had to warn them very earnestly against so imperiling the safety of us all; but Joe Punchard's admonitions were more effective than mine, for in a harsh whisper he roundly abused them, threatening with many offensive terms to leave them to their fate if they did not instantly cease and obey me as their captain.

Their intelligence being penetrated with some notion of the exceeding danger of our situation, the noisy ones kept silence and agreed to follow my behests. This threw on me a task of great hazard and responsibility, for we were strangers in a strange land, and I had no knowledge of our whereabouts, nor a clearly defined plan of action. Gathering them in a knot about me, so that all could hear my lowest whisper, I put to them the situation as I conceived it.

"By God's mercy we have succeeded thus far," I said, "but the greatest of our dangers lie still before us. I know nothing of this country, nor does any of us, and in a few hours day will dawn, our escape will be discovered, and there will be a hue and cry after us for miles around. What we want to do is to make the coast and borrow a boat in which we may set sail for England."

"Ay, ay," was the general grunt.

"Ay, indeed," I went on, "but we know not in what direction the coast lies, nor would it be safe for us to attempt to reach it yet. When our absence is known, the Frenchmen will assuredly suspect that the coast will be our aim, and they will have it watched for miles, so that even if we found a boat and got to sea (in which we might fail), we should certainly be espied and chased and caught. What we must do, as it seems to me, is to strike into the country and find a hiding place where we may lie until the first alarm has passed, and then endeavor by some means to learn of a secluded fishing hamlet whither we may steal our way by night. Can you suggest a better plan?"

For a brief space there was silence; then the bosun said:

"If we can not tell the way to the coast, neither can we know if we be going inland, and so we may stumble into the very danger we ought to avoid."

"There is the north star above us," I replied, "and by going south it would appear that we shall go away from the sea. I propose, then, that we turn our backs on the star and march southward, trusting to find some wood or perchance some ruin where we may lurk a day or two."

"And our bellies empty," groaned Tolliday.

"Let us hope not," I said. "We may come upon some fruit gardens where we can find enough to keep us from starvation. But if we must fast, then I warrant we, being Englishmen, can endure our pangs for a day. Time is passing; 'tis gone midnight, if I guess right, and since move we must, I speak for moving at once."

No other course suggesting itself, we set off, and, having the good luck to strike a road, we marched along in dogged silence for what must have been a couple of hours. We passed but one house, and that was in total darkness, and if any person in it had been awake, our passage would not have been heard, for we were all barefooted but three, myself and two others.

After pausing a while to rest, we set off again, and tramped on until there was a hint of daybreak in the sky. Then, being utterly weary (for none of us had enjoyed a full night's sleep for months), we looked about for some spot where we might rest without danger. We found ourselves between open fields, somewhat cut up by low stone dykes, but with no buildings or copses that offered even a temporary shelter. We had perforce to continue on our way, and about half a mile farther on our eyes were gladdened by the sight of a large, low, dismantled farmhouse lying somewhat back from the road. It appeared at first to be a total ruin, and bore the marks of fire upon its blackened walls: but on entering we discovered one room that had some portion of a roof over it, and, better still, a quantity of straw spread about the floor. We were gathering this up to make rough beds of it, when we perceived a trap door in the floor, and it occurred to me that if it led down to a dry cellar, such as were not uncommon in farmhouses in England, this would prove a more secure refuge than the room on a level with the road.

Lifting the trap door, I found that it was even as I hoped. The cellar beneath was large, and dimly illuminated through a grating let into the wall just above the level of the ground. I perceived, too, that it had a door, so that in the unlikely event of our re-entrance by the trap door being prevented, we could still escape into the open. There was straw also in the cellar, and it did not take us many seconds to decide that here we would lay down our tired bodies and gain some sleep. My purpose was, after resting, to go exploring alone, trusting to my knowledge of the French tongue to procure some food and also to learn something of the lie of the land, for there must assuredly be a habitation somewhere in the neighborhood.

We all descended into the cellar, closing the trap door after us, and gladly stretched our limbs upon the straw. It did not appear necessary to keep a watch. The farm had clearly not been inhabited for many years, and there was no reason to fear that our rest would be disturbed. Even when the pursuit of us should be begun, it was in the highest degree unlikely that it would tend in this direction. The road was hard after a period of dry weather, and we had left no foot tracks to betray us. But as a precaution I went out by the cellar door, ascended a short flight of steps and made my way to the upper room again, where I spread some straw on the trap door, to hide it from any chance visitor. Then I returned to the cellar. Our fatigue was so great that in a few moments we were all asleep.

I was awakened by a touch on my arm. I sat bolt upright in an instant. Runnles was leaning over me, with his finger at his lips. The other men were already awake, and seeing, I suppose, a look of inquiry on my face, Runnles whispered:

"I wakened them first, 'cos they was snoring."

And then I became aware that it was precisely the unexpected that had happened. There were people in the room above. I heard footsteps and voices, and then felt no little alarm when another sound reached my ears--a sound that I could not mistake. It was the sound of muskets being stacked.

We looked at one another in mute dismay. Had our pursuers hit upon our tracks at once? It seemed scarcely credible. Yet for a minute or two I waited in a kind of paralysis, expecting the trap door to open and a posse of armed soldiers to descend. My anxiety on this score soon vanished, however, for I heard a heavy thump on the trap door above, and guessed that either something had been thrown upon it or that one of the intruders had unwittingly chosen it for his seat. This, with the previous stacking of the arms, seeming to indicate that the visitors intended to make some stay, and had no suspicion of our presence.

I determined to set my fears finally at rest (and, I must own, also to satisfy my curiosity) by stealing out and taking a peep at them, if they had left the door open. Whispering my comrades to remain perfectly silent, I slipped off my boots, quickly opened the door, and went very cautiously round to the front part of the house.

The first object that caught my eyes was a horse standing tethered in what had been the ruins of a barn adjoining the farmhouse. Creeping up to the door, which had been left ajar, I peeped in, and saw a party of French soldiers seated on the floor, eating bread and sausages, and drinking from little tin cans. My mouth watered at the sight of this food after more than twelve hours of fasting, but I was not conscious of this till afterwards. The party consisted of seven men. One, somewhat apart from the rest (it was he who had sat himself on the trap door), was clearly an officer. He was a tall, lean man of some forty years; he had unbuttoned his coat and laid his hat, in which there was a white cockade, beside him. At a respectful distance from him sat the others of the party.

For some time they ate their meal in silence, the men, I suppose, not daring to converse in the presence of their captain. But by and by the officer, his hunger being some whit appeased, unbent a little from his dignity and addressed a stout little sergeant among the party.

"It is twelve years since I was here before, Jules," he said, and there was a noticeable air of condescension in his tone; it was as though he did the sergeant a mighty favor in speaking at all.

"Yes, monsieur," said the sergeant, as if humbly inviting him to continue.

"Yes, twelve years ago," the officer repeated. "I have reason, truly, to know it again. Those were the days of the Conversions, Jules. You don't know what the Conversions were? I will tell you. There were cursed Huguenots in the country then, Jules, bad citizens, unruly rascals every one of them, and our good king commanded that they should instantly return to the true faith. Some of them were obstinate, and they, see you, had to be converted. We called it conversion by lodgings, and, my faith, it was excellent sport. They quartered some of us on any household that was unwilling to obey the king, and there we remained until they saw the error of their ways.

"My faith! some were hard to convert. The owner of this place, for instance. We were here for a month, and never lived better in our lives. The fool! He had a pretty daughter, too, and I fell in love with her. The farmer objected, and one day had the insolence to strike me. That was treason, of course, and the least we could do, especially as he was so obstinate in the matter of his conversion, was to burn his farm. He shot one of my men while we were at the work, and--well, we hanged him. That was twelve years ago."

The sergeant laughed. I, who had heard something from my father of King Lewis' treatment of his Huguenot subjects--of the Dragonnade, as it was called, and the sufferings of the poor people at the hands of the brutal soldiery--I, who knew of this, was shocked at the callous levity of the captain's speech; and I could have struck the fat, foolish face of the sergeant for his chuckle.

"What fools men are!" the captain went on. "Who would have supposed that these rascals of deserters would make for the very place where they would most readily be discovered! But all these peasants are simpletons. If you, now, were to desert, Jules, you would not return to Meaux, would you? You are a townsman, and have more sense. But these peasants--bah! cattle, no more."

I thought the sergeant's laugh at this rang a trifle hollow. He was not a soft-hearted man in appearance, but perhaps he had some fellow feeling for poor men dragged from their work at the plough to serve in the army of the Grand Monarque. His next words surprised me, for I had not understood the captain's reference to deserters.

"Shall we give them something to eat, *mon capitaine*?" he asked.

"Decidedly not," said the officer with an oath. "They have led us a pretty dance, and what's the good of food to men about to be shot!"

"But they may fall from exhaustion before we reach Rennes," suggested the sergeant, "and that may cause delay. They have had nothing for near twelve hours, *mon capitaine*, and marching best part of the time."

"Well, give them a crust," said the captain, lazily throwing himself back on the straw; "but it is waste, sheer waste."

The sergeant rose and, taking some scraps of food, crossed the room and disappeared from my sight. I knew now that the deserters of whom they had spoken were actually in the place with them, and found myself pitying the fate of men who had had the ill luck to fall into the hands of so coldly brutal an officer as this captain.

Then I turned about with a start, having the strange feeling-- for I heard nothing--that someone was moving behind me. It was Runnles. He came towards me stealthily, wearing that meek, shy look of his, and told me in a whisper that Joe Punchard had sent him to see what had become of me. At the sight of him a fantastic notion buzzed into my head. I caught him by the sleeve and whispered eagerly in his ear, his eyes becoming two round O's with excitement as he listened. He stole away again, and I turned once more to my business of eavesdropping.

"They eat like pigs," I heard the captain say to the sergeant, who had returned to his lair on the straw. "These peasants never lose the ill manners bred in them. And those English dogs who have escaped from prison--how do I know they are peasants, too, Jules?"

"I can not tell, *mon capitaine*," says the sergeant.

"Why, because you may be sure they have done a foolish thing, like these deserters of ours. They are seamen; depend upon it, they have made straight for the coast, and we shall soon hear that they have been taken."

I could not help smiling at the ingenuousness of the captain's reasoning.

"My faith!" he went on, "I wish we were going from Rennes to St. Malo instead of from St. Malo to Rennes. I should have loved to join in the hunt for the rascals, and I doubt not you, Jules, would be glad enough to get some portion of the reward offered for their capture. Ah, well! the others will have the luck; but I would give something to see those English dogs when--"

And here I pushed wide the door.

"Am I permitted to enter, messieurs?" I said in my best French, and giving the captain a pleasant smile. Lying at full length with his head on his arms, he could not clearly see me. The men stared at me, but did not move nor speak, waiting dutifully for their officer. He raised himself on his elbow.

"Who are you?" he asks, looking me up and down from my bare feet to my unkempt head.

"I, monsieur," said I steadily, though my heart was thumping at a furious rate--"I, monsieur, am one of the English dogs--at your service."

This announcement was sufficiently startling to account for the temporary paralysis that seemed to have fallen on the party. They stared at me, speechless. During that moment I had thrown a rapid glance to my left. The three deserters were lying against the wall; between them and me were the stacked muskets of the soldiers.

While the men were still fixed in their astonishment, I sprang three paces to the left, caught up the muskets in both arms, and dashed towards the door. That released them from the spell; the men jumped to their feet and rushed after me. What happened to the captain I learned afterwards from Joe. He suddenly found himself heaved up into the air: four brawny arms had shoved up the trap door on which he was lying, my dash for the door having been the signal I had communicated to them through Runnles. When the officer came sprawling down on the straw again, some feet away from his former position, he was pounced on by Joe and the bosun, who made short work of tying him up with his own sword strap.

Meanwhile the rest of my comrades had run out of the cellar door, and joined me just in time to receive the charge of the six Frenchmen who had followed me from the house. Fortunately for us, what with surprise and haste, the Frenchmen had not drawn their swords, so that the fight that ensued beneath the ruined wall of the farm was waged on fairly even terms. And when it comes to a contest in which nature's weapons are employed, I never yet met combatants to match sturdy English tars. There were six Frenchmen, and my comrades (Joe and the bosun being busy with the captain) numbered seven, but of these Dilly was old and Runnles was small, and, coming up in the rear of the rest, they two had no part in the fight. Nor had I, for when they engaged my arms were full of the muskets; and when I had laid these on the ground I saw that one of the Frenchmen, evidently foreseeing how the matter must end, left his fellows and ran fleetly towards the horse, which was looking with serene indifference at the scene. I sprinted after him; he had only a few yards' start, and knew that he was pursued, for he swerved out of the direction in which he was running, seeing, no doubt, that he would not have time to untether the horse before I was upon him. He turned aside, leapt a low dyke into a field, and picked up his heels so nimbly that, though I was pretty quick of foot, I was by no means sure of my power to overtake him.

But he had left me the horse. Quickly untethering it, I mounted, and set off after the runaway. And then my practice in cross-country riding about Shrewsbury served me well; I did not hesitate to set the beast at the dykes that divided the fields; he took them gamely, and after five minutes of as mad a steeplechase as I ever enjoyed I came up with the fugitive. He sprang aside, drew his sword, and seemed to be for showing fight: but when I wheeled the horse and threatened to ride him down he saw that the game was up, and, sullenly surrendering his sword, marched back before me to the farm.

Then I found that my comrades had already finished the business. They had hauled the Frenchmen back into the room where their captain lay, screeching abuse at Joe and the bosun, who smiled at him encouragingly. The Frenchmen's faces bore marks of punishment; several of them had signs of war upon their sleeves, which they had used to stanch their noses. So loudly did the captain vituperate me that I had to ask Joe to silence him; it was necessary for us to hold a council of war, and quiet discourse was impossible while the Frenchman raved.

Joe chose a way as effective as it was simple. He caught up a handful of straw and stuffed it between the officer's teeth.

And now some of the circumstances reminded me of the similar mischance that had befallen me on the Bristowe road. There also the scene had passed in a ruined building strewn with straw. And the recollection of the indignity I had suffered at the hands of Topper and his fellows, coupled with the sight of the three deserters lying manacled and open-mouthed against the wall, gave me an idea that pleased me mightily. I had once changed clothes against my will; why should not *Monsieur le Capitaine* learn humility in the same way? He was about my height: his clothes would certainly fit me better than Job the poacher's had done; and whereas my former change had been for the worse, the change I contemplated should turn out very much for the better, and so the whirligig of time would have his revenges.

I told my comrades what I had in mind.

"All very well for you, sir," said the bosun bluntly, "but what about us tars?"

"Why, some of you can slip into the Frenchmen's clothes," I replied. "You won't get a fit, I fear, bosun; you are overgrown" (I smiled as the words others had used about me came unbidden to my lips); "but the sergeant there is very much Joe Punchard's figure, and five of you can make shift, I daresay. You would make quite a pretty squad of Frenchmen, and show a little more brawn."

"But what's the good, sir?" objected Tolliday. "We can't talk a word of the lingo, and if your idea be to march through the country till we can find a boat, bless my buttons if we can do it, 'cos the first cuss I say will be the ruin of us."

"I haven't told you all my plan yet," I said. "But first I must speak to these poor fellows here: they are deserters and were on the way to Rennes to be shot.

"Take 'em outside, Joe."

The plan I had in mind when seizing the Frenchmen was somewhat hazy, but it was becoming clearer every moment, and, being spiced with hazard, it appealed to all that was adventurous in my nature.

When I had the deserters out of earshot of their late guards, I asked them if they wished to regain their freedom, knowing well what their answer would be.

"Well," said I, "if I set you free now it may do you no good. You have been caught once and may be caught again. But if you throw in your lot with us there is a chance for you. We are English prisoners who have escaped: join us, and we will try to take you to England."

They demurred to this. They did not want to go to England, where they would be friendless and might starve. They would rather remain in their own country, among their own kin.

"But there is a France overseas," I said. "From England you may perhaps sail by and by for Quebec, where you would be among your own countrymen, and run little risk of being recognized. If you stay here you will sooner or later be captured again and shot. A new land is the place for you."

They discussed this suggestion among themselves, and at length agreed to make the attempt. I then returned to my comrades, and explained to them more fully my design. It was nothing less than to personate the French captain, and to lead my party across country just as he had been doing. The three deserters would exchange their peasant rags for the uniforms of three of the French soldiers, and three of my comrades would wear the uniforms of the rest. I hoped that with courage and address and circumspection we might contrive to keep up the imposture long enough to accomplish our ends.

My comrades, however, looked at the matter in a different light.

"'Tis all very fine," said the bosun gloomily, "but what about the lingo, sir? We may dress up as much as you like, but nohow can we twist our tongues to the jabber of these Frenchies, and I could no more march a score of miles without using my clapper than I could steer without a rudder."

"Then you will have to be wounded in the jaw," I said, "and Joe will tie it up so that you can't open your mouth. We must pretend that we had a desperate fight before we captured the deserters. We must be very careful; I don't make light of the difficulties before us, but we shouldn't be worth the name of English tars if we didn't make the best use of this opportunity that Providence has offered us."

"But what about the rest of us?" said Tolliday. "There bean't enough uniforms to go round."

"Why," I said, with a sudden inspiration, "you shall be just what you are, English seamen who have escaped prison. I shall give out that as we were escorting our deserters we discovered you skulking in a barn, and brought you along with us."

My comrades were aghast at this, but I pointed out that my plan would solve the language difficulty, and that if it succeeded in one part it might succeed in all, whereas if it failed they would be none the worse off. They admitted that this was reasonable, and the humor of the situation suddenly striking them, they began to enjoy it as an excellent joke.

And then Runnles suggested a difficulty which had not occurred to me: it may seem a mark of self-conceit, but it was really mere thoughtlessness. He pointed out that though I spoke French well (little Runnles was a man of tact!), yet it would not deceive a native. He was undoubtedly right, and the suggestion staggered me. Hoping to be reassured, I asked one of the deserters whether I might pass as a Frenchman, and I own I felt deeply chagrined when, with a shrug, he confessed that I would not. But one of his comrades here broke in.

"Pardon, monsieur," he said, "what matters it? That brute of a captain is only a German Swiss; there are plenty such in the king's army; and your French is as good as his."

My spirits rose at this, and having told my comrades what he had said, I determined to lose no more time in putting my plan into execution. The changes of clothes were quickly made, not without some struggles on the part of our victims, and a vast deal of violent language from the captain, whom Joe again half choked with straw. We soon had him and his men rigged up, gagged and manacled as deserters; we borrowed (without leave) kerchiefs of various colors which the Frenchmen had about them, and of them made bandages for those who were to pass as wounded. Joe donned the sergeant's clothes, and the bosun those of the largest of the company, though they were a sad misfit.

It struck us that we should make the imposture more complete if we got a cart in which to convey our wounded men, so when the preparations were otherwise complete I, attired as the French captain, mounted his horse and, accompanied by two of the quondam deserters (now appearing quite respectable infantrymen), set off to find a farm where in the name of King Lewis I might demand what we needed. We had to go some three miles before we came to a likely looking farmhouse, and there, assuming an authoritative and hectoring manner quite foreign to my amiable disposition, I secured a wagon and two horses, for which I gave the farmer a formal receipt.

The sight of his dairy reminded me that I was hungry, and I added to my requisition a good store of food, for which I knew my comrades would bless me. For driver I picked out the stupidest looking yokel I could find among the farmer's men, and then we returned to the ruined farmhouse in triumph and not a little haste, for I was eager to set my teeth in the bread and cheese we were conveying.

Chapter 18
In The Name Of King Lewis

While we were appeasing our appetites, I got from the deserters an inkling of our locality. They had been marching, as I knew, from St. Malo to Rennes, but instead of keeping to the highroad through Combourg, they had taken a short cut that saved several miles. It passed through several hamlets, some of which, they said, could be avoided; but there were others which we must take on our way, and it was in these that we should be put to the test.

I asked the men if they knew of any spot on the coast where we might find a boat to convey us across the Channel, and after consulting together they decided that the only likely place was the little fishing town of Cancale, about ten miles east of St. Malo. It had a harbor on the Bay of St. Michel, whence the luggers sailed forth a little before sunset. I would rather have chosen a smaller place, and one more distant from our late prison, but the men assured me that there was no other so easily accessible, or so likely to furnish the boat we needed; so I determined to put all to the hazard and make for Cancale. It was, as nearly as they could tell, about five and twenty miles from our present position, so that we could not hope to reach it before night, and we had to reconcile ourselves to the prospect of another day's march across country on the morrow.

We set off, a strange company indeed. One of the deserters led the way; behind him went the cart containing the French captain and his men, now passing as deserters, and all gagged; then came seven of my comrades with their hands tied, the other two deserters marching one on each side of them; and the rear was brought up by the bosun, Joe and myself, and the two men being attired as French soldiers and having their heads bandaged, their supposed wounds being sufficient to account for their silence if they were addressed.

Having plenty of time before us, we chose devious and little frequented roads, the deserters who led us being fortunately familiar with the district. We avoided the villages when we could, but towards evening came to a hamlet which it was impossible to shun, since only through it could we gain a ford at a stream that crossed our route.

The appearance of a party of soldiers aroused great interest among the villagers. They came about us, asking who we were and whither we were going. They were greatly excited when they learned that we were escorting deserters and recaptured English prisoners. The real deserters told a glib story of the furious fight they had had with the villains (pointing to the unhappy officer and his men). The villagers threw up their hands with shrill exclamations at this moving recital, and, going up to the cart, gazen openmouthed and not without a secret sympathy at the prostrate forms.

Then they asked why the deserters were gagged. At this I took up the tale, explaining that they were desperate characters, and had used such terrible language against his sacred majesty the king that, as a loyal officer, I had sworn they should not speak again until they were safely jailed in St. Malo. The captain's face was distorted with rage as he listened to this libel: he flung his manacled hands about and made frantic efforts to speak, which Joe's gag was too thoroughly fixed to allow.

"*Voila!*" said I, with a dramatic gesture; and the simple villagers, taking the officer's writhings and gnashings as so much evidence of his desperate wickedness, poured imprecations upon him for his impiety, and declared that no punishment was too great for him. The poor people had, I daresay, no great reason themselves for loving their monarch, but they were anxious that their own loyalty should be above suspicion.

About the English prisoners they expressed their sentiments without disguise. The English were their natural enemies, and they hurled such abuse at my comrades that I felt some anxiety lest these should cast off their cords (which were by no means closely tied) and take summary vengeance on their revilers. Fortunately their patience endured the strain, being aided by their ignorance of the precise meaning of the opprobrious terms applied to them.

The peasants told us we had come far out of the direct road to St. Malo, and pressed us to stay the night in their village. But this I would by no means consent to, for I was on thorns already lest something should mar our plot, and was keeping a wary eye on our wagoner, who, though slow-witted, was clearly in a state of great uneasiness. Professing, then, that having missed our way we must needs hurry on to make up for lost time, I listened patiently to the minute and befogging directions given us for finding the St. Malo road and ordered my party to march. But when we had gone some few miles out of the village, and darkness was settling down, I called a halt, and we rested till daylight in a field, taking it in turns to watch.

During the night I talked long with Joe Punchard about our course. The good fellow was very uneasy, fearing that when it came to negotiating for a boat our scheme would break down.

"Pluck up heart, Joe," I said. "I own we are running a desperate hazard, but so far we have had good luck, and 'tis a case of grasping the nettle boldly."

"But what reason can we give for hiring a boat, sir? If this Cancale is but ten miles from St. Malo we can not say we are sailing thither; 'twould be quicker to go by road."

"Then we'll change our destination, Joe. We may do what we please in this country in the name of the king, and provided there be no soldiers in Cancale we have but to put on an impudent assurance to weather through safely."

I asked the deserters what other port besides St. Malo we might give out to be our destination, and learning that Cherbourg was some sixty or seventy miles to the northward, and by that much nearer home, I determined to make that our aim. This involved another difficulty, for the authorities in Cancale might reasonably say that the prisoners having escaped from near St. Malo, should be entrusted to them to convey back to their prison. But 'tis no good meeting troubles halfway, and I resolutely kept my thought from dwelling on the manifold dangers that bestrewed our path to liberty.

We so contrived our march next day that we arrived at the outskirts of Cancale late in the afternoon, but with time enough, as I hoped, to set sail before night. When I beheld the size of the place my heart sank. I had imagined it to be little more than a village; but found it a regular town (though small for that), its little red-tiled houses clustering thick upon a height overlooking a bay. We had already met and exchanged speech with some of the townsfolk, and to retreat now might awaken suspicion. There was nothing for it but to adventure boldly, and I made up my mind to this the more readily because I had caught a glimpse of half a dozen fishing smacks lying in the little harbor, and a larger vessel of perhaps fifty tons moored to the jetty.

With a word to my comrades to be alert and ready for anything that might happen, I led the way at a quick pace into the town. I had grave misgivings when I noticed that the streets were *en fete*, flags flying at the windows, and people gossiping in knots at the corners. But we had certainly come too far to retreat, so I boldly accosted a red-capped fisherman and demanded to be led to the *mairie*.

As I walked along beside him I asked what was the occasion of the festal appearance of the town, and learned with a disagreeable shock that no other than the redoubtable Duguay-Trouin had that day put into the harbor on the vessel that lay at the jetty.

"A notable visitor, truly," I said, feeling that I had run into a hornet's nest. "But surely that small vessel is not Monsieur Duguay-Trouin's own ship, in which he works such havoc among the English."

"To be sure, monsieur," said the man, "that is an English prize. His own ship lies in the offing there, towards the point; it draws too much water to come into our harbor. And there is another prize out there too: a big vessel, filled, so they say, with a valuable cargo. Oh! without doubt Monsieur Duguay-Trouin is a hero, and the English tremble at his name."

"And why has he honored your little town with a visit?" I asked.

"Why, *Monsieur le Capitaine*, it is because the English admiral Benbow appeared off St. Malo this morning with four great ships, and so Monsieur Duguay-Trouin could not carry his prize there, and indeed had to make all sail to escape."

Here was news indeed! It revived my drooping spirits; surely there must be a providence in the proximity of Benbow. But I devoutly hoped I should not encounter Duguay-Trouin. It was scarcely probable that he would recognize me in my new attire, having paid scant attention to me when I was among the prisoners on his deck, but I trembled to think of the risk we all ran.

"Here is the *mairie*," said my guide, stopping at a house above which a flag was flying.

I thanked him, and whispering Punchard to keep an eye on the Frenchmen, and especially on the wagoner, I stepped boldly in and confronted the *maire*, a little man with a cocked hat over his gray wig.

"Good evening, monsieur," I said pleasantly.

The *maire* rose from his seat and returned my greeting.

"I am taking some deserters to Cherbourg, monsieur," I continued, "and I must beg of you to provide me tomorrow with a smack to convey them thither."

For the moment I said nothing about the prisoners.

"A smack, monsieur!" said the *maire*. "But it is foolish. Does not monsieur know that four English warships are in the neighborhood? Monsieur would run great risk of being captured. I would recommend that monsieur march to Cherbourg; he would then go quite safely."

"That is perfectly true, monsieur," I said pleasantly', "but it is a long and wearisome road; my men are already greatly fatigued by their march from Rennes. The passage by sea would be much easier and more comfortable, and moreover cheaper, and it is the duty of all good Frenchmen to save his majesty expense."

I could see that the *maire* was nettled. His reluctance to accede to my demand was due, not so much to his fears for our safety--for Benbow had higher game to fly at than a fishing vessel--as to his indisposition to provision us for the voyage. Maybe he had had some experience of the same sort before, and knew that, whatever receipts might be given him for commodities supplied, he had little chance of being reimbursed for such services rendered to King Lewis. No doubt it was some recent soreness that prompted his reply to my remark about all good Frenchmen.

"To judge by his accent," he said, with a hint of a sneer, "monsieur is not a Frenchman himself."

At this I affected to be mightily huffed. Laying my hand on my sword, and knitting my brows to a frown, I replied:

"His majesty has honored me with a commission. No doubt if *Monsieur le Maire* has any serious objections--"

"Pardon, *Monsieur le Capitaine*," the *maire* hastened to say, alarmed at my tone. "I was only concerned for monsieur's safety. Certainly he shall have a smack, equipped as befits the servants of his majesty."

"That is well spoken, monsieur," I said. "Is it true, may I ask, that Monsieur Duguay-Trouin is in your town?"

"Not at this moment, monsieur."

I thrilled with relief at this.

"He has gone half a league eastward to the chateau of Monsieur le duc de Portorson, having already sent a message to St. Malo to acquaint the admiral that he was forced to put in here by the appearance of the English warships."

"And did he not fear that in his absence the English might swoop down upon his vessel and the prizes he has captured?" I asked.

"They are hidden behind the point, monsieur. Besides, the highest part of our town commands a view of forty miles of sea, and we have placed a man there who will fire a musket if a strange sail appears."

"Then I hope that we shall after all make our voyage to Cherbourg in safety," I said with an air of satisfaction. "And now, will monsieur be good enough to select the smack?"

Before he could answer, a man who had just cantered up on horseback entered and said:

"*Monsieur le Maire*, Monsieur Duguay-Trouin is supping with *Monsieur le Duc*. Will monsieur kindly acquaint the lieutenant in charge of the brig at the jetty, and say that Monsieur Duguay-Trouin will return before dark?"

"Can not you take the message yourself?" said the *maire*, whose temper I fear, had been ruffled by his interview with me.

The man explained that he had been bidden to ride on without delay to St. Malo; Monsieur Duguay-Trouin, he believed, was concerting a plan to entrap the English vessels, and it was of particular importance that the letter he bore should reach the admiral early. The *maire* then agreed to have the message conveyed to the lieutenant on the brig, and the horseman took his leave.

During their short conversation, which I only partly heard, my brain was whirling with a wild dance of notions the messenger's tidings had suggested. When he had gone, I turned to the *maire*.

"Monsieur," I said. "I think there is much soundness in the advice you gave me just now. It will probably be safer for us to go to Cherbourg by land. In that case, however, I must request you to billet us for the night."

"Assuredly, monsieur," said the little man, delighted at the turn affairs had taken. "Of how many does your party consist?"

"Of seven deserters and five soldiers."

"A dozen," said the *maire*, rubbing his chin. "I fear I shall have to ask some of my fellow townsmen to share in billeting you."

"It is not to be heard of," I said, guessing that he wished to distribute the expense.

Not that I should have had any objection to that; but that it was necessary to the design I had suddenly conceived that we should be all together.

"It will not be safe," I continued. "The deserters are desperate fellows, and will need careful guarding. Besides, I have had the good luck to capture some English prisoners who had escaped, and they are too precious to be allowed out of my sight. My men must take turns at watching during the night; if there were an outbreak, it would not easily be quelled if we were separated."

The *maire* had pricked up his ears at the mention of the prisoners.

"Prisoners, monsieur!" he exclaimed. "You said nothing of them. We have heard about them, and there is a reward offered for their capture. If monsieur would deign to give us part of the reward--"

"We will talk of that again, monsieur," I said. "I am in haste to get to Cherbourg with the deserters; I can trust you, no doubt, to guard the prisoners well until an escort can be sent for them from St. Malo. In consideration of that, no doubt--"

I broke off expressively, and the *maire* doubtless regarded his share of the reward as secure, for he raised no more objections. He accompanied me to the door, looked contemptuously at my comrades (who were in a great state of anxiety, I can assure you, knowing nothing of what I had in mind), and then went on to the wagon where the supposed deserters were lying. On seeing him the captain started up and with many contortions struggled to speak.

"Why are they gagged, monsieur?" asked the *maire*.

I repeated the explanation I had already given.

"Terrible!" said the *maire*, and the captain grew purple in the face.

"You perceive I could not allow my men's ears to be defiled by the language of such a ruffian," I remarked.

"Perfectly, monsieur. Ah, *scilerat!*" he cried, shaking his fist at the infuriate officer, and pouring out upon him a torrent of loyal abuse which I find it impossible to translate.

Then he turned to the bosun, and asked him how he had come by his wound. The bosun was quick-witted enough to take my cue, and, pointing to the captain, whose reputation as the most violent of the deserters was clearly established, he made through his bandages a series of grunts and roars which proved to the *maire's* satisfaction that his jaw was very seriously damaged. And last of all inspecting my comrades, who stood aside with trouble in their faces, he bestowed on them sundry offensive epithets which I was thankful they did not understand, for otherwise I am sure they would have forgotten their part and endangered everything by administering a castigation.

The *maire* arranged to billet us all. Having seen my double set of prisoners securely locked up, and the deserters with Joe and the bosun accommodated in a room hard by, I offered to convey Monsieur Duguay-Trouin's message myself to his lieutenant, saying that I should be charmed to make the acquaintance of the deputy of so renowned a seaman. The *maire* took this as a great mark of condescension. Accordingly I went down to the jetty, not far below the *maire's* house, and accosting the officer in charge, a rough-spun seaman, I gave him the message, and then bantered him in a tone of good humor.

"So the English have been too much for you this time, lieutenant," I said. "It is Benbow, they say; a terrible fire eater, is he not?"

"Bah!" exclaimed the Frenchman. "Let him beware. He is no match for Duguay-Trouin, and we'll beat him again as we have done before, never fear."

"But they say he is bottling up St. Malo," I said.

"So he is," he replied with a laugh: "and while he is bottling up St. Malo we shall slip by to Havre; trust Duguay for that."

I asked him how the prizes had been captured, and he launched forth into a long and vainglorious account (why must the French always boast of their successes?). I affected to be greatly impressed by his tale of daring, and invited him to sup with me, so that I might hear more of his adventures at length. As I had guessed, he replied, regretfully, that he could not leave the vessel.

"I am not to be balked," I said. "I have set my heart upon it: one does not get every day the opportunity of hearing of these glorious exploits at first hand. If you cannot come to supper, then supper shall come to you. Monsieur Duguay-Trouin would not object, I presume, to my bringing a little entertainment on board."

"My faith, no," replied the officer, taking this as a high compliment. "I shall be charmed. I only regret that I cannot invite you, monsieur, but our cook, together with all the crew but four, is on shore for a spell, and I have no means of providing a repast worthy of a gallant captain."

I returned in haste to the *maire*, and informed the *maire* that I should share my supper with the lieutenant, who had not enjoyed a meal fit for a Frenchman for three weeks. The *maire* could raise no reasonable objection, though I doubt not, being economical, he grudged this extra demand upon his hospitality. As for me, I had no scruples at getting, at the King's expense, the best meal possible at such short notice.

While it was preparing, I explained my design to Joe and the bosun. They assented to it with enthusiasm; it was one that mightily pleased them as sailormen; and appealed as much to their sense of humor as to their love of daring.

When the supper was ready, I told off two of the three deserters, with Joe and the bosun, to carry it down to the brig on tables made of boards, each laid on two muskets. The lieutenant received me with open arms, and led me immediately to the captain's cabin. Having placed the viands on the table, the two deserters returned to the deck, to fraternize with the French crew. The other two I kept, ostensibly to wait at table; and I remarked to the lieutenant on their willingness to do their duty in spite of their wounds, of which I gave him a brief explanation.

It was already becoming dusk; we had no time to lose if my design was to succeed, for with the imminent arrival of Duguay-Trouin our fate was sealed.

Chapter 19
I Fight Duguay-Trouin

I had brought wine on board, but before a bottle was opened I said, with a wink at the lieutenant:

"I fear this wine of the country will taste somewhat thin after English rum, monsieur."

"We have a great quantity of it in the hold, monsieur," he said laughing, "and with your leave I will order my men to broach a cask."

He shouted his command to the men on deck. Instantly Joe, who was behind him, threw his arm round the officer's neck, thrust a gag into his mouth, and with the bosun's aid deftly tied his arms and legs together. Then all three of us ran up the companion way. In obedience to the lieutenant's command two of the men had gone forward and were descending through the open hatchway into the hold. While the deserters held the rest of the men in talk, the bosun strolled carelessly after the two, and as soon as they had disappeared, quietly clapped on the hatch and battened it down. Meanwhile Joe and I joined the group at the bulwarks, without awakening suspicion among the crew. At a signal from me the men tripped them up, and in another two minutes they were lying gagged and bound on the deck.

It was scarcely ten minutes since we came on board, and we had done everything without the least noise to alarm the town. Then, leaving the deserters to guard the ship, I returned in all haste with the others to the *maire*.

"What shall we do with our prisoners, Joe?" I asked, as we hurried along.

"Leave 'em locked up, sir, and lock the *maire* up with them in case of accidents."

"But I think we will bring the captain and the sergeant," I said. "You see, they have got our clothes."

"But these are better, sir," he replied, "and you make a rare fine captain, smite my timbers if you don't."

"Still, we will bring them; a taste of prison may do the captain, at any rate, a world of good."

And so, when we got to the *mairie*, I unlocked the door where the prisoners were confined, told my comrades in a few words what had happened, and bade them go forth into the street, when Joe and the bosun had loosed their bands and hasten to the harbor.

The *maire*, learning that I had returned, had followed me in, and hearing these words of English, and seeing Joe and the bosun untying the cords, he cried to me to know what I was about. The bosun instantly laid hands on him and began to truss him up. He gave one shout of alarm, which Joe deftly checked with a gag made of the bandage he had stripped from his head, and then he was laid on the floor beside the Frenchmen. Then we seized the captain and sergeant, and having locked the door again, marched them among us at a brisk pace to the harbor and on to the brig.

"Now, man, we have no time to lose," I said, as we stepped aboard. "'Tis nearly dark, and Doggy-Trang, as you call him, may return any minute. Luckily the tide is fast ebbing.

"Cast off, Joe; Bosun, run up the sail. And we are only just in time. Here they come."

And indeed we had escaped only by the skin of our teeth, for I saw a number of French seamen coming down the streets and a horseman behind them. No doubt it was Duguay-Trouin himself, and his coming had caused his men to turn out of the cabarets. The brig was already moving from the jetty; the practised hands of my comrades were at work with the sails; and as the vessel slipped away quickly on the ebbing tide, from sheer lightheartedness and pleasure at the success of our trick they made the welkin ring with their cheers.

I was as hilarious as they. The Frenchmen were crowding on the jetty, shouting, cursing, actually screaming to us to come back. I mounted the bulwarks, and, clinging to the shrouds, took off my hat (or rather the captain's) and waved it gaily towards Duguay-Trouin, who, having dismounted, had pushed through his men, and was evidently angrily demanding an explanation of the extraordinary scene he had arrived in time to witness. The townsfolk and fishers were flocking down now in great numbers; the shouting increased to a veritable pandemonium, and as we scudded away farther and farther into the growing darkness I heard the scurrying of feet on the cobble stones and the creaking of blocks as the sails were run up on the smacks in the harbor.

They were going to pursue us, then! I laughed aloud. With nine good English tars aboard an English brig I thought I could snap my fingers at Duguay-Trouin in a smack.

But there was one danger, which, after the flush of jubilation had died down, I was quick to appreciate. Duguay-Trouin's privateer was lying off the point a few miles northward, and if, in answer to a signal, she were to join in the chase, I saw that our chances of getting away were small enough. Even as the thought struck me, two musket shots were fired from the harbor. These were doubtless a signal, but they could scarcely convey any real information: the capture of the brig at its moorings was too unlikely a thing to have been provided against. But the shots would set the privateer on the alert, and we must run no risks of encountering her. So, instead of running straight out into the channel, we stood away up the coast, keeping the brig close-hauled. She proved somewhat slow in working to windward, but we were now almost totally enveloped in darkness, and by hugging the shore were not so likely to be descried from the privateer as if we ran out to sea.

Unluckily this gave the pursuers some advantage of us. Looking in our wake, I by and by discerned three smacks in full chase, and perceived that they were steadily overhauling us. The brig carried a brass gun, and I thought it well to get her ready for use, though I was determined not to fire save in extremity, since the flash would apprise the privateer of our direction and bring her on our track. But the distance between us and the leading smack grew less and less, and knowing that we dare not allow them to close in upon us (for doubtless their crews vastly outnumbered ours and would overpower us if they got the chance to board), I at length, when our enemy was within about half a cable's length of us, called to the bosun to fire, aiming to hull her just below water line.

He set his match to the touch hole, and the round shot flew forth. I could not tell whether the smack was hit or not, but 'twas clear that she had suffered little or no damage, for she came on as fast as ever. The bosun reloaded in all haste, and fired again when she could not have been above fifty yards distant. This time I knew the shot had struck her, but she still came on, and as she was now below our line of fire I feared it would come to push of pike after all. But a moment or two afterwards I rejoiced to see that she was losing way: our shot had gone home. The other two smacks overtook her, and then began a dropping fire of musketry from all three.

Clearly it was no longer expedient to hull them merely. Their speed was so much superior to the brig's that even if we hit one or other of them they might close in before their pace was much checked by the inrush of water.

Loath as I was to spill blood, I bade the bosun now load the gun with grape, and my qualms were banished when I heard cries of pain, and learned that Runnles and another had been hit by musket shots. The smack that was leading was coming up directly in our wake.

"Give it her, Bosun!" I cried.

"She shall have it," he answered, and immediately she was swept by the grape shot from stem to stern, yells and execrations telling that the bosun had not aimed in vain. She at once paid off before the wind: 'twas clear the steersman had been hit; and before another man could take his place and bring her head round the smack behind crashed into her.

I had good hope that the chase was now ended, and we might go rejoicing on our way to the white shores of England. But I was reckoning without Duguay-Trouin. For a few moments we drew away from our pursuers; but then I saw that the third smack had cleared herself from the one she had run into and was again sailing swiftly in our wake, having apparently suffered no injury. The bosun had already re-charged the gun with grape, but when he fired, at a range which forbade the possibility of missing, there were only one or two cries instead of the chorus we had heard before.

"Burst me if they be not lying down in the bottom," said Joe, standing at my side, "and the shot have passed clean over them."

"And 'tis no good firing again," I said. "We can't depress the gun enough to hull her or hit the men, and the shot will only cut holes in the rigging. Would we had tried round shot and brought down her mast."

"'Tis all hands to repel boarders now," returned Joe, "and there'll be a few broken heads afore we are done."

Runnles meanwhile had had the good sense and the ready wit to load three muskets apiece from the ship's armory. We each of us took one, having the other two in reserve at our feet. The smack came on bravely, and I could now see that her deck was swarming with men. She had deflected somewhat from her straight course, and was coming up on our larboard quarter, whither we hastened to meet the attempt to board us. In another minute the vessels touched, and a few shots were fired from the smack, but without damage to us, for the impact had set her rocking, so that 'twas impossible for the Frenchmen to take good aim. Next moment they threw grapnels into our rigging, and the vessels were locked together.

The whole of our company, save Dilly at the wheel, was spread along the bulwarks, and at my word twelve muskets sped their slugs among the men endeavoring to swarm up our side. There were cries and groans enough now, and not merely from the enemy, for while the foremost of them was attempting to board, others beyond fired at us, and I knew from the bosun's bellow of rage that he for one had been hit. We snatched up a second musket each, but before we could turn to fire them, three of the Frenchmen had gained a footing on our deck.

Making a rush for these, we shoved them by main force back over the side, only just in time to meet another group who had scrambled up. It was no longer possible to fire. We clubbed our muskets and dealt about us lustily, cheers and yells and groans mingling in a babel the like of which I had never heard before. I reckoned that there were at least three Frenchmen to every one of us, and Duguay-Trouin was with them; I heard his voice shouting encouragement. 'Twas lucky that their deck was lower than ours, for if we had been level I doubt not we had soon been overpowered by the weight of numbers. But they, being below us, and crowded to boot, could not use their superiority to advantage, and though they did what mortal men might to get at us, we beat them back time after time.

Joe, beside me, was a host in himself. 'Twas clear fighting and not coopering was the trade he was born to; he cut and thrust and jabbed and smote with his musket, and more than once drove a Frenchman backward by mere shoving with his mighty shoulders, breathing hard, shouting loving farewells to the men he heaved into the smack or the sea, some of them, I fear, never to fight again. But in truth we all fought with might and main; we knew how much depended on the issue.

And let no Englishman ever despise the French as an enemy, as 'tis the fashion with some vainglorious folk to do. I have fought them, and I know, and I say they are gallant fighters, and as brave as men can be.

How long the light continued I could not tell; but all at once, as it seemed to me, the enemy disappeared; there was no one in front of me to hit.

"Fling off the grappling irons," I shouted, and in a trice we disengaged them and cast them back whence they came. The two vessels broke apart, and though ere we had left the smack behind, a volley of bullets fell among us, hitting three of our men, and giving me a burning wound in the leg, the fight was over. We hailed our victory with a true English cheer, and I own I felt no little pride in having worsted so renowned a captain as Duguay-Trouin.

But I was by no means sure that we were wholly out of peril. The sound of firing must have been heard for miles around, and we could not tell but that Duguay-Trouin's own vessel, and maybe others, too, were making sail towards us. Dilly had now set the course of the vessel due north, but the wind was against us, and we had still many hours to sail before we gained the open Channel. A big red moon was peering above the horizon, and (having stanched my wound and done what was possible for my comrades who were hurt, none seriously, thank God!) I looked anxiously for signs of vessels.

By and by, as the light increased with the whitening moon, I did indeed behold a large vessel under full sail beating towards us, and I made no doubt 'twas Duguay-Trouin's privateer. The bosun said her course would bring her athwart ours, and I felt how barren our late victory would prove if she came to grips with us. 'Twas clear she was outsailing us, and the seasoned mariners among my comrades foretold that in a couple of hours we should be at her mercy.

We had spread all the canvas we could carry, and could only wait and hope. I sat on a coil of rope, suffering much pain from my wound, and trembling with anxiety as I watched the vessel drawing nearer and nearer. A shifting of the wind helped us to mend our pace a little; two hours, three hours, four hours passed, and still the enemy had not come within range of us. And then, as day began to dawn, I gave up hope, foreseeing a speedy end to the chase and an enforced surrender.

But a cry from Runnles, who had gone aloft, raised my drooping spirits.

"Four sail, sir, on the larboard bow," he shouted.

I sprang up (forgetting my wounded leg), and looked eagerly across the sea. By and by I discovered four vessels of a large size bearing down upon us from the west. Whether friend or foe I could not tell until I saw the privateer change her course and at last head directly back towards the shore. Then a great shout of thankfulness broke from the throats of us tired men. We could no longer doubt that these were English ships, and we were alive with excitement when we saw two of them part from the others and go in chase of the privateer. Would they catch her? We forgot our fatigue and wounds, so fascinated were we in watching the pursuit, and the other two vessels were within hailing distance of us almost before we were aware. English colors were now flying at our masthead, and a voice through a speaking trumpet called to know who we were.

"The brig Polly of Southampton," roared the bosun in reply, "run a-truant from Doggy-Trang. And who be you?

"Ads bobs, sir," he added in a breath to me, "there be a white flag at her fore topmast."

"What's that mean?" I asked.

But I had my answer from the other vessel.

"The frigate Gloucester, with Admiral Benbow aboard."

And then Joe Punchard danced a pirouette ('twas a comical sight, he being so bandy), and shouted:

"'Tis my captain, my captain, dash my bowlines and binnacle."

And he caught the arm of one of the deserters, and danced him round the deck till he was dizzy.

Chapter 20
The King's Commission

I have had many happy moments in my life, but none happier, I do think, than when Admiral Benbow clapped me on the shoulder and cried, in his big quarterdeck voice:

"Why, my lad, we must have you a middy, and you shall serve the King."

I was in the admiral's own cabin on the Gloucester, whither I had been taken when my wound was dressed. Mr. Benbow and the captain were both there, and to them I had to tell my story, from the time of my setting forth from Shrewsbury to the late fight with Duguay-Trouin. Some little concernments of my own (the fight with Topper in the barn, and my rescue of Mistress Lucy on the highroad) I kept to myself, but the rest of my adventures I related as I have set them down here, though, to be sure, more shortly. The officers found much entertainment in my narrative, and in particular they were mightily tickled at the notion of escaped prisoners capturing themselves. The admiral was good enough to speak in high praise of my doings (far beyond my deserts), and then he told me that though he could not himself make a midshipman without a warrant from a higher power, he would use his interest in my behoof, and had no doubt that all would fall out as I most ardently desired.

I had to wear my leg in a sling for a week or more, but then I got about as nimbly as ever. In all but name I was a junior midshipman, for the admiral said I must learn betimes the duties of the rank which was to be mine as soon as he could compass it. And I set about doing so with zest, for I was now turned eighteen, and there were boys in my mess four years younger who were veterans in seamanship and ship drill compared with me.

My messmates welcomed me with much kindness; while I was laid up of my wound they had heard of my adventures from Joe Punchard, who was a prime favorite aboard; and they all declared they wished they had had my luck, though they agreed with me when I reminded them that a nine months' imprisonment was after all a long price to pay. They told me

I should certainly get a good share of prize money for the recapture of the Polly of Southampton, and probably also for the other prize of Duguay-Trouin's that was retaken. The two frigates sent in chase of the privateer had failed to come up with her, but they had seized the prize lying off the point, which proved to be an Indiaman richly laden.

The knowledge that I should soon have some money of my own was very grateful to me, and I felt a natural elation of spirits at the wonderful change that had come over my fortunes.

I hoped that while I was on the admiral's ship I should see and take my part in a good set battle between our squadron and the French; but in this I was disappointed. Admiral Benbow was on his way to Dunkirk, to lie in wait for the French admiral Du Bart and pursue him if he should put to sea. We cruised off the port for upwards of a month without any encounter with the enemy; and when at last, towards the end of August, we gave chase to some of their vessels which had slipped out, we failed to overtake any of them save a small privateer of ten guns, which struck her colors on the first demand we made.

And then in September we learned that peace was proclaimed. The treaty about whose terms the diplomatists had been wrangling for seven or eight months had at last been signed at Ryswick, and the war was at an end. But none of the officers believed that the peace would endure. 'Twas impossible, they said, that Dutch William would ever be a friend of French Lewis, and they prognosticated that the lifelong struggle between the two kings would yet be fought out to a bitter end.

Regarding war, as did all lads of my age, rather as a stage for the display of gallantry and prowess than as the dreadful scourge it really is, I wished for nothing better than that I should soon have an opportunity of serving under the brave admiral. He was already a hero to me, and not to me only. All the world knows of his courage and daring and skill, but only those who were closely connected with him know the full worth of that great-hearted man. The sailors loved him. He would go and sit down with them in the foc'sle, chatting with them rather like a brother than a high officer, yet without loss of dignity or respect. Bravery and seamanship he rated at their true value, whether in peer or peasant; but he never could abide the fops and fine gentlemen who thought they became officers merely by donning epaulets. With them he had no patience, and in consequence he was as much hated as loved. The tars were his to a man: but the officers were either his dear friends or his bitter foes.

Towards the end of September we ran into Portsmouth harbor, and the ships were then paid off. I learned that some time must elapse before the prize money was distributed: but being eager to get back to Shrewsbury and see my good friend and especially to acquaint Captain Galsworthy with my wondrous good fortune, I was glad to accept the advance of twenty pounds which the admiral offered me when I told him of my wish. I spent five pounds in buying a befitting suit of clothes, devoting much care to the cloth and the cut. The admiral laughed when I went to take leave of him, and jokingly said that he hoped I was not going to shame him by turning into a beau and a lady-killer.

"I smoke you, by gad!" he cried with another laugh, when to my confusion I felt my cheeks go warm.

And the truth of it is I had determined to pay a visit to Mr. Allardyce on my way home, and the wish to cut a different figure from that in which I had first appeared to the ladies of his family had entered not a little into the consideration of my new garments. Why do I say "the ladies"? Let me be honest and say 'twas Mistress Lucy I had in my mind.

There was no question of tramping to Shrewsbury afoot. I took passage to Bristowe in a coasting vessel, and there, after having a chat with old Woodrow (who told me that his friend Captain Reddaway had sworn to shew me a rope's end for deceiving him if I ever came athwart his hawser), I booked a seat in the new diligence that ran between Bristowe and Worcester, and there indulged myself in the luxury of a postchaise for the journey to the Hall. And I warrant you I was as proud as a peacock when the chaise swung in at the gate, and rattled up the drive to the door.

'Twas Susan who opened it. She stared at me for a moment, then burst out a-giggling, and left me standing while she rushed into the house with a cry of "Measter, here be Joe come back, dressed like a lord!"

"The deuce he is!" came the answering roar, and down came Mr. Allardyce, pipe in hand, with his wife and Mistress Lucy close behind him.

"How d'ye do, sir?" says I, advancing, feeling my face glow with pleasure at seeing my kind friends again as much as any other emotion, I am sure.

"Come back for a job, Joe?" cries Mr. Allardyce, gripping my hand heartily. "Ah! you impostor! We know all about you, you young dog, don't we, madam? Joe! Humph!"

"You can't shorten it like that, sir," said I, laughing, and giving a hand to the ladies in turn.

And I don't know whether 'twas due to the suit of clothes, but certainly I felt, as I shook hands with Mistress Lucy, none of the shamefaced awkwardness that had overcome me when I stood before her in rags and she called me "poor man."

They had me into the room where I had begged work of Mr. Allardyce, and despatched Susan (still giggling) to bespeak a meal of Martha the cook.

"And you must give an account of yourself, Mr. Bold," says Mr. Allardyce, putting out a chair for me and pushing a pipe into my hand.

"With all my heart, sir," said I, "but first will you please enlighten me as to how you know my name?"

"Why we learned it a month after you left us," he replied. "'Twas Roger found it out.

"He is not here, hang it!" he said, his face falling a little. "We could not keep him at home after you had gone, and now he's carrying an ensign in the foot regiment of General Webb.

"Well, 'twas he found out all about you. Having set his heart on going into the army, he must needs go into Shrewsbury to take lessons in fencing from a Captain Galsworthy he had heard of. And it appears that during his very first bout with the captain he tried a *botte* that you had taught him. The captain drops his point, and stares a moment, and then cries 'Ads my life! The only man in the world that knows that *botte* besides myself is Humphrey Bold. Where in the name of Beelzebub did you learn it?' And so it all came out, and the whole story of the villainous doings of those Cluddes and Lawyer Vetch--"

"Stay, sir," I interrupted; "Mr. Vetch is a very dear friend of mine, and I would lay my life he is innocent of any share of the trickery that lost me my father's lands."

"Maybe, maybe: I know the story of the will," said Mr. Allardyce. "Roger was wild with excitement when he came back, and nothing would satisfy him but that he must go to Bristowe and see if he could learn any news of you. But he could learn nothing, and--"

"My dear," says Mistress Allardyce at this point, "you are keeping us waiting so long. Lucy and I want to hear Mr. Bold."

"That's an extinguisher," cries he with a jolly laugh.

"Light my pipe, Lucy, my dear; it will last a good half hour, and maybe that will be long enough for Mr. Bold's story."

But in truth he had smoked another couple of pipes before I had finished, and gave no heed to Susan when she appeared at the door and said that my meal was ready. I have heard that a speaker's eloquence depends much upon his hearers and the bond of sympathy betwixt him and them, and sure I spoke with a freedom that surprised me. Certainly no man was ever better favored in his audience; Mr. Allardyce let his pipe go out more than once. And the ladies hung on my words, Mistress Lucy sitting forward in her chair, her lips parted, her eyes kindling, and a ruddy glow suffusing her cheeks. The room rang with Mr. Allardyce's laughter when I described our march across country with the gagged Frenchmen, and I vow I could almost hear the beating of Mistress Lucy's heart as I told of our fight with Duguay-Trouin.

When I had ended my tale, Mr. Allardyce tugged at the bell rope, crying:

"Egad, we must drink the health of Mr. Midshipman Bold," and when Susan appeared, with surprising celerity (I believe the minx had been listening at the door) he roared at her for keeping me waiting so long a-fasting.

"And what do you think of that, Lucy?" he cries, turning to his niece. "Didst ever hear such a tale of ups and downs and derring do?"

"I *love* Joe Punchard," said Mistress Lucy, and that set her uncle a-laughing again, though I confess it somewhat mystified me.

My kind friends insisted that I should stay the night with them, and we sat up talking to a late hour. I longed to ask how things stood in the matter of the guardianship of Mistress Lucy, but the subject was ignored by tacit consent so long as the ladies were in the room. When they had retired, however, Mr. Allardyce drew his chair alongside of mine, and said:

"Humphrey, I am worried out of my life. We are almost in a state of siege here. Ever since that attempt at kidnapping Lucy that you so happily frustrated I have never felt easy about her. She never goes forth unattended now: those morning rides are at an end. I have taken two more menservants to act as special guard for her, and they two, or myself and one of them, always accompany her, with well primed pistols, I warrant you. Men have been seen at various times lurking about here, and I have taken pains to track them, and went so far as to commit one of them for loitering with intent to commit a felony. But I had no proof, and an attorney fellow in Shrewsbury named Moggridge threatened me with all sorts of pains and penalties if I did not at once release the villain."

"But what does the law say to it, sir?" I asked.

"The law is uncommon slow to say anything, confound it! My lawyer in Bridgenorth was at first all for an accommodation, as he called it; he wanted me to make terms with that rogue Cludde, and a host of letters passed between him and Moggridge, who is Cludde's attorney. But that failed; of course it did, since I wouldn't give way, and now my man has filed a bill in chancery to make Lucy a ward of court, with me as her guardian. The other side is opposing, and the case will not come on till next sessions and maybe not then. My man says we are bound to win, the court, as he declares, being very jealous of the rights of minors, especially where property is concerned. But meanwhile we live in constant fear of the girl being carried off, and if they once get her there will be precious little chance of getting her back."

"Can we not imprison Dick Cludde for the former attempt?" I suggested. "Now that I am back I could give evidence against him."

"He is away with his ship, and will be careful, you may be sure, not to show his nose again in these parts while there is any danger."

"But the other fellow, Vetch--has he been seen hereabouts? I have often wondered what became of him after he left prison."

"What is he like?"

"A tall, thin, weasel-faced fellow, with a sour look."

"No, I have not seen or heard of him."

"If I could hear of his whereabouts I would have him arrested for his complicity in my kidnapping. I own I should feel more secure of Mistress Lucy's safety if I knew he was laid by the heels. Could you give me a warrant, sir, which I could execute if ever I met him?"

"I will certainly do so, though I doubt if he'll ever give you the opportunity. Villains of his stamp are uncommonly clever in running to earth. But you shall have the warrant."

"I shall see his uncle tomorrow," I said. "May I mention Mistress Lucy's affairs to him? He was accounted a good lawyer until that unhappy business of my father's will, and as he has no reason to love the Cluddes, or his nephew either, I am sure he would give the best advice he knows."

"Do so, by all means; 'twill be some comfort to know that my man is taking the right course."

We sat till near midnight, and Mr. Allardyce recovered something of his usual good spirits before I rose to say good night. As he shook hands with me he broke into a sudden laugh.

"Egad!" he cried, "I had forgot to ask you whether you still have that crown piece you were so loath to part with."

"Indeed I have," I said, laughing too. "It is slung about my neck, and there it will remain until I return it with interest to Dick Cludde."

"Dick Cludde!" says he. "What! is he concerned in that, too?"

And then I told him what I had hitherto kept to myself--that incident upon the road when Cludde flung the coin at me.

"On my life, Humphrey," he said, "I should not care to have you for an enemy."

And then we parted.

I left next morning, promising to see my friends as often as possible before I received the summons which I hoped for from Admiral Benbow. Mr. Allardyce lent me one of his horses, which he was kind enough to place at my service while I remained at home. In my breast pocket I carried a warrant in due form for the arrest of Cyrus Vetch.

There was a great surprise awaiting me at Shrewsbury. I asked the little maid who answered my knock at Mr. Vetch's door for Mistress Pennyquick, and felt some astonishment that the door had not been opened by the good dame herself, for she had no maid when I left her, doing all the housework herself. The girl stared at me.

"Is Mistress Pennyquick within?" I repeated.

"No, sir: but would you like to see Mistress Vetch?"

I was minded to refuse, and thought of going on to Mr. Vetch's offices where I knew I should find him at this time of day. I felt a certain annoyance at Mr. Vetch marrying ('twas unreasonable, I admit), and wondered whether poor old Becky had been dismissed, or was dead. But while I stood hesitating, I heard the well-remembered voice from the interior of the house--"Tell the man the coffee is not fit to drink, and if I have any more of it I'll say goodby to Mr. Huggins and see if Mr. Martin can serve me better."

"What, Becky!" I cried; "d'you think I'm a grocer's boy after all?"

There was a scream, and my old friend came flying towards me, her cap (with lilac trimmings) shaken askew by her haste.

"Oh, my boy!" she cried, flinging her arms about me. "Drat the girl!

"How many times have I told you to ask visitors into the parlor!

"Oh, my dear, precious boy!"

"'Tis not her fault," I said, giving the good creature an answering hug; "I asked for Mistress Pennyquick."

"Which my name is Vetch, and has been for six months come Saturday. He would have it so, though I told him Vetch wasn't a name to my taste. But there! What was a poor lone widow to do? A lawyer have got such a tongue!"

"You look ten years younger, Becky," I said.

"I feel it, Humphrey," she said solemnly, and then bade the maid set wine and biscuits in the parlor, and never to forget to ask a gentleman in instead of keeping him at the door, gaping like a ninny!

Of course I had to tell my story to her, and again to Mr. Vetch when he came home to dinner. The lawyer looked much the same as when I left him, save that he was certainly neater in his dress. He was delighted to see me, and when he heard of the good fortune that had befallen me in gaining the interest of Mr. Benbow he declared that I had taken a load off his mind, for he had always been oppressed with the fear that the loss of the will had ruined me. His business, I was glad to hear, was a trifle better than when I was with him, though it would never be what it had been.

"Fiddlesticks!" said his wife. "You have no spirit, Mr. Vetch, and what you would be if I didn't keep you up, the Lord alone knows."

I will not dwell on my visit to Captain Galsworthy. He was looking older, I thought: but after I had told him my adventures, nothing would satisfy him but that we should have a bout with the foils. I was careful to let the good old man get the better of me, and when we had finished he shook his head and declared that my skill had declined.

"But we'll get it back, we'll get it back," he said. "You must come to me for half an hour every day, and we'll soon rub off the rust."

He told me of the six months' lessons he had given Roger Allardyce, and foretold a creditable career for that young soldier, not so much for any sign of military aptitude in him (though the captain owned he had the making of a good swordsman) as because he had doggedly refused to say anything about me. He knew, I suppose, that I should not wish the tale of my mischances to be told by any lips but my own, and could not have pleased the captain more than by declining to answer his questions. I never knew a man nicer than Captain Galsworthy on the point of honor.

I remained about a month in Shrewsbury, seeing old friends, among them Nelly Hind and Mistress Punchard, whom I rejoiced with news of their brother and son, and paying many visits to my newer friends at the Hall. I was able to assure Mr. Allardyce that the procedure of his lawyer had the full approval of Mr. Vetch, who was careful to say, when giving his opinion, that it was given in a private capacity and without prejudice to his brother in the profession.

One day I received through the post a letter with a great red seal. I tore it open eagerly, and could scarcely believe in my good fortune when I saw it was nothing less than a lieutenant's commission in the King's navy, accompanied by an order to join my ship the Falmouth, Captain Samuel Vincent, at Portsmouth, as soon as might be. I had not expected to be rated higher than a midshipman, though when I had mentioned that to Mistress Vetch, she tossed her head and declared she had looked for nothing else.

"Midshipmen, as I have heard tell," she said, "are but little boys fresh from their nurses' apron strings, and the King had the good sense to know that you are too tall for any such childishness."

"I don't suppose the King knows anything about me," I said laughing.

"That I will never believe; the King knows everything," said the simple creature.

You may be sure I rode off at once with my great news to the Hall, and received very hearty congratulations there. But I could see that Mr. Allardyce was in some perturbation of mind, and by and by he took me aside and said:

"That weasel-faced rascal you spoke of was seen about here yesterday, Humphrey. One of my men told me that he saw such a man as you described in close talk with a low innkeeper in Morville. I have not acquainted the ladies; 'tis no use alarming them; but I don't like it, my boy."

This was a mighty disconcerting piece of news, especially now that I was on the point of going away for I knew not how long. While I remained within close call I flattered myself on being an efficient protector of Mistress Lucy, and I had that warrant always in my pocket to use against Cyrus Vetch if ever I set eyes on him. And now I would willingly have resigned my commission, dearly as I prized it, if I could have found any reasonable ground for remaining to defend her still. But I knew 'twas impossible, if for no other reason, because I was little more than a pauper, having indeed only enough of my twenty pounds left to carry me to Portsmouth. So I could only fume inwardly, and long that war might break out again, and that I might capture many of the enemy's vessels, and win heaps of money and early promotion to the rank of post captain, and return with my laurels thick upon me to lay all at Lucy's feet. You may smile at such ambitions in a youngster; but can you truly say you have not dreamed such dreams yourself?

'Twas with a full heart I set off in the dusk of evening to ride back to Shrewsbury. I rode slowly, my mind being filled with forebodings, and I was only roused from my preoccupation by the sudden appearance of a horseman at the turning of a byroad leading from Bridgenorth. He was riding rapidly, and we both reined up at the same moment to avoid a collision. And at that moment my heart leapt with furious exultation as, in the fading light, I recognized my old enemy, and my friends', Cyrus Vetch.

"Hold, you villain!" I cried, pulling my horse against his and drawing my sword. "I have you now, and you will come into Shrewsbury with me."

Fear struggled with anger in his face. He was in no mind to show himself in Shrewsbury, where there was that matter of his uncle's cash box to answer for, to say nothing of a matter more nearly concerning me. But he could not pass me, and seeing that there was no other way out of it he whips out his sword and deals a savage cut at me. I easily parried the stroke, and not being disposed to spare him, I ran my own weapon under his guard (he having no skill in sword play), and through the fleshy part of his right arm, so that he cried out with the pain, his sword dropping to the ground.

"Now, sirrah," says I, "you will ride before me into Shrewsbury, to which you have been overlong a stranger."

"I will not," he cries, with a scream of rage. "'Who are you to order my goings?"

"No matter as to that: we will see where the right lies when we get to the town. And since I have no wish to cheat the hangman, I will tie my kerchief round your arm."

He raged and swore at me as I made the bandage, but was helpless, and soon I had him riding at a foot pace in front of me, he knowing very well that he could not escape, wounded as he was, without risk of being thrown from his horse.

I had a comfortable sense of satisfaction as I rode behind him, my eyes fixed on his back. He had much to answer for, and any one of his crimes would send him to the plantations. Then I remembered that he was Lawyer Vetch's nephew, and thought of the good old man's grief when he should see his flesh and blood in the felon's dock. And the idea came to me that by merely holding over him the threat of punishment for his undoubted villainies we might draw from him a confession of what we only suspected--his theft of my father's will. I did not reflect for the moment that Mr. Allardyce would have something to say in that matter, and already saw myself reinstated in my father's property (though I meant to cleave to my new profession), when suddenly I noticed that Vetch was swaying in the saddle. Thinking him overcome with faintness from his wound, I cantered up to assist him, but just as I reached him he suddenly pulled his horse across the road, and I saw a pistol in his left hand. While I was ruminating he had quickly unbuttoned the holsters, which I had stupidly neglected to examine.

Immediately I wrenched my horse aside. The sudden pull caused it to rear, and the poor beast received the shot intended for me, and fell to the ground. I was up in an instant, but Vetch was already galloping madly away, leaving me by the side of Mr. Allardyce's dying horse.

To pursue the fellow afoot would be but a fool's errand. The spot at which this mischance happened being about a mile from Oldbury, my best plan seemed to be to ride thither and hire a horse at the inn and then ride back to the Hall and acquaint Mr. Allardyce with what had befallen me. This I did, and found my friend much less vexed at the loss of his horse (though 'twas a noble animal) than at the escape of Vetch. He sent off a man at once to Bridgenorth to ask his lawyer to raise a hue and cry after the fugitive, and promised to take like measures in Shrewsbury. I spoke of it to the town authorities and to Captain Galsworthy, and since I was leaving on the morrow, he agreed to enlist some of his old pupils in the business, who would ride here and there about the neighborhood and try to track Vetch down. And thus, having done all I could, I set off next day once more for Bristowe, to take ship for Portsmouth.

Chapter 21
I Meet Dick Cludde

Captain Samuel Vincent gave me a reception warm indeed, but not in the way of kindness. After making me repeat my name, he asked me under what captain I had served as a midshipman, and when I said that I had never been a midshipman, and was proceeding to explain the manner of my appointment he cut me short.

"Not a midshipman!" he cried, running together all three syllables of the word. "You bin to school, I s'pose?"

"Yes, indeed," I said, "at Shrewsbury."

"Now hark to me," he cries, again interrupting me. "I never went to no school, and I hain't got no philosophies nor any other useless cargoes in my hold, nor Mr. Benbow neither; and if ever you say a word against Mr. Benbow you'll wish you wasn't Humphrey, nor Bold, 'cos you'll wish as how you'd never bin born. I bid you good mornin'."

I left him, in a fine heat of resentment, thinking that a few years at Shrewsbury school might have improved both his language and his manners. But when I came to know him better, and to understand the motive of his rough address to me, I forgave the bluff seaman heartily. He was a keen partisan in the feud that then divided the navy, the one faction being for Benbow, the other against him; and being ignorant of my antecedents, he supposed from my not having been a midshipman that I was one of the fine gentlemen who were foisted on the King's service by their high connections and despised plain seamen of the Benbow school. I might have undeceived him very soon had I so pleased, but I thought it best to win his approval by the manner in which I performed my duties, leaving the other matter to time. As it happened, my fidelity to Mr. Benbow was shown very clearly before long.

'Twould be a dull story to relate the trivial incidents of my first year of service in the navy. I spent five months at sea, and seven on shore, and Captain Vincent being a martinet. I had to work hard for my pay of four shillings a day (on shore it was cut down to two shillings). My diligence in studying navigation pleased him; and when a little affair in which I had been concerned came to his ears, he took me, in a sense, to his heart.

I had gone one day with Lieutenant Venables, of our ship, into a coffee house in Portsmouth, whither the officers of the fleet much resorted. The first man I set eyes on was Dick Cludde, who was, as I learned afterwards, a lieutenant of the Defiance, which had lately come into port. With him was his captain ('twas the Captain Kirkby I had seen in the inn at Harley), also Captain Cooper Wade, of the Greenwich, Captain Hudson of the Pendennis, and a number of junior officers.

Cludde greeted me with a puzzled stare; 'twas clear he had not heard of the change in my fortunes, and maybe believed me to be still scouring the cook's slush pans aboard the Dolphin privateer. I saw him turn to Lieutenant Simpson, of the Pendennis, who knew me, and guessed by the quick glance Simpson gave me that Cludde had asked him concerning my appearance there.

Venables and I sat down to our coffee, and 'twas not long before we knew, by the loud voices of the others, that they had laced theirs with rum, or maybe were pretty well filled with wine to begin with. And, as it always happened when officers of the fleet met together, they were soon hot upon the subject of Mr. Benbow, his rough manners, his rustic speech, and his outrageous lack of respect for his betters. After a little of this talk Venables says to me:

"Come, Bold, we are better away from this."

"You are right," says I, and we both rose and put on our hats.

Cludde saw the action, and, taking courage I suppose from the presence of his boon fellows, he said, in a tone loud enough to reach my ears:

"That's one of his doings. Simpson tells me that that fellow is a lieutenant on the Falmouth, through Benbow's interest; he comes from my town Shrewsbury, and a year or two ago was a charity brat, with scarce a coat to his back."

At this I swung round and took a pace or two towards the table where Cludde was seated. Though I had much ado to curb my anger, I said quietly:

"If that is true, Cludde, you know who is the cause of it."

"I did not speak to you, sirrah," says he.

"But I speak to you," I said. "You may say what you please about me; I will settle my account with you in good time; but I advise you not to say too much about Mr. Benbow, who is not here to answer for himself."

"Oho, you sneak out of it that way, do you?" says he. "I'll say what I please about Mr. Benbow without asking leave of you or any man. Benbow is a low-born scut--can you deny it? Wasn't his father a tanner, and don't his sister keep a coffee shop?"

"And what then?"

"What then? Why, this: that he ain't fit to be in the company of gentlemen," and then he told a foul story of Benbow which angered me past all endurance.

I strode up to him, and before I could be prevented I planted my fist in his face with such force that he toppled backwards over his chair and came to the floor.

"Now you can swallow that lie," I cried, standing with clenched fists over him.

I was now in the midst of a great hubbub; the officers had started from their chairs, shouting and cursing, some of them helping Cludde to his feet.

"You will answer for this, sir," says Captain Kirkby.

"With all my heart," I said. "Mr. Venables will meet Mr. Cludde's man and make the arrangements."

And with that I went from the house.

I ever regarded dueling as a barbarous and foolish way of settling a quarrel. If men must fight, let them use their fists, and so be quit of it for a bloody nose and a few bruises. But I could not avoid the duel with Cludde without suffering the imputation of cowardice, and when Venables came after me and said that he had arranged with Simpson that we should meet next morning at daybreak on the Southsea Common and settle the matter with rapiers, I was quite content. 'Tis true that ere the day was over I regretted in cool blood that things had come to this pass; but I could not think I was in the wrong, and believing myself more than a match for Cludde in swordsmanship I resolved to disarm him quickly, when his friends would no doubt declare him satisfied.

In the chill of dawn we met within sound of the surf, and having stripped to our shirts, faced each other with the length of our two swords between. Cludde was three or four inches shorter than I, but well made and muscular, and in mere strength I daresay there was little to choose between us. But after a pass or two I knew (and the knowledge surprised me not a little), that I had no mean swordsman to deal with. His riposte came quick upon my lunge; he had a very agile wrist; 'twas clear he had had much practice in a good school; and being determined not to do him a serious injury I put myself at some disadvantage and had much ado to avoid his point. He was beset by no such scruples, I could see, and would willingly have taken my life, which made my task all the harder.

Finding him thus proficient in all the ordinary tricks of sword play, I saw myself in a difficulty. I had no doubt that I could bring things to a speedy end by employing the special *botte* which Captain Galsworthy had taught me; and if we had been fencing for sport I should already have used it to disarm my adversary. But fighting as we were (at least, as he was) in deadly earnest, I could not be sure that my *botte* would not be too successful, and that, instead of merely striking his sword from his hand, I should not run him through. The caution I displayed was mistaken by him (and by his friends also, I suspect) for weakness, and gaining courage therefrom, he pressed me so hard that, unless I had gone instantly to the extremity I wished to avoid, I could not have parried the thrust which pinked me in the shoulder.

"He is hit!" cried Venables, running between us.

"You are now satisfied, Mr. Cludde?"

"If Mr. Bold will apologize," says Simpson, after a glance at his principal.

"I am ready when Mr. Cludde is," I said bluntly.

Certainly I would not apologize; besides, I was annoyed to think that, through my own forbearance, the fellow had drawn blood (though 'twas but a scratch). And so we set-to again.

This time I no longer pursued the same purely defensive tactics, and before many passes had been exchanged I saw an opening for my *botte*, took instant advantage of it, and sent his sword spinning from his hand. Cludde was too good a swordsman to be ignorant that I had purposely spared him, and I saw by the look in his eyes that he knew it and would fight no more.

"Mr. Cludde is now satisfied, I presume?" said Venables, at a look from me.

The contest was of course over. At that moment I own I felt tempted to take Cludde's crown piece from the string whereon it hung about my neck, and return it to him; but as a second thought showed me that to do so would be in a manner to heap humiliation on a beaten enemy, I forbore, conscious at the same time of an inward assurance that I should yet find a fitting time for that act of restoration.

The duel was much talked of among the officers of the fleet, and when Captain Vincent heard of it he, as I have said, took me to his heart. By it I was sealed of the tribe of Benbow, and became, in my worthy captain's eyes, one of the elect.

In October of the year 1698 we were stirred to excitement by the news that Mr. Benbow had been ordered to take a squadron to the West Indies, and there was much eager speculation among us as to the vessels which would have the good fortune to sail with him. I hoped with all my heart that the Falmouth would be one of them, for I was weary of the humdrum life of idling on shore or aimless sailing up and down the channel. The admiral's was a peaceful mission, and no fighting was expected, but I felt a great curiosity to behold new scenes. To my vast delight, when the admiral came down from London, Captain Vincent told me that the Falmouth was to be one of a squadron of four, the others being the Gloucester, the Dunkirk (both fourth rates of forty-eight guns), and a small French prize called the Germoon.

We set sail on the 29th of November, touched at Madeira to take in wine and other stores in which that bounteous isle is prolific, and after a tranquil voyage reached Barbados on the 27th of February. We proceeded to Mevis and the Leeward Islands, and steering our course thence to the continent, made the highland of St. Martha, and so to Cartagena, where we obliged the governor to deliver up two or three English merchant ships which they had seized at the time of the hapless Scotch settlement at Darien. Thence we stood away for Jamaica.

Joe Punchard (who was on board the Gloucester, having returned to his old vocation of body servant to Mr. Benbow) had prepared me, in a measure, before we left Portsmouth, for the wondrous beauty of these western isles, but I might say, as the Queen of Sheba said of the glory and grandeur of King Solomon, that "the half had not been told." I was struck dumb with admiration as we threaded our way through a narrow channel between irregular reefs lying off the harbor of Port Royal. The spacious harbor itself was a noble sight, but the background was even more picturesque--the light, two-storied houses with their piazzas painted green and white, the varying hues of the gardens, filled with palms and cocoanut trees, and the lofty minarets of the Blue Mountains, towering to a great height behind. Such scenes were a new thing to my untraveled eyes, they were in very truth the revelation of a new world to me.

Our arrival was the occasion of great festivity; all the inhabitants of Spanish Town, the capital, from the governor downward, were lavish in their hospitality; and for some days it was one round of balls and banquets, to which we came with unjaded appetites and vigor after our long voyage. And I warrant you that the officers of Collingwood's regiment then in garrison were soon mighty jealous, for the ladies of the place, English and Creole alike, preferred us naval men to them as partners. I confess I nearly lost my heart a dozen times, and the thirteenth might have been fatal, only it chanced that her name being Lucetta reminded me of a certain Mistress Lucy at home in England, whom the others had, so to speak, elbowed out of my recollection. My wandering fancy being thus recalled to her, I remembered that her estates were in Jamaica, and she had lived here during all her childhood, and then I was for seeking out the house, and assuring myself that her interests were being well guarded.

But I learned that her estates lay on the north side of the island, two good days' journey distant. They were being managed by a careful Scotchman named McTavish, who sent large and regular consignments of sugar and tobacco to the port for shipment to England. I would have gone a thousand miles to see Mistress Lucy, but had no interest in the excellent McTavish, and so I remained in Spanish Town.

After a week or two of high revelry, the admiral, yielding to the entreaties of the governor and merchants, sailed to Puerto Bello to demand satisfaction of the Spaniards for several depredations which they had committed on their ships, goods, and men. We had but a rough answer from the admiral of the Barlovento fleet, he alleging that whatever the Spaniards had done had merely been in reprisal for similar doings of the Scotch settlers on Darien, and he could not be persuaded that the Scotch and English were two separate nations, and as often (in those times) enemies as friends. But after several messages he assured us at length that if we would retire from before the fort, our demands should be satisfied. This was an instance of the notorious perfidy of the Spaniards, for after our departure, notwithstanding their solemn promises, nothing was effected.

We returned to Port Royal the 15th of May, where, having intelligence that the insolent pirate Captain Kidd was hovering on the coast, Mr. Benbow went in quest of him, unluckily without success. After that we spent several months in cruising among the West Indian islands, and receiving then orders to return home, Mr. Benbow, leaving the Germoon for the service of the governor of Jamaica, set sail for New England, our squadron being increased by three other king's ships which happened to be then in Port Royal harbor. When we had made Havana, the admiral, thinking the Falmouth too weak to be trusted in the dangerous seas about the New

England coast, ordered Captain Vincent to return in her to England, and we sailed into Portsmouth harbor towards the end of August, two years, all but three months, since our departure.

I stayed there but long enough to replenish my wardrobe and to draw my prize money, which, added to what I had left of my pay, amounted to the respectable sum of four hundred pounds, and then, having leave from my captain, I set off once more for Shrewsbury.

As before, I broke my journey at the Hall, to see my good friends the Allardyces, and especially to give to Mistress Lucy some kind messages entrusted to me by old friends of hers in Jamaica.

They were rejoiced to see me; Mistress Lucy was greatly interested to learn that I had but lately come from scenes she knew so well, and we talked for a long time about friends and acquaintances of hers whom I had met. And when I was alone with Mr. Allardyce I did not fail to inquire how things stood in the matter of her guardianship. He told me that no more had been seen of Vetch, and indeed the espionage upon the house had ceased, Sir Richard being resolved apparently to abide the issue of the action at law. The bill in chancery had been filed; answers had been put in by Mr. Moggridge on behalf of Sir Richard; and Mr. Allardyce hoped that the proceedings might drag along for a couple of years, when Mistress Lucy would be of age and her own mistress. And so 'twas with a light heart that I went on to Shrewsbury, to tickle the ears of my old friends there with the tale of my wanderings.

Chapter 22
I Walk Into A Snare

Cruising on shore is a flat and sorry business to a man who has obeyed the call of the sea, and I was glad enough when, soon after Christmas, I was summoned to rejoin my ship. There were already whispers that war was like to break out again ere long between England and France, owing to the machinations of King Lewis, who had procured from the king of Spain on his death bed a will appointing the Duke of Anjou to succeed him. 'Twas not to be expected that our good King William, having striven all his life to prevent Europe from being swallowed up by King Lewis, would tamely submit to see a great kingdom like that of Spain disappear into that ravenous maw; and when the new parliament met in February, 1701, it was significant that their first resolution was "to support His Majesty and take such effectual measures as may best conduce to the interest and safety of England." There was a widespread suspicion that the French proposed to invade our shores from Dunkirk, and Admiral Benbow, who was then commanding in The Downs, was ordered to use his utmost diligence to frustrate any such design.

In common with every officer in the fleet I hoped that the French would take the sea, so that we might have the pleasure of thrashing them. But in this we were disappointed: I suppose they were deterred by the knowledge that the channel was swarming with our ships; for, besides Admiral Benbow off Dunkirk, there was Sir George Rooke in The Downs, and Sir Cloudesley with six and forty vessels at Spithead. Whatever be the reason, we saw nothing to alarm us; and toward the middle of August Admiral Benbow was ordered to proceed once more to the West Indian station, with two third rates and eight fourth rates. The French and Spanish both had large fleets in the Indies, and 'twas to secure our possessions against attacks in case war should be declared, that Admiral Benbow was sent out again.

Since it was not expected that we should set sail for several weeks, I obtained leave from my captain to go to Shrewsbury and take farewell of my friends. With war imminent, and the possibility that I might never return; I should not have been happy without seeing them once again and leaving with their blessing. You may be sure I took the Hall in my way, for having been almost wholly at sea since my last visit, I had not heard anything from the family, and I was anxious to know whether the chancery case had yet been settled. Mr. Allardyce was not at home when I rode up to the door; but I was taken to Mistress Allardyce, who astonished me beyond measure by bursting into tears when she saw me.

"Good heavens, ma'am!" I cried, imagining all kinds of ill, "what is amiss?"

"Oh, Mr. Bold," says the good lady, "I am so glad to see you. We are in such trouble."

"Have the Cluddes got her?" I asked, Mistress Lucy being uppermost in my thoughts.

"No, it is not so bad as that, though I fear that will be the end of it. But she has left us, and I tremble to think of the poor child so far away, and among strangers."

"Among strangers! Pray, ma'am, explain," I said, glad enough that my first fear was unfounded, but marveling much at what had happened.

"She left us six months ago," Mrs. Allardyce went on. "She has gone back to Jamaica."

"To Jamaica!" I said. "What on earth induced her to do that, ma'am?"

"'Twas that dreadful law case, Mr. Bold. The squire lost the day. I do not understand it myself, he will explain it all to you when he comes home: he has indeed gone to Bridgenorth this very day to see his lawyer about it. Oh, Mr. Bold, I am so distressed! If I only knew she was safe I could bear the separation so much better."

"I do not think you need be uneasy on that score," I said. "She has friends in Jamaica, as you know; the people there are all very kind; and you may be sure they will see to her happiness."

"I am so glad to hear that," said the lady. "After all, she is no longer a child; she is twenty now, Mr. Bold, and has a will of her own, and great self reliance. We had one letter from her, to say that she had arrived safely; that was three months ago: I suppose there has not been time to receive another."

"There has been time, certainly," I replied, with some misgivings. "Vessels leave Port Royal every week. But her estate is situate a long way from the port, and maybe it is not convenient to send letters often."

"'Tis the absence of letters that makes the squire so uneasy. But for his being unwilling to leave me, I am sure he would have sailed to Jamaica himself to make sure that all is well. He dotes on Lucy. 'Tis a thousand pities that Roger's military duties will not permit of his going out. Do you think that Jamaica is a healthy place to live in, Mr. Bold?"

We were still talking when Mr. Allardyce returned. He was heartily glad to see me, and at once poured out his tale of trouble. The Court of Chancery, it appeared, had made Miss Lucy a ward, but instead of appointing Mr. Allardyce to be her guardian, it had given that office to Sir Richard Cludde, her paternal uncle. Mr. Allardyce spoke of the judge with the most bitter obloquy; he was a cross-grained, dried-up old mummy, said the squire, without a drop of good red blood in his veins.

"He was prejudiced against us from the beginning, and when our counsel said that Lucy herself entreated to be placed formally under my guardianship the old wretch refused to listen, and said that girls were better seen and not heard. I suppose he has a nagging wife, and serve him right!"

"And there is no appeal?" I asked.

"Oh, the wretch said we might appeal if we pleased, but meanwhile 'twas the order of the court that Lucy should pass under Cludde's guardianship. But he had not reckoned with Lucy. While I was in London about the miserable business she was with Mistress Allardyce at Bath, where madam had gone to take the waters. 'Twas lucky Cludde did not know that, for as soon as the decision was made, he posted off with the decree in his pocket, making no doubt that he would seize her here and carry her off in triumph. Ha! ha! you should hear Giles tell how he raved and cursed when he found she was not here. He demanded to know where she was, but not a man or maid would tell him; I've raised their wages all round. Meanwhile I had posted to Bath, and no sooner does Lucy hear what has happened than she jumps up and cries: 'I'll not have him for guardian for all the judges in the country. Uncle, I'll go back to Jamaica; please find me a ship at once.' Egad, I like spirit in a woman.

"Well, being only a stone's throw, you may say, from Bristowe, it was no long matter to arrange as she wished. I own I was loath to let her go, but 'twas clear that Cludde would get hold of her if she remained in the country, and there was no better way to avoid that. ''Twill not be for long, uncle,' she says when I bid her good-by. 'In a few months I shall be of age, and then I can snap my fingers at the Lord Chancellor himself.' And that's one consolation, Humphrey; she will be of age before the year's out."

"But will not Sir Richard go after her?"

"Not he. He doesn't know--at least I hope not--where she is. And he's crippled with the gout, and made it ten times worse by rushing across country in such desperate haste in the wettest month I've known for a score of years. He came in his coach to see me, and couldn't stir out of it, his foot being so swathed in flannel. He roared himself purple, threatening me with imprisonment for contempt of court and what not, but I laughed in his face, and told him that Lucy was a Cludde already, and would change her name for a better one when the time came. That hit him on the raw, Humphrey my boy; he went away fuming, and I don't think he will drive over to see me again."

And then, being somewhat cheered by this recollection of his victory over Sir Richard, he asked me how I had been faring. When he learned that I was about to sail for the West Indies again, he gave a gleeful chuckle.

"I wish you luck, my boy," he cried, slapping me on the back, "both in love and war."

"Sir!" said I, conscious of flushed cheeks.

"Give Lucy my love," he said, "and remember, my lad, that 'tis a very serious matter to marry a ward of court."

And then he chuckled and laughed again. Seeing that I had never so much as hinted that any such idea as he suggested had entered my head, I was somewhat taken aback by the old gentleman's perspicacity; for if the truth must be told (and it will out, sooner or later) I had quite resolved in my own mind that as soon as I attained captain's rank, and had gained some store of prize money, as I had no doubt I should do, I would endeavor to settle Dick Cludde's hash so far as his matrimonial project was concerned.

"I will warn off all trespassers, sir," I said soberly in reply to Mr. Allardyce's remark, and my answer seemed to give him great delight.

Having said my farewells to my friends in Shrewsbury also, I hastened back to my ship. We set sail in the last week of August, being escorted down the channel by Sir George Rooke and Sir John Munden with a large fleet. On the second of September we left Sir George off Scilly, and on the twenty-eighth made St. Mary's, one of the Azores, and remained there some eight days, during which Mr. Benbow (who was now promoted vice admiral) called his flag officers and captains together on board the Breda, his flagship, and communicated to them his instructions. The junior officers and some of the men were allowed to go in detachments for a few hours on shore, and it was on one of these trips that I heard a piece of news that interested me deeply.

I was strolling along with Mr. Venables when we encountered Joe Punchard and a group of men from the Breda. Seeing me, he touched his cap, and begged that he might have a few words with me in private. I went aside with him, and he began:

"That there young lady, sir--wasn't she kin to Dick Cludde--Mr. Lieutenant Cludde, begging his pardon?" (I had told Joe how 'twas Mistress Lucy had saved me from a horse whipping when first I appeared at the Hall.)

"To be sure, Joe," I replied, "she is his cousin."

"That be bad, sir," says he, "and 'twill be worse, by all accounts."

"What do 'you mean?" I asked.

"Why, sir, one of the men yonder be Jonathan Tubbs, Captain Kirkby his man, and he was just a-telling of us how Mr. Cludde, when he's in his cups (which is pretty often) tells a bragging yarn as how there's a mighty pretty girl out in Jamaicy a-waitin' to be spliced as soon as he comes to port; and she's a cousin of his, with a fine property; and he'll invite all the officers of his ship to the wedding and take 'em teal shooting next day, and--"

"That's enough, Joe," I said. "You had better go and tell your friend Jonathan Tubbs not to repeat things he hears when he's on duty."

Joe instantly touched his cap, begged my pardon, and walked away. I must have worn a very sober countenance when I rejoined Mr. Venables, for he looked at me oddly, and asked if I had had bad news. I evaded the question, and he did not press me. It was indeed bad news in this respect; that 'twas clear the Cluddes knew of Mistress Lucy's whereabouts. Indeed, for all I knew, Sir Richard himself might have got well of his gout and made the voyage to secure his ward. It wanted but a few months to her coming of age, and while I knew that Dick could not wed her during her minority, I saw that the very shortness of the time left would make the Cluddes eager to get her under their influence. I had never met Dick since that duel of ours on Southsea Common, having deliberately avoided him; but I said to to myself that I would certainly meet him when we arrived in Jamaica and make it clear to him that he would interfere with Mistress Lucy at his peril.

Much as I loved the sea, I now wished heartily that the voyage was over. But I had to curb my impatience. 'Twas the third of November when we arrived at Barbados; we made Martinica on the eighth, and next day came to anchor in Prince Rupert's Bay, on the northwest end of Dominica, where we supplied ourselves with water and other refreshments. Thence we sailed to Mevis, and proceeding to Jamaica, arrived there on the fifth of December, and anchored in Port Royal harbor.

I immediately got leave from my captain to go ashore, and inquired of the harbor master whether one Sir Richard Cludde had lately come to the island. My worst fear was relieved when I learned that it was not so, but I could not rest until I had satisfied myself of Mistress Lucy's well being, so

I hired a horse and rode out to Spanish Town, being well nigh choked, I remember, with the dust my steed's hoofs raised from the sandy road.

And here I had news that gave me the greater shock, for that it was utterly unexpected. I made my inquiries from a merchant with whom I had struck up a friendship during my former visit (he was indeed the father of the Lucetta I have spoken of) and he told me that Mistress Lucy was certainly living on her estate on the north side of the island, but added that 'twould not be hers much longer, for 'twas coming into the market by order of her guardian. This was surprising enough, and I asked to whom the instructions to this effect had been committed. My friend then said that they had been brought from England some months before by a lawyer named Vetch, who was armed with a power of attorney.

"Cyrus Vetch?" I cried, not doubting it, but overcome with sheer amazement.

"His name is Cyrus, I believe," replied my friend. "He stayed here a few days, and made himself very pleasant, though I can't say I took to him myself."

"He is a thorough-paced villain," I said. "Is he still in the town?"

"No, he is at Penolver." (This was the name of the Cludde estate.) "He is a masterful fellow, too; he dismissed old McTavish, who has stewarded the estate since Mr. Cludde's death; the poor old fellow feels it very sorely, for though he is a pretty warm man, like most of his countrymen here, he won't take no other stewardship, though he could have one for the asking, but moons about here in idleness."

"Does Mistress Lucy write to her friends here?" I asked.

"No, and they are displeased at her silence; but I suppose she thinks it scarce worth while to write when she will soon be here in person. She will, of course, return to England when the estate is sold, and is to make a match with her guardian's son, so they say. My word! he'll be a lucky fellow."

This news of Vetch's presence was staggering. As Sir Richard's attorney he had, I supposed, full power to administer the estate, or to sell it if he pleased; but I thought it a monstrous proceeding if he did this without Mistress Lucy's consent. I had no belief in his honesty, and suspected that he would take a pretty picking of the purchase money for himself. The absence of letters from Mistress Lucy was disquieting. The presence of the man who had been Cludde's companion in the abduction must be obnoxious to her, and it seemed strange that she had not written to her friends in Spanish Town, and had allowed the report of a projected marriage with Cludde to pass unchecked.

A notion that she might be under some constraint put me in a ferment, and I resolved to ride to Penolver and see for myself how matters stood, and to let Vetch know that, even though I could not dispute his legal status, he would at least have me to reckon with if he subjected Lucy to any annoyance or duress.

Returning to the port, I begged leave of Captain Vincent to go for a few days' visit to a friend on the north side of the island, not acquainting him with any particulars, because I felt that Mistress Lucy would not like her affairs discussed. He demurred at first, saying that we could not tell when we might have to put to sea; but on my reminding him that the work of refitting and cleaning after the voyage would take some time, and promising to return within a week, he yielded.

I set off early next morning, being provided by my merchant friend, Mr. Gurney, with a trusty companion and guide in the person of a smiling negro. At first I had purposed to ride alone, but my friend said that, while I had only to follow the direct road for about half my journey, which could take me through the well-settled parish of St. John, afterwards I should run great risk of losing my way in the cockpit country, maybe stumbling upon a settlement of wild maroons, or stepping into one of the impassable sink holes whose grass-grown surface gives no warning of the treacherous chasm below.

We rode till eleven o'clock, when the air became too hot for comfortable traveling, and entered a rest house kept by a black friend of my companion. He met us at the door, his face shining with heat and good temper.

"Good mornin', Massa; hope I see you well," says he. "Hi, Jacob, where you bin dis long time?"

He led the way most obsequiously into a large room with a sanded floor. It was cool and dark after the outside air, being shaded with green jalousies at the windows. I sat down, glad to escape from the heat, and Jacob went off with the host to enjoy a chat and prepare me a meal. Drowsy with the warmth, I was half dozing when a rough voice aroused me with a start.

"Mornin', yer honor."

My eyes being now accustomed to the dim light, I saw a man seated at a table at the farther end of the room. He was a burly fellow, with a look of the sea dog about him.

"Good morning," I replied.

"Ridin' far, yer honor?" said the man again.

"Massa Humf'y Bold ridin' jest as far as Missus Cludde's at Penolver," said my guide, coming at this moment into the room with a plate of jams and part of a fowl. "Massa Bold a king's officer, and don't want do no talk wiv common man. Me do talk for massa."

I laughed at the negro's officiousness, which the man did not appear to resent. He said nothing more to me, and I soon knew by his snores that he had fallen asleep.

After a light meal and a long rest, we set off again, and came at dark to another humble roadside hostelry, where I was glad to put up for the night. I had not yet gone to sleep when I heard the trot-trot of a horse, and wondered a little, as the sound died away in the distance, who could be riding so late. A brilliant moon was shining, and I thought that perhaps I had done better if I too had pursued my journey through the night, and rested during the day. But it was too late to think of that now; I was very tired, and with the faint sounds of the trotting horse still in my ears I fell asleep, not awaking till the sun was an hour or two above the horizon.

'Twas towards evening next day when, after riding through a wild hilly country, densely clad with tropical vegetation, amid which the only road was a horse track, my guide told me we were approaching our journey's end. The road broadened, and by and by ran between large fields of pasture land. Then we came beneath a thick grove, and were jogging along carelessly, when my horse suddenly stumbled and went down with so violent a shock that I was jerked from the saddle. Before I could get upon my feet, rough hands seized me, in a trice cords were lashed round me with a dexterity that identified my captors as seamen, and I was forthwith hauled along at the heels of as villainous a crew as I had ever seen. And I knew from sundry moans and howls behind me that Jacob had been dealt with in like manner.

Chapter 23
Uncle Moses

Since my former kidnapping at Bristowe I had learned that 'tis mere folly to fly into a rage and rail at fate or your enemies. So, affecting a cheerful tone, I said:

"Why, sure this is scurvy treatment to deal out to a king's officer, my friends."

"No friends of yourn," replied one of the men.

Another laughed and said: "Strap me if we ha'n't caught a tolly, mates."

"Tolly," as I learned afterwards, was the cant name by which king's officers were known to the buccaneers. The fact that I was an officer, of which they had apparently been ignorant, seemed to give the men much pleasure. Some of them, no doubt, had once been king's men, and knew without any telling the gravity of their offense. I wasted no more words on them. They took me to a wooden shanty standing by itself, tied me to a staple in the wall, shut and padlocked the door, and went away.

Left to myself, I sought for some explanation of this new addition to the catalogue of my mischances. What were buccaneers doing on this estate? Had they quitted for the nonce their usual work of snapping up cargo ships? Had they made a raid upon the house and served Vetch as they had served me? I had no pity for him, but the thought of the sore straits in which Mistress Lucy might be filled me with disquiet and alarm.

And then another explanation flashed into my mind. Was it possible that the men had been hired by Vetch himself in pursuance of some villainous scheme for keeping Mistress Lucy in his power? I thought of this until it became a conviction. Mistress Lucy's friends in Spanish Town were surprised and hurt at the absence of news from her; her silence must be due to Vetch. His motive was not far to seek. Cludde had been boasting of the bride awaiting him in Jamaica; I could not doubt that Vetch was holding her in durance until Cludde should arrive, and, her minority having expired, she could be cajoled or forced into a marriage with him. It was essential to the success of this piece of villainy that she should be kept from communication with her friends, and nothing was more natural than that Vetch should hire a gang of buccaneers to assist him in accomplishing his end. I marveled at his audacity, and burned with rage at my utter helplessness.

It did not occur to me at first that Vetch would know who it was that his hirelings had entrapped. I supposed that he had established a system of ambushing, so that whoever should arrive at the place might be prevented, if need were, from having speech with Mistress Lucy and learning of the restraint in which she was held. But on considering this matter further I doubted whether even Vetch would have dared to go this length, for if people came from Spanish Town and did not return, it would certainly be suspected that something was wrong, and I could scarcely believe that no notice would have been taken of it by the authorities, civil or military. This made my capture the more surprising, for while I did not doubt that Vetch, if he had heard of my coming, would not scruple to lay by the heels one who had defeated him in his former design on Mistress Lucy. I was at a loss to understand how the identity of his visitor could have become known to him.

I lay awake all night, plagued by the heat and the multitudinous insects, but still more by my anxieties. In the morning I heard footsteps approaching, and the door being thrown open, I saw that my visitor was Vetch himself.

"So 'tis indeed Mr. Humphrey Bold," he said, with a grin of malice. "I scarce believed in my good fortune. I did not expect to be honored by a visit from Mr. Humphrey Bold."

I knew not what to say to the insolent wretch who stood smiling there; 'twas clear that he had expected me, which was very puzzling, since none but my friend Mr. Gurney in Spanish Town and Captain Vincent knew of my errand. Then all at once I remembered the seaman in the hostelry, and my guide's telling him my name, and the horseman riding by at night; 'twas clear to me now that the man was a spy of Vetch's, kept on the road for this very purpose of riding ahead of a visitor and giving intimation of his approach.

"I need not say," continued Vetch, "how charmed I am to see one who is endeared to me by many old associations."

"You villain!" I cried, finding my tongue now that I had light upon his doings. "You have had many lucky escapes, but by heaven you shall not escape this time."

"Escape!" he said, opening his eyes in feigned astonishment. "'Tis you who will not escape again!"

"You will release me," I said.

"In my own good time," he answered. "A hothead like you will benefit by a period of quiet meditation."

"You will release me at once," I said. "You dare not keep me here. There are those in Spanish Town and Port Royal who know where I have come: they will seek me if I do not return to the ship within the expected time, and then you will find a halter round your neck, Cyrus Vetch."

"Not at all," he said with a bland smile. "A messenger will leave here tomorrow with a letter saying that my old friend and schoolfellow, Humphrey Bold, is sick with a fever. He will have every attention, and a report of his condition shall be sent to his captain--Captain Vincent, is it not? I fear Mr. Bold may not have recovered before the fleet sails; it is likely that he may be very ill indeed; 'tis possible he may die! And Captain Vincent shall know how tenderly he was nursed--yes, by Mistress Lucy Cludde--"

"Don't name her name, you hound!" I cried hotly, stung at last into fury.

"Gently, Mr. Bold," said he; "you will but aggravate your distemper. Mistress Lucy Cludde will nurse you--in my letter; and your captain will think it most natural and commendable seeing that you are her guest, and that it may be regarded there is some slight relationship between you. And if you should happily recover, why, she may herself accompany you to port and restore you to your comrades. But that will not be till I please."

I cried out on him as a scoundrel, though vexed with myself for such mere windiness of utterance. The truth is, want of sleep and the discomforts of the night were like to throw me into a real fever, and the dismay I felt at this possibility helped me to pull myself together. When I spoke again 'twas calmly, without heat.

"You are playing a fool's game," I said. "You are exceeding your rights as representative of Sir Richard Cludde, and you may be sure you will be called to a heavy account if you deal wrongfully with the estate or its owner. Pull up before it is too late; there are sundry things against you in England that will not dispose the courts to show you mercy."

"Hark to him!" cries Vetch with an evil sneer. "He turns preacher! You fool! Who are you to foist yourself into the concerns of your betters--a fellow only saved from the gutter by charity! While the girl is a minor I will deal with this estate as I please; and when she comes of age, then--"

He paused, an inscrutable look upon his face.

"Then Humphrey Bold may go hang," he said, and with a smile that made me feel wondrous uneasy he shut the door upon me and departed.

Of all the mischances I had suffered, this was, I thought, the most afflicting. In the others it was only myself that was concerned, and a man who sets out to conquer fortune must expect his share of buffets by the way. But my own ill hap was as nothing compared with the dangers I felt to be hovering about Mistress Lucy, and to know myself helpless when she was in sore need was as a crushing weight upon my heart.

I was not left long to my reflections. Presently Vetch returned with two villainous-looking ruffians, seamen by their build, who at his orders bound my hands behind me and then conveyed me across a stretch of pasture land to a wooden house that stood in the angle of a field. They took me up a flight of steps on to a veranda, through one room into another, furnished with a table, a chair, and a bed, and there left me.

"I warn you once more," I said to Vetch before he went. "You are dealing with a king's officer, and if you think this outrage will go unpunished you are mistaken, and very grievously. And I tell you, Vetch, that if Mistress Lucy suffer a jot at your hands, either in herself, or in her property, you shall hang for it, as sure as my name is Humphrey Bold."

He smiled, swept me a bow and was gone.

The chamber in which I was left was an inner apartment, such as are common in the houses in Jamaica, enclosed by other rooms, to defend it from the heat. It had but one door, and was illuminated by a little window high up in the partition wall. Escape was impossible save through the door, and I knew by the sound of voices from without that the two men had been stationed there to keep guard over me. They brought me some food by and by, one of them carrying it into the room, the other standing at the door with a musket in his hand, and I perceived that he had a hanger at his belt. To attempt to overpower them and escape would be madness; but I thought it might not be impossible to prevail on them by means of a bribe to help me, and with that ultimate design I resolved to open friendly communications with them.

"What house is this?" I said.

"Look 'ee, master, drink your bumbo and say nought," he growled.

"Come, come," I said pleasantly, "you are a tar, as any one can see, and as good a seaman, I doubt not, as ever slept upon foc's'le. Two years ago I was a swab myself--"

"Splutter and oons!" cried the man, interrupting me, "who be you a-calling swab, I'd like to know!"

"No offense," I said, "I was just going to tell you of the fun we had, my mates and I, when we were prisoners in France, and how we escaped and had a running fight with Duguay-Trouin--"

"That's a good un!" he cried.

"Hark to him, Jack: says he had a fight with Doggy Trang."

"Let's hear about it," cries the man he had called Jack.

Whereupon I launched out into the story of our escape, made them laugh heartily by my description of our dealings with the French captain, and so brought them, as I thought, to a more reasonable temper.

"And now, seeing that we're in a manner shipmates, you won't refuse to answer a simple question, I'm sure," I said. "What house is this?"

"No harm in that, Bill," says Jack. "'Tis the house of the second overseer of this 'ere plantation, and much good may it do you to know it."

Having thus broken the ice, I succeeded, before I had finished my meal, in drawing sundry other information out of them. I learned that the place of my imprisonment was some two miles from Mistress Lucy's house, being situate at the extreme verge of the sugar plantation. The men knew nothing about Mistress Lucy, or of what went on at the house, having recently been brought up by Vetch, along with a dozen or more shipmates, from a brig belonging to their employer that now lay in a cove on the north of the island some ten miles away. They made no bones about acknowledging that they had formed part of the crew of a buccaneer vessel and had been hired by Vetch for a month's service on shore, which suited them very well, since they had nothing to do, good pay, and were given a liberal allowance of bumbo, which was, I discovered, a concoction of rum and water, sugar and nutmeg.

"Well, now," says I, thinking the time had come for my proposal, "I don't ask you what pay you are getting, but whatever it is, I will double it if you'll let me loose, and help me to get down to Spanish Town."

"Come up, now!" says Bill, "d'ye think to gammon us? We know what a lieutenant's wages is, we do, and 'twould take a dozen of you together to pay us enough for that there job."

"And you shall have it," I said.

"Ay, and a dose of irons into the bargain," said the man. "No, no; we don't want no lobsters up from Spanish Town; not if we know it.

"Besides, we knows what king's officers be, don't we, Jack?

"We've bin on king's ships, Lord love you, and we knows where the pay goes to. Once you get to Spanish Town you'd forget all about us; we've bin done like that afore."

And then what must I do but produce a handful of silver and show it them as earnest of my promise. I could not have done a stupider thing. At the sight of the money the men fell upon me, and emptied my pocket (despite my resistance) of every stiver it contained; so that I was now, as once before in my life, bare of everything save my clothes and Cludde's crown piece, which was hidden under my shirt. Then, with many a chuckle, the scoundrels left me, to meditate on the exceeding folly of trying to make terms with buccaneers.

So three days passed. I was never allowed to quit my room; Jack and Bill guarded it by day, two other men by night. I became more and more miserable and anxious. I could get no news from my jailers, nor did I ever see the overseer in whose house I was; and I suffered from a constant dread that Vetch's plans, whatever they were, were maturing, and that it would soon be too late for any intervention.

On the third night of my imprisonment in the overseer's house (the fourth since my arrival) I was very restless. My enforced inactivity, and the lack of fresh air, were producing the natural effect; every night I slept less, waking frequently, to toss and heave until I sank again into a troubled slumber.

In one of these intervals, I heard a scratching sound--just such a sound as a mouse makes behind the wainscot. I had not noticed it before, and it caused me nothing but irritation now, for when a man is wakeful, such sounds, however slight they may be, become magnified to his overstrung nerves. I endured the sound for a time; then shooed to scare the gnawing animal away. But it did not desist for an instant, and at last, vexed beyond measure, I got out of bed, groped my way to the spot whence I thought the sound proceeded (it seemed to come from the floor) and stamped heavily on the boards.

My action was heard by the men outside the door, and one of them cried out angrily to know what I was about.

"'Tis a wretched mouse will not let me sleep," I replied.

"And what can you expect, you fool, when your room's over an empty stable?" he said. "Curse me! what a fresh-water fair-weather fowl you be!"

The scratching having ceased, I went back to bed. But in a few moments it recommenced, at what seemed to be a spot nearer to me, and, marveling somewhat at the persistence of the beast (for a mouse is easily scared), I covered my head, and so endeavored to shut out the annoyance.

I think I must have dozed again, for suddenly I found myself sitting bolt upright, straining my ears as a man does when he is suddenly wakened from sleep and is not sure whether 'twas by an actual sound or by a sound heard in dream. And in a moment my doubt was resolved; assuredly I heard a sound, and 'twas like a human voice, but muffled. I listened intently; it appeared to come from beneath me. While I was wondering who could have chosen the stable as a place for conversation in the dead of night I could have sworn (though half-believing it must be an hallucination) that I beard my own name. In a trice I was out of bed, and groping my way under it, my hand struck against something projecting from the floor, and at the same moment I heard distinctly, and as it were in my very ear, a low whisper, "Massa Bold, Massa Bold!"

"Who is there?" I whispered in return, and, clutching the thing my hand had touched, I felt it move.

I tightened my grasp upon it; it was round, and as I discovered by laying my other hand upon its top, hollow. Struck by a sudden thought I bent my face down, and whispered again into the hole, "Who is there?" afterwards turning my ear upon it.

"Massa Bold, lill Missy sends a letter."

The words came clearly up the tube.

"Me poke it up," said the voice again.

I withdrew my ear, and waited in a tense breathlessness of amazement. Then I heard a slight rustling, and placing my hand on the tube, I felt a small piece of paper thrust against it. Grasping this, all my frame thrilling with excitement, I whispered again:

"Who are you?"

"Me Uncle Moses," said the voice. "Good night, sah; come again tomorrow."

And then all was silent.

Picture if you can my state of mind as I crept back into my bed and lay down again, the precious note in my hand. I was trembling with happiness: Lucy knew of my presence, and had written to me. And yet I was doomed to lie in a tantalizing impatience until the dawn should give me leave to read her message. I had no more sleep that night, wonderment, conjecture, pleasure, hope, setting up a whirl in my brain.

As soon as there was the faintest tremor in the darkness I sat up and, unfolding the paper, sought vainly to decipher it. Never had time seemed so long to me as I waited for the oncoming of the beneficent light of day. And at last, lifting the paper almost to my eyes, I was able to make out the words.

'Twas in French, and I blessed the chance which enabled me to understand it, and the woman's wit that had prompted Lucy to choose this disguise. She said she had learned of what had happened through the gossip of the servants; the man who had heard my name in the rest house had mentioned it. She told me that she was virtually a prisoner. She knew not what Vetch intended (she did not name him, but wrote of him as *cet homme mechant*), but she was kept under strict surveillance; her movements were dogged; and though she had three times endeavored to make her escape along with the old nurse who had accompanied her from England, she had always been prevented, and those who had assisted her had been terribly punished. Uncle Moses, her father's bodyservant, who was devoted to her, had been whipped almost to death, and she dared make no further attempt, for the sake of the poor black people.

Dick Cludde had come up from Spanish Town, she told me, and crushing down her repugnance to meet him, she had besought him to interpose. He had seemed troubled, and had gone away, as she thought, to plead with Vetch, but she had not seen him again. It was after that that she had heard of my imprisonment. She thanked me for coming to help her; she knew that was my purpose; had I not helped her before? and she prayed that I might find some means of escaping, so that I might take her away and save her from the wicked man who had her in his power.

I ground my teeth as I read all this, and vowed that if I could but get free I would wreak a vengeance on Vetch that he would not easily forget. But the knowledge of my impotence wrought me to a pitch of fury that for a time almost bereft me of my senses, and I could only rage and fume in desperate misery. My guardians, when they came in to attend to my wants, seemed to be conscious of my state of mind; they eyed me with suspicion, and the man at the door took up his musket ostentatiously, though neither said a word to me.

After a time my passion subsided, and with recovered calmness I saw that my only chance of doing anything for Lucy depended on my patience and self restraint. I waited eagerly for night. The negro had said that he would come again, and this could only mean that Lucy had some hope of our being able between us to devise some means of escape. The man ran a great risk; if the buccaneers heard us speaking they would discover him, and then all hope would be lost. Fervently as I longed to hear his voice again, I was consumed with anxiety lest he should come too soon, or that by some accident, some incautious movement, he might reveal his presence.

The day passed and when I went to bed I lay in restless impatience, straining my ears to catch the slightest whisper, and starting up several times in the belief that I heard him. At last, when all was silent save for the heavy breathing of the men outside the door, I caught the faint sound made by the pushing of the tube (a length of sugar cane, as I afterwards learned) through the hole he had bored in the double floor. I stole noiselessly out of bed, and crept cautiously to the place beneath it.

"Is that you, Moses?" I whispered.

"Yes, massa, me's here."

"Is Mistress Lucy well?"

"Welly miserable, sah. Missy say Massa Bold take care; she say 'God bless Massa.'"

Inwardly I blessed her for her thought of me; then I said:

"We must both be careful, Moses. Now, I must escape from this, and you must help me."

"Yes, Massa, me want to help, but dere is no way for po' Uncle Moses."

"We must find a way; we must," I said in a fierce whisper. "Could you come up and help me if I burst open the door? Are you strong? Could you knock a man down?"

"Me plenty strong, sah, but what good dat? Massa might get away, but what den?"

"Why, we could get among the trees in the darkness, and you could lead me to the road, and perhaps find me a horse, so that I could ride to Spanish Town."

"No, no, sah, me berry much 'fraid in dark, sah. Me shake like leaf now, sah; but in forest, wiv de bugaboos, me melt all away to water."

I had heard of the dread with which the negroes regarded the bugaboos, the evil spirits of the woods, and knew that there was but a poor chance of escaping if my guide were in a state of panic terror. Moses had shown unusual courage in coming alone in the darkness to the stable beneath me, and there was a tremor in his voice which showed that even now but little was wanted to make him go howling away. I thought it best not to risk so inopportune and fatal a calamity, so I bade him go away and come again next night, by which time I hoped to have been able to think out a plan that offered reasonable prospects of success.

Chapter 24
I Make A Bid For Liberty

I slept heavily when Uncle Moses had gone, making up for my wakefulness the night before; and next day I was more composed in mind, and readier to take thought. Ignorant as I was of the plantation and the country round, I saw that to escape in the night without a guide would be to court disaster, and a timorous guide like Uncle Moses, with his fear of the bugaboos, might lead me to my undoing. Therefore my flight must be contrived by day. The door of my chamber was opened three times, when the guards brought me food, and 'twas possible that, with the negro making a diversion outside, I might seize such an occasion to fell one of the men and evade the other. But this plan scarce promised success, for the house was situate in the sugar plantation, and doubtless many negroes would be at work, and the overseer would be at hand, with possibly others of the piratical dogs whom Vetch had brought up from the coast.

There was one period of the day, however, when few people, if any, would be astir, and that was the middle part from eleven till about three, when work ceased, everybody seeking shelter from the heat. I could reckon on my guards being sleepy and sluggish then; and, moreover, seeing that during several days I had given them no trouble, they would be quite unprepared for any violent outbreak. True, my door was always locked, but looking at it, I did not doubt that if I threw myself upon it with all my strength it would give way. And if Uncle Moses had the courage at the same time to tackle the men, there was a chance that we might seize their arms and make good our escape before they had recovered from their surprise. At any rate, I saw nothing better.

Being resolved on this first step, I had to consider the next. What should I do if I escaped? Should I endeavor to make my way to Spanish Town and return with a force of tars, or of soldiers from Collingwood's regiment then in garrison, sufficient to deal with Vetch's desperadoes? This idea I soon dismissed. I felt that time was of the greatest moment. I did not know the exact date of Mistress Lucy's coming of age, but 'twas very clear that it was not far distant; it might be, indeed, within a few days, and I had such a belief in Vetch's villainy that I feared he might force Lucy into a marriage with Cludde the very moment she was free from the authority of the Chancery Court. Cludde had arrived, I remembered, and was perhaps still at the house awaiting the day of Lucy's enfranchisement, and I clenched my fists at the thought.

It would take me a full day on a swift horse to reach Spanish Town, even if I rode at peril of sunstroke through the hot hours, and another day, perhaps two or three, to return with assistance; and it was in the highest degree unlikely, first that I should be able to get a horse, and if I did, to ride the whole length of the estate without being intercepted. And further, supposing all happened as favorably as I could wish, at the news of my flight Vetch would without question carry off Mistress Lucy to the brig that lay on the coast, and would sail to England or elsewhere, secure in the knowledge that I could not pursue him.

I can relate the course of my reasoning in cold blood now, but on that day of anxious pondering every other consideration was outweighed by the feeling that I must not go far from Mistress Lucy. And so I resolved that if I got free I would ask Uncle Moses to lead me to some spot near by, difficult of access, where I might lurk while concerting some means of assisting her. It passed my wit to conceive of any plan that promised success; but certainly I could do nothing while a prisoner, and to be free was my one consuming desire.

How impatiently I waited for the dark needs no telling. And some words I overheard pass between my jailors, as they talked over their supper, drove me to such a state of desperation that I had almost there and then dashed myself against the door and ruined everything.

"'Twill be summat new for Parson Jim," says Jack.

"Ay, 'tis many a year since he tied a knot o' that sort," replied the other.

"D'ye reckon he can tie it safe and proper, seeing he bean't no more a parson?" asked Jack.

"Never you fear," says Bill; "once a parson always a parson, as I've heard tell. 'Tis no matter he's a swab and a tosspot like you and me, only worse, and fit for nothing but a Newgate galley; he'll read the words o' the book, if so be he's sober enough to see 'em (though to be sure his talk is always most pious when he's drunk), and they'll be lawful man and wife, same as if they'd bin spliced by the Pope of Rome himself."

This wrought me into a very fever of apprehension. I could only guess who Parson Jim might be; the buccaneers gathered all manner of strange recruits; it was enough that there was talk of a marriage, and I was sick with dread lest after all I should be too late. And when at last I heard the welcome rustle below me, the first words I spoke through the tube were an anxious inquiry for Lucy's welfare.

"Missy lots better now, sah," replied the negro, and with the vanity of youth I inferred that she was better for the knowledge that I was near.

"Is Mr. Cludde at the house?" I asked.

"No, sah; Massa Cludde gone yesterday."

That was good news, at any rate, for I supposed him to have returned to Spanish Town, perhaps to make preparations for his wedding, and it must be four or five days at earliest before he could be back.

"And when is Mistress Lucy's birthday?" I asked.

"Missy's bufday Friday, Massa, but oughter be Fursday."

"What do you mean?"

"Missy keep bufday one day after proper time, sah, cos her muvver die on proper bufday, and Massa and Missy too sorry to be jolly dat day, sah."

"Does Mr. Vetch know that?" I asked, with no little anxiety, for 'twas Tuesday night, and if Vetch knew that Lucy came of age on Thursday the time was perilously short.

"No, sah; Massa Vetch t'ink de proper bufday be Friday, and he hab told all de black people dey shall get drunk Saturday, 'cos dere will be wedding in de house."

There was confirmation of the suspicion my jailors' talk had bred in me. I lost no time now in imparting my plan to the negro. He gave a low groan when I had finished.

"What's the matter?" I said. "Are you afraid?"

"Yes, Massa, I am 'fraid. S'pose we get away, dere be dogs at the big house, and dey will let 'em loose on us and follow on horseback. We shall be cotched, and dat will be de last of po' Uncle Moses."

This was a staggering blow, and I own I felt for the moment an utter despair. In the depths of the forest land, could we but gain it, we might elude the search of men, but not the unerring scent of bloodhounds.

"Are there horses we could make off with?" I said at length.

"No, Massa; all de horses but two at de big house be gwine to take sugar to de coast tomorrow, and dose two are kept for Missy and Massa Vetch."

This had an element of comfort in it, for if we could not find horses for ourselves, neither could our pursuers, save these two, which might not be at hand, and I did not doubt we could outstrip any man on foot. I pointed this out to the negro, and when he replied that we had still to reckon with the dogs, I tried to hearten him by showing that some time must elapse before the beasts could be fetched from their kennel and put upon the scent. And then I asked him whether slaves had never run away from the estate without being caught.

"Not when old Massa was alive, nor yet when Massa McTavish was de boss; but some did run 'way when Massa Vetch come, and dey was not cotched."

"Well, then, why should not we do the same? Do you know where they hid?"

"In de swamp six mile 'way," he said.

"Yes, dat is it," he added, with a new eagerness in his tone, "we will run to de swamp. I never thought of Massa going where de niggers go. De dogs will not run on de swamp 'cos dey 'fraid of being drownded."

"Then how can we?" I asked, wondering.

"I know all about dat, Massa," he said. "De slaves what run way dey wear swamp shoes. I make some for massa and me, and den if we get dere befo' de dogs cotch us, we shall be safe."

I was getting desperately uneasy lest our whispered conversation, which had lengthened itself out, should be heard by my jailors. So I now brought it to an end by reminding Uncle Moses of the part he was to play on the morrow and giving him a message to Mistress Lucy.

"Tell her that with God's help I shall be free tomorrow, and beg her to shut herself in her room, and see no one. If mortal man can save her, she shall be saved."

And ere I went to sleep I prayed very fervently that all might be well with us and her.

When morning broke, I was conscious of a great agitation of mind, which I schooled myself to hide from the eyes of my guards, forcing myself to eat the breakfast for which I had no appetite. It would have eased me to pace up and down my room, but I forbore even from this, so that no restlessness might provoke their curiosity or suspicion. I sat for hours on my bed, awaiting the time for our attempt. The men brought me my midday meal: one of them made a brutal remark on my pallor; and then the door was shut, and they settled themselves to their usual siesta.

'Twas about an hour later when I heard the tube pushed up through the hole in the floor. Uncle Moses was below. The critical moment for which

I had been longing was come, and my limbs trembled uncontrollably, as they had not done since the time when I saw my first sea fight on the deck of the Dolphin. As we had arranged, I allowed time for the negro to mount the steps and come through the veranda into the room adjoining. Then, gathering my strength, I took three strides across my chamber and dashed my right shoulder against the door. It flew outwards with a crash, the force of my impact being such that the lock tore a great piece out of the jamb.

I rushed blindly into the next room, and lost a few moments in the endeavor to grasp the scene. But my jailors lost more, for the crash had wakened them from a sound sleep and, seamen though they were, the event was so sudden and unexpected that they were taken perfectly aback, and were still looking about them in a dazed bewilderment when Uncle Moses and I threw ourselves upon them. We got them just as they were staggering to their feet. A blow from my fist sent one spinning against the wall; at the same moment the negro, whom I had barely yet seen, caught the other man by the middle and, by a feat of strength which amazed me, hurled him through the doorway into the room I had just quitted. I hoped they were stunned; we could not wait to see, and we had no means of binding them.

The noise must have awakened everybody in the house; indeed, I heard shouts from the rear; no doubt the overseer, and the two buccaneers who had been on guard during the night, would in a few moments be upon the scene. Snatching up the men's muskets and bandoliers that lay on a bench against the wall, we dashed into the veranda, sprang down the steps, and made off across the plantation.

We had not run a hundred yards when we heard a bellow behind us, and, turning, I saw a man at the head of the steps lighting the match for his musket. I was pleased at this, for it would give us another hundred yards' start before he could fire. The muskets of these days can not boast of great precision, but those of fifty years ago were infinitely more cumbersome and clumsy, so that I did not fear he would hit us, unless by some unlucky chance. And indeed, when his weapon flashed, we were quite two hundred and fifty yards away, and the slug went very wide. He would have done better, I thought, to pursue us at once on foot.

But as we sped on side by side, I heard a great horn blast that seemed to set the welkin ablaze. 'Twas the signal that a slave had run away, and I could not doubt that Vetch would immediately suspect what had actually happened. Before long, beyond question, he would be hot upon our traces.

"How far to the forest?" I asked of the negro.

"More'n a mile, massa," he replied.

And then, as I ran, I looked more closely at the man whom fate had made my comrade in this desperate adventure. He was an older man than I had expected; very powerfully made, as his cast of the buccaneer had proved; but his hair was white, and, short as was the distance we had run, I could see that he would soon be laboring for breath. But it was two miles to the big house, as he had called Mistress Lucy's abode, and I did not despair of reaching the edge of forest land before Vetch could make up on us, even if he started the very moment he heard the alarm. If once we gained the forest, we might perhaps blind our trail in a stream, and so gain time enough for our further flight to the swamp.

We were running on a broad track that divided the sugar plantation, and here and there negro laborers who had been roused from their noontide sleep by the horn blast and the shot rose up to see what was afoot. None of them offered to interfere. They stared at us for the most part in silence, one or two of the older people crying out that it was Uncle Moses on the run, and wondering at his companion being a white man.

I took little note of them, for I was already anxious on behalf of the old negro. We had six miles to go; could he hold out? 'Twas two miles from the big house to the house we had left; a horseman could cover the distance in little longer than it would take us to reach the forest; and then we should have but one mile start in a race of six. The odds were heavily against even me, in strong and lusty youth; how much more heavily against Uncle Moses, who was perhaps three times my age!

Already I was slackening my pace to keep with him. And we were cumbered with the muskets we had seized--heavy weapons, and, when I came to think of it, likely to prove of little use to us, for we could not pause in the race to light matches, nor, once they were discharged, should we have time to recharge them. Yet I dared not suggest we should fling them down; they were our only weapons save for a knife that Uncle Moses carried at his belt, and perchance if it came to a fight at close quarters we could wield them with some effect as clubs. So we pounded on, saying never a word, I husbanding my breath, the negro panting hard.

We came to the edge of the forest land bordering the estate, and when we had plunged into it for some little distance Moses was fain to stop to recover his wind.

"Dey hab not started yet, massa," he gasped.

"How do you know?" I asked.

"'Cos dere is no sound of de dogs," he replied.

"Should we hear them three miles away?"

"Oh, yes, massa; de wind carry de sound miles and miles."

"We have luck on our side, then. Can you run again?"

"Yes, massa. Po' Uncle Moses hain't no chicken now, but he hain't done yet."

And then we set off again through the forest, at a more moderate pace now, for the way ran no longer clear. The word "forest" to a stay-at-home means a tract of soft, springy turf, with tall trees and pleasant glades and clumps of bracken that shelter rabbits and other small creatures of the woodland. But the forest of the West Indies bears to our English forest the relation of a giant to a dwarf. The fronds of the bracken grow to feet where we have inches; weeds that with us would shelter a mouse would there oonceal an elephant, and a creeping plant which in England would delay a man only while he kicked its tendrils aside grows in Jamaica to such a strength and tanglement that it would obstruct the passage of a troop of horse.

This was somewhat in our favor. We could run where horses might not. But I took little comfort from this, for where we went the dogs would certainly follow. And we had not gone above a mile, as I reckoned, when the howling sound came to our ears--a deep-toned baying, faint and mellow, stealing through the umbrageous foliage like the horns of some fairy host. The hounds had found our scent.

Uncle Moses groaned. Doubtless he knew full well the fate of unhappy slaves who had been recaptured in flight. He quickened his strides for some yards, then, stopping, he held his hand to his side and begged me to go on alone.

"But I can not," I said. "I do not know the way; and besides, I will not leave you. Give me your musket. We have still a good start, and after you have rested a little you will be able to run again."

I took his musket, and when we set off again we were lucky to come upon a stream swirling athwart our track. We stepped into this and walked through the water for some distance, until we had, as I thought, effectually blinded our trail. And no doubt it was so, but Uncle Moses told me that it would only delay our pursuers for a little; they knew the direction of the haven for which we were making, and even if the dogs were at fault the horsemen would still press on. We wasted no more time in deflecting from our course for any such vain manoeuvers, but ran straight on.

Alas! the old man's strength was failing. He staggered, and but for my arm would have fallen. I think his collapse was due partly to terror, for the baying of the hounds was growing upon our ears; the pursuers were gaining fast upon us. I had perforce to wait patiently until the poor negro had somewhat recovered, and meanwhile the deep-mouthed baying sounded ever nearer, and the precious minutes were fleeting by. When we set off once more 'twas at little above a walking pace, and every moment I dreaded the appearance of the pursuers at our heels. And I noticed with alarm that the forest was thinning; apparently we should soon reach open country, and lose what little advantage we had in being out of our enemy's sight.

I asked anxiously whether 'twould not be better for us to turn aside into the thickets and try to hide; peradventure the dogs and the horsemen would go past. But the negro said 'twould be useless; we could not deceive the dogs, and we should be no safer than rats in a barn.

We had come to the end of what would in England be called a glen- -a narrow gorge, with shelving banks rising to the height of some ninety feet, and overgrown with shrubs and creeping plants. No doubt in the rainy season 'twas the bed of a torrent; the bottom was sandy and pebbly, and hard to the feet. We had gone but a little way along it when Uncle Moses sank down, and, looking at his livid face, his panting nostrils and starting eyes, I feared that the hand of death was upon him. 'Twas clear that he was utterly spent; he could not even stagger to the farther end of the gorge; and with the bitter pangs of despair I heard the fierce baying of the hounds, and had almost resigned myself to the inevitable end.

I glanced round to see whether the pursuers were in sight. I saw, not them, but something which flashed a wild hope through me. Some little distance back a tree hung over the sandy bottom, its roots partially laid bare by the washing of the stream which had now disappeared. The trunk was inclined at a sharp angle; but little force would be needed, I thought, to topple it over until it lay athwart the path which the pursuers must follow. Its foliage was thick, and though I did not flatter myself 'twould put an end to the pursuit, I thought it might serve as a check, and enable Uncle Moses to gain strength enough for a last attempt.

Dropping the muskets by the negro's side, I ran down the gorge, scrambled up the bank to the base of the tree, and swarmed along the trunk to the farthest extremity. It was a tall tree, of a kind I did not know, and my weight upon its tapering top must have exerted a considerable force upon its loosened lower end. Catching a branch that seemed strong enough to bear me, I dropped with a jerk. There was a movement of the trunk, and I heard a wrenching sound below, but the roots still held fast. I climbed up again with the quickness I had learned at sea, and again threw myself down.

This time I produced the effect I desired; the roots gave way, and in a moment I found myself on the ground, somewhat scratched and bruised, but sound of bone and limb. The fallen tree lay full across the gorge, its foliage completely filling the space, save for a narrow gap between it and the ground, through which a man or a dog might crawl, but not a horse.

I ran back to Uncle Moses, lifted him to his feet, and, assisting him with one hand, the muskets clasped in the other, I led him up the gorge with what haste I might. We had gone but a little way when I heard the shouts of men mingled with the baying of the hounds, and immediately afterwards these latter forced their way beneath the tree and ran with lolling tongues towards us. Knowing nothing of the ways of bloodhounds, I expected the two dogs would fly at our throats like foxhounds at a fox, and I loosed the negro's arm and stood with musket upraised to defend myself and him. But to my surprise Uncle Moses called to them by name, and they answered him with a bark and fawned on him.

"Dey won't hurt us," he said. "Dey hab done their work; dey lub po' Uncle Moses."

"Will they come with us?" I asked, with wondering delight.

"Dey will do anyt'ing for Uncle Moses," he replied.

"Then let us get away into the forest again as soon as we can, and take them with us. How far is the swamp now?"

"'Bout a mile, Massa."

"Come, then; we may have time to get to it before the men can overtake us. They cannot get their horses over the tree."

And we made off, the dogs accompanying us willingly, in spite of the cries and calls of the baffled horsemen on the other side of the tree. Issuing from the gorge, we struck into the forest, and heard our pursuers cursing us and the dogs as they tried to follow us. By the help of my arm Uncle Moses managed to struggle along, and after about a quarter of an hour we came to the edge of the swamp.

Then he took from his back, where they had been strapped, two pairs of shoes in shape similar to those which our trappers in America adopted from the Indians for marching over snow, but slighter and shorter. These we donned, the negro showing me how to fasten mine, and then we stepped on to the morass, the oozy red soil squelching beneath our feet. The hounds came with us for a few yards, but, the ground becoming softer the farther we went from the edge, they halted, whined as though loath to part from friends, and then ran back to meet Vetch and one of his buccaneers, who stood helpless at the brink. They fired at us, but we were already out of range, and with the sound of their execrations still in our ears we trudged slowly but steadily towards the other side of the swamp.

Chapter 25
I Spend Cludde's Crown Piece

Thankful as I was for my wondrous escape, my mind still misgave me, both as to our own ultimate safety and as to what might befall Mistress Lucy. I did not know the extent of the swamp, and maybe Vetch and his companion would go back for their horses and, circling round it, circumvent us. Uncle Moses relieved my fears on this score, telling me that, while the swamp was little more than half a mile across, it stretched laterally for several miles, and we should reach the haven whither we were making long before the swiftest horses could complete the circuit.

On the other point, the well being of Mistress Lucy, he could give me no reassurance. 'Twas Wednesday: she came of age tomorrow; even if Vetch was not aware of this, but believed that Friday, the day of her birthday celebrations, was the actual birthday, it gave us terribly little time to concert any movements on her behalf. And so my joy of having recovered my freedom was tempered by uneasiness.

It was heavy going across this sagging morass. Uncle Moses told me that we were in no danger of sinking into it so long as we took short and rapid steps; but we were both mightily fatigued, and my feet as I lifted them seemed heavy as lead. The negro was in far worse case than I, and had I not grasped him firmly by the arm and fairly pulled him along, I think he would never have gained the other side. Towards the middle the surface of the swamp was nothing but liquid ooze, and once or twice, in spite of our swamp shoes, we sank in it up to the ankles. But at length we reached more solid ground; then Uncle Moses said we must strike off to the right, and after a tramp of two miles or thereabouts we should come to a well-concealed spot where he had no doubt we should find fugitives of his color.

As we neared the place he put his fingers to his mouth and blew a whistle of three quick notes that reminded me of the piping of a thrush. And immediately I started back: a black man had risen almost from beneath our feet. So well hidden was he in a low-growing bush that we might have passed within a yard of him and been none the wiser. I perceived that he carried a long knife in his hand.

"Hi, Sam!" said Uncle Moses, stepping in advance of me.

I stood leaning on one of the muskets while the two men spoke together in tones too low to reach my ears. But I knew from his gestures and his manner of looking at me that the stranger was loath to comply with the request Uncle Moses was putting to him. His demeanor said, as plainly as words, that he distrusted me; I was a white man, and doubtless the poor runagate had too much reason to regard all white men as his enemies. But Uncle Moses took him by the arm and appeared to plead with him; and by and by the man left us and went away.

"Him gone to ask his brudders if we may go where dey are," said Uncle Moses, coming to my side.

Then he flung himself on the ground and lay at full length upon his face, with his arms outstretched in an attitude of utter prostration. I sat down by him, clasping my knees, and mused with down-bent head.

After what seemed a long while the negro returned and told us that we might accompany him. He led us back toward the swamp, threading his way through the rank vegetation along an invisible path that wound about like the coils of a snake in most bewildering wise. But it was firm to the tread, and his bare feet had no need of swamp shoes. Finally we came to a little island copse slightly above the general level, and there, well screened from view, we found a group of about a dozen negroes. They had constructed for themselves little huts of grass and branches of trees, and in the midst a pot was boiling on a fire of sticks. They cried a greeting to Uncle Moses, and I was not a little amazed when one of them came grinning up to me and said:

"Massa Bold, we bofe free now. Huh! dat debbil nebber cotch us no mo'."

'Twas Jacob, the man who had escorted me from Spanish Town and been captured with me. He told me that he had been put to work in the plantation, but had run away on the second day, along with another man.

"Dat him ober dere," he said, pointing to a burly, pleasant-featured negro who was in close conversation with Moses. "Dat Noah! Ah! he hab dreful time--pufeckly dreful, 'cos he help Missy."

"What did he do?" I asked, feeling a most friendly disposition towards a man who had done anything for Lucy.

"She want to run away, too," he said; "ebery one want to run away. She got on horse, and Noah was leading her round about, but dey cotched him, and den, oh, lor', didn't dey jest beat him!

"Say, Noah, show Massa Bold your po' back."

The man left Uncle Moses, and, coming to me, turned about (he was naked to the waist) and displayed to my sickened gaze a score of long, raw wounds upon his back. They had begun to heal; I learned that his companions had anointed them with grease, and plastered them with leaves from a plant that grew abundantly in the forest.

"Dat is what Massa Vetch do," he said with a dark look, "and his friend he look on and cry to him to gib me mo'. He say, teach me a lesson, and I learn it--oh, yes, I learn it. And now I show how to teach lesson back."

His pleasant face was darkened with a glare of utter savagery.

"Black man can teach jest as good as white. Come 'long o' me, massa; I show massa somet'ing."

Wondering, I followed him past the huts, through the copse, into a little clearing, when I saw a white man stripped to the shirt and tightly bound to a tree.

"Dat is him!" cried Noah excitedly. "Dat is de white debbil what say gib me mo'. I teach him lesson: he nebber want no mo'."

His tone already sent a shiver through me, but as he went on to explain the nature of the lesson he intended, I shuddered with horror.

"Dis berry night we burn him up!" he cried. "Massa Bold see? We tie him up to de bough of de tree, and we light a lill fire, jest a lill one, and first it warm his feet, and den it get bigger, and creep up and up, and bimeby it come to his head, and den he burn all up. Oh, yes; dat is a proper lesson for white debbils to learn!"

"You will not do anything so horrible!" I murmured.

"Hobbible! Hain't my back hobbible? He laugh when he see ole whip come whisk! whisk! on my po' back; well, den, I laugh when I see de fire go creep, creep, and when I hear him holler. Oh, yes, it will be a proper lesson, no mistake 'bout it."

And then the poor bound wretch, whose head was hanging forward as though he were already *in extremis*, lifted his eyes and saw me.

"Bold! Humphrey Bold!" he shrieked in a harsh, gasping whisper. "Save me! Save me from these monsters!"

I started forward, scarce believing my eyes. In the pinched, haggard features of the man who was lashed to the tree I recognized my old enemy, my whilom schoolfellow, Dick Cludde.

"Save me! Save me!" he cried again and again.

"For God's sake, loose him!" I cried, turning to the negro.

God knows Cludde had done me harm enough; but for the working of a gracious Providence he had ruined my life; but all remembrance of this fled from me as I beheld his pitiful plight and mortal terror, and heard his altered voice screaming for mercy.

"I know him; he was once a friend of mine," I cried, and God forgive me the lie. "Let him go; don't torture him any longer."

Noah laughed in my face.

"What for me let him go?" he said. "'Cos he is a white man? He is a white debbil; he shall hab his lesson."

"But it is murder. You would not murder him?"

"And he murder me! De whip cut me twenty times, and if I die, what den? Noah is only a black man: it is not murder to kill a black man! Dey kill me: I lib for teach him lesson."

"Let him go," I cried, "and I will give you money--twenty dollars."

"No!"

"Thirty--forty dollars!"

"No!"

"Forty dollars is a great big lot," said Uncle Moses, who had joined us and saw my desperate eagerness to save the man.

"No!" said Noah again, his mouth tightening with inflexible determination.

"Uncle Moses," I said, "can't you bend him? I will give anything if he will but spare the man. I am a king's officer; you know that what I promise I will do; and he is your mistress' cousin."

"Noah, my son," said the old negro, "listen to Massa. S'pose you burn de white man, what good to you? He die, oh course, and nebber can do nuffin' to black mans no mo'; but you will only be pleased a lill tiny while, and if you let him go you gwine hab dollars what will last long, long time."

"No!" returned Noah. "I will teach him lesson, and be pleased for ebber and ebber."

And he walked away and began to gather up some sticks and carry them to the tree where Cludde, utterly exhausted, seemed to have fainted away.

I asked Moses what sum would purchase Noah's freedom, ready to spend my last penny to prevent the hideous scene for which preparation was being made. He told me five hundred dollars, and I bade him go to Noah and promise that the money should be his as soon as I got back to Spanish Town. He returned downcast from his mission.

"He say dat is all talk," he said. "It is for bimeby, but he want rebenge now; black man don't fink nuffin' ob bimeby."

"But can't we give him something now as earnest of what is to come? There are our muskets; they will be useful to him, and are worth some dollars; offer them to him, and assure him on the word of an Englishman that he shall have the price of his freedom as soon as ever I can get back to my friends."

He went away with this message, but came back again unsuccessful.

"He say hab plenty guns, and what good guns widout any powder and shots? He hain't got no powder; de guns hain't worth more'n old sticks. Hain't Massa got no money? If he seed de look of silver, now, dat would be somet'ing 'spectable."

But my pockets were empty; all my money had been taken by the buccaneers. And then, with a start of recollection, I remembered the crown piece that hung by a riband about my neck, and with the thought a flash of inspiration shot through my mind. I ran forward to the spot where Noah was already heaping the sticks for the fire, and, tearing open my shirt, I displayed the silver coin.

"Look, Noah," I cried, "you shall have this, and five hundred dollars beside by and by. Listen while I tell you about it."

And then I told how, ever since I had worn that coin about my neck, I had had the best of good fortune. It had brought me friends, and raised me from a lowly position. I had been imprisoned and escaped; I had been shot at, without scathe. I had gained what I prized most in all the world. I fear I exaggerated; certainly I had never before ascribed any talismanic power to the coin which I had kept for no other purpose than to humiliate the man who had humiliated me. But in this extremity I saw the possibility of working on the negro's superstitious mind, and I would have racked my invention to give the piece the most marvelous virtues under heaven.

But I had said enough. With a stare of wonderment Noah took the coin in his hand, turned it over, examined it, handled it as though it was a sacred object. I lifted the string from my neck.

"There, take it; 'tis yours," I said, handing it to him, and then, by a happy afterthought, I myself slipped it over the negro's head. He saw the white coin lying on his dusky breast, a smile overspread his face, most wondrously obliterating all the lines of malice and hate; and then, turning swiftly, he went to the tree, with me at his heels, and cut the cords.

Cludde fell fainting into my arms, and as I laid him on the ground and begged for water (not a drop had passed his lips for thirty-six hours), I wondered whether he would ever know how I had paid the stored-up interest I had vowed to pay.

Chapter 26
We Hold A Council Of War

For some time I was in doubt whether the agonies Cludde had suffered would not prove fatal. He lay long unconscious, and when his eyes at last opened he shrieked aloud, with so wild a look in his eyes that I feared his reason was gone. But I, who had not left his side since he was loosed from the tree, spoke to him quietly, assuring him that he was safe, and gave him water to drink, and by and by he was soothed to quietude and slept like a tired child. And then I lay beside him, worn out with the stress and agitations of this long day, and together (strange chance!) we who had been mortal enemies found repose on the bosom of mother earth.

Night came down upon us, and the stars were blinking in the dark vault above when we awoke. Uncle Moses brought us food--birds the negroes had snared and roasted, and root plants they had grubbed up; and as we ate we talked.

"Bold," said Cludde huskily, "you've returned good for evil. You don't want my thanks; you hate me."

"I wonder if I do," I said, and pondering the matter, I came to the conclusion that I rather despised than hated him; but I did not tell him so. "How did you come to this strait?" I asked him.

"I came up to see Lucy, and happened to arrive just after that nigger had been caught. Vetch was flogging him, told me he was an insolent and lazy scoundrel, and I agreed he ought to be taught a lesson--"

"Even if it killed him," I interrupted.

"Why, he's only a black fellow," said Cludde.

"And black fellows are flesh and blood, like you and me."

"But they haven't our feelings; come now, you won't say that?"

I would not argue with: him, and he went on--"I came to the house, and Lucy refused to see me. I hated you then, Bold; Vetch told me that you had been up, and I guessed you had put a spoke in my wheel."

"I never saw Mistress Lucy," I said.

"What? Why, Vetch told me that you had proposed to her, and been sent away with a flea in your ear."

"That was a lie. But go on: I will tell you about myself presently."

"Well, I plucked up courage to go to the house again, and this time I was admitted and saw Lucy, and by heaven, Bold, I had no inkling of what had been going on."

"You might have guessed, knowing Vetch, whom your own father had sent out here," I said.

"But not for this," he said eagerly. "I beg you to believe me, Bold. I know there is much against me, but after that business at the turnpike I told Vetch I would countenance no more tricks of that sort--though I own I helped to arrange your kidnapping at Bristowe."

"'Twas an insult to Mistress Lucy to send Vetch out here," I said, refusing to compromise on this matter. "But go on, let me hear how you came to this."

"Lucy told me what tricks Vetch had been playing, and begged me to help her to get away from him, and burst into tears, and I can't stand a woman's tears. I sought Vetch, and I told him that he had gone too far, and bade him remember that, whether she married me or not, she is my cousin, and I wouldn't have her worried.

"'You've got my father's power of attorney,' I said to him, 'but that don't authorize you to do what you are doing.'

"And then the scoundrel rounded on me, and asked me with his infernal sneer what I thought he had come out to Jamaica for, and then, by heaven, Bold, he said that he was going to marry Lucy himself!"

At this I broke into a shout of laughter, the idea seemed so ridiculous; but my mirth gave place to a hot fit of anger when I remembered that the fellow had Lucy in his power.

"I laughed, too," said Cludde, "but 'tis no laughing matter. The villain has a parson to his hand--a besotted Cambridge fellow who has sunk to buccaneering with the pretty crew Vetch has about him. I said I'd see him hanged first; I've been sick of the fellow this long time; and then he threatened me, and in his blazing temper told me about the will which he stole--"

"You didn't know it?" I cried, astonished.

"Why, I'm not a saint, Bold," he said, "but I'm not so bad as that. Vetch told Sir Richard that his uncle had burned the will among some old papers by mistake, and was afraid to confess it, but he tells me now 'twas he stole it and hid it, and says that if I attempt to interfere with him he'll produce it and turn us out of our property--which is yours, Bold; and swear that he stole it at Sir Richard's request. And then I called him a villain to his face, and said I would go instantly back to Spanish Town and proclaim him for the scoundrel he is, and he laughed and said I should never get there alive.

"But his horse was standing by; he had just come in from riding; and before he knew what I was about I was in the saddle and galloped off. In my hurry I took the wrong road. The horse carried me into the forest and stumbled over a root, and down I went, and lay dazed for a time, and when I got up I wandered about, utterly lost, and fell among these niggers. You know the rest."

I fell silent, thinking of Vetch's villainy, and of the extremity of peril in which Lucy lay. That she would willingly wed him I did not for a moment believe; but in her helpless position I feared what she might be compelled to do under constraint.

"I know we have treated you very ill," said Cludde.

"I was not thinking of that," I said, interrupting him. "You can make amends, Cludde."

"And I will, Bold, on my honor I will, as soon as ever we get back to England."

"Before then," I said. "'Twill be too late then. You must help me to save Mistress Lucy."

"But what can we do? Her birthday is on Friday--"

"On Friday?" I said, to test his knowledge.

"Yes, Vetch told me so. She will be of age then, and even supposing we could escape his people we could not get to Spanish Town and back in time. I only wish we could do something. I would give a great deal to see Vetch get his deserts."

"We must get help from Spanish Town: we must do something ourselves--you and I and the niggers. We must attack the house."

"'Tis impossible. He has a score of cut-throat ruffians in his pay."

"At the house?"

"A dozen or so at the house, the rest about the plantations and on the road, to guard against surprise from Spanish Town or any of the settlements."

"Will you help me loyally, if I can find some means of rescuing Lucy?" I asked, for Cludde's attitude to me was so altered that I was not without suspicion of his sincerity.

"With all my heart; but we can do nothing."

"At present I see no way," I sorrowfully admitted; "but help her we must. Good heavens! Can we leave her at his mercy, and not make an effort on her behalf? We may fail, but let us at least do what men may do."

Then Cludde made me tell him what had happened to me. He fell asleep before I had finished my story, but I lay for long hours pondering this baffling problem, and wishing that I had Joe Punchard and my messmates of the Dolphin instead of negroes, whom I could scarce trust. 'Twas clear, as Cludde had said, that we were no match for the ruffians whom Vetch had about him; in open fight we should be worsted, and maybe hasten the very catastrophe I dreaded. Even if we should attempt a surprise by night I could not hope for success, for the least check would turn the negroes into a pack of howling cowards. We could only succeed by a ruse, and though I cudgelled my brains until all my thoughts were in a whirl I could invent no plan which had the least promise.

And it was Wednesday night! If we had not rescued Mistress Lucy within forty-eight hours I had a strong presentiment that 'twould be too late.

I sank at last into a sleep of sheer exhaustion. When I awoke, day had dawned, and with the return to consciousness there came a sudden recollection of something told me by Uncle Moses--something that explained the fact that only two horsemen had ridden in pursuit of us. All the horses of the estate had been employed in conveying sugar to Dry Harbor. They had been gone a day; when would they return?

I sprang up in haste to get an answer to this question; for on it depended the chances of a plot which had flashed upon my mind. Uncle Moses told me that, if the usual course were followed, the wagons would return on Friday, either empty, or with loads of salt fish, which formed the staple of the negro's food. I asked what men would accompany the convoy, and learned that the wagoners were negroes, and that one or two white men would be in charge.

This information threw a ray of hope upon my dark forebodings. If we could but win to a position where the returning convoy might be intercepted, I made no doubt we could overpower the white men--overseers of the plantations; as to the negro drivers, I held them of little account. There was one possible danger: that the customary escort might be augmented by some of Vetch's buccaneers. But I saw no likelihood of this, for however careful Vetch might be in his watch over Mistress Lucy, he would have no reason to be specially vigilant over the conduct of the ordinary operations of the estate.

The question was, could we by any means come unobserved at a place where the wagons could be intercepted? I put it to Uncle Moses, who answered me readily enough, not seeing the drift of it. If we crossed the swamp, and retraced our way through the forest, we could skirt the whole length of the plantation without fear of being discovered until we arrived within a very short distance of the road to Spanish Town. We should then have to cross the road in the open, but having crossed it, we should come in less than a furlong to another clump of woodland, and passing through this, avoiding the plantain groves which filled that portion of the estate, we should reach the rough track leading to Dry Harbor, at a point about three miles from the big house. 'Twas a round in all of some twenty-five miles, and, as Uncle Moses assured me, if we were reasonably cautious we should run no risks save at the crossing of the road.

In great elation of spirit I now took into consultation Cludde with Uncle Moses, Noah, and Jacob, all of whom I felt I could trust, because all had suffered. I told them what I proposed, and whether it was the story I had told of the wondrous good fortune that had befallen me through the crown piece, or whether their own native courage and their thirst for revenge influenced them, I know not; but certain it is that the negroes agreed at once to follow my lead.

Considering then how the rest of my party should be made up, I decided, with the assent of Uncle Moses, to take only two more men, these being all who had fled from the Cludde estate. I thought it better that none but those who had a personal interest in the welfare of Mistress Lucy, and who had reason to deplore the iron rule of Vetch, should be enlisted in the enterprise. The sixth and seventh members of the expedition having been brought into the council, we talked over the details of the scheme so far as we could foresee them. My general plan was to surprise the convoy, to conceal ourselves--myself and Cludde--in one of the wagons, and, thus gaining the house unsuspected, to steal our way in and then act as chance might order.

Since we knew not how we might be taxed if we should succeed in reaching the house, and a march of twenty-five miles in the heat of the day would greatly impair our energies, we decided to set off at once (this being Thursday), and spend the night in the forest at a spot not far distant from the road. The negroes by themselves would never have consented to this plan, so great was their dread of bugaboos, but they derived courage from the companionship of white men, and, to stiffen their resolution, I told them how, when wearing the crown piece about my neck, I had escaped by night with nine companions from a place with stone walls ten feet thick. This impressed them greatly--Noah in particular; and in the evening, when we halted for our bivouac in the forest, he came to me holding the string on which the coin was suspended, and put it into my hand, saying:

"Dis white man's duppy. Massa hab it dis time; Massa got through stone wall, get through anything. Den I hab it again when Massa done wid it."

I smiled and was hesitating whether to sling it round my neck or to give it back when Cludde asked me what was the meaning of this strange talk. As I did not answer at once, Uncle Moses broke in.

"Massa gib dat silver so dat you not be burned, sah. Noah will hab eber so much more bimeby, 'nuff to buy him free, sah."

Cludde looked at me inquiringly.

"'Tis true, Cludde," I said. "I had to buy you off."

"But I don't understand," he said. "A crown piece?"

"Oh!" said I, feeling a little uneasy lest he should probe this matter of the crown piece too far, "the negro has the mind of a child. The price of his freedom is five hundred dollars: he wouldn't take my word for that sum, but the sight of a coin was enough."

"But you told me the buccaneers stripped you of your money," he said, with a look of puzzlement.

"So they did, but I happened to have this crown piece slung about my neck under my shirt, and it escaped their attention."

"Egad, I should never have believed you were superstitious," he said with a laugh, and I laughed back, glad enough that I had escaped further interrogation.

I returned the coin to Noah, assuring him that I had no further need of it, and he went away well pleased, assured of the protection of the white man's duppy--the token of the good spirits which he venerates as much as he fears the bugaboos.

I was not to get off after all. When we lay side by side on the grass, Cludde was for a long time silent; then he said abruptly, with a keen look at me:

"Bold, do you remember I flung a crown piece at you when I passed you on the Worcester road years ago!"

"I believe you did," said I, prevaricating.

"Is that the coin?"

"Why, Cludde," says I, "there are thousands of crown pieces in the world."

"Is it?" he persisted.

"Why should you suppose it is?" I said.

"Why did you keep it? Come, I must know."

"Oh, confound you, Cludde," I said, "why don't you let me go to sleep?"

"You had some design in keeping that coin," he said; "I want to know what it was."

"Well, if you insist," I said, "I meant to keep it until I could return it to you with interest. But Fate, you see, has found a better use for it."

"Bold," says he, after a silence, "you're a good fellow and a generous--"

"Belay there, Cludde," I said, anxious to cut him short, "we'll cry quits over all the past. *Intus si recte ne labora*--you remember the old school motto. We're friends, and all we have to worry about now is how to dish Cyrus Vetch; and as we shall be none the worse for a long sleep, I'll take first watch, and wake you when you've had three or four hours."

And with a grip of hands we closed the enmity of a dozen years.

Chapter 27
Some Successes And A Rebuff

We lay all next day in the forest, maintaining an irksome silence, and continually on our guard against intrusion. Uncle Moses told me that the wagons would not leave Dry Harbor on their return journey until the heat of the day was past--a circumstance which favored our design. The spot we had determined on for the ambush was five miles from our lurking place, and we should have cover all the way save where we must needs cross the road. When the time came for our setting forth, I went myself to the edge of the woodland to spy out and see if the coast was clear. Not a soul was in sight; we were at the portion of the estate which was given over to pasture; if it had been sugar land we must have inevitably met negro laborers.

I was about to return and acquaint the others that we might safely start when I heard a trotting horse, and from my place of concealment among the trees, I soon afterwards saw a horseman appear from the direction of Spanish Town and ride by towards the big house two miles or more away. He was beyond doubt one of Vetch's gang: 'twas impossible to mistake the thick ungainly figure, and the exceedingly nautical way he had of sitting his horse. 'Twas lucky indeed that we had not already begun the crossing, for he must have seen us, the road being straight: and for that same reason I deemed it well to delay a little, lest he should chance to look back. And so 'twas a good half hour later when, nothing further having happened to give us pause, we ran in a compact body for the edge of the forest, crossed the road and a long stretch of grass land, and arrived at the clump I have before mentioned, where we stood a little while to recover breath.

And then we were amazed to hear the sound of singing--amazed, for it was not the uncouth singing of negroes (who in happy circumstances delight to uplift their voices in psalms) nor yet the boisterous untuneable roaring of rough seamen, like Vetch's buccaneers, but a most melodious and pleasing sound, which put me in mind (and Cludde also) of the madrigal singers of our good town of Shrewsbury. And as it drew nearer there seemed to be a something familiar in the tone, though being quite without ear for music, as I have confessed, I could not tell whether it was a known tune or not.

With one consent, we had waited, held, I suppose, by the same feeling of wonderment and curiosity. The sound continually approached; 'twas from the direction of Spanish Town; and from our vantage ground we should soon see the singer as he passed along the road. But before he came within sight, the words of the song came distinctly to my ears, and though I knew not one tune from another, I started with a thrill of delight.

"What's that for?" cries out Salem Dick.

"What for, my jumping beau?

Why, to give the lubbers one more kick!"

Yo ho, with the rum below.

Thus rang the voice, and there ambled into view Joe Punchard, perched upon a mule, and on mules behind him two negroes, their countenances shining, their teeth flashing, with a happy smile.

"Joe!" I cried, in defiance of all caution.

"Ahoy ho!" he cried in return, pulling up his mule. "Who be that a-calling of Joe?"

I broke away from Cludde's detaining arm, and ran to my old friend.

"Ahoy ho!" he shouted jovially when he saw me; but when I put my fingers to my lips he dismounted clumsily, and met me with the whispered question, "What be in the wind, Master Bold?"

I could not have taken ten minutes to possess him with the necessary facts, so rapidly did I tell the gist of my story.

"Bless my buttons!" he ejaculated, "I reckoned there was somewhat amiss. When I heard talk of you being ill, I was most desperate uneasy, knowing you was in the latitude o' Vetch. And I said so to my captain, and begged him to let me fetch a course this way to make sure as you weren't run aground or wrecked on a sunken reef. My captain he laughs and says you'd steered clear so often that he'd no fears of you not coming safe to port; but seeing I was set on it, he give me leave, and to make things reg'lar, as he said, he told me being in these parts to keep an eye lifting for the buccaneers as are said to be somewheres on this coast. And sink my timbers, it do seem as how I'm on a rare voyage of discovery!"

I told him quickly of the purpose I had in view, and he at once volunteered to join our party. But this I could not allow. I had no doubt that the horseman whom I had previously seen riding to the house was carrying thither news of his approach, as my own arrival had been heralded. He would be expected, and if he did not appear Vetch would be suspicious, and might despatch men in search of him, and the footprints of his mule would bring them upon our track. I urged him to go forward with his guides to the house, where it was possible, if they left him free, that he might prove a useful auxiliary if our ruse succeeded. To this he readily agreed, declaring he would anchor at Vetch's door, and would not slip his cable until I came up on his quarter. And he clambered to the saddle again, called to the negroes to come on astern, and set forth again towards the house, and as I rejoined my party among the trees I heard his jolly voice ringing out:

"I 'llow this crazy hull o' mine

At sea has had its share;

Marooned three times an' wounded nine,

An' blowed up in the air."

We had wasted some eight or ten minutes on this interview, and 'twas high time to speed on our journey if we were to reach the place of ambush before the convoy. As we marched, I told Cludde the purport of my talk with Joe, and he agreed that the course I had insisted on was the right one, though he feared Punchard would have a sorry time when he came within the clutches of the man who bore a long-standing grudge against him. I confess that I had clean forgotten the matter of the barrel rolling, and being now reminded of it, felt greatly concerned at having sent poor Joe into the very jaws of danger, but 'tis idle to repent, and I could only hope that we should get to the house in time to prevent any irremediable harm.

'Twas nigh five o'clock when we came to the copse fringing the road (a rough cart track) from the coast.

Noah went out stealthily to inspect the road for traces of the convoy, and told us that we were in time; the wagons had not yet come up. We waited patiently, and I took advantage of the interval to repeat the instructions I had previously given to the negroes. About half an hour after our arrival we heard a creaking in the distance, and soon the convoy came in sight-- three six-horsed wagons, with two negroes in each, and two overseers on horseback, carrying long whips, and riding side by side in the rear. These two Cludde and I marked for our own, leaving the negroes to deal with the men of their color. We two separated from the rest of the party, so that the attack might be made on the whole line at the same moment.

When we came opposite to the two riders, I gave a shrill whistle, and with Cludde at my side dashed from among the trees. So sudden and unexpected was the assault that the overseers had no time to defend themselves. Cludde and I hauled them from their saddles and held them fast while two of the negroes brought from the wagons ropes wherewith to bind them. The negro drivers let forth a yell and dropped their reins when the rest of our party sprang out from the copse. The convoy halted and Uncle Moses in a very little time made the drivers understand that they must either do what we bade them or be trussed up and left in the woods. With night approaching this latter alternative had too many terrors to make it acceptable, and the men professed themselves willing to render utter obedience, the more readily in that Vetch and his gang of desperadoes were well hated by all the hands upon the estate.

One of them, who Uncle Moses told me, was a bad character, we bound and placed with the overseers in one of the wagons, which we then drew into the copse out of sight from the road.

Cludde and I deliberated for a moment whether we should mount the overseers' horses and ride on with the wagons. But we decided not to tempt fate. Before we reached the big house we should have to pass that of the principal overseer of the estate, and though the sky was already dusking, and it would be dark before we arrived, there were many chances that we might be seen by the buccaneers or others as we came within the bounds, and being in our officers' habiliments we should be marked and the alarm given. So we resolved to get into the first wagon, and cover ourselves with the sacking it contained as soon as we came to the borders of the plantations. Uncle Moses seated himself beside the driver of the first wagon, Noah on the second, and the rest of our party got into this wagon and likewise hid under sacking.

The stables, as I had learned from Uncle Moses, lay beyond the big house, so that our driving by would awaken no suspicion. In order that we might gain the further advantage of darkness, Uncle Moses drove slowly, and there was but a glimmer of twilight when we reached the house of the overseer. He had heard the rumbling of our wheels, and was standing at his gate as we came up. Seeing only the wagons and no horsemen, he cried out to know where the rest were. The negro beside Uncle Moses (who shrank back to escape recognition) made ready answer that the third wagon had broken down, and would come on presently with the overseers. The white man rapped out an oath, declaring (with what truth I know not) that the cursed wagon was always breaking down, and we drove past. Two of the buccaneers were smoking at the gates of the big house when we came up, and they hailed us in rough sailor fashion, but showed no curiosity; the work of the estate was no concern of theirs.

Uncle Moses had told me that there would certainly be a number of the buccaneers in the kitchen of the big house, where they took their supper and often sat far into the night drinking and dicing. As we drew near, indeed, I heard through the sack that covered me ('twas very sticky and fraught with the cloying smell of sugar) loud sounds of merriment proceeding from the house. Instead of driving past in the direction of the stables, the negro, obeying his instructions, pulled up his horses when the wagons came opposite the kitchen door.

I did not need Uncle Moses' call to know that the moment had arrived. Flinging off the sack that smothered us, Cludde and I sprang from the wagon, our companions doing likewise, and we burst headlong into the kitchen.

The merry sounds that we had heard were explained, but in an unforeseen way. In the middle of the room sat Joe Punchard, tied to a chair. Around him were half a dozen of Vetch's villainous crew engaged in the pleasant sport of baiting their prisoner. At the moment of our entrance they were rubbing the dregs of molasses into his red hair. I learned afterwards from him that he had been seized on approaching the house, and, Vetch being absent at the time, had been carried into the kitchen for a preliminary inquisition. They knew, doubtless on the information of the horseman I had seen, that he was a seaman from a king's ship, and charged him with having come to spy on them, shrewdly hitting the mark, though they could hardly have believed in their accusation, seeing that he had approached quite openly with no companions but a brace of negroes. He had suffered many indignities before we arrived, and he confessed to me that, though he had endured many a buffeting in the first years of his life at sea, he had never spent so distressful a couple of hours as those when the buccaneers put him to the question.

They were, I say, rubbing a filthy black semi-fluid into his hair at the moment when Cludde and I, with our negroes behind, made a sudden irruption into the kitchen. We had our muskets with us, and seizing mine by the barrel, I brought the stock down on the head of the fellow nearest me, and he dropped heavily to the floor. Springing past him, I cut Joe's cords with my knife, and then turned to assist my companions in the fight that was raging. The five buccaneers were sturdy villains, and after the first shock of surprise they were more than a match for Cludde and the negroes. One had wrested the musket from Cludde's hand, and now had his arms about his body, endeavoring to throw him. The rest had drawn their hangers and were pressing hard upon the negroes, who made play with their knives, but were not equal to their opponents.

The entrance of Joe and myself into the fray, however, turned the tide of battle in our favor. Joe had caught up the chair to which he had been bound, and wielded it like a flail, with every swing of it breaking a head or snapping an arm. And my musket took a heavy toll. The room rang with the din of battle--the shouts of the men, the whoops of the negroes, the clashing of our weapons. For half a minute it was perfect pandemonium; then finding the odds hopelessly against them, the two buccaneers who were not by this time on the floor dashed through the open door and fled, pursued by the negroes, who had no doubt long scores to pay off against them.

In the midst of the uproar I had not lost sight for a moment of the main purpose of my errand, and as soon as I saw that the issue of the fight was decided I called Uncle Moses to my side and asked him eagerly to lead me to his mistress' sitting room. We went along a passage and up a flight of stairs to the floor above, coming then to another corridor which was in darkness.

"Missy's room at de end," said the negro.

With beating heart I hurried along behind him, and we came to an open door. I knocked upon it, and entered. The room was dark, but the window was open, and the jalousies not having been closed it was possible to see that no one was there.

"Missy gone to bed," said Moses; "de bedroom is just dar."

He pointed to a closed door in the wall. Loath as I was to disturb Mistress Lucy, I was still more anxious that she should know of my presence; so I went to the door and rapped briskly upon it. There was no answer. I rapped again, more loudly, but still without result. She was either fast asleep or-- and the thought struck me with a chill--she was no longer there.

"Where is Mr. Vetch's room ?" I asked, beset by a great anxiety.

"I show Massa," replied Uncle Moses.

He led me from the room, and along a passage that branched from the other. There was a thread of light beneath a door at the end.

"Dat is Massa Vetch's room," said the negro.

I went to it and tried the handle. The door was locked. I thumped upon it with my fist, and was answered with a curse.

"Settle your drunken quarrels yourselves," cried the well-remembered voice. "What is it to me if you break each other's skulls?"

Clearly he had heard the uproar and taken it to be a brawl among the buccaneers. 'Twas like Vetch to shut himself aloof from the disputes of his hirelings; he was ever careful of his skin. Affecting a harsh and surly voice I cried that the quarrel was over and asked him to open the door: I had news from Spanish Town. Another oath saluted me; then I heard the sound of movements within, and the door was thrown open.

Instantly I sprang in, the negro at my heels; he closed the door behind me; and I stood once more face to face with Cyrus Vetch.

His sallow cheeks blanched when lie saw me. No doubt 'twas the apparition he least expected. He whips out his sword and springs back to have space to cut at me; but I parried the stroke with my musket, and he skipped back and entrenched himself behind the table. I own that I could have cheerfully slain him there and then but for my anxiety concerning Mistress Lucy's whereabouts. There was Vetch, glaring at me from behind the table, upon which, as I now saw, there were books and money, and two lighted candles.

"You have no right here," said Vetch, and his voice was unsteady, "breaking into my house--"

"Your house!" I replied. "And as for right, I have the right of every honest man to catch a villain and present him to the hangman."

"Mind your words, sir," cries the fellow, and I saw by his manner that he was desperately anxious to gain time. "I warn you I am steward of this estate by virtue of authority deputed to me by Sir Richard Cludde, the guardian appointed by the Court of Chancery."

"Your stewardship and Sir Richard's guardianship ended yesterday," I said curtly.

"You mistake," says he, beginning to recover himself, "I tell you again that this is an unwarrantable intrusion, and you stand there at your peril."

"Stuff!" I cried impatiently. "'Tis you who are an intruder, a trespasser; you are in this house against the will of the owner, who is now of full age. But I won't bandy words with you about that. You and I have other accounts to settle, Cyrus Vetch, and if you do not yield at once, I swear I will show you no mercy."

I advanced towards the table, and Vetch lifted his sword as though to defend himself. But his courage failed him, and indeed his was a hopeless case if it came to a tussle, as he very well knew. Incontinently he dropped his sword point, and with a shrug of the shoulders, said:

"I will not fight a couple of bullies. I yield now, but let me tell you, Humphrey Bold, the law will have something to say to this."

"It will indeed," I said grimly. "Hand over your sword."

He took it by the blade; I placed my musket against the table and reached forward to take the hilt, but with a sudden swift movement he swept the candles to the floor and the room was in total darkness. I sprang forward, but before I could vault over the obstructing table Vetch had dashed through a door behind him that opened on to the veranda. I was after him in an instant, and he escaped me by no more than an arm's length. He had leapt over the rail of the veranda, and I halted for a moment, supposing that he must at least twist his ankles after a fall of some fifteen feet. But I was amazed to see him swarming down one of the pillars that supported the veranda.

I followed him in desperate haste, but the fellow was always very light and nimble, and the fear of death lent him a marvelous new agility. My heavier frame was slower in descending; yet I could not have been much more than fifteen seconds behind him; but he had vanished. There were bushes and palms growing to within a few feet of the house. I ran among them, but could not hear his footsteps, nor had I any means of judging of the direction of his flight. Mad with disappointment, I rushed blindly on, and in a moment collided with a man, whom seizing, I knew by the howl he emitted, no less than by the feel of his bare skin, that I had laid hands on a negro.

"Which way did he run?" I cried, shaking the man in my hot impatience.

"Oh, Massa, I dunno nuffin'," said the trembling wretch.

I hurled him aside and sped off again, very soon encountering other negroes, who in spite of their dread of the dark, had been drawn from their huts, I doubt not, by the noise of the altercation.

"Where is your mistress?" I asked one of them.

He could tell me nothing. I asked the same question of another man whom I met within a few yards.

"I see Missy going to Massa Wilkins' house," he said. "Two men take her."

Wilkins was, I knew, the name of the principal overseer. Uncle Moses coming up with me, I bade him lead me at once to Mr. Wilkins' house. We ran on as fast as our legs could carry us, the other negroes shuffling along behind, uttering cries and yells which angered me beyond endurance. We had come some distance in the wrong direction, and I fumed in vain and bitter rage at the loss of time.

Coming into the road that led to the house I heard the sound of galloping horses, and though I continued to run until I was breathless and dripping with sweat I knew I was too late. The thud of the hoofs grew fainter and fainter. Without doubt Vetch had seized Mistress Lucy, and was hurrying her away; the villain had baffled me; Lucy, snatched from me, was hopelessly beyond my reach.

Chapter 28
I Cut The Enemy's Cables

At the door of the overseer's house stood Patty, Mistress Lucy's old nurse, wringing her hands and weeping bitterly. She told me through her tears that Vetch had set Lucy before him on his own horse, and that he was accompanied by two of his desperadoes. I broke away from her as she was imploring me to save her "dear lamb," as she called her mistress, and ran back in the direction of the big house to find a horse and lead a pursuit.

The whole place was in commotion. All the negro workers on the estate seemed to have flocked together, many of them carrying flares which threw a lurid glow upon the scene. Before I reached the house I was met by Cludde and Punchard, who had laid the captured buccaneers in pound. I rapidly acquainted them with what had happened, and was going on to the stables to find horses when one of the negroes told me that there was none there, the only saddle horses being those which were now carrying Vetch and his companions to the coast. But the wagons were still where we had left them; in the excitement of the past half hour they had been forgotten. The horses were draught horses, and did not promise good speed, but we had no others; and I cried to the men to unyoke the teams, while I ran to the kitchen for a weapon.

I seized a couple of the buccaneers' cutlasses, and hastening back, gave one to Cludde. We had no time for saddling up; throwing ourselves on the horses' bare backs, we set off with Punchard and Uncle Moses along the road, urging the beasts to a pace which I feared they could not long keep up.

As we drew near to the place of our ambush I remembered the overseers we had left tied up there in the wood, and their horses which we had tethered. Bidding Punchard and the negroes ride on, I flung myself from the back of my sweating steed, ran into the wood, and soon returned with the saddle horses. Within three minutes of our halt Cludde and I were galloping on, at a pace which soon outstripped our more heavily mounted companions. Vetch had had but ten or fifteen minutes' start of us, and his horse carrying a double burden, I hoped we should overtake him before he could convey Mistress Lucy aboard his brig.

Luckily the moon had risen, and was throwing a light, dim but sufficient, upon the track. Birds clattered out of the trees as we sped past; wild creatures of the wood, terrified at the unwonted disturbance of the night, scurried across our path. In spite of the moonlight, and because of the deep shadows it cast, we narrowly escaped being dashed from our horses by low-hanging branches of the trees on either side.

So we raced on for mile after mile without pause or mitigation of our pace. The track wound about in baffling curves, so that we could see but a little distance ahead. Once or twice I thought I caught a glimpse of moving objects before us, but 'twas but a trick of the moonlight. We dared not stop to listen for sounds of the fugitives; I felt that every second was of vital import, and 'twas not until we had come into a stretch of country clear of trees, our horses' hoofs falling silently on the soft turf, that we caught the faint rustle of the sea. I knew not how far distant it was; sounds carry far and are deceptive at night; we smote the flanks of our horses and rode as for a wager.

Suddenly a shrill whistle cut the air.

"A signal!" I said to Cludde, riding at my side. "Are they calling assistance?"

"'Tis a call for a boat, without doubt," he replied. "They have got to the shore."

Sick with fear that we were too late, I pressed my horse forward at a mad and reckless gallop, outpacing Cludde altogether. We were now again among trees, and, having come out of the moonlight, I could not at first see more than a yard or two ahead. But on a sudden the dim track before me was wholly blotted out by a dark figure. It loomed larger as I approached, and my heart leapt with the hope that it was Vetch's overburdened horse dropping behind. The rider could not escape; there was a bank on either side of the track. I was within a dozen yards of him when he reined up as if to dismount and seek the shelter of the woodland, and then I perceived with distress that whoever it might be it was not Vetch; the horse had no second burden.

Next moment there was a flash and a roar; a bullet grazed my arm; finding himself closer pressed than he thought, the fellow had turned in his saddle and fired at me. He uttered an oath when he saw me riding towards him unchecked. I was level with him, I drew my horse alongside; and raising my cutlass above my left shoulder I brought it down with a swinging cut upon the man. With a cry he toppled from his saddle, and I shot past, in a headlong rush towards the now thunderous rumbling of the sea.

'Twas but a few moments afterwards that I found myself falling as it seemed into space. In my heedless and impetuous course I had come unawares to the edge of a cliff. My horse fell, flinging me clean over his crupper. I had given myself up for lost when I was suddenly caught as by outstretched arms, in the entangling foliage of a shrub, and as I lay there, dazed, I heard a sickening thud far below me, and guessed that no such friendly obstacle had saved my poor horse from death.

Barring the shock, and a few scratches, I was unhurt, and with great thankfulness of heart for my merciful deliverance I crawled carefully out of the shrub, and set to scrambling up the steep slope to the top. There I met Cludde pale and shaking with horror. My involuntary cry as I fell had warned him. He reined up in time to escape my mishap, and hearing shortly afterwards the thud as the horse came to the bottom, he believed that I must be a mangled corpse.

"Too late!" he gasped, clutching me by the arm and pointing down to the sea.

Clear in the moonlight lay the dark shape of a brig with bare yards. At that very moment a boat was drawing in under her quarter, and as we stood helpless there we saw a cradle let down over the side, a form placed in it and hoisted to the deck, and then the boat's crew mounting one by one.

'Twas not until Uncle Moses came up with Joe that we found the circuitous path by which Vetch had reached the shore. We raced down, but Vetch, you may be sure, had left no boat in which we might follow him. We came upon his horse, quietly cropping the plants that grew at the foot of the cliff. The moon shining seawards, we were in shadow, so that had Vetch been looking from the brig, he would not have seen me as I raged up and down in impotent fury, nor my companions as they sat themselves down, troubled, like myself, but not with the same yearning.

My grief and rage bereft me for a time of all power of thought. All that I was conscious of was the fact that Lucy was gone, irrevocably, as I feared. But by and by order returned to my confused and gloomy mind, and, observing suddenly that the tide was running in, and that the breeze was blowing inshore, I felt a springing of hope within me.

'Twas clear that the brig could not put to sea against both wind and tide; she must lie where she was for several hours; was it possible that even now something might be done to rescue Mistress Lucy? Could we by some means win to the brig and snatch her from the villainous hands that held her captive? I dashed back to my companions and put this throbbing question to them. They shook their heads; we had no boat to convey us to the vessel, nor if we had could we have overcome the crew by main force. Uncle Moses said that there were some fifteen or twenty men aboard, well armed; she carried three brass guns; whereas we were but four, unarmed save for our two cutlasses. And even supposing our party were ten times as large, we could do nothing without means of transport; and the buccaneers could bring their guns to bear upon us if we exposed ourselves to their view, and with the turn of the tide could mock us and sail away.

But on a sudden a thought came to me. Might we not at least render the departure of the brig impossible? Though with any force we might gather 'twas hopeless to think of capturing her, if we could but strand her we should at any rate gain time, and maybe bargain with Vetch for the release of the lady. He would know that he had put himself beyond the pale of mercy if he should be caught, his hope of gaining the estate must be dead; we might work on his fears and the fears of the men with him, and secure our object by paying them a price.

I took Cludde with me to the top of the cliff to gain a clearer view of the vessel's position. Keeping in shadow, we saw that she lay some little way out in a narrow bay overhung by cliffs, the seaward end appearing closed, owing to a bend in the shore. The tide was fast coming in; the wind, which at the foot of the cliffs had seemed but a light breeze, was blowing strong at our altitude.

"Cludde," I said, "I am going to cut the cables."

"'Tis madness!" he replied, in an accent of amazement and protest. "You would be sure to be seen in the moonlight."

"The moon is sinking," I answered. "'Twill be down behind the cliffs in an hour."

"But the sharks! These waters are infested with them."

"'Tis the only way," I said with resolution, "and sharks or no sharks I must make the attempt. With the wind and tide the brig, if I can but cut her cables, will drift up the bay and run on the shoals, and then 'twill be impossible to get her off for some hours."

"You cannot cut the cables unperceived. When they feel her riding free they will suspect the cause, and you're a dead man."

"I must take my chance. 'Twill be dark soon, and maybe luck, that has been against me so long, will turn with the tide. I am going to do it, Cludde, and as we have an hour or so before the moon goes down, come with me along the cliff to find the most convenient spot for the venture."

We went along together, and had walked but a few yards when we came near to breaking our necks. A part of the cliffs had fallen, leaving a wide gap, and coming suddenly to this, we barely escaped plunging headlong down. The long slope was strewn with great numbers of stones small and large. We managed to scramble down the one steep side, and up the other, without having to go a long way round, and came at length opposite the brig, and saw by the manner of her rocking that she rode on two anchors, one from the bows and the other from the stern. There were several men on deck; we heard their voices and laughter. I thought of Mistress Lucy doubtless imprisoned in the cabin, and vowed that before many hours were past she should be free, if mortal wit and mortal arm could achieve it.

We settled on a place for me to take the water--a little beyond the brig, where the cliff dipped low. With all my heart I hoped the tide would not turn before the moon went down. We did not care to leave the spot and return to the others, lest when I came again I should lose my way in the darkness and come to some mishap. But while we were waiting on the cliff edge for the setting of the moon I bethought me that our company would be none the worse for strengthening, for if the brig were stranded as I hoped, some means might perchance be found (though I knew not what) of gaining possession of her. So I sent Cludde back to Uncle Moses to bid him ride back to the house and bring up, afoot or on horseback, a great force of the negroes of the estate, with whatever arms they could find. I reckoned (but wrongly, as it proved) that curiosity, the courage of numbers, and their common hatred of Vetch, would outweigh their dread of bugaboos, and bring them at once.

When Cludde had departed on this errand, I sat by the edge of the cliff, waiting with scant patience for the slow sinking moon to disappear. At last it was gone; all around was darkness and silence, save for the washing of the tide and the rustling of the trees in the wind. I stripped off my coat, left it with my cutlass on the grass, and, taking my knife between my teeth, crept into the water and struck out towards the brig. I swam silently; indeed, I had little need to exert myself, for the tide carried me in the direction I would go. And so, with a few minutes, I came safely under the vessel's side.

I heard voices on the deck above me, and though I could not catch what was said, I distinguished Vetch's clear, high-pitched tones. Doubtless the crew were keeping a careful watch on the shore, but very likely they had heard the crashing of my horse when he fell, and Vetch might be flattering himself that the beast and I had shared the same fate and that he would set eyes on me no more. I waited but long enough to be sure there was no uneasiness among the crew; then, with much pains to avoid splashing, I crept close along by the hull until I found the fore cable.

When considering my plan on the shore, I had to decide which of the two cables to attempt first. The vessel lay with her head to the sea. If I cut the cable over the stern, the tide running in, the position of the brig would alter so slightly as not to be at once perceived, and I might have time to deal with the other cable before anyone was aware of it. On the other hand, supposing I were by some unlucky chance espied, the cutting of the second cable would be beyond possibility, and no harm done. Whereas, if I began with the fore cable, the brig would swing round immediately, and the movement could not escape the notice of the crew, however heedless, and if they looked over the side they might spy me and so defeat my full purpose. Yet it seemed that by adopting the latter course I could not fail utterly; with the fore rope cut the vessel might drag the other anchor, so that, indeed, it might not be necessary to cut the second rope at all. The risk to me was perhaps greater, but so would be the success; accordingly I had decided to begin my work under the bow of the vessel.

Winding my legs about the part of the rope that was in the water, I began to saw gently with my knife at the part above me, only my head and shoulders showing above the surface. The tide and the sea breeze put some strain on the cable, but every now and again it slackened as the bow sank with the long rocking of the vessel.

This set me thinking. If the rope snapped when it was taut, those on board would feel the spring of it, and I should be without doubt discovered before I could sever the other: whereas, if the severance was made when the rope was slack, there would be no shock, and the men would be aware of nothing until the vessel swung round on the tide. I so timed my knife work, therefore, that the last strand was cut through when the bow was dipping. The moment it was done I sank down to the water level, and after waiting a moment to see in what direction the vessel would swing, I went wholly under, and swam along in the opposite direction towards the stern, keeping as close to the hull as was safe.

When I came up for breath, I heard a great uproar on board. The crew were flocking to the bows to see what had happened to the anchor. Meanwhile with a few more strokes I reached the other rope, and was hacking away at it steadily when I heard one cry out that the cable was cut, and immediately afterwards the voice of Vetch as he rushed out of the roundhouse. I felt pretty secure in the darkness under the stern sheets, but the strain upon the cable here was much greater now that the other was gone, and when I cut it through the vessel gave a jump, I heard oaths and a great scurry of feet on deck and some one let down a flare to discover the perpetrator of the mischief.

You may be sure I dived under water as quickly as might be, but not before I was descried, and my head had barely disappeared when a heavy object fell with a great splash within a few inches of it. I swam along like a fish beneath the surface, making towards the shore; but when for the sake of my lungs I had perforce to come up, a perfect fusillade spattered all around me, and it seemed a miracle I was not hit. I swam on; the tide was bearing the vessel away from me; the flare lit but a narrow space of water, and I doubt whether my head could now be seen and made a target. Though I heard the muskets roaring and slugs plopping into the water, not one of them touched me, and in a minute or two I gained the beach, pretty breathless, but marvelously content.

As I shook the water from me I heard lusty swearing from the deck of the drifting vessel, and from the tone of some of the voices guessed that the lookout was in very hot water. And amid the deeper voices of the buccaneers Vetch's shriller tone was quite audible to me, as he shouted for someone to drop a kedge anchor over the side and stop the cursed drifting. This was done, but I was in no fears for the result, for under the force of wind and tide combined there was a considerable way on the brig, which no light anchor would avail to check. And in a few minutes I knew for certain that I was right.

There came a great shout: "She's aground!" and the dark shape, which I could now barely distinguish from where I stood, ceased to move.

Satisfied that for a time at least I had prevented Vetch from putting to sea, I clambered up the cliff and set off to rejoin my companions, not venturing to go back for my coat, lest I should lose my way in the dark. They had been eagerly watching the issue of my device, the success of which pleased them mightily. Cludde made me strip off my dripping garments, declaring that if I stood in them (the night being chilly) I should catch my death of cold.

"That's all very well," I said; "but I shall be colder still stark naked."

"You must just run about and slap yourself," cries Joe; "Mr. Cludde and me can help--me particler, my name being so. And it won't be for long, 'cos when that black Moses went off to do your bidding (he was a bit scared of some foolishness he called bugaboos), I told him to bring clothes and blankets from the house, knowing that the likes o' that wouldn't have come into your own noddle."

"True, it did not," I confessed. "I am lucky in having an old mariner like you to look after me."

"Ay, and there be old mariners aboard that brig, too. See, they bin and dropped a couple of boats out, to tow her off."

This gave me a start, and I watched with great anxiety the efforts of the buccaneers to haul their vessel off the shoals. She was not more than fifty yards from the cliff where we were standing, which somewhat overhung the bay, and from our elevated position we could see clearly what was going on. I suppose it was a full hour before they gave up the attempt, and 'twas clear that having failed a good many more hours must pass before 'twould be possible to float her, for the tide, which had been at the flood when she ran aground, was now ebbing, and Vetch could not (any more than King Canute) command that.

I think if I had been Vetch, with so much at stake (for if we got the better of him, be sure there would soon be a halter about his neck)--I think if I had been in his place, with nigh a score of stalwart daredevils at my beck, all armed and trained to desperate deeds, I should have waded ashore wi' 'em and made some effort to run us down. He must have known that there could be but two or three of us, and with a little manoeuvering and stealth there was a chance that he might have got upon us and done us mischief.

But Vetch, as has more than once appeared, was never a fellow to run into jeopardy; and our very weakness, I doubt not, persuaded him that he had nothing to fear in way of assault, and need only bide for the next flood to carry him out beyond our reach.

Many times during that night I thought of Mistress Lucy, and wondered whether she, below decks, had guessed from the movement of the vessel, and the commotion and uproar, that we were still working for her behoof. She told me afterwards that, having locked herself in the cabin, she was in a stupor of grief, and felt, when the vessel moved (believing that it was putting out to sea) that nothing could save her now. But when she heard the shouts and the firing, a wild hope sprang up within her; she was possessed with a strong assurance that something was being attempted for her sake, and she clasped her hands and prayed that it might have a happy issue.

Chapter 29
We Bombard The Brig

'Twas not very long before Uncle Moses was back, bringing welcome blankets, in which I rolled myself while my clothes were drying at a fire Joe kindled in the wood. The old negro said that we could not expect any reinforcements before daybreak, the people being quite unwilling to march during the night so far from their homes. He had brought back with him, however, Noah and Jacob on horseback, and indeed I suspected that without them even Uncle Moses himself would not have conquered his dread of the bugaboos and faced the night journey a second time.

Some three hours after daybreak the dusky recruits came dropping in with weapons of all sorts--firelocks, knives, bludgeons--and with food, of which I for one was mighty glad, being sharp set after my swimming and a cold night. The negroes made a great clamour as their numbers increased--there were soon pretty nearly a hundred of them, all the able-bodied men on the estate and a fair sprinkling of women, too. 'Twas hopeless, the noise being so great, to expect that Vetch would not get a shrewd notion of the size of our force, and I saw no reason for attempting to conceal it; indeed, I nourished a secret hope that, being a coward at heart, he would be daunted at sight of us, and yield up Mistress Lucy on terms. But this hope soon took wing.

The tide had now left the brig high and dry on the sand. She had heeled over, but not enough to make it possible for her crew to use their brass guns against the negroes who crowded the top of the cliff. They made some attempt to train the guns, but desisted when they saw that the utmost elevation would reach no higher than halfway up. But the cliff top was well within range of their muskets, as one unfortunate negro, approaching the edge too closely found to his cost. A shot struck him on the leg, and he ran howling back, causing his companions to scuttle like rabbits into the woodland.

We had discussed during the night what course we should follow in the morning, but without arriving at any conclusion. I hoped that we should find ourselves in a state to make an organized assault on the brig and carry it by main force; but this idea was speedily dashed when I came to take stock of our forces and armament. We had but eight muskets among us; I counted more than twenty buccaneers on the sloping deck of the brig. Though we so greatly outnumbered them I saw that a direct assault could not succeed. From the vantage of the deck they would have us at their mercy; and though fifty disciplined men, even unarmed, might perhaps swarm up and overcome them by sheer weight of numbers, I believed that the negroes would have no stomach for so desperate an undertaking.

And my former gloom and trouble of mind descended upon me, when I saw the tide begin to creep up again. Unless we could do something before the flood the buccaneers would without doubt get the vessel off, for she had not sufficient way on when she struck to run her deep into the sand, and they had only to jettison a part of her cargo to float her.

I walked apart with Cludde and Punchard, all three of us at our wit's end. With only eight muskets we could not fire fast enough to keep the deck clear of men, and our store of ammunition was scanty; further, I doubted whether the negroes were sufficiently practised with firearms to make good marksmen. It seemed that we should ere long see the buccaneer vessel slipping out of our reach.

'Twas a chance act of Joe Punchard that drew me out of my heaviness, and set my wits a-jump. We were walking along the cliffs, and came to that gap I have before mentioned, where Cludde and I had nearly broke our necks the night before.

"'T'ud ha' saved a deal o' trouble if that there barrel had rolled a bit further," says Joe, and he picks up a stone and shies it out to sea, for the mere easement of his temper. My eyes followed the flight of the stone idly, but when it flopped into the water a notion came to me which I was quick to impart.

"By Jupiter, Cludde," I cried, "we'll bombard 'em!"

He stared at me as though he feared my wits were astray, but when I pointed to the innumerable stones strewing the cliff side, from boulders of great size to nuggets no bigger than an apple, and showed how easy 'twould be for our negroes to cast them on to the very deck of the brig, his face changed, and I saw a light in his eyes that reminded me of the time when he was one of the ringleaders in the prankish tricks of the Shrewsbury Mohocks. Then all at once he fell sober again.

"But what's the good," he said. "We can clear the deck, 'tis true; but be never a whit the nearer to capturing the vessel."

"I don't know that," said I. "If we clear the deck they go down below; if they go down below they will not be able to keep so good a lookout upon us; and while the niggers are stoning the deck we may get a chance to creep up and be among 'em before they know it."

"But they would see us from the portholes," he persisted.

"True, if we are fools enough to approach 'em broadside," I said. "The bow is pointing shorewards; if we make for a point exactly opposite and go in single file in a line with the vessel's keel, they will not see us unless they put their heads clean out of the portholes and look down and aslant, and they will not do that with the chance of getting a broken skull."

"Smite my timbers," cries Joe, "'tis a pretty ploy, and would tickle my captain mightily. We'll do it, sir, and all I wish is that the niggers can aim straight."

We lost no time in putting things in trim for the venture, and indeed 'twould not be long before the tide washed the brig and rendered the attack I proposed impossible. Gathering the negroes, we set them to collect stones of a fair size (but not too big, for I did not wish to break holes in the deck with jeopardy to Mistress Lucy), and pile them up so as to be handy. And since I have ever believed that folk, whether black or white, work more willingly if they see the aim and purpose of their toil, I told them as they set about the task what our intent was. It pleased them, and they worked with a will, being indeed childishly eager to begin the bombardment before the time was ripe.

When a sufficiency of missiles had been collected, I ranged the negroes along the cliff so that, while they could see the brig, they could scarcely be seen from it. They were stupid enough to be sure; from what I saw of negroes then and since I cannot but think they are no better than children in intelligence; and in their eagerness to begin this merry sport, as they regarded it, they went a deal too near the edge of the cliff and exposed too large a portion of their bodies.

There was nothing for it but to place them in position ourselves, which I did, Cludde and Joe assisting (the latter with some roughness of handling and of speech), and we marked out a line for them beyond which we forbade them to advance. Then, all being ready I gave the word. Instantly some three score stones, none less than a pound in weight, hurtled down, many of them falling on to the sand, a dozen, maybe, finding the deck, and two or three striking the buccaneers.

There was a roar from below, which the negroes answered with a wild whoop, and then a dozen muskets flashed, and the slugs whistled over our heads or embedded themselves in the cliff. Another shower of stones fell, a greater proportion this time hitting the mark, which filled the simple negroes with such joy that they pressed forward in full view from the ship, many of them exposing the whole upper half of their bodies.

What ensued taught them a lesson. A second fusillade burst from the vessel; two of the negroes fell with howls of pain; the rest scurried back in dismay, and some few took to their heels and fled squealing into the woods. I called them back and rated them soundly for disobeying orders, and then we placed them again in a secure position and the bombardment recommenced.

I reckoned that within a minute or two five hundred stones had been hurled from the cliff, and though many more fell upon the sand than upon the deck I saw that the effect was answering my hopes. Some of the crew retreated to the lee side of the masts; others crouched under the guns, whence they fired their muskets, slowly and with difficulty, doing us no harm; others again took refuge by the break of the poop, and in the round house and the forecastle.

One man with great boldness tried to climb the rigging to the cross-trees, no doubt with intent to get a better aim. But he instantly became the target for a perfect hurricane of stones, and he dropped to the deck and crawled painfully away. In a few minutes not a man was to be seen.

Bidding the negroes continue to throw, but not so rapidly, I lay down on the cliff top and took a good look at the vessel. So far as I could discover, no one was so posted as to be able to see below the level of the deck and I deemed that the time had come to attempt the second and more hazardous part of my plan. Leaving Uncle Moses to superintend the activities of the main body of negroes, I crept down the gap with Cludde, Punchard and a score of the men who possessed arms of a sort, and came (not without some perilous stumbles) to the sea line, immediately opposite to the bow of the brig. Then those of us who had muskets lit our matches, and I set forward across the sand, bending almost double, and making straight for the figurehead, the others close behind me in single file. Stones were still falling from the cliff, and I was in fear, as we approached the vessel, lest some of the negroes should be hit and betray us with a cry. But we arrived beneath the bow without this mishap and undiscovered, and crept round to the larboard side, where we were sheltered by the intervening hull.

We made for the cable to which the kedge anchor was attached, and I began to swarm up, any sound that I may have made being smothered by the clatter of stones on the planks of the deck. I gained the poop without being seen, but immediately afterwards I heard a yell from the roundhouse, and the men who had sheltered there began to pour out.

But having seen the uselessness of their fusillade against the cliff they had allowed their matches to go out, so that I was for the moment safe from musket shot. When I fired and brought down the first man, the rest hesitated, and seeing my companions clambering up behind me they scuttled back into the roundhouse again. The instant Joe Punchard reached the deck he swung round one of the brass guns to command the roundhouse. It was already loaded, as the buccaneers knew, and Joe cried out that he would send them all to Davy Jones if they showed their noses outside the door.

The shower of stones had now ceased, and the men who had gone below were swarming up to meet this unlooked-for boarding party. Cludde and I, with our negroes, were upon them before they had time to collect their wits. And then ensued as pretty a bit of close fighting as ever I was engaged in. We laid about us right lustily with our clubbed muskets, and I will say for the black men that they were not a whit less doughty than the white. Our first success had, I suppose, given them confidence; and Noah, with his firm belief in the virtue of the talisman slung about his neck, threw himself into the very forefront of the struggle, dodging the cutlasses of the buccaneers with great agility, and slipping in under their guard with shrewd thrusts of his knife.

They still outnumbered us, I think (for you may be sure I was too busy to count them); but they were disheartened, no doubt, as any men would be, at this rude and sudden onslaught on their security, and with their comrades cooped up under the menace of the guns they fought without the confidence that goes so far to win victory. Moreover, they lacked leadership. The master of the brig, as I afterwards discovered, was in the roundhouse, and Vetch (in this equal to himself) was not to be seen, having ever a tender regard for the safety of his skin. And so, after some few minutes of it, the buccaneers turned tail and fled for their lives into the forecastle, where they barricaded themselves.

Leaving Cludde to keep an eye on them, I rushed down the companion to find Vetch and to assure Mistress Lucy that her troubles were at an end. And there was Vetch, trying to batter down the door of the cabin in which she had locked herself. His design, I guessed, was to seize her and use her to extort terms from us. He had the advantage of me in that I was coming from the full daylight into the dimness of below decks, and before I had reached the ladder foot he fired his pistol at me, the bullet striking my thigh. I fell to the floor; he sprang over my body and up the steps; I cried out to Cludde to seize him, and to Mistress Lucy that the fight was over, and then all things became a blank to me.

When I came to myself, I knew by the lazy rocking of the vessel that it was once more afloat; I was lying on a bench beneath a porthole, and when I turned my head to see more particularly where I was, Mistress Lucy came towards me, her eyes shining with kindness.

"Mistress Lucy!" I cried, trying to rise, but wincing at an exquisite pain in my leg.

"Don't move," she said. "The surgeon said you were to lie quite still."

"The surgeon!" I repeated, scarce believing I had heard aright.

"Yes, you are surprised," she said with a smile; "but that is not the strangest of the many strange things that have happened of late. One of the crew of this vessel was once a surgeon; he took his degrees in Edinburgh, he told me--"

"And that's true," said a harsh voice, and there entered the cabin one of the buccaneers--a big bottle-nosed fellow, with a face of purple hue. "And how are ye the noo, Mister?"

"Mighty shaky!" I said. "What is wrong with me?"

"A bit wound in the dexter femur," he said, "within a hair's breadth like o' your femoral artery and kingdom come.

"But ye'll do fine," he added, feeling my pulse. "Man, ye've good blood in your veins, and me having a good hand at the cutting, we'll verra soon have ye on your two feet again; and the lassie will no like be fashed at that, I'm thinkin'."

"I am to thank you then for cutting out the bullet," I said, and then, remembering how I had come by it, I cried: "Have they got that villain?"

"Meanin' Vetch?" says the man. "Hoots! Ye'll no catch him; he's a slithery man, yon. He was up and awa' before he could be stoppit, with a wheen o' yelling niggers after him. Aweel, I'm no that sorry mysel', for he wasna just what ye would call a gentleman."

I suppose that something of what I was thinking showed in my face, for the Scotchman continued:

"I had naething against him as an employer, ye ken; he was sound wi' the siller; but his dealin' wi' sic a bonny lassie kind o' affrontit me, and I'm well enough pleased ye got the better of him in that regard. I mind o' the time when I had a wee-bit lassie mysel'."

And then the besotted fellow began to weep, and comforted himself with a long pull from a flask he took from his pocket. 'Twas plain that the drink had been his undoing, and indeed, before I parted company with him in Port Royal some days later, he told me with maudlin tears the story of his declension from surgeon on a king's ship to buccaneer, and preached me many an impressive sermon on the text of the bottle.

Mistress Lucy had withdrawn while we were talking, and Sandy MacLeod, as he was named, dressed my wound again with a hand as tender as a woman's. And then Joe Punchard came down to see me, Cludde remaining on deck to keep an eye on the crew. Vetch had sprung overboard, and run fleetly as a deer to the shore, and though the negroes on the cliff sped after him with yells, they had a round of half a mile to go over rough ground, and could not catch him. I would fain have him in my power, so that he might receive his desserts at the hands of a jury, and be deprived at least of further opportunities of mischief, but my vexation at his escape was solaced by the knowledge that Mistress Lucy's safety was secure.

I talked things over with Joe, and we decided to sail the brig round the coast to Port Royal, and hand Mistress Lucy over to her friends in Spanish Town. The management of her estate gave us some concern. It could not be left without a responsible head, and the overseers, being, as I learned from her, men whom Vetch had put in when he dismissed McTavish and the other white men whom he had found there on his arrival, were scarcely to be trusted.

As the result of a consultation with Mistress Lucy, she asked Cludde (who had begged and received her forgiveness) to return to Penolver and take charge until we should have had time to reengage McTavish and send him up from Spanish Town. Mistress Lucy being now of age, Vetch's brief authority had come to an end, and I supposed that he would make his way to Dry Harbor and take ship to England. I could imagine the rage of Sir Richard when his emissary should return and report the total failure of his scheme. 'Twould sort with his violent and overbearing character to make Vetch a scapegoat (a man in the wrong must ever have someone to kick); and I wondered to what new villainy Cyrus would turn for his livelihood.

We had some trouble with the buccaneers when I told them they would be required to work the brig to Port Royal. They felt a very natural reluctance to come within reach of the merchants and shipmen who had suffered from their depredations. But I took it upon myself to promise them good pay and immunity from arrest, provided they joined a king's ship forthwith, and being seconded by Sandy MacLeod the surgeon, who had much influence with his comrades, I brought them to acquiesce. And so, having bade farewell to Cludde and the friendly negroes, Uncle Moses and Noah (Jacob would accompany me), we waited a few hours until the old nurse Patty had been sent up from the house and then we unfurled our sails to a favoring wind, and in the course of three days made the harbor of Port Royal.

During the voyage I saw almost nothing of Mistress Lucy. My wound kept me to my cabin; she did not often stir from hers, and 'twas Patty who bestowed on me the ministrations that are so pleasant to a sick man. I own I was somewhat disappointed in this matter. 'Twas nothing that Mistress Lucy had not uttered a word of thanks to me for what I had done for her (she was much more affable with Joe Punchard); her refraining spared me embarrassment, for a man of my nature is ill at ease under any demonstration of gratitude; but there were many other things we might have talked about, and the mere sight of her would have been a comfort. But, as I say, she saw me but seldom, and spoke very little, and I felt a spasm of jealousy when I learned that she spent hours on deck chatting with Punchard, who for his part, when he came to see me, spoke of her with all the adoration of a worshipper.

And when, on arriving at Port Royal, I was carried ashore, and Mistress Lucy came and took leave of me, she said nothing but a mere "Goodby, Mr. Bold," though to be sure she looked on me with wondrous kindness.

And when she was gone I could not forbear heaving a monstrous sigh at the thought that she was now a lady of great property, whereas I was but a second lieutenant, poor on eighty pounds a year.

Chapter 30
The Six Days' Battle

My wound kept me laid up for a fortnight, and hobbling for another, so that I was unluckily prevented from accompanying my captain in a little expedition in which he gained much credit and a goodly portion of prize money. The Falmouth was sent by Admiral Benbow, with the Ruby and the Experiment, to cruise off the Petit Guavas. 'Twas the middle of May when they returned (with four prizes, one a very rich ship), and meanwhile things had happened which mitigated my disappointment.

We learned in April from Rear Admiral Whetstone, who had joined the vice admiral, of the death of King William and the accession of the Princess Anne, and knowing how much the new queen was under the influence of the Earl of Marlborough's lady, we had little doubt that England would soon be at war with France. A few days before my ship returned to port we had advice of the rupture between the two countries, and when Captain Vincent informed the admiral that Monsieur Chateau-Renaud was at the Havana, with six and twenty men-of-war, waiting for the great treasure fleet from Santa Cruz, we looked forward with lively anticipation to the imminent conflict.

And it chancing that one of the second lieutenants of the flagship was sick, Mr. Benbow with great kindness appointed me, being now perfectly recovered, to fill his room. I parted with regret from Captain Vincent, whom I esteemed a better commander than Captain Fogg, of the Breda, but I was greatly delighted at the prospect of serving under Mr. Benbow's eye, and in hardly less degree at being on the same ship as Joe Punchard, who had returned to his duty as the admiral's servant.

It was nigh two months before the vice admiral hoisted his flag and set sail. In the interim he had despatched Rear Admiral Whetstone to intercept Monsieur du Casse, who, as he was informed, was expected at Port Louis, at the west end of Hispaniola, with four men-of-war, to destroy our trade for negroes. At length sailing orders were given to the fleet, and on the evening before we departed we attended a grand entertainment given by the new governor, Brigadier General Selwyn, who had arrived towards the latter end of January.

All the important people of the colony accepted the governor's invitation, and among them was Mistress Lucy. I had seen her many times since I had recovered of my wound, and, I own, was somewhat piqued at her conduct towards me, for though always perfectly kind, she was no more cordial to me than to a score of my fellow officers. Indeed, if any one was favored more than another, it was Dick Cludde, who had, since his breach with Vetch, cast off his bad habits, and appeared to be on an excellent footing with his cousin.

I had always thought him a lubber, and the good qualities he now showed annoyed (I am ashamed to say) as much as they surprised me. 'Twas clear that he was humbly paying his court to the lady, and feeling myself debarred by my poverty from entering the lists against him, I could but stand aside and fume at his greater advantages. Lucy danced much with him at the governor's ball; she was so beset by would-be partners that when I, who had somewhat morosely hung back, approached her to ask her for a place on her card, she hummed, and pursed her lips, and said she feared I was too late, and then, with a pretty air of relenting, announced that she could give me one dance towards the end.

I was standing, gloomily watching her dance with Cludde, when I felt a tap on my arm, and saw Mistress Lucetta Gurney (whom I have before mentioned) smiling up at me from behind her fan.

"Why these black looks, Mr. Bold?" says she.

"Because you have not favored me with a dance, Mistress Lucetta," said I, with a very low bow.

"Fie, Mr. Bold," cries she, "when did you ask me?"

"I ask you now," I said, and with that I took her under my arm and strode among the dancers with so fierce and determined an air (as Mistress Lucetta told me) that, being more than common tall, I was much observed and humorously criticized by the company. I suppose I carried the same fierceness into my dancing, for after footing it for the space of a minute, Mistress Lucetta begged me to stop, saying she had no fancy for dancing with a whirlwind.

"Take me to a seat, Mr. Bold. I am going to talk to you," she said.

And talk to me she did, in a way that mightily surprised me.

"Do you think I don't see through you, Mr. Bold?" she said. "You are most desperately jealous of Mr. Cludde; you know you are; and of every other man in the room; and you show it, which is a very, very silly thing to do. Oh, don't speak; you would only tell me stories. Listen to me. Lucy is a dear friend of mine, and I know all about everything. You are a disgrace to your name, sir."

"Why, what have I done?" I asked, amazed at the sternness she had suddenly thrown into her voice. And she burst into a ripple of laughter.

"I do think you are the stupidest man alive," she said. "Is not your name Bold, and are you not timid, and backward, and humble, and despondent, and a great big baby! Why, Lucy thinks the world of you; she is never tired of hearing that red-haired man Punchard talk of you; and yet you are glum, and scowl at her, and glower at the men who are cheerful and try to amuse her, and whom she doesn't care a button for. Oh, Mr. Bold, 'tis you who ought to change your name, for to be sure you will never persuade her to change hers."

"But Dick Cludde!" I stammered, taken aback by this plain speaking.

"Is going to dance with me, sir," she said, springing up as, the dance being over, Dick came to claim her for the next.

I wandered into the governor's beautiful garden, and, pacing up and down, pondered what the lively Lucetta had said. Was it true that Lucy did not care a button for the men who courted her so assiduously? Was Lucetta seeking to make a fool of me? Did Lucy's apparent indifference mask another feeling? My thoughts made a flying circle of perplexity and I could not anywise come at a resolution.

And then I remembered again how far above me Lucy was in worldly position, and how I had nothing, barring a few hundred pounds of prize money and my paltry eighty pounds (or less) a year. What had I to offer her? And besides this, I felt a scruple (even supposing my chances were not hopeless), against seeking to engage her while she was so far from the relatives whose advice she would naturally seek. 'Twould savor much of fortune hunting, I thought, if I sought her hand so close upon her coming of age.

The upshot of my meditations was that I must cleave to my former resolve, and wait at least until I should have been promoted to captain's rank, and then seek her at her uncle's house and put my fate to the hazard.

Whether my resolution would have survived a dance with her I know not. When I went back to the hall to claim her I found I was too late: she was dancing with a young popinjay of Collingwood's regiment. I watched them gloomily, in high dudgeons, though 'twas my own fault, and I did not even get an opportunity of bidding her farewell.

Next day ('twas the eleventh of July) we sailed out of Port Royal, amid salvos of artillery, the merchant ships in the harbour being all dressed with flags. The Breda, in which I was now serving, led the van, and the squadron consisted, besides another third-rate, of six fourth-rates, a fireship, a bomb vessel, a tender and a sloop. Mr. Benbow designed to join Rear Admiral Whetstone, but we were soon spoken by the Colchester, from which we learned that Monsieur du Casse was expected at Leogane, and making for that place, we arrived on the twenty-seventh.

We saw several ships at anchor near the town, and one of them being under sail, we pursued her, and found her to be a man-of-war of fifty guns. She did not stay to try conclusions with us, but ran ashore, and then her captain, to prevent her from falling into our hands, blew her up. Next morning we had the good fortune to capture with ease three other French ships and to sink a fourth; and perceiving that a vessel of eighteen guns was being hauled inshore under the guns of the fort, the admiral sent the boat in, which burned her to the ground, and brought off some other ships with wine and stores aboard.

We came next day before Petit Guavas, and saw three or four small ships in the harbor called the Cul, which was so strong by its natural position, and so well defended, that Mr. Benbow thought it not advisable to run any risk there for vessels of little value. We continued for three days in the bay, and sailed from thence for Cape Donna Maria, on the west side of Hispaniola, where we learned that Monsieur du Casse was gone to Cartagena. 'Twas clear that the Frenchman was in no mind to encounter us, and there was a good deal of grumbling among our men at the wild goose chase on which we appeared to be engaged.

Falling in with Rear Admiral Whetstone, who had taken three ships of the enemy, Mr. Benbow despatched him back to Jamaica to look to the safety of that island, being resolved himself to cruise about until he should come in touch with the fleet of Monsieur du Casse.

On the tenth of August we left Cape Donna Maria, the Breda being accompanied by the Defiance (of which Captain Kirkby was commander, and Dick Cludde first lieutenant), the Falmouth (with my friend Captain Vincent), the Ruby, the Greenwich, the Pendennis and the Windsor. Early in the morning of the twenty-ninth we came over against the coast of Santa Martha, and espied ten ships sailing under topsails westward along the shore, and soon perceived them to be the French. Four of them were great vessels of sixty or seventy guns.

Some of our ships being three or four miles astern, Mr. Benbow flew the signal for action, and went on under easy sail so that the others might come up with us. He had disposed his line of battle with the flagship in the center, the Defiance at the extreme left, and the Falmouth at the extreme right.

On board the Breda we were all desperately eager for the fight, and I could not watch without admiration the coolness with which Mr. Benbow made his disposition, and the particular order and cheerfulness that prevailed among the men. Our consorts were long in coming up, and I observed the admiral to grow very uneasy as he watched them through his perspective glass. He bit his lips, and frowned, and at last broke out into indignant speech, especially against the Defiance and the Windsor, which were making but little haste to come into their stations.

He was ever a man of quick temper, and his habit of speaking his mind freely accounted in some measure for his unpopularity with some of his captains. But to my mind he was fully justified in the bitterness with which he now spoke of Captain Kirkby of the Defiance and Captain Constable of the Windsor. Evening was drawing on, and though the enemy was stronger than we, both in numbers and armament, Mr. Benbow made no doubt we should give a good account of ourselves if only the captains would loyally support him.

At length, to bring on an engagement before night, the admiral ran alongside of the enemy, being to windward, and steering large, not intending to attack before the Defiance was abreast of the headmost ship. But before this was done the Falmouth opened the fight by firing on a great Dutch-built ship in the rear, and the Windsor and the Defiance immediately did likewise, though they had not arrived at the appointed stations. Cursing with vexation at this violation of orders, the admiral saw himself forced to open fire upon the nearest French ship, which had already given us a harmless broadside.

And then to our amazement we saw the Defiance and the Windsor, though they had received but two or three broadsides apiece (in one of which Dick Cludde got a severe hurt) luff out of gunshot, so that the two sternmost ships of the French were free to lay upon the Breda. I think I never saw a man in such a passion of anger as Mr. Benbow was then. He mingled hot reproaches of the erring captains with words of cheer to our gunners, and though we were the target for three of the enemy's ships, he bade Captain Fogg keep us in touch with them and swore that he would fight the whole squadron single-handed.

'Twas four o'clock before the action became general, so sluggish were our vessels in coming into line, and the firing continued till nightfall, by which time we on the Breda had suffered severely. We kept the French company all night, and during the night watches the admiral, believing that if he led himself on both tacks the captains for very shame could not fail to follow his example, altered the line of battle accordingly, the Defiance coming next to the Breda. At daybreak the Breda was near the enemy, but only the Ruby was up with us, the rest of the squadron lying three, four, and five miles astern, and there was little wind. We were within gunshot of the French, but they were civil enough not to fire, and indeed 'twas clear as the day went on that they were not eager to fight us, for on a sea breeze coming up they got into a line and made what sail they could.

One ship set off with the Ruby in pursuit, plying our chase guns on them till night; but the other ships again delayed to come up with us, and we were left to keep the enemy company.

Next morning at daylight we found ourselves on the quarter of the second ship of the enemy's squadron, within point-blank shot, the Ruby being ahead of us. The French ships fired at the Ruby, which returned their fire; and the two French vessels which were ahead fell off, and there being little wind, brought their guns to bear on our consort. Mr. Benbow gave orders that we should send our broadside upon the ship that first began, which our gunners did with such right good will that they brought her masts and rigging tumbling down, and shattered her so that she had to lower her boats to tow her away. But the Ruby had suffered in no less a degree, and the admiral ordered Captain Fogg to lay by her and send his boats to tow her off.

This action had lasted for nigh two hours, during which the Defiance and Windsor had come abreast of the rear French ship and though within point-blank range had never fired one gun at her. The admiral ground his teeth and swore he would court martial the captains when we came to port. Meanwhile a gale had sprung up, and the enemy again made all sail, and we set off in chase. At two in the afternoon we got abreast of two of the stern-most of the enemy's ships off the mouth of the Rio Grande, and in hopes to disable them in their masts and rigging we began to fire on them, as did some of our vessels astern; but the Frenchmen, seeing the Breda so ill supported, paid no heed to any other, but pointed wholly at us, doing much hurt to our rigging, and maiming some of our men.

After the fight had continued upwards of two hours, the Frenchmen drew off out of gunshot, and we made what sail we could after them, but they used all possible shifts to evade fighting, our men shouting after them derisively as cowardly curs. Darkness put a stop to the pursuit, but again we hugged the enemy all night, hoping that next day would see the conclusion of this long-drawn battle.

When the third morning dawned, we spied the enemy about a mile and a half ahead. Of our ships the half-crippled Ruby was nearest, the Falmouth next; the rest were but indifferently near, the Greenwich indeed lying full three leagues astern, though the admiral had never struck his signal for battle night or day.

For many hours the wind blew easterly, but at three in the afternoon it shifted to the south and gave the enemy the weather gauge. In tacking we fetched within gunshot of the sternmost of them, and for half an hour or so we kept up a brisk bombardment; but our line was still much out of order, and some of our ships being even now three miles astern, nothing more could be done.

And so another day passed. The other vessels had not come within speaking distance of us, and it seemed that all hope of bringing the enemy to a decisive engagement must be abandoned.

The dawn of the fourth morning found the Frenchmen six miles ahead, and one less in number, for the great Dutch ship had separated from the squadron and was out of sight. The Defiance and Windsor, ever the most dilatory of our vessels, were at this time four miles astern. About ten o'clock, the wind then blowing east nor'-east, but very variable, the enemy tacked, and the admiral fetched within range of two of them, giving them his broadside and receiving from them many shrewd knocks. Then, tacking also, he pursued them with what speed he might, and about noon contrived to cut off from their line a small English ship, the Ann galley, which they had taken off Lisbon.

This small success cheered our drooping spirits a little; but a complete victory seemed further off than ever, for the Ruby proved to be so disabled that the admiral ordered her to return to Port Royal, so that we had five ships against the enemy's nine. During the day our vessels drew somewhat closer to us, the Falmouth being the foremost, and we gained some four miles upon the enemy by sunset.

Ever since we had first sighted the Frenchmen, Mr. Benbow had snatched but a few hours' sleep each night, and was becoming worn out for want of rest and for bitter mortification at the ill conduct of his captains. 'Tis true the enemy had shown no disposition to stand, and the light winds had not favored the overhauling of them, and I was very sure that in the case of Captain Vincent, at any rate, 'twas sheer ill luck that prevented him from giving the admiral support. But I had other ideas of the behavior of the captains of the vessels that hung back most. Captain Kirkby of the Defiance and Captain Wade of the Greenwich I knew to be of the anti-Benbow party, and though I had not the same knowledge of Captain Constable of the Windsor and Captain Hudson of the Pendennis, I suspected that they were infected by the same blight, for I could not believe that officers of the English navy could be arrant cowards.

On the night of the twenty-fourth I had the middle watch. Towards two o'clock Joe Punchard came to me, smoking a pipe, and looking more miserable than I had ever seen him.

"Twill break my captain's heart if we have another day of it," he says gloomily. "He looks five years older than he did when we left Port Royal. He can't sleep, and if he do fall into a doze he starts up like a child out of a bad dream. He swears he will court martial the captains, every man jack of them, when we get to port, but that won't win us the battle, and he has set his heart on giving the Frenchmen a drubbing. And he's took a notion that he'll never get through alive, which is so uncommon unlike him, being mostly so cheery, that it gives me the dumps bad."

I was saying what I could to cheer the good fellow when the lookout cries he sees a sail ahead. The admiral rushes out of his cabin and orders the drums to beat to quarters. In an instant, as it seemed, the decks were full of men. 'Twas a clear night, with very little wind, and we could see one of the French ships within hail of us. We gave her a tremendous broadside from all three decks at once, with double shot, round below, and round and partridge aloft. She returned it hotly, striking down many of our good fellows; I myself narrowly escaped one of the shot, which hit a man at my side, carrying away his right arm clear from the shoulder.

We kept up the duel of firing for near an hour, and then I heard a great cry go up that the admiral was wounded, and by and by Joe comes to me with tears streaming down his cheeks, and says that the admiral's right leg was shattered to pieces by a chain shot, and he was carried below. But while he was still talking to me we heard a great shout and there was Mr. Benbow being hoisted in his cradle on to the quarterdeck, and crying out "Good cheer, my hearties! The Frenchmen have given me a knock, but we've got 'em now and by God! we'll beat 'em!"

And then they cheered him again, and he, sitting in his cradle, making nothing of his dreadful pain, gave orders and shouted encouragement for a good three hours.

When the morning light showed us the ship we had been fighting, she appeared a mere ruin; her main yard down and shot to pieces, her fore-topsail yard shot away, her mizzen mast by the board, all her rigging gone, and her sides bored through and through with our double-headed shot.

And near by us stood my old ship the Falmouth, which in the darkness had assisted us very much in crippling this great vessel of seventy guns, the sternmost of the French squadron.

Soon afterwards we saw the other ships of the enemy bearing down upon us before a strong easterly wind; at the same time the Windsor, Pendennis and Greenwich, ahead of the enemy, ran to leeward of the disabled ship, gave her their broadsides ('twas like flogging a dead horse), and then stood to the southward. Whereupon up comes the Defiance, and passes like the others; and while we were still in our amazement at this sudden bravery, the battered ship fired twenty of her guns at the Defiance, whereupon she ports her helm a-weather and runs away right before the wind, lowering both her topsails without any regard to the signal for battle.

This was more than our men could stomach; breaking all discipline, they pursued the coward ship with groans and curses. I glanced at the admiral, sitting erect on the quarter deck, and his pale face was drawn with a look of utter despair.

The enemy, seeing our other two ships stand to the southward, clearly expected them to tack, for they brought to with their heads to the northward, preparing to meet their fire. But when they perceived that our dastard captains had no such intent, but were beyond doubt running away, they bore down upon the Breda and ran between us and the disabled ship, firing all their guns, shooting away our main-topsail yard, and shattering our rigging.

"For God's sake, Mr. Fogg," cried the admiral, "fire a couple of shots at those villains ahead and mind them of their duty!"

This the captain did, but the others took not the least notice of his signal. He stamped and swore like a madman, and I went hot with shame to think of what opinion the Frenchmen must have of us. And with our rigging all shot away we had to lay by and look at them as they brought to, remanned their own shattered ship, and took her in tow. Sure never did English admiral before or since suffer such undeserved humiliation.

Our men set to work diligently to refit the vessel, and this being done by ten o'clock, Mr. Benbow ordered the captain to pursue the enemy, who was then about three miles distant, and to leeward, having the disabled ship in tow, and steering northeast, the wind being sou'-sou'west. We made all the sail we could, the battle signal always flying at the fore; and the enemy, taking encouragement from the behavior of some of our captains, now showed the first signs of waiting for us. Whereupon the admiral ordered Captain Fogg to send to the other captains and bid them keep their line and behave themselves like men.

And when our boat returned from this errand there was Captain Kirkby in it. He came aboard the Breda and went up to the admiral, who never left the quarterdeck. There were high words between them; I learned afterwards that Captain Kirkby pressed Mr. Benbow very earnestly to desist from any further engagement, alleging that he had tried the enemy's strength with little success for six days together.

"And whose fault is that, sir?" roared the admiral.

Then, with difficulty curbing his anger, he bade Captain Fogg signal to the other captains to come aboard, so that he might know whether they were all of the same mind as that craven.

They obeyed this signal with wondrous alacrity. They came aboard, and for two mortal hours the admiral, racked and almost fainting with pain, reasoned, expostulated, pleaded, showed them that now they had the fairest opportunity of success, seeing that our ships were all in good condition, and only eight men killed in all the squadron save those the Breda had lost; that we had plenty of ammunition; that three or four of the enemy's ships had suffered injury and one was quite disabled and in tow. 'Twas all in vain. The most of them concurred with Captain Kirkby's opinion, that it was undesirable to continue the fight, nor could any reasoning turn them. And then they put their names to a paper, formally giving their opinion, and (though I did not know this till afterwards) Captain Fogg and my own old commander, Captain Vincent, signed with the rest.

After this there was no more to be done. If the admiral had been unwounded I believe he would have stood out against them all and fought the enemy single-handed: but he had no assurance of being in a fit state to direct the battle; 'twas clear the captains had no mind to fight; and rather than imperil the whole squadron and let the French boast of a victory he resolved to venture no further. And so we let the enemy depart unmolested, and returned to Jamaica.

On the way I had the privilege of some talk with the admiral. Deeply mortified as he was at his own ill success, his personal grief was outweighed by his sense of the national disappointment which must attend the frustration of his design.

"And 'tis my last fight, Bold," he said to me. "I shall not live to meet the French again, and 'tis a sore trial to me to go out of the world a failure."

"You are not a failure, sir," I said. "'Tis those rascally captains who have failed and are disgraced forever; and be sure our people will do you justice."

"You think so?" he said, with a pleased look. "'Twas King William that called me 'honest Benbow,' and if I keep that name with the country I am content. I may die before we make Port Royal; if I do, you will take my love to Nelly, my lad?"

"I will indeed, sir, but I hope for better things," I said. "There be good surgeons in Spanish Town, who will use all of their skill to preserve a life so valuable to the country."

"We shall see," he replied. "This plaguey leg will have to come off; maybe I shall return home with a wooden leg and stump about as port admiral somewhere!

"At any rate, I hope I shall live long enough to see you a captain. You have done well, my lad, and there will be a few vacancies, I warrant you, when the court martial has done with those villains."

Before we reached Port Royal a French boat overtook us with a letter to the admiral from Monsieur du Casse, who, being a brave man, felt for the distress of his brave foe.

"Sir" (he wrote), "I had little hope on Monday last but to have supped in your cabin, but it pleased God to order it otherwise; I am thankful for it. As for those cowardly captains who deserted you, hang them up, for by God, they deserve it."

Our return to harbor was a melancholy affair. There was universal rage against the unworthy captains, and universal grief at the plight of the admiral. His broken leg was taken off, an operation which he bore with wonderful fortitude, and being of a robust constitution, he gave the surgeons at first good hopes of recovery. From his sick bed he issued a commission to Rear Admiral Whetstone to hold a court martial for the trial of the four captains whom he accused of cowardice, breach of order, and neglect of duty; and of Captains Fogg and Vincent on the minor charge of signing the paper against engaging the French.

The trial began on the eighth of October. Among the officers who gave evidence (much against his will) against Captain Kirkby was Dick Cludde, who was carried wounded before the court. Kirkby and Captain Wade of the Greenwich were found guilty on all the charges and sentenced to be shot. Captain Constable was cleared of cowardice, but convicted on the other counts, and he was cashiered from her Majesty's service, with imprisonment during her pleasure. Captain Hudson of the Pendennis was lucky, as I thought, in dying before the trial which must have branded him with indelible disgrace.

As for my old friend Captain Vincent, and my new commander, Captain Fogg, they alleged in their defense that they had signed the paper only because they feared if we engaged the enemy, that the other captains would wholly desert and leave the Breda and the Falmouth to their fate; and Mr. Benbow himself testifying to their great courage and gallant behavior in the battle, the court was satisfied with suspending them from their employment in the queen's service. The sentences were not executed at once, it being decided that the officers (except Vincent and Fogg) should be carried to England to await the pleasure of the queen's consort, Prince George of Denmark, who as Lord High Admiral had the power to ratify or quash the decrees of the court martial.

I was not myself present at the trial of these officers. On arriving in the harbor, the admiral was informed that, taking advantage of his absence, a buccaneer vessel had appeared off the north coast, and was doing much damage among the merchant shipping. Many planters who had suffered in their property had sent requests to the governor to take immediate action against the buccaneers, which he was unable to do until Mr. Benbow's return, Rear Admiral Whetstone not thinking himself justified in diminishing his own squadron with risk to the general safety of the island.

But on the day before the court martial was to meet Mr. Benbow sent for me, and ordered me to cruise along the north shore in search of the pirate vessel. He did not give me a ship of war for this purpose, thinking that this would only serve to warn the buccaneers, who no doubt had spies in the principal ports. But the brig in which we had brought Mistress Lucy being still in the harbor, the admiral instructed me to fit her out as a trader, and send her to sea with a dummy captain and a skeleton crew, and then to join her secretly with some thirty picked men from the queen's ships.

This mark of his confidence gave me very great pleasure, and I set about my preparations with zeal, being busy with them during the days of the trial. Knowing how strongly attached I was to Joe Punchard, Mr. Benbow insisted that he should accompany me, declaring with only too much truth that he himself had little need of Punchard's services while he was fixed to his bed.

I had, of course, paid a visit to Mistress Lucy immediately on reaching port. She took me very severely to task for leaving the port without a word of farewell, and seemed to find it a demerit in me that I had returned without a wound, praising Dick Cludde very warmly for the part he had taken in the fight. I answered with some heat that if I was not wounded 'twas from no shirking of duty, and I would have desired nothing better than that we should board one of the French vessels; 'twas no pleasure for a man to stand idle on deck while guns were shot off. And being now wrought to a certain degree of anger, I reminded her that I had given proof that I was no coward, and hoped the queen would not show herself so ungrateful to those who served her well as some other ladies I could name.

This outburst (foreign to my wonted mildness of temper) brought a color to her cheeks and a gleam to her eyes, and in quite a changed voice she said:

"Indeed, and I am not ungrateful, Mr. Bold."

And then I craved her pardon (for which, as I learned, Mistress Lucetta Gurney called me a fool), and inquired how her own affairs were prospering.

Mr. McTavish, she told me, had gone back to her estate as steward, she heard from him every week, and he gave excellent reports of the plantations. I asked her whether anything had been heard of Vetch, and whether any vessel conveying her produce from Dry Harbor had been molested by the buccaneers. She said she had no news of either the one or the other, and I inclined to believe that Vetch had accepted his defeat and vanished out of her life for ever. When I told her of the commission intrusted to me by Mr. Benbow she looked a little troubled, and besought me to have a care of myself--a departure from her former indifference that surprised me. I could only answer that I would not court danger, and that as for taking care of myself I must do my duty and leave the rest to Providence.

Long afterwards I learned that she sent privately for Joe Punchard, and extorted from him a solemn promise that he would watch over me day and night, see that I did not take a chill or expose myself to danger, and bring me back unscathed, on pain of her lasting displeasure.

"I had to promise," said Joe when I taxed him with it. "I couldn't help it. I would ha' sworn black was white, the mistress have got that way with her. Thinks I to myself, 'Mr. Bold beant a baby, nor I beant a nurse; but I'll commit black perjury to make her happy,' and so I would, sir."

And having taken my leave of her, and of Mr. Benbow, and Cludde, and other my friends, I left the harbor in a boat at sunset on October twelfth and joined the brig off Bull Bay, where she had lain awaiting me.

Chapter 31
The Cockpit

The brig, whose name was the Tartar (a very fitting name for one that had been a privateer) was manned with thirty able seamen whom I had myself been permitted to pick from the man-of-war's men in the harbor. As lieutenant I had a quartermaster named Fincham, a very excellent officer. We sailed with a fair wind until we reached Port Antonio on the northeast side of the island, but then the wind fell contrary, and we had to beat up along the north coast at a creeping pace that vexed me sorely.

We did not expect to have any news of the buccaneers until we had fetched past Orange Bay, but from thence onwards I knew that we should have to search every inlet save those that had an anchorage for large vessels; and our slow progress was the more vexing because I feared that the buccaneers might get wind of Mr. Benbow's return and sheer off. I hoped they would not do this, for I was burning to justify the admiral's confidence in me by bringing the pirate craft into harbor.

One morning, when we had been a week at sea, we sighted a wreck on a small island off Blowing Point; the islet has since totally disappeared in one of the volcanic disturbances that afflict those latitudes. We drew in towards the derelict, and then spied a man on deck waving his shirt very energetically to attract our notice. I sent Fincham with a boat's crew to bring him off, and learned from him when he came aboard that he was the sole survivor of the barque Susan Maria, which was set upon a week before by a buccaneer vessel and carried to this islet, where she had been plundered and burned, many of her crew being killed, the rest taken away to be sold to the Spanish planters in Hispaniola. The man had been left for dead on the deck, but he had come out of his swoon, and had since supported himself on some moldy cheese and biscuits which the buccaneers had not deemed worth taking when they stripped the vessel.

He told me that the buccaneer vessel was a light brig carrying six guns and a crew of at least sixty men of all nations, her captain being a Frenchman. She had sailed away to the westward. I had little doubt that this was the very vessel I had been sent in search of, and though she was stronger than I supposed, I was hot set to find her and see for myself whether we might not attempt to put a stop to her mischievous career.

We lay becalmed for the rest of that day, but a light easterly breeze springing up towards morning, we clapped on all sail and worked steadily along the coast. I examined the chart very carefully for likely anchorages, and used my perspective glass constantly; but we saw no sign of the pirate, nor indeed of any vessel, all that day.

Towards dusk we approached the entrance of the cove whence I had sailed the brig of which I was now in command. We heaved to behind a headland about two miles to the east of it, out of view of any vessel which might be in the cove or at the mouth, and waited for darkness. I had no reason to suppose that the pirate lay within the cove, though 'twas likely enough; but it behooved us to go as cautiously as if we knew she was there for certain. Considering her strength, if it should come to a fight, 'twas clearly good tactics to choose my own time and manner of attacking her.

About the end of the second dog watch I lowered a boat, and with Joe Punchard and half a dozen picked men, together with the sailor we had rescued, set off with muffled oars up the cove to reconnoiter, leaving Fincham in charge of the brig. The moon was rising, but there was a deep shadow beneath the cliffs, and by keeping well within this I trusted to escape observation. The cove was about two miles long, and after rowing half the distance I caught sight of a dark shape before me, as nearly as I could judge, almost at the same spot as my brig when I cut her cable. We drew a little closer, till we could see every spar clear in the moonlight, and the man of the Susan Maria told me that the vessel was beyond doubt the pirate of which we were in search. We lay on our oars for a while watching her, and listening for sounds from her deck, but hearing nothing, and judging that her captain would feel perfectly secure, I thought that all things favored an attempt to cut her out that night.

We pulled back to the brig and immediately prepared two boats for the expedition. I selected twenty-four men for the job, leaving ten to guard the brig. 'Twas a question whether Fincham or Punchard should be placed in charge of the second boat, but Joe pleaded so hard to have a hand in the venture (animated as much by his love of action as by his promise to Mistress Lucy, of which I as yet knew nothing) that I decided to leave Fincham in command of the vessel. If the buccaneers numbered sixty, as I had been told, we had heavy odds against us; but with the advantage of surprise I hoped that our twenty-four picked men would prove equal to more than twice their number of a mixed lot who had nothing but their common crimes to hind them together.

'Twas about four in the morning, under a waning moon, when we again came within sight of the enemy's vessel. We rowed dead slow in order to avoid noise, and had come within half a cable's length of her, and I was on the point of ordering my men to give way for a dash, when I was surprised to hear voices from the deck, and the creaking of davit blocks. 'Twas clear the buccaneers were letting down a boat. I whispered my men to ship oars, and waited with no little anxiety.

Had our approach been discovered? I could not think so, for the most confident enemy would scarcely throw away their advantage of position by seeking us out under the shadow of the cliffs when they might securely await our attack and surprise us in turn. Then what could they be about? I could just see the boat as it was lowered over the side, and then immediately afterwards a second boat followed, and men crowded into both and pulled away for the shore. They came full into the moon's rays, I saw them land, cross the beach, and disappear.

My first thought was that the vessel was delivered into our hands. I reckoned that the boats had carried close on forty men; those who were left would be no match for my tars; it seemed that my task was made miraculously easy. But then, reflecting that the buccaneers must have some errand on shore, it flashed upon me that their destination was Penolver, and their object to plunder the house and estate. There could be no other explanation of their quitting their vessel at this dead time of night.

And here I felt a conflict between duty and inclination. The latter prompted me to make off at once after the landing party and do what might be done to save Lucy's property. But my orders were to deal with the buccaneers, and I felt that I should not be justified in interfering on behalf of a private person, however dear to me, until my first duty was fulfilled.

It was a question then whether I should first attack the ship or capture the boats on the strand. To accomplish the latter we should have to overpower the men who had no doubt been left in charge, and there would certainly be some noise that would alarm the men on board the vessel, so that although the possession of the boats would cut off the return of those who had landed, it would also make the capture of the brig far more difficult. On all grounds it seemed better to wait until the landing party had gone too far to return in time to help their comrades, and then cut out the ship. When that was in our hands I should be free to go ashore and set off in pursuit of the ruffians who, I was convinced, were marching for Lucy's house.

Ordering my men to put me alongside Punchard's boat, I arranged with him the manner of our attack. I would make for the larboard, he for the starboard side, and we would board as nearly as possible at the same moment. This being settled I whispered the word to go, and the two boats crept along the shore in shadow as silently as we could until we came directly opposite the enemy's vessel. Then I, having the tiller of the leading boat, brought her round and steered her straight for the ship. 'Twas scarce to be hoped, in spite of our muffled oars, that our approach should be wholly unheard; and we were no more than ten fathoms distant when the alarm was given. There was not sufficient way on the boat, the tide being between flood and ebb, to bring us quite to the vessel, but after a few more strokes I ordered the men to ship oars and seize their arms, and we came under the brig's counter just in time to escape a volley from the deck.

We swarmed up, half a 'dozen of us together, the men shouting and cursing as Jack tars will, and met with a very warm reception. The enemy was assembled in full force to beat us back, the watch below having had time to tumble up, though to be sure they were half dazed with sleep, and maybe drink. If they had been wide-awake I will not answer for it that we should not have been repulsed; even as it was, several of my crew were driven headlong back into the boat and the sea. But the rest gained a footing on deck, and I warrant you they kept it. We were at too close quarters to fire; 'twas a brief hand-to-hand encounter with cutlasses and clubbed muskets, and what with the clashing of the weapons and the cries of the men we made a great din and hurly burly.

But the enemy had lost their sole chance of success when they failed to dislodge us before Joe's men arrived. 'Twas but a minute before his boat came round the bows to the starboard side, and then the crew swarmed up, with Joe at their head, and fell upon the rear of our assailants. Thus hemmed in between our two parties the buccaneers saw 'twas vain to contend longer. They flung down their arms and cried (in many tongues) for quarter; and within five minutes of our first setting foot on deck we had them securely battened down below.

And now having accomplished, by fortune's favor, my first duty, I resolved to make all speed after the fellows who had landed, hoping fervently that the noise of our engagement had not reached their ears and put them on their guard. There was hot work before us, I well knew, if they numbered forty, as I had reason to believe. I could not leave the brig wholly unguarded; yet I was loath to diminish my own little company; in the end I decided to leave a boatswain's mate in command of a party of five (three who had had a ducking and two who had received slight hurts in the fight) and to take Joe and the other eighteen hot-foot to Penolver.

I had left instructions with Fincham on our brig to sail into the inlet in the morning to support us, and I told the boatswain's mate to communicate with her as soon as she appeared. Thus I had no anxiety about the security of the prize and the prisoners during my absence.

These arrangements made, we set off for the shore, taking two of the six men to row back to the brig the boats from which the buccaneers had landed, which we found hauled up on the beach, but no one in charge of them. Either they had been left unattended because the leader had no fears for their safety, or the men set to watch had taken alarm from our doings on the brig and had decamped. I hoped they had not gone ahead of us to warn their fellows, which indeed did not seem very likely, for they would be loath to venture alone into a strange country. If the buccaneers had had warning of what was happening behind them and hastened back, or if we should miss them and they returned to the cove before us, they would at any rate be unable to recapture their vessel, lacking their boats.

I reckoned that 'twas near two hours since the main body of the buccaneers had departed; by this time they must be three parts of the way to the house, if that was their goal; so we set off at a great pace to follow them up. The sun was not yet risen, though the darkness was lifting; and the air being cool, we could march without discomfort.

We had not gone very far, and had come to where the track runs between thin clumps of trees, when Joe Punchard suddenly left my side and darted into the woodland. His bandiness was no check upon his running. In a few seconds he was back, shoving before him a seaman much larger than himself, having one hand upon his neck and the other grasping his arm behind his back. He thus propelled the man towards us at a quick trot, crying out to me:

"Here be one of the villains, sir, and I reckon 'twill be well to make him speak."

Without slackening our pace I made the captive walk by my side and questioned him. He had been left, as I suspected, in charge of the boats, alone, and at the noise of our assault he had run up the path, intending to overtake his comrades and give them warning of what was happening. But being out of his element, his heart failed him when he came into the wild wooded country, and he had been skulking behind the trees when Joe espied him. He was a Frenchman.

I learned from him that some weeks before, his vessel had been joined by an Englishman, who had proposed to his captain an expedition to an estate some ten miles inland. The captain had been at first reluctant to undertake the expedition; 'twas work for landsmen, he said, not for sea dogs, and having heard rumors of a buccaneer brig having been captured in that very cove by a horde of negroes led by a white man, he was loath to leave his vessel. But the Englishman had worked upon his fellow countrymen among the buccaneers by tales of large sums of money lying in the house in question; he had been steward of the estate, he said, and had been forced to leave behind the hoard he had gathered, on being attacked by a villainous enemy that coveted his wealth. But it was too securely hidden to have been discovered by the interloper.

These compatriots of his had insisted on the captain holding a council of the whole crew, at which the proposal was put to the vote and carried; and the captain's last objections were overcome by the promise of a quarter of the hidden money, the Englishman to have a quarter, and the remainder to be divided among the crew.

My suspicion being so fully borne out, I forced the pace, for though I foresaw a tough fight, my men were all sturdy fellows, who were not like to feel any distress after a march of but ten miles. I only half believed the story of hidden gold. The produce of the estate would generally, I thought, be paid for, not in specie, but in bills of exchange, which would be in the hands of duly appointed agents at the port. It seemed more likely that Vetch had some other motive: what, I could not guess. But whatever his design might be, I counted myself very lucky in having come to the neighborhood in time to frustrate it.

When we came within a mile of the estate we saw a dense cloud of smoke rising into the air at the spot where, as I judged, the house stood. This seemed to confirm my suspicion; Vetch was indulging his venomous spite by burning the residence of Mistress Lucy. We sprang forward at the double, and coming in sight of the house, I saw with relief that it was yet intact, the smoke arising from the outbuildings, which were already almost burned to the ground. Then we heard musket shots, and as we drew nearer loud shouts. The plantations were utterly deserted, there was not a negro visible of whom we might ask what was toward; so we skirmished forward to a place among the trees where the front of the house was in full view.

The veranda was packed with men, and around them smoke was swirling, but the smoke of musketry, not of a conflagration. Some were firing at the shuttered windows, others hacking with axes at the doors and walls. 'Twas clear that the attack had only just begun, for the light timbers of the house could not long have withstood the tremendous battering they were now receiving. It amazed me that the assailants had met with any resistance at all; McTavish and his overseers must be men of mettle to attempt to hold the house against such odds. Even in the few seconds I allowed myself to observe them I saw two or three of the buccaneers fall, shot, I had no doubt, by the defenders within. But mingled with the yells of rage there now arose a cry of triumph; a panel of one of the doors had given way under the fierce strokes of an ax wielded by a man whom I knew by some instinct to be the captain. 'Twas manifest that we had come but just in time.

Calling to my men to follow me closely, I led them at the double straight across the open grassy space that separated us from the house. The buccaneers were so intent upon their work, and the noise was so deafening, that they were not aware of us until we came within a few yards of the veranda. Then a great shout of warning was raised by those of the men who, having been wounded, had fallen out of the fight. Some of the storming party swung round, caught sight of us, and rushed to the head of the steps leading to the veranda as we reached the foot. Luckily for us they had discharged their muskets, whereas my men had theirs loaded, and had lit their matches during the few moments we had waited at the edge of the copse.

Knowing ourselves outnumbered by at least two to one, I cried to my men to halt and fire. Several of the foremost of the buccaneers fell, but those behind had not been hit, and when I gave the order to rush up the steps they stood in close array with clubbed muskets to meet us.

The next few moments were filled with such a wild commotion that 'twould be vain to try to describe all that happened. Joe Punchard, seeing that it was impossible for all of us to mount by the steps, had with great readiness of wit called off half a dozen men, and they were now scrambling up the pillars supporting the veranda. Finding my ascent blocked by the crowd, I slipped over the balustrade, and, taking advantage of my great height, leapt at the rail of the veranda and began to haul myself up.

At that desperate moment I saw one of the buccaneers with his musket uplifted, preparing to bring it down with crushing force upon me, and caught sight of Vetch behind him sword in hand. I thought my end was come, for I had not yet secured my footing, and was powerless to protect myself. But suddenly there was a deafening report from the room beyond; the buccaneer pitched forward on to the rail, his musket falling from his hand. My life was saved by the man's body lurching against me, for being between Vetch and me, he prevented my old enemy from using his sword arm.

With a desperate heave I threw the buccaneer against Vetch, and in a trice was over the rail and on the veranda. Vetch's face was fixed with terror, as, drawing my sword, I rushed at him. There was no escape for him now; his slipperiness could not serve him; and I will do him this justice, that, finding himself driven into a corner, he stood against me and fought with a courage of frenzy. But he was no swordsman; with a few simple passes I disarmed him, and flinging his sword over the rail I caught him by the neck and arm and held him fast.

Meanwhile the resistance of his hirelings had been broken. My sturdy men had forced their way up the steps or climbed up the pillars, not without loss, and the defenders in the room behind firing a succession of shots, the buccaneers had scattered to right and left to escape being taken in front and rear at once. Their ranks being thus weakened my men pressed upon them with redoubled vehemence. I caught sight of Joe Punchard in the melee, his red head a flaming battle signal, wielding an iron belaying pin, every swing of it leaving the enemy one man the less.

The buccaneer captain, with the furious courage for which the West Indian freebooters have ever been notable, threw himself wherever the fight was thickest, striving to stay the rout, with cutlass in one hand and pistol in the other. He hurled his pistol at Joe, but he saw the movement and nimbly ducked, to the discomfiture of the man behind him, who received the weapon full in his chest (Joe being short) and staggered back in a heap against the rail. Joe was erect again in time to catch the captain's cutlass on his belaying pin, which it struck with such force as to be shivered to splinters. Ere the captain had time to spring back, a half swing from Joe's formidable weapon caught him on the neck, and he fell like a bullock under the pole ax.

This was the signal for a general stampede. With their leader gone the buccaneers could not rally, and every man sought how best to save his skin. Some tumbled down the steps, others swung themselves over the rail and dropped to the ground, and as they rushed this way and that to find safety, they were pursued not merely by my men, but by crowds of yelling negroes, who had emerged from their concealment with wondrous rapidity when they saw the tide of battle turn against the buccaneers, and were now ready enough to join in the shouting.

The veranda being clear of the enemy, the half-battered door was thrown open, and to my amazement Dick Cludde came towards me with Mr. McTavish, three overseers, Uncle Moses, and Noah, all with smoking muskets in their hands. A bare word of greeting passed between us, for Noah, seeing Vetch helpless in my grasp, sprang forward with a shout of savage joy and but for my intervention would have plunged his knife into the wretched man. Fending him off, I pushed Vetch into the room, and shut the door, keeping out all but McTavish and Cludde.

Vetch was pale and discomposed, his lips twitching, his eyes ranging restlessly between Cludde and me. I felt no pity for him.

"This man," I said to McTavish, "led his ruffians here under promise of a share in a large sum of money they would find. Is there any truth in it?"

"There is no that much money here at this present time," replied McTavish, "but when I came back to the estate a while ago and looked into matters, I couldna just make out where two thousand pounds had gone. 'Twas in specie, too, for I happened to know that the coin had been sent up from Spanish Town--a verra large sum to keep in an up-country house."

"Where is that money?" I asked, turning to Vetch.

He was more composed now, and his wonted look of alertness had returned.

"Let me understand," says Vetch. "You accuse me of--"

"Of appropriating money that did not belong to you," I said, filling up his pause.

"A serious accusation," he said, drawing his brows together. "And when did this appropriation take place?"

"We are not playing a game," I said impatiently. "Where is the money which you stole, and which you used as a lure for your ruffians?"

"We are not playing a game, as you say," he replied, becoming more and more collected as I waxed hotter. "You accuse me of stealing, I answer, when did I steal, and what are your proofs?"

"You heard what Mr. McTavish said," I replied, with difficulty curbing my anger. "Two thousand pounds are not accounted for; you were here when the money was received; it disappeared during the time you held Mr. McTavish's place; you bring your desperadoes here to secure it. 'Tis useless fencing with us."

"During the time I held Mr. McTavish's place," he repeated musingly. "That was for several months last year, until the day when the owner of this property came of age--the day when Mr. Humphrey Bold by trickery gained access to this house and threatened my life. Has it gone from your recollection that I held Mr. McTavish's place in right of a power of attorney from the legal guardian of the estate, and that whatever I may have done I was empowered to do? Does it not occur to you that the money you charge me with stealing was appropriated to the payment of the men whom I felt impelled to engage for the defense of this property against the unlawful designs of Mr. Humphrey Bold?

"You will bear me out, Mr. Cludde, when I remind you that the owner of the estate had fled from her lawfully-appointed guardian, aided and abetted in her flight, I doubt not, by this upstart himself. I am ready to account for my administration of the property to Sir Richard Cludde, and to no one else, and I say you have no right to call in question anything I may have done in his name."

The fellow's impudence fairly took my breath away. For some moments I could do nothing but look at him, and he returned my gaze without blinking, the old sneer playing about his lips. The brazen coolness with which he ignored his recent attack on the house and sought to put me in the wrong filled me with sheer amazement. I began to wonder again whether, after all, the tale he had told to the buccaneers was a lie, and he had come back to the house with no further design than to wreak his spite upon it.

And yet this could hardly be, for he could easily have set fire to it, and then the question flashed upon my mind suddenly, why had he pressed home the attack on this particular room, when all the rest of the house lay open to him? Did not that point to the probability that the money he had spoken of was actually here, in this room?

'Twas vain to bandy more words with the fellow. I called in Joe Punchard and one of my seamen, and bade them take him to the kitchen and tie him up. He flushed and bit his lip when I gave this order, but he saw 'twas folly to resist. When he had gone I told the others what I had been thinking, and suggested that we should search the room. A bureau stood against the wall; this was the only article of furniture in which money could be secured, and Mr. McTavish, who used it constantly, assured me that there was but a small sum in one of its drawers, which he had himself placed there.

We looked around in perplexity. The walls were of wood, not of lath and plaster, so that there were no nooks and crannies in which he could have bestowed his hoard. The floor also was of single planking, forming the roof of the room below. There seemed no possible place of concealment here. Could there be any spot on the veranda that might have served his purpose?

I went out; the veranda was empty, the men who had been injured (and some who were dead) having been removed. If my reasoning was correct, the hiding place must be on the inner side, otherwise the assailants could have obtained what they came to seek without attacking the room. We looked carefully along the base of the wall where it met the floor of the veranda at first in vain.

But just as I was almost prepared to give up the search and try elsewhere I noticed that at one spot the nails of the flooring seemed newer than at other parts. Calling to Cludde, with his assistance I prized up one of the boards, and the secret was instantly revealed. The board rested on one of the broad wooden pillars supporting the veranda. A hole had been cut down the center of the pillar, and there lay the missing money--doubloons and silver dollars.

Leaving McTavish to gather them up and count them, Cludde and I went down to the kitchen. Vetch was tied to a chair (as Joe had been tied months before), and Joe was sitting over against him, with a cutlass on his knees. I told Vetch briefly that the money was found.

Even now his bravado did not desert him. He repeated we had no right to call in question any action of his and that none but Sir Richard could claim an account of his stewardship. I did not reply, as I might have done, that the money, being found in the house after Mistress Lucy had come of age, was patently hers, and in attempting to recover it he was no better than a common housebreaker. I bade Punchard collect our men in readiness to march back to the brig, and strictly charged him that he should have every care of Vetch on the way.

Then I saw a shadow of fear cross the villain's face. He knew that to brazen it out longer would avail him nothing, and 'twas his inward vision of the hangman, I doubt not, that caused him to go white to the lips.

Cludde went from the room to gather his few possessions in preparation for our despatch. Vetch struggled with himself for a moment, then said huskily:

"Bold, you must let me go. I will make it worth your while. Your father's will--is not destroyed; let me go--and I will tell you where it is."

"I will make no terms with you," I said.

"But what do you gain by refusing?" he cried. "You are only a lieutenant; promotion is slow; money would help you on. You have your revenge on me--and lose your property, for I vow I will tell you nothing unless you let me go."

"I would not let you go for a king's ransom," I said. "The wrongs you have done me are nothing; but for your villainy I should not be a king's officer today. I could almost forgive you. But nothing in the world could persuade me to forget the wrongs you have done to a helpless woman--the indignities you put upon her, the villainous designs you harbored against her. No, you have done your rascally work--you shall take your wages."

He said no more then, but presently, when Cludde returned he made an appeal to him.

"Dick," he said, "you and I are bound by long friendship--"

"Which you have killed," said Cludde, interrupting him.

"But you will not forget all the past--our school days, the merry times we had then and after, all I have done with you, and for you. For a dozen years we were as close as brothers; you won't turn against me now?"

"I know, but--Lucy--'twas unpardonable," Cludde stammered in great discomfort. "I'm not spotless--done things I am ashamed of--but you carried things too far--you wanted to force her to marry you--"

"And do you think she will marry you now, you fool?" cried Vetch, with a flash of his old fiery temper.

"I could wish her to wed a better man," says poor Cludde.

"Even so good as Mr. Humphrey Bold," says Vetch with a sneer.

Cludde looked at me. If he intended to say anything 'twas prevented by the entrance of Joe Punchard with news that all was ready.

"Bring him along," I said, glancing towards Vetch.

Joe unstrapped his legs, leaving his arms still bound, and they followed us from the room.

We set off on our seaward march, having just time to regain the brig before the day became oppressive. We took with us, as prisoners, such of the buccaneers as had been caught; what became of the rest I never knew. Vetch marched with them, amid a guard of our men.

On the way I learned from Cludde how it happened that he was at the house at a time when, but for him, the buccaneers' attack might have been successful before I came on the scene. Being convalescent from his wound, and learning that Mistress Lucy wished to consult Mr. McTavish about selling the estate (for she had determined to carry through the negotiations begun by Vetch), he had offered to carry a message to the steward, intending to remain at the house for a few days for change of air. He had seized the opportunity also of bringing to Uncle Moses and Noah charters of freedom from their mistress, in reward for their services to her and to hers. Cludde insisted on her accepting from him the five hundred dollars which I had promised Noah for his life, and she handed it back as a present for the negro.

We were talking about all these strange things that had happened, when suddenly we heard a commotion at the head of the column. Running hastily forward, I saw Punchard and several of my men rushing at full speed across a tract of scrubby land in pursuit of Vetch. He had persuaded the buccaneer beside him, whose hands had not been bound, to cut his bonds.

I joined in the chase; Cludde hung back; I think that after all he would not have been ill pleased, for old friendship's sake, if Vetch had got away. Vetch had had but a few yards' start, but he was a swift runner, and I doubted much whether any of us could overtake him. We could not bring him down with a shot, for my men, though their muskets were loaded, had not kindled their matches, so that before they could fire he was out of range.

Foremost of the pursuers was Joe, bounding along like a deer, furious (as he afterwards told me) because he regarded the escape as due to his own negligence.

We had raced on for maybe half a mile, and still had not lessened the distance between us and the fugitive, when I suddenly saw him sink above his ankles into the earth. He uttered a terrible shriek; the man running beside me, who knew something of the country, cried out "A cockpit!" in accents of horror and stopped short. But the agonizing cries of the poor wretch who was sinking inch by inch into the horrible hole whose treacherous surface had beguiled him were more than I could endure. 'Twas not a death for the foulest villain on earth. Heedless of the warning shouts of my crew, I dashed forward, hoping to reach Vetch in time to rescue him ere he was sucked under.

To venture directly on the spot where he was sinking would, I knew, be certain death to me. But when I reached the edge of the cockpit I flung myself on my face, thinking with my outstretched arms to seize him. He turned his head and saw me. To this day I shudder as I see again the anguish, the mute imploring entreaty, that spoke out of his ghastly features.

I could not reach him.

I crawled forward, and my hands began to sink. Joe Punchard behind was shouting to recall me. Vetch was up to his shoulders. Half my body was on solid ground, and with a prayer on my lips I was edging forward inch by inch to make one final effort, when I felt my feet held fast; I was hauled back with great violence, just as Vetch, with a scream that rang in my ears and ran through my dreams for weeks afterwards and haunts me still, disappeared forever.

—

Chapter 32
I Become Bold

The flags were at half mast when we sailed into Port Royal Harbor, with the pirate brig in our wake; and my dark foreboding was confirmed by the first news we had when we stepped ashore. Admiral Benbow was dead. Sturdy fighter as he was, he had contended gallantly for near a month against the fever that ensued upon the amputation of his leg, but 'twas not Heaven's will that he should live for further service to his country. In the presence of Death, the great leveler, all detraction is hushed, all enmities are extinguished; and even some who had thwarted and criticized the admiral sincerely deplored his loss. He had won no great victories, done nothing to dazzle the eyes of men; but I make bold to say that, in the long roll of England's worthies no name will ever shine more brilliantly to a seaman's eyes than that of honest John Benbow.

Rear Admiral Whetstone, to whom the command of the West Indian squadron fell, was pleased to compliment me on my dealings with the buccaneers, and appointed me first lieutenant of the British frigate on which the officers under sentence of the court martial were to be conveyed to England.

When we sailed out of Port Royal (you may be sure I had Joe Punchard with me), we acted as convoy to a large merchant brig, richly laden with produce of the island, and with a freight more precious to me in the person of Mistress Lucy. She had not waited for the completion of the business connected with the sale of her estate, having perfect confidence in the integrity of Mr. McTavish, who would remit the price to her in due course. From a mercenary point of view the time was not well chosen for the disposal of her property, values always diminishing in time of war. But the island was associated for her now with so many unpleasant incidents that she was glad to sever the last tie that bound her to it and return to her happy life with the Allardyces.

'Twas a bleak day in December when we sailed into Plymouth Sound. As soon as we had spoken the port a boat put off hearing a paper sealed with the seal of Prince George, the Lord High Admiral. And there fell to my captain a duty which sure no man could have performed without compunction. I was truly thankful no such dreadful task was ever mine. The prince ordered that the sentence of the court martial should be executed upon those two unhappy captains, Kirkby and Wade, on the deck of the vessel, with a full muster of the crew. When they were drawn up in lines according to rank, the whole ship's company, from the lieutenants and master's mates down to the grommet and the boy; the captain, pale as death but in a firm voice, gave the word of command at which, with one volley of muskets, the souls of those two cravens and traitors were sped into eternity. Their crimes were flagrant, the sentence was most just; but I hope and pray no Englishman will ever do the like again.

The same papers contained news of a more agreeable nature. Considering the high terms in which Mr. Benbow had spoken of Captains Fogg and Vincent, and the recommendation he made on their behalf, the prince was pleased to command that the sentence of suspension should be remitted, and that they should be again employed in the Queen's service. I was sorry that I could not be present when this good news was conveyed to them; they had remained in Jamaica, and did not learn of the prince's clemency for several months. I never saw Captain Fogg again; but I had the pleasure to serve with Captain Vincent seven years later, when we each commanded a vessel in Admiral Baker's squadron that cruised about the Irish coasts in search of Duguay-Trouin. He retired from the service soon afterwards, and lived for twenty years longer in much contentment. 'Tis sixteen years (so fast does time fly) since I was bid to his funeral.

We continued to Portsmouth, where, the ship being paid off, I hastened with Mistress Lucy, her faithful nurse and Joe, to be in time to keep Christmas at Shrewsbury. My good friends Squire Allardyce and his lady were in the seventh heaven of delight when I restored Mistress Lucy once more to their arms, and overwhelmed me with their praises when they heard from her a full recital of what they were pleased to call my heroic deeds on her behalf. In truth I think there was little of the heroic in anything I had done, but just my plain duty, and what any man of honor would have attempted for any woman in like circumstances.

The squire made a comical grimace when (after the ladies had disappeared) I expressed this opinion.

"Ads bobs!" he cried, "what are young fellows made of nowadays! Have you spirit for nothing but fighting the French, Mr. Humphrey Bold? I could have sworn there would be a Mistress Bold by this time."

I reminded him that I was as yet only a lieutenant on eighty pounds a year (though I looked for my captain's commission when Prince George should have had time to overlook Admiral Whetstone's report).

"But hasn't Lucy enough for you both and a large family to boot?-- though to be sure she made a precious bad bargain over that estate of hers. D'you want her to be snapped up under your very nose? Why, young Cludde will have her yet, if he has turned out such a paragon as you would make it appear."

But I corrected him on this point, for on our journey to the Hall Mistress Lucy told me (what had been a secret hitherto) that Dick Cludde and Lucetta Gurney would one day make a match of it. In the end the old gentleman pished and pshawed and called me a young fool, but I learned from Mistress Allardyce afterwards that in the bosom of his family he laid this also to my credit.

I stayed at the Hall one night, as did Joe Punchard (who, between Susan and the cook, spent a merry evening, and made Giles turn black with jealousy), and then set off with him to see my older friends in Shrewsbury. Mr. Vetch and his good lady welcomed me right royally. They were in excellent health, Mistress Vetch fine in a new magenta-colored cap, and I was right glad to learn that the lawyer's practice had grown quite to its former prosperity, and that he was spoken of as mayor for the next year. (This honor, however, he did not attain to, the election falling on Mr. William Bowlder the tanner.)

I warrant you I had to tell over my adventures until my tongue was aweary, my wits being sore put to it, moreover, to avoid the mention of Cyrus, for I was resolved that the lawyer's declining years should not be vexed by the knowledge of his nephew's villainy and dreadful end. But Fate was against me in this. I had strictly charged Joe Punchard to keep silence on all that pertained to Cyrus Vetch; but having his pockets well lined, and being of a generous and social disposition, he made a great feast on Christmas eve, to which he invited certain friends of his mother, Nelly Hind among them, and some who had been 'prentices at the same time as himself.

And in the height of their entertainment, good ale flowing very freely, Joe, usually the most abstemious of tars, was a little overtaken by the liquor he had drunk, and, with no other object than to heighten my reputation, must needs tell how I had ventured into the jaws of death (so he put it) to save the man of all others who had done me the most ill. And next day Nelly Hind meets Mistress Vetch at the church door and pours the whole tale into her ears; and by and by Joe comes himself with a very doleful countenance and begs Mistress Vetch not to let her husband know, and very humbly asks my pardon, vowing not to drink more than a quart in future even though the Queen should bid him do otherwise.

But Mistress Vetch bore an old grudge against Cyrus for the tricks he had played on me, and the trouble he had brought on the lawyer, forgetting, good soul, that but for this same trouble she would still have been (so far as one can tell), Becky Pennyquick and a widow. She declared to me that she would not have the matter hidden up, quoting against me the Bible text that says a candle is not put under a bushel, but set on a candlestick to give light to the whole house. And so that the light might dazzle as many as possible, she invited a dozen neighbors to dinner on Boxing Day and sprung the story on poor Mr. Vetch as he sat at the head of his own table. ('Tis marvelous what strange ineptitudes mar the characters of excellent good folk.)

Luckily our good friend Captain Galsworthy was among the guests. He ever treated poor Becky with a sort of good-humored tolerance, and now, perceiving the shadow that crossed the lawyer's face, he broke in upon the dame's loquacity with a tremendous tirade against the captains who had behaved so treacherously towards Mr. Benbow (the story of whose last fight he had already drunk in from my lips).

"How can you wonder at it," he cried, "when you remember the covetous spirit that overspread the kingdom before Dutch William came to rule us--when men perfectly scrambled for the revenues of the crown, and made their private fortunes out of the nation's treasure! 'Tis a matter of years, ay, generations, to undo all the mischief that springs from such corruption; and when money, oftener than merit, gained admission to a command, no wonder that such scoundrels as Wade and Kirkby were trusted with our men-of-war.

"By God, sir!--" and here he raised his clenched fist, no doubt to bang upon the table; but being seated at the corner, very close to the wall (the party being a large one for the room), he drove his elbow clean through a wooden panel beside the fireplace. He swung back, full of consternation and remorse.

"And now see what you have done, with your profanity and all!" cries Mistress Vetch, her cap sidling upon her head as she shook it with vexation. "You was always a violent man; 'tis no thanks to you that poor Humphrey hasn't been killed over and over again, for 'twas you and no one else as taught him to fight. And who'll pay the bill for your breakages? That's what I say!"

Mr. Vetch did his best to soothe his angry spouse; I fear he suffered a good deal at times from her unmannerliness, though to be sure she was an excellent housewife and had a heart of gold. And Captain Galsworthy, saying never a word in reply to her outbreak, rubbed his elbow and said with a rueful smile:

"'Tis assault and battery, Vetch; I'm sorry: but I wonder why they call it the funny bone!"

Mistress Vetch would, I am sure, have given her views on this question had not Mr. Pinhorn, the surgeon, who was at the other side of the corner from the captain, suddenly called out:

"I say, Vetch, I fear you'll have to choose another receptacle for your secret documents."

"He has no secrets from me, I would have you know!" cries Mistress Vetch in high indignation, not knowing in the least what had occasioned his remark.

"I don't doubt it, madam," said Mr. Pinhorn, with a comical twist of the mouth; "but maybe he stowed that paper there before you and he was made one."

He pointed to the hole made by Captain Galsworthy's elbow, and there, sure enough, was the white end of a folded paper showing.

"Dear me," says Mr. Vetch, getting up from his seat. "I knew nothing of it."

He goes to the broken panel, brings out the paper, and as he looked at it turned so ghastly pale that Mr. Pinhorn clutched a decanter of brandy and began to pour some of it into a glass. We were all struck silent with wonderment; even Mistress Vetch being tongue tied. Then Mr. Vetch turned to me and, holding out the paper with trembling hand, tears standing in his eyes, said:

"God be thanked for all His mercies!"

'Twas my father's will, dusty, gnawed at the edges, but indubitably the will which had disappeared seven years before. Remembering the hiding place in which Cyrus had secreted the money at Penolver, it was no mystery to me that he should have fashioned a similar receptacle for the will he had purloined.

There is no need to tell of the congratulations showered upon me; My hand was wrung by my kind neighbors until it tingled with numbness. Mistress Vetch fell into hysterics--mercilessly ignored by Mr. Pinhorn. And as for Captain Galsworthy, he seemed incapable of doing anything but repeat his question, chuckling aloud "Can anyone tell me why 'tis called the funny bone?"

The party soon broke up, to carry the news far and wide through Shrewsbury. And I, after an affecting five minutes with the lawyer, suddenly stuffed the paper in my pocket, flung on my hat, and ran out with furious haste to saddle my horse. Mistress Vetch came to the door as I mounted.

"Mind you speak the villain plain," she cried.

I laughed joyfully and galloped away up Pride Hill. The tale of my discovery had already got abroad; the people came to their doors and cheered me, and some little fellows of the school stood in the middle of the road and waved their caps and shouted "Huzzay for Captain Bold!"

But I did not ride straight on towards the Wem Road and Cludde Court, as Becky had supposed I intended. I turned into Dogpole, rode helter skelter down Wyle Cop in the very course where Joe's barrel had rolled, and never drew rein until I came to the door of the Hall. 'Twas opened to me by Roger, home from following the campaign in Flanders--a strapping fine fellow, near as tall as myself.

"Gad, but your horse is in a sweat!" he said by way of greeting. (We laughed at it afterwards.).

"Where is Lucy?" I said.

He stared at me for a moment, then burst into a hearty roar.

"Up you go," says he, clapping me on the back. "Egad, and I'll go and find the squire."

That is more than forty years ago. My hand is weary with writing: why should I tell you more? There is indeed little more to tell, for from that time, thank God, there have been no mischances in my life. Yet maybe those who have read my story patiently hereto (if any there be) may like to have it rounded off--*totus, teres, et rotundus.*

A few weeks after I regained possession of my little property Sir Richard Cludde died--of gout and other diseases, said Mr. Pinhorn; Mistress Vetch said of rage. His estate had been much impoverished, and his widow was now left almost penniless. She was my father's sister, and, my own lot being happy, I could not endure to think of her in penury and distress. So I made her a small allowance through Mr. Vetch (and I can vouch for it this was a secret his wife never knew) --sufficient to keep her from want. She never saw me, made me no acknowledgment, and to the day of her death maintained, in the little house she took next St. Michael's Church, the haughty bearing which had always won her such dislike.

Lucy and I were married on St. Valentine's day in the year 1703. Less than three months afterwards I was appointed to command the Pegasus, a third-rate of forty-eight guns, and ordered to the Mediterranean with Admiral Sir Cloudesly Shovel. From that time until I retired in the year 1713 I was almost continuously on service, having but brief intervals to spend with my wife. I was at the taking of Gibraltar by Sir George Rooke (which we have yet in possession, and may we ever keep it), and in the famous sea fight off Velez Malaga in 1704; next year I entered Barcelona with Sir Stafford Fairborn; in brief, I had a share (though humble) in many of our notable transactions at sea during those memorable years when we fought King Lewis.

But when peace was concluded in the year 1713, both Mr. and Mrs. Allardyce being then dead, I thought it was high time I settled down at home, especially as there were two sturdy boys growing up to plague their mother. Accordingly I retired with the rank of captain and a considerable fortune. We purchased the estate of Cludde Court and made great additions to it, and our boys every day rode into Shrewsbury to school, and did it more credit than their father.

Captain Galsworthy was a frequent visitor, and though he was past eighty, insisted on giving our boys their first lessons with the singlestick. He died in the year '15, leaving fragrant memories to us who loved him.

Joe Punchard is with me still. He regarded Lucy's injunctions as binding on him for life, and clave to me all through my naval career, though he lost a leg at the taking of Port Mahon in 1708. He retired when I did, and came to Cludde Court as our lodge keeper, where he would entrance my boys with sea songs and his tales of p what he had gone through on sea and land with me and with Admiral Benbow, whom he ever cherished as a matchless captain. His own naval career, he says, began with a wooden barrel and ended with a wooden leg, and sometimes, over his pipe, he shakes his head and declares that I had all the chances, he all the mischances. But he is gone seventy years of age, and is apt to be a little forgetful.